Crunchy with

Chocolate

Edited by
Carol Hightshoe

I0561328

WolfSinger Publications ⟨ Security, Colorado

Acknowledgements

Purple Haze © 2021 by Beth W. Patterson
Of Myths and Mercy © 2021 by Miriam Thor
A Found Dragonel © 2014 by Joyce Frohn
First Published in *The Lorelei Signal*, 2014
Our Dragon Neighbor © 2021 by Cara Brezina
Egg Snatcher © 2021 by Allison Rott
The Dragon Queen © 2021 by Rose Strickman
A Squeaky-Clean Reunion © 2021 by Mary Jo Rabe
Dragon in Distress © 2021 by Gustasp Irani
Our Last Battle © 2021 by Birgit K. Gaiser
Blacktooth 500 © 2020 by Gwen C. Katz
First Published in *Hear Me Roar*. Poise and Pen Publishing, 2020
Here by Choice © 2010 by Gerri Leen
First Published in Life Without Crows, Hadley Rille Books, 2010
The Fool's Fiddle © 2021 by Austin Charles Roberts
The Dragon's Choice © 2021 by Annie Percik
Domain of the Dragon © 2017 by L.H. Davis III
First Published in *Electromagnetism,* 2017
Meal Ticket © 2021 by Gregg Chamberlain
Dragon Life © 2021 by Barbara G. Tarn
A Thread of Adventure © 2021 by Sally Jo
Domestic Dispute © 2021 by Fred Phillips
Madras © 2021 by Mabel Ginest
The Princess and the Dragon © 2021 by Karen G. McCullough
The Beggar Prince © 2021 by Mark Bruce
The Wyvern and the Dragon © 2021 by Claire Davon
Nog, the not so Terrible © 2021 by Kevin David Anderson
Tied to the Whim of a Tender Tyrant © 2015 by S.H. Mansouri
First Published in *From the Dragon Lord's Library V2*, 18thWall Productions, 2015
Slay the Dragon: Ten Pence a Go © 2021 by Samuel Poots
Memories of Dragons Slain © 2007 by Ken Goldman
First Published in *You Had Me At ARRGH!!!,* Sam's Dot Publishers, October 2007
Dragons are Forever © 2021 by Jean Martin

Copyright © 2021 by WolfSinger Publications
All stories copyrighted to their individual authors

All rights reserved. No part of this book may be used or reproduced in any
manner whatsoever without the written permission of the copyright owner.

For permission requests, please contact WolfSinger Publications at:
editor@wolfsingerpubs.com

All characters and events in this book are fictitious.
Any resemblance to persons living or dead is strictly coincidental.

Cover Art copyright 2021 © Lee Ann Barlow

ISBN 978-1-944637-05-7
Printed and bound in the United States of America

Table of Contents

Purple Haze

Beth W. Patterson

The cave was the perfect amphitheater. Once the entrance tunnel widened into an ancient chamber, the acoustics created the best natural reverb. The squawk of a bat, the sustain of a guitar, or the roar of a beast all sounded like a million bucks.

The light scaffolding framing the subterranean auditorium was more impressive than any arcane portal as recounted and recorded by men. Red, green, and blue bulbs swiveled on their mechanical fixtures, shooting beams like accusatory pointing fingers. Stalagmites stood at attention in front of the stage beneath it, as if some basilisk had created a captive audience eons ago.

And in the center of it all was a beast the size of a city bus on his urban dais. His glimmering amethyst scales overlapped one another, triangular but gently rounded at each corner like guitar picks. Being a dragon meant his body had built-in smoke machines and pyrotechnics. His ever-changing stage light eyes of amber, cyan, and magenta took in everything like search beams.

The dragon's raw energy was enough to supply electricity to his lair without the use of a power grid or generator. The occasional drip of water onto the limestone floor was no hazard. There was no way he could have survived for a geological span of time without a hint of magic.

The monster had been in touch with human desires for millennia. He had no more use for the gold he'd guarded centuries ago than he did for the treasures he currently held. The power he gained was in the withholding precious things from mortal men.

But who came in search of a sacred chalice or a magical sword these days?

Now he hoarded the intangible. Well, maybe with the exception of a couple of objects he fancied. He had the second largest collection of Paul Reed Smith dragon-inlay guitars in the world. It seemed unlikely a creature his size would be able to hold one of these prized instruments without crushing it, let alone play it, but the dragon had an extra talent that allowed him to coax sounds from a guitar beyond any human…

Human! Just like that, one such mortal was standing only meters away from his scaly snout. Had his mere thoughts summoned this person into his lair? The dragon was so surprised, he forgot to roar a warning. The easygoing-looking black man was unarmed and relaxed, with a wild mane of hair and a familiar grin the dragon knew from somewhere. He seemed so utterly unfazed the great lizard was too curious to roast him on the spot.

The visitor was also holding his guitar upside down and backwards. Was he from some mirror parallel universe? The dragon snorted steam in irritation. Everyone knew that sort of thing was fantasy bullshit.

"Who are you to enter my lair?" the wyrm thundered.

The human shrugged. "I am a just a man like everybody else, Alexander the Great or Napoleon. I'm just this guy."

"Hmmm, your name is 'This Guy'?" drawled the beast with dry rhetoric. "Never mind. That's what I'll call you." The newcomer had no response to that, which the legendary creature found frustrating. He roared, belching a jet of flame dangerously close to the man's oddly configured guitar.

The intruder known as This Guy simply laughed. "Do you think setting my guitar on fire is going to scare me?"

The beast narrowed his spotlight eyes. "Wait a minute. I recognize you. But you died decades ago."

The man spread his arms wide, the gold French braiding of his black military jacket catching the stage lights. "And yet, here I am," he replied with a slight bow. "Honestly, I don't know why I'm here. I don't think I'm a ghost…" He pinched himself experimentally, wincing. "Maybe I'm a manifestation of people's collective memories. It doesn't really matter, does it?"

"Well, perhaps you've heard of me," the dragon rumbled. "They call me Haze. Of course, that was back before the word was used to mean 'pollution.' I'm a bit of a musician myself."

The creature sat back on his haunches and picked up a guitar, the instrument looking like a tiny Christmas tree ornament compared to the massive reptile. Haze closed his eyes, took a deep breath, and seemed to concentrate on something. In a single fluid motion, he dwindled in size. Like a balloon deflating, he shrank to the proportions of an elephant, then a moose, and finally a professional basketball player, allowing him to wrap his digits around the guitar neck. His claws retracted with a click.

The dragon struck a chord, then screamed right into a two-handed tapping solo.

This Guy clapped in genuine appreciation. "That's a pretty impressive lick," he murmured. "I recognize it, even though it was after my time. I can see how you would like an eruption, with all of that fire breathing. But Mister Haze, are you experienced?"

Haze had no response to that. He only drew back his lips to reveal a fearsome set of choppers. Even human-sized, he was not a reptile to be reckoned with.

"Of course I'm experienced," he snarled. "I've lived my life on my own terms and become a dragon who actually does something interesting. No razing villages, no amassing piles of trinkets I can't even use. Now *this* equipment—" He paused to indicate the stage, light rigging, speaker system, and arsenal of instruments "—this is something even better. Why live as a hermit if I can't rattle the foundations of my cave? Who's going to complain about the noise?"

"I get it," This Guy murmured. "It's hard to be creative when people are always trying to box you in. Now don't think anything bad, but…where'd you get all this stuff, anyway?"

Like all dragons, Haze had twenty-seven bones in his neck alone, and he snaked his upper body downward to meet the man at eye level. There was suspicion in his eyes, but a hint of world-weariness in his tone.

"Ever since the eighties, these wanna-be guitar gods have gotten it into their heads they can take down monsters with their playing. They probably studied the covers of their Yngwie Malmsteen records, looking at a painting of a man blasting a three-headed dragon, and thought, 'Cool! I can do that!' Armor-clad challengers gave way to big-haired men with tight pants and eye makeup. And then some genius designed a video game, likening skills on a fake guitar to heroic deeds! How does pressing some buttons instead of learning a real instrument earn you the lauds of making the word a better place?" Haze noticed his emotions were causing tiny flames to fly from his mouth like flecks of spittle. He took a deep breath and reined in his emotions, though he wasn't sure why.

"Somehow these arrogant hominids figured out how to find

me. They'd come to my lair, I'd lay them to waste, and I'd keep their equipment," the lizard finished.

"What about the stage and all those lights?"

Haze flashed an odd magenta color. "I spared one man's life. He was a disgruntled worker at a chain of music equipment outlets called GuiTarget. He actually offered me a box of bon-bons in exchange for my services. I ripped off the roof of the warehouse and helped myself to the biggest merchandise before incinerating the rest of the store."

This Guy took a seat on the stone floor, gazing up at the beast with eyes full of genuine sympathy. "What do you truly want, my scaly friend?"

"I want people to leave me the fuck alone…" Haze began with a snarl, and even as the words tumbled from his jaws, he wasn't sure he meant it. He actually liked This Guy. He was the first decent human being ever to pay him a visit, and the man didn't even judge the dragon's monstrous nature.

"Why are you so angry?" This Guy didn't wait for an answer before continuing, "I mean, you wouldn't have this attitude about humans if they weren't constantly pissing you off, right?"

"I'm not angry. Why would I be angry at such an inconsequential bunch of short-lived mortals?"

"Look, man, I can tell. You're purple. And it's the color of rage. You see, I have synesthesia…"

"You rock stars got all kinds of diseases, with all your promiscuity."

This Guy threw back his head and laughed. "Naw, man, it means I hear colors and see sounds. And right now, you are furious. For centuries, people have been trying to prove their worthiness by attacking you while you were just minding your own business. You could pick them off one by one, but now you have a chance to wield power over all of humanity."

"I don't *need* to wield power over anyone," the dragon snarled. "I'm already a dragon. It's in my nature to hoard things."

"Yeah, but this is more than draconian nature, isn't it?" This Guy shook his head. "Look, I get it, man. People suck. I'm a person, and I still had to deal with prejudice from all sides. Music was what transported me, and I made quite a lot of it in my time. But nobody gets to hear it anymore, unless they pirate my records and…what came after that? I heard something about eight-tracks, cassettes, compact discs, and airwaves. Isn't that crazy? Music used to be everywhere.

"And that's why I'm here. You see, I know you have more than a groovy guitar collection. You control all the copyrights in the world now. You want things no one else has."

Haze snorted. "Don't be daft. There are plenty of public domain songs for people to enjoy…" A distant discordant jangling of an acoustic guitar coming from somewhere interrupted his argument.

Haze gingerly set his guitar onto a stand and drew himself back up to his full size. He slunk to the entrance of his cave, with the mortal visitor scurrying close behind. The harsh winter sunlight momentarily blinded them both, but as their eyes adjusted, they spotted another musical challenger. The interloper was clearly trying to recreate a bygone era, clad in only a toga and bawling out a song too old for anyone to claim ownership. This Guy recognized it as "The Riddle Song," sometimes known as "I Gave My Love a Cherry." This invasive folkie was either unperturbed by the massive piles of human bones that littered the mouth of the grotto, or he was high as a kite.

"Oh, shit," muttered the legendary guitarist. "I know what happens next. Sometimes a guitar must suffer to make a statement. It gets the tension out. But even after I died, I saw how this scenario played out in a movie. You don't have to do this, man…"

But it was too late. Haze reached one foreleg out and closed his talons around the neck of the instrument. The toga-clad man struggled for a moment before losing his grip, sprawling onto the hard stone. The dragon lifted the guitar high in the air, dipped his long neck, opened his jaws, and blew a jet of flame onto the unfortunate balladeer.

The toga was the first thing to combust, followed by the minstrel's hair. Like valiant special effects of an eighties action flick, the rest of him melted into a puddle. When the smoke cleared, there was nothing but a blackened skeleton on the ground, gaping jaw and empty eye sockets somehow conveying a lingering dismay.

This Guy coughed and gagged at the stench of sulfurous dragon flame, charring flesh, and burning hair. He lit a cigarette, perhaps to dispel the odor. He tried not to look at the remains of the charred bard who had one bony arm outstretched, still reaching for his guitar.

Haze examined his newest acquisition. "Nineteen forty-three Martin 00-18. Not bad. It'll be a nice addition to my collection." He tucked it against his chest, cradling it as tenderly as if it were a new hatchling, then made his way back into the concert hall of his lair. This Guy trotted in his wake, careful to avoid the swishing spiked tail.

"You see?" the reptile said, reverting to human size before placing his new treasure among the other instruments. "People can still make music if the songs are old enough. Too bad most of those tunes are so annoying. So back to the copyrights. What does that have to do with you?"

Real or not, This Guy trembled slightly over the fiery execution he had just witnessed. "I wanna make a deal," he finally said. "How long has it been since you've jammed with anyone?"

The beast snorted, sending twin jets of smoke across the stage like a fog machine. "I'm a solo artist."

"Look, man, I didn't become some sort of icon on my own. I played backup for a lot of people before I did my own thing. Come on…aren't you the least bit curious to feel the synergy?"

The dragon actually did, very much, in fact. "So what's this deal?"

"We just *play*. If I show you up, you have to release all of those songs back to the proper copyright owners. If you run rings around me, you get to blast me." His voice quavered slightly on the last phrase.

"You'd take that chance?"

"Do you think I'm jiving?" This Guy challenged. "I jumped out of an airplane once, got hurt, and only then did my life take a turn for the better. Why even bother with life if you don't take chances?"

The man sauntered over to the rig on the opposite side of the stage. "Mind if I use that sweet, sweet Marshall amp over here? It would bring back such fond memories." Without waiting for a response, he plugged in and played a few bars of a march that suddenly got Haze's attention. "What's the point in having this big electric church if you don't have a congregation?"

The dragon's scaly jaw gaped. "How did you know the

Dragon National Anthem?" he demanded.

This Guy grinned. "All national anthems are draconian," he smirked.

"Very funny," the dragon grumbled. "Okay, if you're so hell bent on us playing together, why don't you get us started?"

The man commenced a funky groove, embellishing it with teasing licks. It was catchy, but not threatening.

It was so very *inviting*.

Haze had a plan, of course. He'd had centuries of musical experience, but even if this mere mortal had something on him— that damned *humanity* making music so raw and expressive—the dragon planned to roast This Guy no matter what.

All it took was one little victory to defeat a dragon. And Haze was going to make damned sure he didn't give it to the enigmatic human. He was impatient, of course, ready to upstage this silly mortal, even if This Guy never played anything the same way twice. But there was something that tickled the recesses of his mind as they dissolved from a spar to a dance.

Haze had millennia of experience on This Guy. He'd heard eons' worth of stringed instrument music, from the lyre of ancient Greece, the doshpuluur on the steppes of Tuva, the valiha of Madagascar. He had witnessed the evolution of necked chordo-phones: the oud and the lute, the microtonal buzuq, the vihuela de mano and the cittern. He knew every riff from classical guitar to speed metal.

But something was different. Haze was definitely firing notes at machine gun speed, but This Guy was managing something the dragon had never considered. The man was channeling raw emotion.

The trading of solos became tedious, and soon they locked into a groove. It was reminiscent of covens raising the energy for a ritual. It was the ebb and flow of tides, something greater than either of them.

The wyrm had once been a force of nature, wandering the earth until he had tired of humanity. He could pick up any genre and had a preternatural memory for music.

But do I have my own style? the great beast wondered.

He thought back on his own emotions. If purple was really the color of anger, then he would tap into his rage, for he'd had eons of it building up inside him. He thought of his peers, slain just so mortals could prove their prowess.

All this he channeled into a new kind of music he never knew existed, let alone lived in his head. It felt even better than razing a village. He longed for the old feeling of wreaking havoc, but every time he opened his jaws to demolish his challenger, something stopped him.

This Guy was beginning to tire. Maybe he was an imprint of memories, but people remembered the flesh and blood human. He was still a man who had too often become run down at the ends of his tours when he still lived.

And there was no doubt Haze was the greatest guitarist ever to exist.

~ * ~

Many hours later, they had both shed their instruments and were lounging on some silken pillows Haze kept in an apse behind the stage.

This Guy got to his feet, strode over to the dragon, and held out his cigarette for the dragon to light. Haze barely opened his mouth and shot a flame so thin and precise it didn't even singe the human's prodigious fingers.

The man took several puffs in silence, just watching the smoke curl toward the ceiling. "Since this is probably my last cigarette, I might as well enjoy it," he said at last.

"You've run out of them already?" Haze said absently.

"I have a whole pack in my pocket. I mean, it's curtains for me, right?"

The huge lizard just gave him a blank look.

"Well, I've seen how story songs and movies end. Whoever plays with the most virtuosity wins. You've had centuries of practice on me, man. So you might as well just smoke me. Go ahead. You've still got all those copyrights, and the world is none the wiser. I'll be gone in a flash."

Haze drew up to his full massive size spreading his wings and dwarfing the stage. He let out a roar that carried overtones of feedback shrieks.

"I'm waiting."

The dragon bared his teeth, gnashing them like cymbals.

"Man…are you *stalling?*" This Guy's expression was unreadable, but his eyes might have held a twinkle.

"Me? Never!" Haze boomed.

The dragon was totally stalling.

"Of course if you roast me," the man went on, "it'll destroy the little recording device I have hidden on me somewhere. It sure would be a shame to lose the only recording in the world of a famous dead musician jamming with a legendary beast. There are some way-out moments on there, and no one else in the world has ever heard them. And you can still own it."

"What? Give it to me now!" Haze demanded. The man withdrew a slender silver box from his coat pocket and placed it in the massive claw.

"Fool!" the dragon said with a laugh. "Why in the world would you just hand it to me, since I'm going to incinerate you anyway?"

"'Cause there's more where that came from, and you know it."

The beast's spotlight eyes swirled from red to cyan to yellow, but they would not meet the man's gaze.

"No matter what you do, music still lives on in people's hearts and minds. We humans are on earth for mere seconds compared to mythical creatures. You've lived a long time, and have all the moments in the world. Why not just experience them to the fullest?"

The beast drummed his claws on the floor, then bent his long neck until he was face to face with the rock star.

"So…wanna do this again?" This Guy finally asked.

"Same time tomorrow?" Haze pressed.

"I'll be there with frills on. Oh, and about those copyrights?"

"I'll make a call next week if you hold up your end of the bargain."

"You got it. Now, ya take it real easy, ya hear?" This guy donned a wide brimmed leather hat, picked up his guitar, and faded like a hologram.

Haze sighed, then picked up a jeweled conch shell and held it to his ear.

"Hey, Rumblesnort? Yeah…I know, it's been about three hundred years since we last spoke but…you'll never guess who I just got to play with? And he's coming back tomorrow…Well, yeah, you can bring your lute, but times are changing, and…you know what? Never mind. Bring the freakiest instruments you have. He'll love it."

~ * ~ * ~

Beth W. Patterson was a full-time musician for over two decades before diving into the world of writing, a process she describes as "fleeing the circus to join the zoo". Beth often incorporates her musical experiences into her stories and loves it when people try to guess which parts are real or fictional. She is the author of the books *Mongrels and Misfits, The Wild Harmonic,* novelette *The Spirit of Rodeo,* and a contributor to over sixty anthologies.

Patterson has performed in twenty countries across five continents. Her playing appears on over two hundred albums, singles, soundtracks, commercials, and voice-overs (including eight solo albums of her own). More than a hundred of her compositions and co-writes have been released. She studied ethnomusicology at University College, Cork in Ireland and holds a Bachelor's degree in Music Therapy from Loyola University New Orleans.

Beth has occasionally worn other hats as a body paint model, film extra, minor role actor, recording studio partner, record label owner, producer, and visual artist. She is a lover of exquisitely stupid movies and a shameless fangirl of the band Rush. She lives in New Orleans with her husband Josh Paxton, jazz pianist extraordinaire.

You can find her at www.bethpattersonmusic.com.

Of Myths and Mercy

Miriam Thor

Paige woke to the sound of someone banging on her door. She was out of bed and heading to open it before she made a conscious decision to move. It was never good when someone came to her home in the middle of the night, but as a healer, she would help in any way she could.

When Paige opened the door, her breath caught in her throat. Brevin, a local shepherd, stood there with his twelve-year-old son, Vallen, in his arms. Burns covered the boy's entire right side, and his leg was twisted at an unnatural angle.

"Help him, Paige," Brevin begged. "You have to help him."

Mouth dry, Paige nodded.

"Of course," she said, stepping back. "Put him on the cot over there." She pointed at the bed she used for her more serious patients.

As Brevin hurried to obey, Paige tied back her brown hair and rolled up the sleeves of her sleep dress. It was going to be a long night.

"What happened?" she asked Brevin once his son was settled.

"This morning, Vallen and I led our sheep to graze near Benaro Lake in the hills," he said quietly. "Around sunset, a dra-dragon attacked our sheep."

Paige's mouth dropped open. A dragon? In Bryolan?

"I told Vallen to just let it have them," Brevin continued, "but he wouldn't. He used his sling to throw stones at it instead. One got it in the eye. That must've made it mad 'cuz it spit fire at him. He tried to dodge, but a sheep got in the way, and…" He held out a hand to indicate Vallen's injuries.

Paige stepped closer and surveyed the boy, concerned that he hadn't stirred.

"How long ago was he attacked?"

"Several hours," Brevin replied, his voice shaking. "I got him here as quick as I could, but—"

"You did well, Brevin," Paige assured him. "How long has he

been unconscious?"

"Since it happened," the shepherd said. "He hasn't woken up since."

Alarmed, Paige reached for her magic and using her finger, drew the rune that allowed her to assess a patient's condition. The rune hovered in the air, glowing dark green, as she sensed not only Vallen's burns and broken leg, but also a contusion on his head and bleeding beneath his skull. She stifled a curse. The boy must have hit his head on something when he fell.

Despair rose in Paige, dark and choking. Healing Vallen's burns alone would be a challenge, especially after she expended so much magic aiding in a childbirth that afternoon. There was no way she could heal the bleeding in his brain, too, and the boy's life force was starting to fade. She needed help, but the only other healer in the village had gone to visit her daughter. No one else could—

She cut herself off mid-thought as Ellie's words came back to her.

I want you to promise you'll ask me if you need help.

Paige took a deep breath. She knew Ellie meant what she said. It didn't matter that it was the middle of the night or that her friend was the Baroness of Laveny. Paige's mother had been Ellie's maid since she was a baby, so the two of them had grown up together. Despite the difference in their stations, they were friends. If Paige sent for her, Ellie would come.

Looking down at Vallen's young face, Paige knew Ellie was his only hope. She turned and met his father's anxious gaze.

"I'll start healing your son," she told him. "But, I won't be able to do it alone. I need you to go to the Manor House and tell Baroness Elliana that Paige needs her help."

"The baroness?" Brevin cried. "I can't deliver a message to the baroness, especially not at this hour!"

Paige put a hand on his shoulder. "I understand your reluctance, but without another healer, your son is going to die. She's the only one I know of who is close enough to help."

Brevin glanced at his son, then gave her a firm nod.

"Very well," he said and headed for the door.

Satisfied, Paige turned back to her patient, determined to keep him alive until her friend could get there.

~ * ~

Elliana woke to the sound of a man screaming her title outside the door of her chambers.

"Baroness! Baroness, please!"

Ramono, the soldier guarding her chambers that night, said something in response, too quietly for her to make out the words. Then, the man screamed for her again.

Puzzled, Elliana got up and walked toward the commotion. Not wanting to be seen in her sleep dress, she reached for her magic and pictured herself in the clothes she planned to wear the next day. By the time she reached the door, she was clad in a green silk dress, and her blonde hair was pulled up.

She smiled. Being one of the kingdom's most powerful mages had its perks. Feeling more prepared now, Elliana opened the door to her chambers. In the hall, she found a commoner being dragged away by a young soldier who usually guarded the gate.

"What is going on here?" she asked Ramono.

"Please excuse the noise, my lady," he replied as the man continued to call for her. "This man came to the gate claiming he had to see you immediately. Since Terry is so inexperienced, he escorted him up here. When I refused to allow him to see you, he began yelling. I'm having him brought to the dungeons until morning."

Elliana frowned. The man was clearly desperate. What if his request couldn't wait until morning?

"Stop," she ordered, her eyes on Terry. "Let him go."

The young soldier obeyed at once. The commoner staggered forward and fell at her feet.

"Please, Baroness," he said before she could speak, "my son has been badly hurt, and Paige asked me to tell you she needs your help."

Elliana's eyes widened. It had been half a year since she'd made Paige promise to ask her if she needed help, and her friend hadn't requested it once. If she was doing it now, it must be serious.

"Right," Elliana said. "Let's go."

Reaching for her magic, she imagined herself and the commoner on Paige's doorstep. The next moment, they were there. The man gasped in shock, glancing around in disbelief. Shaking her head at him, Elliana walked straight through the door, where she found Paige kneeling next to her patient. Her friend's face was ashen as she drew runes in the air with a shaky hand. Elliana was at her side in an instant.

"Stop," she said, knocking her hand aside to prevent her from completing the runes.

Paige turned to looked at her.

"Ellie," she said, her shoulders slumping in relief, "I'm so glad you're here. There's bleeding in his brain. I've stopped the worst of it, but it still needs a bit more. His burns don't want to heal, and I haven't even started on the broken leg."

"Okay," Elliana replied, eyeing her friend with concern, "I'll take care of him. Don't worry."

Paige nodded and looked around. "Where's Brevin?"

Assuming that was the boy's father, Elliana said, "Outside. I think me transporting us here by magic unnerved him."

"I can't imagine why," Paige said, her voice dripping with sarcasm. "I'll check on him." She stood up and took a couple of unsteady steps toward the door.

Concerned, Elliana used her magic to move a chair behind Paige and pushed her into it.

"He's alright," she said. "You rest. I'm sure he'll come in any moment."

As if on cue, Brevin burst into the house.

"My son…How's my son?"

"Your son will be fine," Elliana told him. "Now, why don't you get yourself and Paige some water? You both look like you could use it."

"Yes, Baroness," Brevin said and hurried to do so.

"I'm okay," Paige insisted.

Elliana rolled her eyes and knelt beside the patient. She ran some magic through him to assess the damage, then got to work. She healed the brain-bleed and broken leg in a matter of seconds. To her surprise, the burns resisted at first, but with an extra pulse of magic, she healed them as well. She stood up just as Brevin returned with two cups of water.

"Your son is well now," Elliana told him. "He'll probably sleep for a while, but you can bring him home."

The man dropped both cups. Elliana caught them with her magic and floated them over to a table.

"Thank you, Baroness," Brevin said, falling to his knees. "How can I ever repay you?"

"No need," she replied. "Just give Paige her usual fee."

"What…but…"

"I insist," Elliana said. "Now, do you need help bringing your son home?"

Brevin's face blanched, probably remembering her preferred mode of transportation.

"No thank you, Baroness," he said, walking over to pick up his son. "Paige, I'll bring your payment by in the morning."

"Sounds good, Brevin," Paige said. "Thank you."

When the man was gone, Elliana studied her friend.

"Are you sure you're alright?"

Paige nodded. "I just overused my magic a little. I wasn't expecting the burns to take so much out of me."

"Yeah, I noticed the way they resisted healing," Elliana said. "It was bizarre."

"I think it has something to do with dragon fire," Paige replied. "I've never heard of—"

"Did you just say *dragon* fire?" Elliana interrupted, sure she'd misheard.

Paige's eyes filled with worry. "Yes. Brevin said a dragon attacked their sheep in the hills."

Elliana's mouth dropped open. "There's a dragon in Laveny?"

"According to Brevin," Paige replied. "And given those burns, I'm inclined to believe him."

Elliana nodded, torn between excitement and worry. Growing up, she'd heard stories about dragons. Her favorite had been the one about dragons and humans sharing a magic language. She'd been sorely disappointed to learn dragons were considered ancient history, or even myths. If there really was a dragon in Laveny, she would love to meet it. Although if it was attacking her people and their livestock, there was little chance of that meeting being friendly. Regardless, that was her problem to deal with.

"I'm glad you asked me for help," Elliana told Paige. "But, we need a more efficient way for you to contact me. Poor Brevin almost ended up in the dungeons." She thought for a moment, then summoned a rock from outside. She poured some magic into it and handed it to Paige.

"Here. Just touch this with your magic, and I'll know to come."

Paige smiled. "Thanks, Ellie. And thank you for coming tonight. I know it's late."

"No problem," Elliana said with a shrug. "You sure you're okay?"

Paige gave her a pointed look. "Yes, and if you ask me that one more time, I'll—"

"Alright, alright," Elliana said, holding up her hands. "I'll head home then." She paused. "Do you know where Brevin and his son were when they were attacked?"

"Near Benaro Lake," Paige replied. "Why?"

Elliana smiled innocently. "Just curious."

Paige narrowed her eyes. "Tell me you're not going to do what I think you are."

"I don't know what you're talking about."

"Yes, you do," Paige snapped. "You plan to go face the dragon by yourself, and that's—"

"The best option I have," Elliana filled in, abandoning her ruse. Paige knew her too well to let her get away with it. "The dragon already injured one of my people. I can't let it hurt anyone else."

Paige crossed her arms. "Ellie, it's a dragon. There hasn't been a dragon in Bryolan in living memory. You have no idea what it might be capable of."

"All the more reason for me to go after it," Elliana retorted.

"Yes, but not by yourself," Paige argued. "A dragon may be too much, even for you."

Elliana frowned. She'd never faced a human mage she couldn't defeat, but her friend had a point. Dragons had been gone from the kingdom so long that only children's tales remained. She had no idea what she'd be facing. Having other mages to back her up would be beneficial, but the handful of mages who were strong enough to do so all served the Crown directly. It could take days for them to get here. Her people couldn't wait that long.

"I'll be fine," Elliana said with confidence she didn't feel.

Paige sighed. "At least let me go with you."

Elliana stared at her friend, wondering if she'd lost her mind. Paige had to use runes to wield and amplify her magic. She wasn't even powerful enough to use it instinctually. How did she expect to be useful against a dragon?

She tried to keep her incredulity hidden, but some of it must have shown on her face because Paige added, "I know my magic isn't that strong, but I could be of *some* help. It would be better than you going alone."

Elliana was pretty sure she could fill a book with all the reasons that wasn't true. The most important one was her friend could easily get hurt, or even killed. That was unacceptable.

"Look," Elliana said, "I'll send a message to Ren. I'm sure he'll send mages to back me up soon."

"And you'll wait for them to get here before you go?" Paige asked, her tone a mixture of hope and skepticism.

"Of…of course, I will," Elliana said.

Paige slowly got to her feet. "Alright. Good luck then." She walked toward her bed. "Thanks again for your help, Ellie."

"Any time," Elliana said. "Good night."

With barely a thought, Elliana transported herself back to her chambers at the Manor House and sighed. She hated lying to Paige, but she knew her friend wouldn't have let it go if she'd admitted she was going by herself.

Though she had misgivings, Elliana knew she had to go. Even if she sent a message to Ren now, which she planned to, it could take days for him to convince his father, King Crios, to send reinforcements. She couldn't wait that long, not with her people in danger.

Telling herself her friend would understand, Elliana sent a message to Ren, then went to start getting ready. At sunrise, she would leave to face the dragon.

~ * ~

Renaldor woke up to something tapping his head. Blearily, he opened his eyes and looked around. In the pre-dawn light, he saw a roll of parchment hovering above him. Every few seconds, it tapped his forehead.

Renaldor stared at in confusion. As the Crown Prince of Bryolan, he wasn't accustomed to being accosted by parchment in his bed. Sure, some mages were capable of such a thing, but who would have the audacity to send him a message that way?

After a moment's reflection, his cousin's face flashed through his mind. Yes, Ellie would certainly be audacious enough to do this, but only if her message was really important.

Moving slowly so he didn't disturb his wife, Renaldor grabbed the parchment and walked over to his desk. Yawning, he lit the lantern and read Ellie's message. By the time he finished, he was wide awake.

There was a dragon in Bryolan, specifically in the hill country of Laveny, and his cousin was on her way to confront it. Confound Ellie with her overconfidence and sense of duty. She couldn't wait for other mages to get there and back her up. Of course not. She had to go on her own to face a dangerous creature he'd always thought was a myth.

Renaldor looked at himself in the mirror. His light brown skin looked paler than usual, and his black hair was slightly disheveled. He ran his fingers threw it, then headed to wake up his father and the kingdom's chief mage. He had to get reinforcements to his cousin before it was too late.

~ * ~

Treading lightly, Elliana stepped behind a tree. It had been about an hour since she transported herself to the shore of Benaro Lake. Since then, she'd been searching the surrounding area on foot. She would have preferred to scan it with magic, but she was afraid the dragon would sense it. So far, she'd found some broken trees and a few gouges in the earth, but she hadn't seen hide nor scale of the dragon.

Peering around the tree, Elliana surveyed the clearing she'd just found. Her heart skipped a beat. Lying on the other side of the clearing was the most beautiful and terrifying creature she'd ever seen. The dragon was the size of several houses with bluish-green scales that shimmered in the sunlight. The beast's large wings were folded against its body. With its head on the ground and its eyes closed, it appeared to be asleep.

Taking a deep breath, Elliana considered how she should approach the dragon. Somehow, she didn't think the confident strut she used when challenging other mages was a good idea, but she also didn't want to appear subservient. She had to strike a balance between the two, kind of like Paige, now that she thought about it.

Elliana squared her shoulders and dropped her chin a fraction. Then, she strode into the clearing, watching the creature carefully for signs of movement. It didn't so much as twitch.

In the middle of the clearing, Elliana came to a halt. Should she wake up the dragon? It didn't seem like the way to make a good first impression, but the alternative was to wait until it woke up naturally. Who knew how long that would take?

Decision made, Elliana cleared her throat.

"Excuse me, dragon," she said, feeling a bit ridiculous.

The dragons in the children's tales she'd heard could always speak, but so could the bears and eagles. She figured it was better to talk to the dragon and find it incapable of speech than to treat it like an animal and find it intelligent. Still, it felt odd to address the creature like a human.

Elliana waited several seconds. When the dragon didn't stir, she increased her volume.

"Excuse me, dragon."

This time, the beast lifted its head and looked at her. For the first time ever, Elliana had to fight the urge to step back.

"I am Elliana, Baroness of Laveny, a fief in the kingdom of Bryolan," she said, her voice firm but hopefully non-threatening. "Yesterday, you attacked one of my people. I've come to ensure that doesn't happen again."

The dragon stared at her for a long moment. Then, it turned its head skyward and opened its massive jaws. Smoked drifted out of its mouth.

Afraid it was about to spew flames, Elliana reached for her magic and pictured the beast shutting its mouth. Much to her surprise, nothing happened. Before she could try again, the dragon's head snapped toward her. Closing its mouth, it rose to its feet.

Elliana gulped. Though her magic had rebounded off the dragon, it had clearly sensed her spell and considered it a hostile act. Things were about to get interesting.

Opening its maw, the dragon blew a stream of fire directly at her. Raising her hand, Elliana shielded herself with her magic. It took a lot more power than she expected. Frowning, she thought about how the boy's burns had resisted being healed, how her magic had no effect on its mouth, and now this. Was it possible dragons were resistant, or even immune, to magic, and anything they created retained a portion of that resistance? That would explain why simply holding back fire was taking so much out of her.

Elliana bit her lip. She should have listened to Paige and

waited for reinforcements, but since she hadn't, she'd just have to do her best. Still maintaining her shield—seriously, how long could the beast continuously spout flames? —she used her magic to uproot a tree and sent it flying toward the side of the creature's face. It twisted its neck, allowing the tree to hit the back of its head. The stream of fire shifted a bit, but otherwise she might as well have thrown a flower at it.

Elliana stared at the creature in dismay. Just how strong was this beast?

As if in answer to her question, she suddenly felt an invisible force grip her entire body. She pushed against it with her magic, but for the first time in her life, she found herself fighting a power much greater than her own.

Elliana's jaw dropped. The dragon could use magic, too? It was her last thought before she was thrown backward into a tree, and the world went black.

~ * ~

Paige leaned forward, urging her horse to go faster. There was smoke rising from the clearing ahead, and she knew what that had to mean.

Paige had known Ellie was lying about waiting for reinforcements the moment the words left her mouth. Her friend was many things, but an accomplished liar wasn't one of them. Paige had known better than to argue with her, though. Once Ellie got determined to do something, she'd do it, come death or disaster, no matter what anyone said.

Knowing that, Paige had slept for a couple hours to replenish her strength, then left on her horse before first light. She knew, as far as magic went, she wasn't the most reliable backup, but she was better than nothing. She just hoped she wouldn't be too late.

When the air started feeling hot against her face, Paige jumped off her horse and ran toward the clearing. She arrived just in time to see an enormous bluish-green dragon stop spewing flames and throw Ellie backward, presumably using magic. Her friend's head hit a tree with a thud.

Stifling a gasp, Paige looked at the dragon. Its eyes were fixed on Ellie, and it didn't seem to have noticed her. As quietly as she could, Paige moved further back into the trees and ran in Ellie's direction, her mind racing. She had no hope of facing the dragon in combat, but if she could pull her friend under the cover of the trees and heal her, they might have a chance. At the very least, Ellie should be able to transport them both to safety.

When she was directly behind the tree Ellie had hit, Paige steeled her nerves and sprinted to where her friend lay. Without looking at the dragon, she grabbed Ellie under the shoulders and tried to drag her backward. Her friend didn't move.

Fighting against her panic, Paige tugged harder. Ellie still didn't budge. Heart sinking, Paige realized the dragon must be holding her in place somehow. Trembling, she glanced toward the dragon. It was watching them, looking ready to attack at any moment. Since she didn't have time to assess Ellie's injuries, Paige drew the rune for *heal* in the air. It hovered, glowing dark green, for a moment before sinking into Ellie.

Paige felt the drain on her magic immediately. She was already weak from healing Vallen the night before, and apparently, Ellie's injuries were serious. Dropping to her knees, Paige poured her magic into her friend, all the while expecting them both to be burned to a crisp.

After what could have been a minute or an hour, Paige felt her magic stutter, then stop. Ellie still hadn't stirred.

Tears filled Paige's eyes. Her best friend was going to die, either from her current injuries or from being unable to escape, all because she was too weak to save her. What kind of healer was she?

Desperate, she turned her gaze to the dragon. She found it sitting on its haunches, regarding her with its head tilted to the side.

"Please," Paige said, "have mercy. She just wanted to protect her people."

The dragon stared into her eyes for a long moment. Then, to her astonishment, the rune she'd drawn before appeared in the air, glowing the same bluish-green as the dragon's scales. The creature looked at her with what appeared to be a question in its eyes.

Paige's mouth dropped open. A dragon powerful enough to easily defeat Ellie was asking for her permission to heal her friend. Why in Bryolan would it do that?

Pushing her questions aside, Paige nodded and pointed at Ellie, hoping the creature would understand. The dragon's eyes seemed to soften, and the rune sank into Ellie. Instantly, the color returned to her cheeks, and her eyes flickered open.

"Ellie," Paige said, weak with relief.

"Paige?" Ellie asked, looking around. "What happ—" Her eyes widened when she spotted the dragon.

"It's okay," Paige rushed to assure her. "The dragon healed you."

Ellie's eyes flicked to the dragon then back to her, looking worried for her sanity.

"It did," Paige insisted, then frowned.

After what the dragon had done, it seemed rude to keep calling the creature an 'it.' Before she could contemplate an alternative, a string of bluish-green runes appeared in the air.

Ellie sat up. "Are those…runes?"

Paige nodded absently as she examined the glowing symbols and realized they had to be a message. The dragon was trying to communicate with them.

"But where did they—" Ellie began.

"Shush," Paige told her. "I need to concentrate."

Ignoring the glare she knew Ellie was sending the back of her head, Paige studied each rune carefully. She only recognized four: *hurt, mend, two,* and *connect.* It wasn't a lot to go on.

Frowning, Paige wished she'd learned runes beyond those needed for healing and tried to figure out what the dragon meant. After a minute, she took her best guess.

"Yes, the two of us are connected." She pointed at herself and Ellie. "We're friends."

The dragon's head tilted in confusion.

Paige bit her lip. Not only could the dragon not speak Bryolese, it couldn't understand it either. This was going to be a challenge.

After considering her options, Paige reached for her magic and immediately felt lightheaded. She put a hand on the ground to steady herself, grateful that she was still sitting down.

"Paige?" Ellie asked, concerned.

"I'm okay," she replied. "I just forgot I drained my magic earlier."

The dragon studied her. The previous message vanished, and the rune for *heal* appeared again. The creature looked at her inquisitively.

Paige blinked in surprise. The dragon wanted to heal her? The only thing wrong with her was that she'd used too much magic. It wasn't possible to replenish someone else's magic, was it?

Perplexed, Paige pointed at herself and opened her arms wide, trying to show she was willing. The *heal* rune disappeared, and three runes she didn't recognize took its place. As they sank into her, she felt her magic return as if she hadn't used it at all.

"Hey," Ellie said, hackles rising.

"It's alright," Paige said, turning to look at her. "She just replenished my magic."

Ellie's eyebrows shot up. "How's that possible? I can't even do that."

"I don't know how she did it," Paige replied. "It just happened."

"She?" Ellie asked, giving her a puzzled look.

Paige just shrugged. She didn't know how to explain it, but when the dragon's magic had touched her, it was like the creature's consciousness had brushed against her own. Her personality—dragonality? —was undeniably both feminine and kind.

Turning away from Ellie, Paige sent magic to her finger. It felt odd, drawing a rune without using it to amplify her magic, but she pushed aside her reservations and drew the rune for *connect*. She pointed between herself and Ellie, hoping the dragon would understand what she meant.

The dragon's eyes flicked between the two of them, and several runes appeared including the one for *blood*. Paige thought about that for a second, then drew the rune for *not*. She and Ellie weren't blood-related.

The dragon hummed to herself. Then, she made a long string of runes appear.

Before Paige could try to translate them, Ellie said, "Paige, are you...talking to the dragon...with runes?"

"Yes," she replied, awed. "Yes, I am."

Then, she turned her attention to the message and got back to work.

~ * ~

Gripping his sword tightly, Renaldor looked at the mages assembled around him.

"Be ready to dodge as soon as we arrive. Ell...the baroness could very well be fighting the dragon as we speak."

"Yes, Your Highness," they chorused.

"Alright," he said, "Mitano, transport us to Baroness Elliana's location."

The dark-skinned man nodded, and the world spun. When Renaldor felt solid ground beneath him again, he looked around, ready to dodge dragon fire, and saw...Ellie sitting under a tree, unscathed. Her friend Paige, a commoner Renaldor had met a few times, was beside her staring at a string of bluish-green runes hovering in the air. Across from her, an enormous dragon sat on its haunches, watching her calmly.

Renaldor squeezed his eyes shut and opened them again. When the scene before him didn't change, he sheathed his sword and called Ellie's name. In response, his cousin slowly rose to her feet and walked over to him, lacking her usual swagger.

"Hi, Ren."

Renaldor looked between her, Paige, and the dragon.

"What in Bryolan is going on here?" he demanded.

"Well," Ellie said, "Paige and the dragon are having a conversation using runes." She sounded like she barely believed her own words.

"What?" Renaldor sputtered. "Why are...How can...What?"

Ellie sighed. "I'm not entirely sure what happened. I was fighting the dragon—losing handily, I might add—and then, it...I mean, she...knocked me out. When I came to, she and Paige were trying to communicate using runes."

Renaldor's head spun. The dragon was strong enough to defeat Bryolan's most powerful mage, and yet, it was currently chatting with a fairly weak healer using runes, of all things. How did any of that make sense?

"Paige only knows healing runes, so it's been kind of slow going," Ellie added. "I don't suppose any of you know any runes?" Her gaze swept over the mages Renaldor had forgotten were standing behind him.

"No, my lady."

"No, Baroness."

"I don't know any," Mitano chimed in, "but my father has a book of common runes. I could transport it here, if you wish."

"Do it," he and Ellie said at the same time.

As Mitano obeyed, Renaldor looked at his cousin. "You know

you're not in charge of the Crown's mages." *Yet*, he added in his mind. When he became king, he planned to change that.

"Of course," she said, the usual fire returning to her eyes. "I just know a good plan when I hear one."

Renaldor gave her a pointed look. "Really? Like going to confront a dragon with only Paige for backup?"

"I didn't bring Paige with me," Ellie replied indignantly. "She came on her own."

"Oh, that's so much better," he retorted, rolling his eyes.

"Here's the book, Your Highness," Mitano said. He walked up and held it out to him.

Renaldor took it and looked at Ellie. "Shall we?"

His cousin nodded, and together, they approached Paige and the dragon.

~ * ~

A small part of Elliana still couldn't believe this was happening. She half-expected to wake up and find this was all a dream caused by her head wound.

The larger part of her, however, knew all of this was real. As she and Ren walked toward the dragon, she studied Paige, kneeling on the ground and patiently trying to communicate with the most powerful being to ever set foot in Bryolan.

Watching her, Elliana realized how wrong she'd been the previous night. As it turned out, Paige had been the perfect person to be her backup. Elliana hadn't needed someone with magical prowess. She'd needed someone with heart, and Paige had that in abundance. Somehow, the dragon had seen that, too.

"We have a book of runes," Ren said, stopping a few paces behind Paige.

"Thank you," her friend said, turning to look at them. Her eyes widened. "Your Highness," she added, inclining her head.

Ren held the book out to her. "Would you please translate so I can talk to…her?" He nodded his head at the dragon.

Paige took the book, frowning.

"Of course, Your Highness," she said, "but now that you have a book, Ellie can—"

"No," Elliana interrupted, "you're more familiar with runes, and she trusts you already. You should be the one to do this."

"Alright," Paige said and opened the book, "what would you like me to say?"

For the next hour, Elliana watched in nothing short of awe as Ren and Paige negotiated with the dragon. Apparently, her name was Twilit Sea, and she was from a distant land where many of her kin thrived. She'd come to Bryolan to explore, never expecting to find an intelligent race residing there, especially not one so small.

By the end of the conversation, Twilit Sea agreed to return to her homeland and report what she'd found. She assured them her race was peaceful and mostly solitary, unless they were provoked. She believed they would want to avoid Bryolan altogether, but if they did come to visit, it would be in peace.

With all of that decided, Twilit Sea drew a rune Paige said meant *farewell*.

"Goodbye to you as well," Ren said. "And safe travels."

After Paige translated that, Twilit Sea looked at them all one more time, her eyes lingering on Paige. One last rune appeared in the air. Then, she unfolded her wings and took flight.

Elliana watched the dragon as she rose higher and higher, then vanished from sight.

~ * ~

As Twilit Sea flew away, Paige watched, confused, as the dragon's final rune floated down to land on the back of her hand. Instead of sinking in and disappearing, the rune simply stopped glowing and remained on her skin. When she rubbed it with her finger, it remained unaffected. It seemed to have become a part of her.

"What does that say?" Ellie asked.

Paige flipped through the book, searching for the unknown rune. When she found it, she couldn't help but smile.

"Friend," she said, rubbing the mark fondly. "It means friend."

"Well, that settles that," the Crown Prince said.

Paige looked at him, confused. "Your Highness?"

"When Ellie comes to court after I become king, I'd officially like to invite you to come, too."

Ellie grinned. "That's a great idea."

Paige glanced between the two of them in shock.

"Me? Your Highness, I can't…I mean, why would you want me there? I'm nobody special."

"Nonsense," the prince said. "I already thought it would be nice to have you around to rein in Ellie. This just seals the deal."

The Baroness of Laveny stuck her tongue out at her future sovereign, then smiled at Paige.

"You should definitely come," she said. "Then, if Twilit Sea or any of her kin come to visit, we'll have a dragon-friend there to negotiate."

Ellie held out her hand. Paige took it, feeling dazed, and let her friend pull her to her feet.

"I'll think about it," she managed to say. She looked at the book in her hands. "Could I keep this book, Your Highness?"

The prince frowned. "Well, it's not mine, so—"

"Here," Ellie interrupted, making an identical book appear in her hand. "You keep this one, and we'll give the original back to Mitano."

As the two of them exchanged books, the prince stared at Ellie.

"How did you…Oh, never mind, I'll take that," he said, plucking the original book from her hand. "Next time, you send me a message about a powerful, magical creature, wait for reinforcements before you confront it."

"I'll…try," Ellie said. Then, her voice softened. "Thank you for coming, Ren."

The prince nodded. "See you later." He looked at Paige. "Both of you."

Paige bobbed a curtsy as he walked back to the group of mages he'd brought with him. Ellie turned to look at her.

"Thank you for coming after me, too. I would be dead if you hadn't."

Paige smiled. "You'd have done the same for me."

"True," Ellie said. "So, do you want a quick trip home, dragon-friend?"

Paige clutched the book of runes to her chest, silently vowing to study it daily.

"Sure," she told Ellie. "But make sure you bring my horse, too."

"You got it."

As the world spun around her, Paige knew she would be ready if dragons ever did come to Bryolan again one day. In her heart, she sincerely hoped they would.

~ * ~ * ~

Miriam Thor grew up in Louisiana. After graduating from high school, she moved to North Carolina where she attended Gardner-Webb University and earned her bachelor's degree in American Sign Language and elementary education. After graduation, Miriam remained in North Carolina for several years. While there, she met and married her husband. Recently, the two of them moved to Alabama. Miriam is currently employed as a sign language interpreter at a school.

In second grade, Miriam's teacher encouraged her to write to her heart's content, so she started doing that and never stopped. Her first short story was published in 2016. She likes to write a variety of genres, but fantasy is her favorite. Occasionally, Miriam also dabbles in poetry, but only when inspiration strikes. Her published works include a young adult fantasy novella entitled *Wish Granted,* a contemporary Christian fiction novella entitled *Her First Noel,* several short stories, and a handful of poems.

When Miriam is not writing, she enjoys reading, doing martial arts, spending time with her husband, and cuddling with her cats. She also loves to eat sweets, especially cookie dough, cheesecake, and anything chocolate.

To learn more about Miriam or her published works, you can visit her website: https://miriamthor17.wixsite.com/author . You can also follow her on Twitter (@Miriam_Thor17) or subscribe to her blog: threecs.org.

A Found Dragonel

Joyce Frohn

"Daddy Atarax, tell me the story one last time, please? My story."

The green dragon nodded his horned head and brought it closer to Dragonel. He looked at the blonde girl in a linen dress. His head was the size of her whole body and twice as wide. "If you're sure you've packed everything." She nodded and patted a leather pack at her side. "It was right after I flew to Jerusalem for Easter, like I always used to. How many years ago was that?"

Dragonel did some fast counting. "About—"

"Never mind. I was feeling old enough then. All the females were running after the skinny males, like they always do. All I was thinking about was a nice hard bed of gold."

"You're not old and you're sort of skinny."

"Thank you for your flattery. I walked into this cave and there were things missing. The sparkling opal egg my first mate had given me (weighed almost as much a chicken egg), the ruby from the ring of Genghis Khan my third mate had given me (at least that was the story she told me) and…"

"Daddy. The story. My story."

"Alright. I heard something crying. On a shelf on the pile of tapestries from Italy my fifth mate gave me, something small was moving, you. A wrinkled, red face stared at me and howled. I shut my ears." Atarax turned to Dragonel and brushed a claw along her shoulder. Her hand reached out and wrapped halfway around one thick-scaled digit.

"I wondered if someone had stolen my treasures and left you as payment? Did the thief think I would eat you? Did some desperate parent think I would be a better parent than they could? I cradled you in one paw and unwrapped the blanket. You were smaller than the smallest new-hatched dragonel, hardly bigger than my smallest digit." He held up the paw and wriggled the small digit by the foot joint. "I wondered how long ago you had been hatched. Or whatever it is humans do? I hope you know.

"There was an idea in my head; maybe you were just what the Healer in the human village needed. Nothing like a new baby or babies, to distract one from problems, or losing the last one. That or massive amounts of rich, dark coal."

"Daddy. You've got to cut back on the coal if you want to lose weight."

"Back to the story. I unwrapped you and touched you with my tongue. You were cold and I knew I was being as bad as some uncaring female. Thinking only of myself and not putting little ones first."

Dragonel brushed a single tear from her eye.

"I figured you were hungry, too. So, I held you in my left front paw and used my right to open my pink brood scales. You were a soft little creature with no milk teeth, no claws. No nothing. So I pulled my own claws over the soft skin. The first milk dripped out, mixed with a little blood. I held you close, and you sucked the milk off my brood scales. When you finished, I pushed the scales back into place and licked away the excess milk.

I knew you needed to be burped. You were far too fragile to be thumped against the floor the way my dragonels were. When I brought you close to my face, you spit up. Squeezing a bit seemed to work. You gurgled and fell asleep." Atarax ignored the smothered giggles. Dragonel snuggled into the crook of his right front leg.

"You were far too soft to tuck under a wing. But I knew I had to keep you warm. So, holding you close, I began to raise my fire. The flames licked at a pile of gold coins until they glowed red. I made a nest of tapestries and silk and put you in. I went to sleep with one arm wrapped around your nest. You did remember to pack those tapestries and what's left of the silk?"

Dragonel nodded.

"It was the bleating of a sheep that woke me. I forgot it was rent day. For a moment I couldn't remember why I had slept in such an awkward position. Then you started crying. I wiped you off on the tapestries and fed you again, then wrapped you in the liner from a suit of armor from a knight and laid you on the shelf I had found you on.

I was hungry, and the bleating of the sheep made my stomach ache. But I thought of my father's words."

"'Chores first, food later. Learn your duty.' What a fuddy-duddy."

"Show some respect. So I dragged an old iron kettle from the back of the cave and filled it from the river. I dropped the soiled cloth in the kettle and put the lid on; I raised my fire and blew at the kettle. When the steam blew the lid off, I knew they were done. I had just started eating, when I heard you crying, so I gulped the rest of the sheep down and hurried to pick you up and feed you.

"I wrapped you in the blankets you had been in when I found you and headed for town. As I walked through the town, my wing tip hit a stack of dried grass. I thought of trying to replace it but decided it might be better to just apologize and give a gold coin to the town leader to pay for the damage. That's usually the best thing. Remember that. I hope you packed enough gold."

Dragonel nodded and pushed deeper into Atarax's leg.

"I sat back on my haunches to switch you to my other paw. The tip of my tail hit something. Then I heard the dog whimpering. It seemed all right. At least, it was moving fast enough. As my first mate always said about dragonels, 'If they can outrun you; they're healthy enough.' I thought maybe I could bribe—convince the Healer to move closer. Without a mate, I needed someone to talk to."

"You'll get someone. I know you will. I've polished your scales and sharpened your claws."

Atarax sighed. "Yes, I hope. I figured out to put my wings up and wrapped my tail around them. The villagers were avoiding me, as usual. I hate dealing with hysterical humans. I'm so glad you can do that instead of me. I sat back and knocked on the window of the Healer's tower with a claw. I said, 'Please open up. It's me.'

"'Lord Atarax. How good to see you,' he said as he pushed back his long, braided hair. 'What brings you here? Have you found someone ill or hurt?' He smiled, for a moment, but the smile didn't light up his eyes. 'Have you come to compare our families and mates? Or to try to cheer me up?' He brushed a tear out of his eye.

"'In a way, both.' I smiled, not showing any teeth. 'I found a human baby.' I held you up in my paw.

"The healer bent out the window and took you. 'A sweet little girl' And I sighed, a female, too bad, the Healer surely would want an apprentice; but maybe…

"I rested my head on the couch the Healer kept there for me.

I watched as the healer diapered you and wrinkled my nose at the smell. 'Is that normal?'

"'At this age; yes. Whoever dropped it off must have just fed her. That'll make it much easier to find out who did this.'

"I had to shake my head. 'I found it when I got back from Jerusalem. I fed it.' I figured it was best not tell him that there had been a clear scent trail, then.

"'But you don't have a litter.'

"'I don't have to.' I thought the healer sounded nervous. "What's the matter?'

"The healer laid you in the empty cradle by the fire and rummaged through a pile of books on the floor. 'She didn't drink any blood, did she?'

"I nodded. 'A little, it comes before the first milk. Why?'

"The healer glanced up from his book. 'It's written that drinking dragon's blood gives a human the ability to understand all languages of men and beasts. At least one writer says so, there is so little written about you dragons by anyone that knows one. So much is lost.' I knew what he meant, there were fewer and fewer of us dragons and more humans and even the books are getting rare. 'Could you please write the book she started?'"

Dragonel nodded. "And I do understand everything. Even if most animals don't have much to say."

"I realized that was why my mates always told me they had to be careful of even the smallest wound during a fight. It wouldn't do for some knight to be able to understand dragons. Those things can be dangerous."

He turned his head to Dragonel, "Watch out for them. I think they could be dangerous to humans, too." Dragonel nodded.

"'That's no problem. I might take her on as an apprentice. An ability like that shouldn't be wasted. Here's the problem. It was in Quenta's book.' He had lifted a battered book off the floor. That was one of the ones that didn't survive. 'That Healer wrote all he could read of it but—'"

Atarax's sides quivered for a moment before he got his emotions under control.

"'The book says drinking dragon's milk can make a human age at the same rate as a dragon.'

"'Is that bad?' I asked.

"The healer looked up from his book. 'Atarax, how old are you? You've been ruler of this town since I was a child.'

"'I tried to count my years and ran out of claws. 'I can't remember how old I am. I'm not very good with numbers. All my mates said that.'

"The healer smiled. 'My mate says that, too. How long does it take for one of your dragonels to grow up?'

"'A dragonel is one year in the egg. They nurse for three years. You said yours nursed that long. Maybe we age at the same rate.'

"'How long does it take a dragon to be able to breed?' The healer asked.

"'At least three hundred years.' I watched the healer's face fall.

"'If he's right, this little one may still be a child when I am long in my grave.' He lifted you up. 'Otherwise, I think I would have liked her as assistant.' He was blinking back tears.

"I decided to change the subject before the healer started crying. Or I did. 'How could you tell it's a girl? It's skin looks the same all over.'

"The healer dried his eyes with his apron. 'I always wanted to ask you how you can tell the sex of dragons for my book. It always seemed to me that your tail would cover your genitalia, but you've told me about being able to tell the difference from a distance.'

"I chuckled. 'You mean you have to see a human's genitals before you know what sex it is? That's why you dress differently, isn't it? Dragons don't need to worry about that. See the pink scales on my chest? That shows I'm a male.'

"'Male?' The Healer's voice was almost a screech. You cried. 'You've told me about nursing babies and...' The healer unlaced her dress and lifted you to her breast. 'Males don't nurse babies. Women do, at least...'

"And then I started to laugh. Like you are now. Like you always do. I was laughing so hard, the herbs hanging from the ceiling shook and the dishes in the cupboard rattled.

"'You're female. You humans have it all backward. Women lay the babies and then nurse them. All of my mates said carrying and laying a clutch of eggs was the end of their job. You females do it all.'

"And then the village headman was knocking on the door. 'My Lord Atarax. What's wrong? I heard you roar.' His face was dark with anger and he was carrying a sword. 'Has this witch angered you?' He turned to the healer who had settled herself and you on a rocking chair. 'Have you no shame? Cover yourself, woman.' She joined me in laughter.

"I winked at her. 'Why do you call me, lord? How can you be sure I'm not a lady?'

"The headman blinked. 'What is the problem here, my lord?'

"The healer buttoned her blouse and laid you back in the cradle. 'The lord of our village has informed me that he found an abandoned babe. We ask your wise opinion as to what we should do.'

"The headman spluttered for a moment. 'Why, have it baptized and then find some loving woman to raise it.'

"The healer stood up. 'Since you and I both will be long dead when this child is grown, there is only one loving parent that should raise it. If you accept the challenge, my Lord Atarax?'

"'Will you two be the godparents? And hire someone to do the laundry?' I asked.

"'We will be honored, my lord,'" the headman said. 'And I am sure that I can find some woman willing to be the wet nurse. What was all the excitement about?'

"The healer laughed too hard to say anything. I smiled. 'I was surprised to find out what sex the child was.' The headman bowed and went to find the priest. I patted her on the head with my tongue, at least she could laugh again. 'I never thought that I would find a nurturing female and such an unusual dragonel in one day.'"

"That headman sounds as stuffy as the one they have now," Dragonel said.

"They all are stuffy but some of them are smart."

"I wish I remembered that healer better."

"She nursed you for three years. But she died when you were barely talking."

"Don't worry, Daddy." Dragonel cinched the straps of her pack tight. "Tomorrow is Easter. You come back with a female dragon and get yourself some dragonels to raise. The world needs more dragons. I'll take these books and move to the Healer's house on the edge of town."

Atarax nodded and patted Dragonel on the head with his tongue. "Remember daughter, don't come here until the babies are a year or two old. By then I should be able to get them to obey. Don't pick mates just because they're skinny and cute. I'm pretty sure that even in humans you need to pick a good mate."

"Yes, Father", Dragonel, said as she walked away.

~ * ~ * ~

Joyce Frohn is married with an adult daughter. She also shares a house with two cats, a lizard and too many dirty dishes. She has been been published in "Writer's Resist", "Nothing Ever Happens in Fox Hollow" and an upcoming anthology, "Dark Cheer: Cryptids Emerging".

Our Dragon Neighbor

Cara Brezina

"There must be some law she's breaking that we can use to force her to get rid of that thing," Heidi Snidman declared.

"And if there isn't, we should draft one immediately," Lori Milliner said.

"It's an outrage this situation should have arisen in the first place," Rich Brouwer added.

Six of the seven members of the Sweet Pea Circle Board of Trustees nodded in satisfaction, which meant the issue was decided. Sweet Pea Circle was made up of the Right Sort of people, after all. They all had credentials and tidy yards and children who were just precocious enough. If the community was united in their opposition to Drusilla Bara and her disruptive activities, she was the one in the wrong. Obviously.

There should be a law.

Typically, only Erika Denk failed to join in the push for intervention. She was paging through a thick black binder, its plastic cover tattered.

"I'm not certain of the appropriate legal action to take in these circumstances," she said, scanning through pages swarming with bylaws and lacking convenient bullet points. "The situation is quite complex, and I'm certain Ms. Bara will appeal the determination of any proceedings that are based on anything less than formidably solid legal grounds."

Six of the seven trustees had stopped listening by the time Erika got to the word *complex*.

"I propose we summon her before the Board of Trustees," Heidi broke in.

"It's a property use issue," Lori said. "That sort of activity does not conform with our community's conditions, covenants, and restrictions."

The atmosphere in the room lightened. It was as if Drusilla and her highly problematic menagerie were already lined up on her long and winding driveway, possessions neatly packed away, waiting for an Uber to convey them out of Sweet Pea Circle's collective memory.

"We'll laugh about this when it's all over," Heidi declared. She was already laughing.

"You'd better take some photos for proof," Rich said. "Nobody would believe it otherwise."

"It's certainly not something I ever expected to encounter in Sweet Pea Circle," Lori said. "You know, really, a—"

Heidi shushed her before she could utter the word *dragon*, and Russell Vilius winced.

~ * ~

Russell Vilius had no desire for the Board of Trustees to embroil itself in a dispute that could require more of his time in addition to the meeting every first Wednesday of each month. Russell worked forty-eight hours a week as a Human Resources specialist, went golfing approximately seventeen times a year, spent every Saturday supporting one of Rusty's or Bella's extracurricular activities, visited his or Michelle's parents for holidays, and puttered about organizing his collection of antique dentistry tools on an occasional rainy weekend. Two weeks ago, he'd been knotting his tie and staring vacantly out the window when he first observed the dragon.

The Vilius family lived on Upper Sweet Pea Circle Drive, which overlooked Lower Sweet Pea Circle Drive as it descended the ridge and curved around the valley floor. Down below lay a swath of green space which Russell had never thought about very much. Until now. The area consisted of several fields, copses of trees scattered about, and a picturesque old farmhouse surrounded by a barn and a few outbuildings. Nobody lived there, but workers visited regularly to mow the fields and perform routine upkeep on the buildings. Russell had vaguely assumed it was maintained by a conservation group.

The pygmy goats had arrived a week ahead of the dragon, conveyed in a gleaming trailer that pulled up in the early afternoon. It disgorged several dozen sturdy little goats into one of the fields, and by evening, the flock was grazing and cavorting as if they'd been lifelong residents.

Nobody saw the dragon appear. According to the surveillance footage recorded at the entrance gateway, no unfamiliar vehicles had passed by in the night. Yet when dawn arrived, the dragon was sunning itself in the pasture adjacent to the barn, which was situated furthest away from the field containing the goats. The tract was enclosed by tight rows of poplars, but they couldn't conceal the dragon's presence from the several hundred houses overlooking the valley.

As Russell watched, the dragon stretched and rested its craggy head on its front paws. A pearly plume of smoke wafted up from its nostrils.

Russell wasn't bothered. His fingers continued the familiar deft movements at his neck. It took him only a minute or two to realize the tie had slipped around the collar of his shirt and fallen to the floor. He swore—almost—and stalked into the windowless bathroom to complete his morning routine.

He was opening the front door when he heard Michelle shrieking. He scooted outside as she surged down the stairs toward him.

"Honey, you won't believe what I've just seen—"

Russell held up a soothing hand as if directing traffic.

"Hush, dear, you don't want to wake the sleeping dragon. Gotta go, don't want to be late to work."

He delivered a kiss to the air a couple feet away from her cheek and proceeded briskly to the car.

Over the next week, the residents of Sweet Pea Circle completely lost their minds over the dragon. The thing was a menace, the children were in danger, the authorities should do something, they were packing their bags to move *right now*.

Nobody moved, including, mostly, the dragon. It spent much of its time arranging itself in photogenic poses in the field and occasionally sashayed into the barn through the two massive sliding doors.

Russell was not particularly fearful the dragon would go on a marauding, murderous rampage. The creature had not yet shown any inclination to violate property boundaries, after all. Russell was more concerned by the prospect all the fuss over the dragon would interfere with his familiar routines.

~ * ~

His apprehensions were realized when the Sweet Pea Circle Board of Trustees began negotiating Drusilla Bara's appearance regarding the contested zoning issue. The woman kept a low profile. It took half a day after the dragon's arrival for the Sweet Pea Circle community to realize the dragon's keeper was also on the premises. Her digital footprint was similarly unobtrusive. The trustees sent out blizzards of e-mails discussing the contested zoning issue— nobody mentioned the word *dragon*—and Drusilla replied to none of them.

Russell Vilius paid them little attention either, until receiving one with the subject line TRIBUNAL DATE FINALIZED followed by a swarm of punctuation marks and emojis. It turned out the upcoming proceedings were not exactly a tribunal. Drusilla's factotum told them she would be willing to see them on Thursday afternoon if they stopped by.

Lori considered the development a huge triumph. Russell thought they'd be arriving on Drusilla's doorstep like supplicants. They might as well be taking along begging bowls.

All of the trustees arrived dressed like they were appearing for a meeting with their CEO, as if to make up for the unconventional circumstances of the so-called tribunal. The farmhouse, which appeared comfortably Kinkade-ish from a distance, seemed more looming and gothic as they approached. The sun grew obscured by the low-hanging smoke. Russell found himself looking upward apprehensively to check for bats flying out from the wide eaves.

"This place does have atmosphere, doesn't it!" Heidi bellowed. Everybody was talking very loudly, as if the volume of their voices would make them more important. Lori stumbled as one of her spike heels wedged between a couple cobblestones of the walkway. Erika frowned at the lack of a doorbell, and her expression darkened further as she looked up to observe the massive door knocker above eye level.

Russell became aware of the smell of sulfur and smoldering charcoal as they stood waiting for Drusilla. After a minute or two, the ground began to shake, and he shaded his eyes against a blinding flare of light. The temperature shot up a couple degrees.

He'd grown accustomed to seeing the dragon pirouette and gently emit a stream of fire from the upper windows of his house.

It had not been so daunting from a distance of nearly a mile off.

Kenneth Golden was nearly doubled over in a fit of coughing by the time Drusilla Bara opened the door. She looked down at him, far down, in mild concern. Drusilla was tall and narrow, with black hair pulled severely back from pallid skin. She wore an extra-long black form-fitting T-shirt, black yoga pants, and neon yellow flip-flops.

"How lovely of you all to stop by," she said with a toothy and insincere smile. "Ethan tells me you are residents of the little village?" She flexed the fingers of her left hand in the presumed direction of the little village.

Russell had expected hints of Transylvania in her accent. Instead, her voice sounded pure Valley Girl, slightly nasal, even if her attitude seemed rooted in the old world.

"We are the trustees of Sweet Pea Circle," Lori announced. "We've come because we're concerned about your livestock situation."

"Don't worry, the goats are fine, thanks for your consideration," Drusilla said. "Very frisky."

A couple of the trustees dropped their eyes at *frisky*, but Lori did not flinch.

"It's actually your other livestock we wish to discuss."

Drusilla tilted her head.

"Other livestock? I don't understand your meaning."

The dragon obligingly smacked its lips in its sleep in the pasture upwind from the farmhouse. A hot breeze threatened to whisk up the hem of Lori's skirt. The vibrations caused the doorframe to rattle.

"That." Lori indicated the direction of the dragon with a thumb.

Drusilla burst out in tinkling laughter.

"*That* is not livestock! Livestock is for eating, check google, you'll see."

Russell whipped his phone out before he realized the advice was rhetorical. He sheepishly slipped it back into his pocket.

"Regardless of the terminology," Lori was saying, "The conditions, covenants, and restrictions of our community forbid keeping backyard animals. We've held extensive debate over families who wished to raise chickens or rabbits, and the consensus has been that these activities are not appropriate for an area with a significant local population density."

She was reading off a notepad filled with dense text Erika Denk had prepared for her.

"You need to check your maps, these rules do not apply to me," Drusilla countered breezily. "The developer bought up all of the property around my family's farm, but my grandfather refused to sell. This land does not fall under your jurisdiction."

The winding layout of Sweet Pea Circle suddenly made sense. Lori cast a desperate glance toward Erika, hoping for a rebuttal. Erika was staring intently off into the middle distance, refusing to meet her gaze.

"But, as a matter of common courtesy…" Lori began, trailing off before managing to formulate a plausible conclusion. It wasn't easy to articulate what the norms of common courtesy dictated in these circumstances.

"My family has been raising these creatures on this land for generations, it's a tradition. You would know that if you'd bothered talking to neighbors."

She waggled her fingers again, presumably in the direction of property owners beyond Sweet Pea Circle.

Lori had paled.

"You mean this isn't the first time one of these, er—"

"What is the precise name of this species, again?" Erika put in.

Russell perked up at this bold direct assault in the game of *don't say the d-word*.

Drusilla gave a smile that showed most of her molars and widened her eyes.

"I thought everyone was familiar with the Greater Promethean Iguana."

The effect was as dramatic as she'd intended. Nobody swooned, but Lori silently mouthed the phrase with eyes bobbling, Erika started scribbling in a pocket notebook, and Russell convulsively entered a search query on his phone.

"Was there anything else?" Drusilla asked. "Thank you, have a good day, buh-bye!"

The latch gently snicked shut in their faces. It would have been much more satisfying if Drusilla had at least deigned to slam the door.

~ * ~

By the weekend, most Sweet Pea Circle residents under the age of thirty had started referring to their community as The Little Village, and most residents over the age of forty had developed symptoms such as elevated blood pressure, headaches, or grinding teeth. Heidi Snidman called an emergency meeting of the Board of Trustees for Saturday afternoon.

Russell sent his regrets, citing a previous commitment. He enjoyed Bella's soccer game that afternoon more than any other he'd ever attended.

Afterwards, he learned the Board of Trustees had determined that they had weighed alternate recourses concerning the GPI (Greater Promethean Iguana) situation. While it was true the Sweet Pea Circle regulations did not apply to the Bara property, Drusilla was subject to Duncan Township ordinances. Heidi was hopeful they could come to an arrangement with the township board of supervisors.

"They're somewhat backward, but basically reasonable," she'd said.

The Sweet Pea Circle Board of Trustees didn't bother with the executive dress code when they showed up for the monthly meeting at Duncan Township Hall, a former one-room schoolhouse. Their petition was the second item on the agenda, following a motion to eliminate the librarian positions in the local public schools.

"We are filing a public nuisance complaint against Drusilla Bara," Rich Brouwer began. He'd been chosen as primary spokesman for the evening because his father had been a plumber. The other trustees hoped his blue-collar bloodline might make him more relatable to the local notables.

The other trustees chimed in with the particulars of their ordeal. The environmental impact, the danger to life and property, the potential negative effects on property values. Rich worked as an actuary, and he displayed four poster board tables of figures to support their case.

Russell looked at the faces of the township supervisors and decided the Sweet Pea Circle trustees were making a good impression. The supervisors didn't challenge a single allegation regarding Drusilla Bara's actions.

The trustees continued with a description of the toll the situation had taken on their daily lives. The myriad health complaints, the psychological torment, the terror that the smells from an incautious neighbor's backyard barbecue would bring disaster.

The township supervisors didn't question the validity of any of the claims, not even the part about Lori taking her French bulldog to the vet for anxiety. Russell started to worry about their impassive stolidity. It was almost as if they'd already made up their minds and weren't bothering to pay attention.

"Any questions?" Chairman Fred Bryce asked after the Sweet Pea Circle people had finished their presentation. Lori was slightly out of breath. There were no questions. Fred sighed.

"This is a complex issue, very complex," he declared. "Do I have any support to table the proposal pending further investigation?"

Within thirty seconds, the public nuisance complaint had been tabled, meaning it was stone cold dead without the faintest hope of resurrection. Ninety-five percent of all proposals brought before the Duncan Township Board ended up tabled.

Rich's poster board displays slipped out of his limp fingers and landed on the floor.

Heidi marched toward Fred as soon as the session was adjourned, glowering ominously as she waited for him to finish small talk with one of the other supervisors.

"I'm afraid I fail to understand, being as we have demonstrated our complaint meets all of the criteria set out in your ordinances, why—"

Fred quelled her with a motion of his hand as if he were patting a large imaginary dog on the head.

"You newcomers don't really appreciate the relationships between landowners outside your own little hive," he chuckled. "We don't base all of our decisions on narrow interpretation of rules and regulations. You people have forgotten the worth of *reputation*."

"...Reputation?" Heidi echoed.

"Exactly. Do you know the Baras have owned that property for more than a hundred years? There have occasionally been disagreements with neighbors, but you have to understand, the Baras are a *solid* family."

"...Solid?"

"The Baras are good citizens who are committed to the welfare of this township. As a public servant, I know I can count on the Baras where it matters."

Realization dawned. Fred Bryce was a white-haired man wearing a polo shirt stretched over an expansive midsection, but she suddenly viewed him as if he were sporting a sharkskin suit, a pinky ring and prestige chronometer peeking out from under a bejeweled cuff.

"They're very generous, you're saying."

Fred chuckled again.

"They hold the township's priorities in high regard. Now, if you'll excuse me."

When Russell returned home, Michelle asked him how the meeting had gone.

"Heidi was right," Russell told her. "They were reasonable. Way more reasonable than she'd bargained for, I'm thinking."

~ * ~

On the day of the derecho, Michelle called Russell at work during his lunch break to urge him to leave early so he'd be home before the severe weather was predicted to arrive. He said uh-huh in all the right places and assured her he'd be on the road by 4 p.m.

He ended up clocking out at 5:40, the same time he always left the office. The sky darkened to dusky gray by the time he turned onto the county road leading to Sweet Pea Circle Drive. What had Michelle said about the forecast? Severe thunderstorms, hurricane force winds, devastating something-or-another. At least it wasn't raining.

A sheet of rain descended on his windshield, drawing a black curtain across the landscape. The wind ramped up to a roar. Twigs and leaves and other debris smacked the SUV and stuck to the glass.

The Sweet Pea Circle families who left their yards littered with toys were really going to regret it, Russell thought to himself.

He was running 20 minutes late by the time he reached Sweet Pea Circle. He inched forward to the gate and carefully maneuvered around the sharp curve where Sweet Pea Circle Drive began its gradual ascent. The barriers on either side were studded with reflectors, but he couldn't see them until the front bumper was nearly touching the guardrail. When the wind did allow an occasional glimpse of the pavement, it looked like he was navigating up a river.

There was a lookout point at the top of the ridge, and he decided to pull over and wait for the tempest to abate, even though he would only have been 25 seconds away from his own door under ordinary circumstances. He gently pumped the brake.

The SUV glided sideways toward the rail.

Frantically blinking icons on his dashboard indicated a half dozen different automated systems were attempting to stop the slide. But the robots were losing. Russell shoved the brake pedal to floor. The SUV meandered toward the barrier in a lazy half spin before barreling through without the slightest pause.

Russell barely registered the tremor of the collision amid the howling storm. The view was equally unspectacular as the vehicle somersaulted over and over down the steep ridge. Everything he saw through the windows was a whirling blur. But the sensation of lost gravity as his stomach flopped up toward his throat, then down to his toes, and back again—that was new to him.

The landing wasn't too easy, either. He heard the roof of the car crunch as it came to rest on the ground. He waited for his head to crunch into his spinal column, but the action sequence had ended. His stomach felt like it was lodged somewhere next to his Adam's apple, and the straps of his seat belt bit into his waist and left shoulder.

The roar of the storm seemed to have subsided. All he could hear was his own heartbeat and the irritating sound of a high-pitched giggle. It took him a minute to realize it was his own voice.

Cut it out, he told himself. The giggling continued.

He finally managed to hiccup to a stop when he noticed a pair of car taillights close to his window. He couldn't imagine why there would be another vehicle in, in…

He realized he must have touched down on one of Drusilla's fields. At least this one was nowhere near the dragon's pasture.

The taillights drew closer, glowing like gigantic, faceted rubies. Russell only had a moment of realization they were actually a pair of eyes before the dragon's paw descended toward him.

He shut his own eyes and gasped as he heard the metallic screeching of the car door being neatly sliced open. The door fell outward with a thunk, and he looked up just in time to see a massive claw retracting. He hastily fumbled out of his seatbelt and tumbled to the ground to avoid having the dragon remove him from the car through the same means.

The huge head descended toward his body, and one glowing eye looked into his. Steam hissed as the rain pelted onto the creature's snout.

Come with me, the dragon said, its voice velvety in Russell's mind. Russell tried to scream, but he couldn't muster up the volition with the dragon's words still reverberating through his skull.

Together, we can ravage the countryside, subdue the populace, and exact tribute beyond your wildest dreams.

Memories that did not belong to Russell flooded through his mind. Many of them involved swooping into cloudbanks like a kid jumping into a pile of autumn leaves.

I am at your command. All you need do is speak these words to me: I abjure thee to bear me beyond these boundaries to freely traverse the land and sea and skies.

The head twitched slightly, toward the direction of the farmhouse, and one giant nostril quivered.

Hurry. Repeat my words.

Russell would have agreed to anything the dragon's voice suggested.

"I—I abjure—" Russell croaked.

A high-pitched, nasal voice interrupted him.

"There you are!"

This was not the condescending and composed woman who had archly insulted the Sweet Pea Board of Trustees in her driveway. Drusilla looked like she'd just sprinted nonstop for over a half mile through a deluge of rain and wind, over rough and muddy terrain. She resembled a sodden ferret, and her right flip-flop was missing. She was wheezing and had to speak at a near shout to be heard through the tumult.

"So *good* of you to rush to Russell's rescue, dear."

She patted the dragon on the cheek. Russell didn't know how he recognized irritated resignation in the creature's expression, but he did.

"Why don't you flip over Russell's car? It's going to be a job towing it out of here."

As the dragon moved to comply, Russell took the opportunity to check whether he was capable of standing up. He managed, shakily.

"Let's get you back to your nest, you really shouldn't be gadding about in this weather," Drusilla was saying to the dragon. Russell stumbled, and she offered him a steadying hand.

"Did you say something about a nest?" he asked as they hobbled toward the farmstead.

"That's right, we came back here so she could lay her eggs. Dragons like to return to their own hatching ground when they're ready to start their own clutch, you know, I don't know whether it's instinct or just sentimentality."

Russell didn't feel qualified to give an opinion.

"But she does get a bit stir crazy sometimes, like any expectant mother," Drusilla continued. "She just couldn't stay put with all this excitement going on outside."

~ * ~

By dawn the next day, the residents were already out surveying the damage. Russell's prediction of a few toys tossed around by the wind had been a spectacular underestimate. No houses had been flattened, but garages, porches, and outbuildings lay strewn in pieces across Sweet Pea Circle. Trees had been uprooted and power lines downed. Dozens of cars had been smashed by falling branches. Rich, the actuary, looked the happiest Russell had ever seen him.

The derecho had provided Lori with the grounds for her next assault against Drusilla Bara. Over lunch, Russell read an e-mail describing the extensive damage she had observed to the Bara house, which appeared to Russell to consist of one of the gutters coming down from the eaves of her roof. She'd learned Drusilla had arranged for an insurance appraisal the next Monday.

However, Lori proposed the Sweet Pea Circle petition the County Board of Commissioners to have the structures officially inspected for code violations, using the fallen gutter as evidence the house was unfit for habitation. According to public documents, none of the buildings on the farm had been inspected since the county began keeping records. If the County Board approved the petition, Drusilla and all other inhabitants (*animals, too!!!* said the e-mail) could be required to vacate the premises until the inspection was scheduled (*that could take months!!!* said the e-mail) and completed.

The next meeting of the County Board of Commissioners was Friday. The Sweet Pea Circle Board of Trustees would have to build its case quickly if they hoped to preempt the appraisal by Drusilla's own insurance company.

Russell didn't bother telling anybody about his encounter with the dragon, the dragon's recruitment effort, the dragon's six-inch-long claws that could rend metal, or the dragon's nest. He figured Sweet Pea Circle was already coping with enough excitement.

~ * ~

The meeting of the County Board of Commissioners took place in the high school cafeteria. Once again, the Sweet Pea Circle trustees dressed for executive success for the occasion. Drusilla even bothered to show up, surveying the proceedings as if she were being forced to attend a variety show featuring dancing Chihuahuas wearing top hats.

Braden Bridges, the chairman of the County Board, had a reputation for his dogged pursuit of accountability and cost-cutting in government affairs. He was widely viewed as a young up-and-comer bound for greater things. At the moment, he was perusing the petition with distaste clear on his smooth face.

"I'm not sure if this issue is worth the attention of the County Board," he stated. "To be clear, this petition pertains to a single house that sustained very slight damage in a devastating storm?"

Lori drew herself up to her full medium height.

"The storm damage brought to light the information this particular house and its outbuildings have apparently never been inspected by county authorities. There's no telling the extent of the decrepitude inside the structures."

"My house and barns were built of mighty oaks, such trees are long gone from the countryside," Drusilla shot back. "My property is littered with the pieces of your rinky-dink little sheds, and you have the gall to question the soundness of *my* home?"

"Please, Ms. Bara, you are out of order," Braden said. "Although your point is valid."

With a querying gesture of his hands, he invited a response from the Sweat Pea Circle trustees.

"I can provide some data tables of trends regarding old farm-houses," Rich put in. "Most farmhouses that were built over a hundred years ago are now demolished or in disrepair. Ms. Bara's house is a statistical anomaly."

"I think he just told us my house is *not* in disrepair," Drusilla observed. "Can we go now?"

"No, what I meant was, if you look at the ratios—" Rich began.

"His point is that we have no idea of the true condition of these buildings that lie at the very heart of our community," Lori intervened. "I'm sure you can understand why we're concerned this situation could be creating an unsafe living situation for the families of Sweet Pea Circle."

"How about you fix your own houses and then you can start worrying about mine?"

"Please, Ms. Bara," Braden said. "Ms. Milliner, I can appreciate your concern, although I'm still not convinced this matter is appropriate for the County Board. We've all had time to review your petition, and if there's unanimous agreement among all County Commissioners and Sweet Pea Circle trustees we should investigate the matter more fully, I'll pass the complaint on to the building inspections division."

"Do I get a vote?" Drusilla asked.

"Please, Ms. Bara. Ms. Atkins, does this issue merit further investigation, yes or no?"

"Yes."

The tally of yeses rolled in without dissent as Braden proceeded down the list. After the final Commissioner had assented, Lori gave an audible sigh of relief.

"Mr. Vilius, yes or no?"

"No," Russell heard himself say.

A pause.

"…Excuse me?"

"No."

Another pause.

"With a failure to achieve unanimous approval, we'll move onto the next item on the agenda."

After the meeting adjourned, Russell found himself at the uncomfortable center of attention. He took refuge in mouthing phrases such as "constitutional protections of property owners" and "standing up against governmental overreach" and "right to due process."

He'd been expecting the arctic blast that emanated from his fellow Sweet Pea Circle trustees. It looked like he'd have a slot opening up on his schedule for the evening of the first Wednesday of every month. He was surprised, though, by the number of people who sidled up to mutter they wished they had his courage of convictions. Even Erika Denk shook his hand very firmly before scuttling away to lurk in Heidi's shadow.

He felt he was owed a word of gratitude from Drusilla Bara, but she merely regarded him out of narrowed eyes for a long moment before sweeping away without speaking.

~ * ~

"Honey, wake up."

The voice came from far away. Russell's world quieted and steadied. He descended back down to earth. The fires died back and faded as he opened his eyes.

He was in bed, in his own house that had escaped damage from the derecho, in Sweet Pea Circle. Not wherever his dreams had taken him. Michelle had laid a gentle hand on his shoulder.

"Were you having a nightmare?" she asked.

He was remembering the dragon's words, something about seeking adventures beyond his wildest dreams.

Russell had never in his life harbored any wild dreams.

Until now.

"Exactly," Russell assured his wife firmly. "It was a nightmare."

~ * ~ * ~

Cara Brezina is a freelance writer who lives in Chicago, Illinois. She has written mostly educational nonfiction books on a wide range of topics, from the history of falconry to the tales from Celtic mythology to the feasibility of time travel. In her spare time, she enjoys bicycling, playing the piano, and gardening. She's an avid life-long reader of fantasy and science fiction, and some of her favorite fictional dragons were created by Tolkien.

Contact her at borealisblue@gmail.com.

Egg Snatcher

Allison Rott

Risingwing's tail swished back and forth as she paced her cave. She walked just on the line where the sunlight came in, and the shadows the cave produced. Winding between stalagmites she kept her eyes in motion and kept her nose in the air.

The drips of water from deeper in the cave were calming, a steady beat with which to count the seconds. She was guarding her Aunt's egg clutch, the red coal covered shells looking a dark smokey grey in the dimness of the cave. The six eggs were nestled in a circle of rocks, partially hidden among the stalagmites.

Risingwing was stretching her dark purple wings when she first heard the footsteps. They were close together, almost a shuffle in some cases, and light footsteps. She jumped up to a stalagmite, crouching and eyeing the different pathways leading through the connected cave systems the Rocky Dragonclan called home. There was no one pattern, and she thought there was more than one sound of breathing. The wind was coming from outside and going down the passages, so she could not identify a scent.

"I'm Risingwing Steelheart and I am watching the clutch of Brighteye Steelheart." She puffed herself up, large as she could, baring her teeth and starting to build a fire in the back of her throat. "Show yourself!" The egg snatchers had never come for a guarded clutch, and her parents had emphasized she announce herself if she had an inkling something was amiss.

"For coal's sake," Rubyeye, another juvenile red dragon came out of one of the passageways, "Risingwing it's just us." The red juvenile was followed by the blue clutch siblings Seeringflame and Whiptail.

"Oh, hey guys." Risingwing jumped down from her perch. She killed the flame and allowed her coiled muscles to relax.

"How long are you going to be watching Brighteye's clutch?" Whiptail approached the clutch, stopping an acceptable body length away and sniffing towards the eggs.

"Not sure." Risingwing watched Whiptail while shrugging

towards the others. "She's with my parents picking up the bison from the human farm, and sometimes that takes a long time."

"So…" Seeringflame curled her tail up onto her back, "you won't be able to come with us to see the glow in the dark fish Rubyeye found in his parents' pond?"

"It's close, you can take a quick peak and then come back." Rubyeye moved to intercept Risingwing's gaze and he smiled at her, the kind that showed off all those perfectly pointed teeth. The kind of smile many of the female juvenile dragons wanted Rubyeye to send their way. Risingwing was no exception, the gaze of those eyes with the red tint, always giving her the feeling of a free dive.

"Well…" Risingwing swallowed, dropping her gaze for a moment. "My Aunt is worried about the egg snatchers you know—"

Whiptail snorted. "These eggs aren't pretty enough for the snatchers to want."

"Hey!" Risingwing growled and jumped right over Rubyeye, using her wings for a little bit of lift, in order to tackle Whiptail. They rolled across the stone floor. "Take that back Whiptail! My Aunt's eggs aren't ugly!"

Whiptail pinned Risingwing to the ground, pressing his prominent forehead scale against hers. "I didn't say they were ugly," he drew out the word as Risingwing snorted some smoke in his face. "Just not pretty."

"Same difference." She growled. She started to puff out again and wiggle, pushing her paws up against his underbelly, not quite able to budge him.

"Let her up Whiptail," Rubyeye bumped his shoulder against the blue dragon's side. "Just because red eggs don't look pretty until a week before hatching doesn't mean they are ugly. Any good egg snatcher would know that."

Whiptail flapped his wings and flew to a nearby stalagmite. "Well, the egg snatcher hasn't come this far north anyway." Risingwing rolled over, shaking off the newly collected dust. He rolled his blue eyes that were a few shades lighter than his scales before looking at Risingwing. "You can totally come look for a few minutes."

"Well…" Risingwing looked over at the clutch, then looked at each of her friends.

"They only glow during mating season," Rubyeye added,

"and that's almost over."

"And they won't glow again for years!" Whiptail jumped to a stalagmite next to Risingwing. She ignored him and looked back at Rubyeye when he began speaking again.

"I would love for you to come look with us." Those eyes looked right into her golden ones, giving her that big smile again. The same lightweight feeling of her heart and stomach during a free dive welled up inside Risingwing.

"Okay." She glanced back at the eggs, throat tightening for a moment. "Just a few minutes. And this stays between us or my parents will ground me til I'm three hundred."

"Two hundred and fifty years is a long time." Seeringflame stood next to Rubyeye. "Maybe you should stay. There is always next mating season." Her navy-blue scales brushed against Rubyeye's red ones. Risingwing bristled.

"I'm coming. But let's make it quick." She jumped to Rubyeye's other side, her back towards her friends and the eggs. She made sure her tail brushed across the length of his tail as she took another couple steps forward. "Last one to Rubyeye's is a rotten egg!" And she was off, running full speed down one of the passageways, not bothering to use her wings down the narrow passages.

The others followed with various grumbles and laughter, mixing with the sounds of their feet as they rushed out of the cavern looking out at the northern range of the Rockies.

~ * ~

The glowing fish were beautiful, neon green and yellow bodies weaving and circling around each other, up and down, pairing off and splashing the surface before going deeper to mate. Risingwing stared at them, for a few moments, she was in awe, all her focus on the pond in front of her. She wasn't even sure which of her friends were on either side of her, didn't see the reflections of her fellow dragons, just the dance of the glowing fish.

"Risingwing?" Her head jolted up to meet Rubyeye's gaze on her left. "Sorry." He chuckled. "I said, isn't it interesting their dance resembles the ones during the spring solstice?"

"Oh, yeah." Remembering the spring solstice reminded Risingwing of the eggs she left behind. Dragons could mate anytime during the year, but they celebrated it during the spring. It was beautiful, to see new and old mates perform in the sky, scales flashing in the sunlight.

She looked back down, her forehead scales lowering slightly as she narrowed her eyes. Brighteye had just performed last spring, and lost her mate to illness a few months later, the eggs being laid a few days later, and she cried the entire time.

"I should get going." Risingwing pushed herself off her haunches.

"It's barely been five minutes," Whiptail added.

"And it took five minutes to get here." Risingwing snapped. "That's ten, and my family could be back any minute." Her stomach twisted; she really shouldn't have left her helpless cousins behind. "I'll see you guys later." She jumped over the pond and started heading through the passageway.

"Guess she isn't all that fun after all huh Rubyeye?"

Risingwing swallowed the growl in the back of her throat from Seeringflame's words. Proving her wrong would have to wait, the guilt from leaving her responsibility stung a lot more than her words.

~ * ~

Risingwing's breath caught in her throat when she got closer to her aunt's cavern. Something smelled off, there were smells that didn't belong in what should be an otherwise empty space. There was the scent of a dragon, but not her parents or her aunt. And even more worrying, was the scent of a human.

She slowed down, crouching behind a large stalagmite. She was silent, thankful the wind was blowing into the cave and not towards the intruders.

"I don't know Smokecloud," she hadn't heard many human voices, except through the films they sometimes watched at school or social gatherings, but she was pretty sure it was an adult male.

"They don't look like much now," Smokecloud's voice was deep, his voice as unfamiliar as his scent to the hiding dragon. "But fire dragon eggs always start to show the beautiful flame patterns about a week before hatching."

"All right." The human sighed. "Then let's get these six eggs out of here."

"First, hand over the gold."

Risingwing listened to the clinking, remembering a trip to the clan's horde, how the gold coins would clink together whenever they shifted.

"All right. Go ahead and load them up."

"Don't!" Risingwing clambered to the top of the stalagmite and then jumped off to glide into the cavern. "Leave my cousins alone!"

The dragon's dark gray tail, a shade matching the stone around him, whipped out towards Risingwing. She flapped hard, and twisted, feeling the air push against her softer underbelly scales. The dragon growled and the human pushed their hat up, a hand going to their back.

It was less than a heartbeat before the cavern was heated with a fireball blasting from Stormcloud's mouth. Stalagmites and stalactites in the fireball's path were scorched, Risingwing's pupils contracted from the sudden light filling the large open space.

A scream covered the sizzle of flame and flesh, the human being knocked back and burning on the ground between the clutch of eggs and the opening to the outside world. The acrid smell filled the air, something about human flesh being cooked, burning to a grey leathery crisp was unappetizing. Her stomach squeezed and her throat burned as she fought the guilt, fear, and the sudden urge to vomit. Something skittered across the floor, and when Risingwing's eyes were drawn to it, Stormcloud knocked Risingwing out of the air with the back of his paw.

She just barely folded her wings before her side hit the ground, hard, the thin hide scraping the ground, and leaving a trail of blood.

"Heh." Stormcloud leaned over her, his neck long even for the grey dragons. Risingwing growled, pushing herself to all fours, feeling blood rolling down her scales. "You think a tiny runt like you is going to stop me?" Her eyes looked away from the green glow, catching on his teeth, nearly as long as her, and then dropping down to his claws, sharp enough to scratch the stone floor. She saw the bulging bag, but the world went sideways again as she rolled away from his claws.

Her breaths were heavy, while his were slow, controlled, even his laugh was perfectly in rhythm to the slow expansion and compression of his chest. "Looks like I can get the money again from a different dealer, huh little juvenile?"

She growled and leapt up; claws outstretched. He moved his face back, tilting his chin to put flesh and scales between her and his eyes. But she wasn't going for his eyes.

She sunk her front claws into the softer grey scales on his neck, feeling a gush of blood flood over her claws. He roared, flinching back and she lost her grip. She flung her wings out, but she couldn't get enough lift with her injured one and she landed hard on her back legs, her tail bracing her so she wasn't thrown to her back.

She was whipped with his tail this time, the crunch of ribs sending a searing pain through her abdomen as she hit the wall near the entrance to the cave. She had no breath, eyelids heavy as she watched Stormcloud touch a paw to his neck, looking at the blood on his claws.

"Stupid little whelp!" He growled. Her eyes looked around wildly as he hunched, one paw reaching for the eggs. The back of his throat was turning yellow, and with that light, she caught sight of the thing that had skittered earlier.

A gun. Near her there was the gun, the thing the human must have been reaching for. Her paws weren't made to be able to pull the trigger, but she wrapped her tail around the handle and slipped the tip of it into the gap near the trigger. Her only hope was this human happened to have loaded their gun with the new scale piercing bullets the adult dragons had talked about in hushed tones.

She raised it, the light in the back of his throat now nearly white, a heat lethal even to dragons. Risingwing had seen humans use guns in movies, so she tried to copy what she had seen. She aimed, held her breath, and then squeezed her tail.

Bang!

The flash wasn't as bright as the building flame in Stormcloud's mouth, and the kickback jerked her tail, but wasn't nearly as bad as being hit by the older dragon.

Crack!

The flame died in Stormcloud's throat, and then his whole body slumped to the ground. The scale in the middle of his forehead had a dark hole in it, the edges cracked, with blood seeping out of it. His chest no longer rose and fell, but rather, he was still.

Risingwing dropped the gun and tried to stand, but her body protested, and she collapsed to the ground as well. She gasped, every breath burning.

"Officer Howard!" Another human ran into the cave, gun drawn, paling as the smell and the sight of his fallen companion hit him. "Backup and medic's now!" He barked into a radio as he pointed his gun towards the small dragon. "What happened!"

"He," Risingwing grit her teeth, "tried to steel my cousins." She let her body sag on the ground.

"And you shot him?" She forced a nod. "Well, he deserved it. Had his claws in at least seven of the illegal egg deals."

~ * ~

Risingwing's parents and Brighteye returned while the cops were still processing the scene. A dragon healer had been contacted for Risingwing and she was resting near the passageways to be out of the way.

"I shouldn't have left." She admitted, a tear clinging to the corner of her eyes nearest her snout.

"But you came back." Brighteye touched her forehead to Risingwing's. "And I owe you big time for saving my eggs little one."

Risingwing thought she could hold back the tears, but they spilled over when she saw the first tear fall from her aunt's eyes. One sob caused enough pain in her ribs to stop that from happening again, but the tears flowed freely for a few minutes while the detectives spoke with the dragon council about the undercover operation and how they believed Stormcloud was the dragon contact many of the bottom smugglers claimed sold the eggs.

The bullets were the new scale piercing ones, not out for mass production, but they had applied for the prototype batch that had pierced scales in the lab. Risingwing had been lucky, she knew that. She thanked the sun fire for the luck. Lucky she came back in time, lucky the undercover agent had the right bullets, lucky the gun hadn't melted because of the fireball, lucky she was able to aim and fire it properly.

She was called a hero, not on the luck, but for the bravery. And that was a title worth having even when being grounded for the next six years, one year for each egg her aunt could have lost due to her walking away.

~ * ~ * ~

Allison Rott, (pronounced 'wrote') lives in Illinois, a train ride away from the Windy City. It is the perfect length ride to catch up on her reading or let her daydreams work on stories. A voracious reader from her own childhood she has never lost her love of stories or the many ways of telling them. She has stories in three anthologies, "The Lingering Rift" in *Foxtales 4*, "Feeding the Universe" in *72 Hours of Insanity: Anthology of the Games*, vol. 7 and "Pocket Watch Problems" in *On Time*.

The Dragon Queen

Rose Strickman

When Elina looked up from applying a new splint to Blaze's wing and saw the plume of smoke, her first reaction was one of overwhelming annoyance. She'd hoped for a summer like the last, a time of untrammeled peace, sunshine and, most of all, solitude. Just her and the flock. No trespassers. They'd just been enjoying a similar period free of visitors this year, and Elina had had high hopes it might continue.

It seemed it wasn't to be. Taking care to finish tying on the splint, she hoisted Blaze onto her shoulder, where he clung on with inquiring cheeps. "We'd better go have a look," she told him. He chirped in agreement.

She exited the East Tower, the ruined edifice that stood closest to the sea bluff, and down the steps to the ancient battlement. Once there, she gently took Blaze down from her shoulder and held him in her arms. There was little chance of the intruders seeing her in her brown-and-gray dress, but Blaze was named for the brilliant red streaks on his blue-green scales. It was better if he was tucked up against her dress rather than preening on her shoulder. Blaze grumbled, but held still as she stealthily approached the battlement overlooking the forest.

Around Elina, the castle spread, stone white-gray in the summer light. The gardens glowed like an intricate tapestry in the courtyard. Directly below her, the thick hedge of shining, transparent glass thorns tangled, dense and impenetrable. Beyond, the vast trackless forest loomed, lush with spring growth. But between thorns and forest was a familiar sight: ragged tents and smoking campfires, men moving around among them, and the murmur of human voices.

"They always choose the same spot to camp," Elina said to Blaze. "No imagination." Blaze yawned and sneezed, shaking his snout in surprise.

Elina ducked behind a rampart and considered the situation. The intruders couldn't fight past the glass hedge to the wall, but that hadn't stopped earlier bands from building siege engines that fired lines onto the battlements. That wasn't a problem: the castle's enchantments always caused the ropes to snap, sending the invaders tumbling down to their doom on the glass thorns. Approach from the sea was impossible, due to the tricky currents and sharp rocks, and no one but Elina and the dragons knew about the secret path down to the beach, hidden behind a thick, iron-banded door deep in the castle.

No, the intruders couldn't break into the castle, but it would take them at least a few weeks to figure that out. Sometimes they were out there for *months*. And Elina had to take precautions the entire time.

She thought wistfully back to last summer, when no one had come at all. That had been *wonderful*. No need to hide her cookfire or avoid lighting windows where they could see, and she could walk the battlements as much as she liked, enjoying the sea breeze and admiring the forest and the castle gardens spread out below. She had laughed and sang and played with the dragons as often and as loudly as she liked, with no fear of anyone overhearing. Yes, last summer had been a golden time, but nothing good could last.

A coarse laugh rose from the camp, and Elina slipped away, heading silently to the nearest staircase down to the gardens. Blaze squawked, and she shushed him, scratching the back of his scaly head and holding him close, taking comfort in his cool little body. His heart quivered against her chest, and she felt overwhelmed with sudden apprehension and protectiveness. Those men couldn't break in, but what if they did?

"We'll just have to wait them out," she told Blaze. Hopefully it wouldn't take long. A few weeks' camping in the wilderness, staring at a blank, empty castle, was usually enough to put off the most determined of would-be heroes.

Accordingly, therefore, Elina took action.

She moved her bedroom that very day, carrying Blaze on her shoulder as she shifted her books, her clothes, her embroidery chest, her lute, her zither and all her other possessions from the highest room of the West Tower, with its panoramic views of forest and ocean, down to the lowest room, the tiny chamber at the foot of the tower. She admitted to herself that it had its charms—the little bedroom was cozy, and opened directly onto the gardens—

but the fact she had to move at all annoyed her still further. However, there was no getting around it: the intruders mustn't see her lighted window, or notice her moving around the tower.

Next, she moved her fire from one oven in the kitchens to another, the one with a hole-filled chimney that would disperse smoke in diffuse, near-invisible strands instead of a single plume. The castle's enchantments provided limitless amounts of food-stuffs, but did none of the cooking, so Elina had to bake her own bread and boil her own porridge, to roast meats and simmer soups, from the raw ingredients provided. The new oven would allow her to continue doing so, without being detected. It would also regularly blow smoke back into her face while she was working with it, making cooking a far more tedious chore.

Preparations over, Elina finished off yesterday's fish stew, mopping the bowl with a heel of bread and feeding fragments to Blaze, before perching him on her shoulder and setting off to the East Tower to await the flock's return.

~ * ~

She stood at the gaping, ragged hole in the seaward wall, watching the dragons return. They came flying in formation from over the ocean: tiny black specks at first, soon resolving themselves into iridescent blue-green dragons, a dozen of them, each about two feet long, their membranous wings glowing in the golden light of sunset. They'd spent all day out fishing over the waves; Blaze had only stayed behind due to his broken wing. The flock had had a successful day, flying low with distended bellies, and they poured into the tower room through the gap in a clatter of wings and a chorus of cheeps, squeaks and chirrups: vocalizations that died as they noticed Elina and her grim expression.

Blaze cheeped solemnly from her shoulder. The other dragons came close, talons scratching the stone floor, and sat back on their hind legs, looking up at Elina, anxious and inquiring.

Regina, queen of the flock and the only breeding female, gave an imperious sort of chattering squeak. Elina nodded. "I'm afraid so," she said. "We've got visitors again."

The flock let out a chorus of annoyed yelps, chitters and snorts. Spots, one of the larger males, was so irritated he turned and bit his own tail. Regina half-spread her wings and chattered at Elina.

"I know," Elina said. "You think I'm any happier about it? But if we follow the usual rules, we should be all right. No flying over the forest, no approaching the south side of the castle. Let our guests think no one's home, and they'll soon be off."

The flock brightened a bit at the mention of the intruders leaving. The smallest female, yellow-spotted Daisy, chittered a question.

"I don't know, Daisy." Elina sat down, allowing Daisy to crawl into her lap. Blaze hissed in jealous fury and half-lunged at the intruder. "Stop that, Blaze!" Elina set Blaze aside. "You can't hog me all the time, wing or no wing. Never mind him, Daisy." She cuddled the tiny female closer. "I think they come because they believe I'm a beautiful princess under an enchantment, and if they break the spell, they'll win a kingdom and get a dragon's hoard."

For a moment, incredulous silence reigned. Then the dragons all burst into piping laughter, rolling onto their backs in sneering mirth.

"I know," grinned Elina. "But that's what they think. If we just make it look like nobody's home, though, they'll soon get bored and leave. It's happened every other year. So, no flying to the south side! And no trying to steal their food," she added pointedly to Nina, the most daring and adventurous of the flock, who had occasionally swooped down to explore the camps of earlier invaders, nearly losing her life on multiple occasions. Regina turned and glared too, and Nina groomed her scales in a rather sulky manner.

Elina played with the dragons for a few hours before heading back toward her new bedroom at the base of the West Tower. Even in late spring, the night winds off the northern ocean were cold, and the East Tower's ruinous state, ideal though it was for dragons, did not appeal to Elina. Besides, it was nice to have some privacy, especially since she could leave Blaze behind with the others (after sternly lecturing the flock against bullying him). She walked the battlement over to the West Tower, breathing in the salt breeze and listening to the booming, invisible voice of the ocean far below.

Once inside the tower, however, with one foot poised on the stairs down to the tower's base, she hesitated. It was almost full dark by now, and she didn't have a light or a noisy dragon with her. Perhaps it wouldn't do any harm to recheck the camp. She padded silently through the tower, exiting the south door, onto the battlements once more.

Sneaking silently, she peered down onto the forest clearing. Firelight gleamed on the glass thorns in weird flickers. The invaders seemed to be in good spirits: music rose, and she listened appreciatively to the lute-played tune and full-throated song. Even intruders had their advantages, she admitted to herself. She'd have to see if she couldn't play that song for the dragons later.

The music came to an abrupt halt at a murmured order from the tall, dark-garbed man nearest the fire. Elina watched as he stood, powerful and limber, and spoke. She couldn't make out his words at this distance, but she knew they were commands, spoken calmly, almost gently, by someone accustomed to obedience. The hairs on the back of her neck stood up, old memories resurfacing.

The men put away their instruments and started preparing to retire. The dark one followed, stretching out his long arms. At the last minute, though, poised by his tent, he paused.

A long, breathless moment passed, while the man stood at his tent flap and Elina sat frozen behind the rampart. Within, her heart thundered. He *couldn't* have spotted her—she *knew* this—but still his face turned, a tiny pale blur in the night, and she was sure he looked at her and s*aw* her.

At last, he turned away. The tent flap closed behind him, and stillness fell on the campsite except for one man left on watch.

More shaken than she dared admit even to herself, Elina turned away, ghosting back to her bedroom deep within the castle.

~ * ~

Insides still crawling from the almost-encounter, Elina dared not spy on the campsite again, but spent the next few days either holed up on the north side of the castle or down in the courtyard, tending the flower gardens. She found she dared not even use the door to the secret beach path. The man's dark, hard gaze was haunting her nightmares, making her shrink back like a barnacle recoiling into its shell.

She stayed in the castle, therefore, tending to Blaze, whose wing was improving rapidly. She read books, embroidered, tended the flowers, and practiced her music—only with the doors and windows firmly shut, however. Mornings and evenings she greeted the flock, before and after they returned from their daily fishing trip, and also lazed with them at their noonday rest, basking in the sun and looking out over the frothy blue waters. Sometimes they saw dolphins leaping through the waves, or the spume of the greater whales further out, here in these northern waters for the summer feeding season.

On the fourth morning, however, Regina seemed agitated, leaping from crack to ruined stone in the broken tower room, chittering with anxiety. When Elina came in, she immediately pounced, launching herself onto the woman's shoulder to chatter into her ear.

"Well, why is that so worrisome?" Elina asked. "Other trespassers have done the same. It doesn't matter how often they circle the castle: there's glass thorns on every side except the north, and that's built directly on the cliffs."

Regina gave an impatient squeak, and chittered on. Elina's confident smile faded. "Really? Hmmm...Perhaps you'd better show me."

With Blaze and Regina riding her shoulders, Elina headed to the eastern battlements. Here one had an excellent view of ocean, thorns and forest alike—and also the construction site built at the cliff's edge. A flight of stairs, built of timber, heading down to the beach.

Regina chattered, half in triumph and half in fear. Elina stood stone-still. "You don't think they know about the path...?"

Regina shrugged her wings, unsure. Blaze puffed himself up, baring his fangs. Elina stroked his spine. "No, Blaze, don't do that. They'd shoot you." She shivered, thinking of the dark man and the unyielding hardness and determination she'd sensed in him.

Maybe they were getting upset over nothing. Maybe the men were just building those stairs to try and see what lay at the bottom of the cliffs. They wouldn't find the beach path if they did. It was exceedingly well hidden, winding into the cliff face itself to emerge within the castle compound through its stout wooden door. Elina had only discovered it due to the dragons' guidance, the day she'd first washed up on the shore. She'd used it frequently since, to go down to the beach to swim, or collect shellfish at low tide, or explore the tidepools, the dragons streaming around her like comets. No one else, in all the years Elina had lived here, had ever discovered it. On the other hand, no one else had thought to go down the cliffs to the beach...

"I'll go make ready," she said to the dragons. "As my mother used to say: hope for the best but prepare for the worst." And with that she headed to the castle workshop.

~ * ~

Nothing in either Elina's new life or old had necessitated mastery of carpentry, and it proved much harder than she'd expected to cobble together a barrier to the door that led to the beach path. She sustained many splinters, cuts and smacks with the hammer before she finally braced a couple of planks against the door. Breathing hard, she stood back to look over her handiwork. It wasn't very inspiring.

"Do you think it will keep them out?" she asked the dragons.

The flock, settled on her carpentry tools, flicked their wings in uncertainty. Regina chittered and suddenly swooped down to pick up several long, curling shavings in her mouth. Sitting up, her stomach looked oddly distended.

"Oh, Regina!" Elina's worries were forgotten in her sudden rush of delight. "You're going to lay eggs!" She beamed in congratulations. Regina hadn't been able to produce a clutch last year, as the fish had been scarce. But this year there would be hatchlings!

If they could outlast the current siege, of course.

There came a heavy flapping, and Regina draped herself on Elina's shoulder. Elina felt the small, hard shapes of the queen's eggs press against her as Regina chirruped in her ear. Elina smiled wanly. "Thanks, Regina. I hope you're right."

~ * ~

Construction of the laddered stairway continued as the men built their way down to the beach. They must have some good craftsmen, Elina thought grudgingly as she spied on their progress from the wall. Her thin little braces seemed more pathetic than ever.

Elina began to scout out hiding places. The cellars were full of nice hideaways, but the trouble was convincing the dragons of the wisdom of using them. The flock didn't like dark, enclosed spaces in general, and were all preoccupied with building a nest for the imminent clutch.

"You should fly out to sea at least," Elina argued one sunny afternoon in the East Tower as the flock swooped around her, adding more material to the ever-growing mass of seaweed, leaves, yarn, seashells, bark fragments and anything else the dragons could carry. "You might be able to escape if…if it comes to the worst."

Regina looked up from rearranging nesting materials and snapped her jaws angrily. She puffed her sides.

"Yes, I know, but better to leave the eggs than all of you die."

Pink-tinged Marta, sitting sentry duty at the seaward wall, trilled a warning. Elina and the other dragons all hurried to join her, the flock settling on broken stones and Elina cautiously approaching the edge of the gaping hole in the wall.

She was not surprised to see the men down on the beach, so far away they looked like stick figures. But even from this distance she could see they were searching the beach methodically, dividing it into quadrants and ranging all over. One figure, which Elina thought looked a little darker than the rest, seemed to be directing operations.

Slowly, Elina looked up. "You need to leave," she said to Regina. "All of you. Now."

Regina spat a little and puffed her sides again. Blaze shook his still-useless wing.

"They're going to find the path!" Elina pointed down at the beach, cold sweat breaking out. "It's only a matter of time. You should all leave, escape—"

The flock erupted in a yattering chorus of cheeps, chirps, squeals and shrieks. The dragons shook their wings and rattled their crests. Their eyes blazed with refusal.

"You…you really feel that way?" Elina faltered.

Blaze hopped over and rubbed against her ankles, purring like a cat. Daisy fluttered to settle on her shoulder. Regina gave an exasperated growl and glared at Elina. *How stupid can you get?*

Elina swallowed back tears. "All right. Then we'll face them. Together."

~ * ~

It took the men two days to discover the beach path. Elina heard their triumphant shouts from the East Tower, where she and the flock now spent most of every day. She pulled herself to her feet, knowing it wouldn't be long now. She clutched the knife at her belt. Around her, the dragons stirred and rustled.

Sure enough, within an hour she heard the men storming around her castle, their voices rising to the tower, their footsteps echoing in her sanctum's peaceful silences. Elina clenched her fists, rage a hard hot stone within, at the violation. But still she stood, surrounded by the dragons, all eyes on the doorway through which the invasion must come.

Heavy footsteps sounded on the stairway: multiple sets of them, hurrying up the stairs. Then the door flew open, and the flock all scattered back, hissing, scuttling over the stones, as the dark man led his followers in.

The thugs ran forward, ready for blood, but the dark man waved them down. He came to a halt, eyes traveling around the room, taking in the dragons, before falling on Elina. His hard mouth twisted in a joyless smile. "Well," he said, "this isn't precisely what I expected."

Elina said nothing. She stood straight and still, watching the men as they streamed into the flock's lair, swords in hand but not yet in use. Tiger, distinguishable by the orange rings around his eyes, snapped at one of the men, and the man cursed and stabbed at the little dragon, blade bright. Tiger shot back, shrieking.

"Stop!" Elina screamed before she could halt the word, half-lunging toward the invader.

The dark man chuckled. "Oh, you care for the creatures? Not at *all* what I was expecting."

Elina, still breathing hard with outrage, turned a fiery gaze on him. "Oh, really?" These were the first words she'd spoken to another human being in ten years, and they were hard with contempt. "And what were you expecting, exactly?"

"A princess being kept captive by an enormous dragon, of course." The dark man shrugged, amused by his own naivete. "With an enormous pile of gold I could steal, once I dispatched of both dragon and princess. But this is even better, really." He turned around, smiling at the ruined tower room covetously. "An enchanted castle, guarded by magical thorns, with self-renewing stores of food and supplies! I never need to worry about feeding my men again, and we have an impregnable fortress from which to conduct our raids. We'll be the richest men of the northern coast!"

His ruffians all raised cheers at this, waving their swords, flashing their teeth. The dragons hissed, rattling their wings. Only

Elina stood still, a motionless flame.

"And all that stands in your way," she said, "is one woman and a flock of fishing dragons."

"Precisely." The dark man drew his sword. It gleamed evilly in the brilliant afternoon light. "You know, you're going to be the strangest woman I've ever killed. What's your name?"

Elina gave him a slow, cold smile. "Women like me don't have names," she said. "Not to men like you. We're the ones who bring you wine in taverns while you roar and brag and tell lies about all your manly exploits. We're the ones you shove against the wall when you've drunk the wine. We're the ones who clean up the mess you leave behind. We don't have names to you, we don't have faces. We certainly never have thoughts or feelings." At this something flashed in Elina's eyes, and even the dark man drew back, arrogant smile slipping. "And when we're kidnapped and forced aboard a ship to serve some captain's lust—when that ship sinks and all the sailors drown—when we find our way alone to shore—and on that shore is an enchanted castle filled with dragons—why then, perhaps, our lives can truly begin. We can…learn things. Things about dragons. Things about ourselves. Things that men like you will never know."

"Very pretty speech." The dark man's smile twisted as he stepped forward. "You have some spirit. Be a good girl and I won't let the men have you before I kill—"

Elina screamed.

It was not a scream of despair or terror. It was a wild, ululating shriek, a war cry, the screech of an owl or a hawk. Or a dragon. And the flock opened their fang-filled mouths and screamed too, an unholy chorus, crests raised, wings spread wide, and flung themselves at the men.

The men raised their weapons, ready to strike down the puny dragons, only to cower back, yelling, as the reptiles—*grew*. Their bodies expanding, their jaws thrusting forward, teeth the size of swords, their wings like sails—the dragons roared like lions, scales glowing with the strength of Elina's rage, and fell on the men like a typhoon.

The bandits screamed as the dragons took hold of them, tearing arms from sockets and heads from necks. They struggled in terror as the dragons seized them and dragged them out of the ruined tower, to fall, shrieking, into the sea. And the dark man fell back, yelling, as Elina and Regina, moving as one being, leaped at him.

He swung his sword, but woman and dragon easily evaded it. Elina ducked—her knife flashed up—and she straightened, bringing the blade up in a pouncing lunge as Regina closed her enlarged jaws on the dark man's head.

Elina's dagger found the dark man's heart just as Regina's teeth snapped his neck. He died in an instant, blood staining Regina's mouth.

Elina let the dark man fall, let the knife fall, as she panted for breath. Around her, the tower room fluttered and rustled as the dragons shrank back to their natural size, the glow of her anger fading from their scales. They clustered around Elina, cuddling close to her ankles, her shoulders and her head, Blaze snuggling into her arms for comfort, as Elina took in the carnage, the room splashed with blood and littered with dismembered body parts.

Regina alone did not come close. She fluttered onto a broken stone, fastidiously pushing away a torn-off finger. She stared at Elina, and a red light flashed behind her golden eyes.

Red light flashed behind Elina's eyes in answer. The whole flock tensed and chittered as Elina's mind tugged all of theirs, one last spasm of shared emotion before the bond subsided once more.

~ * ~

"Oh, Regina!" Elina knelt over the nest, rapt with delight. "They're beautiful!"

Regina, presiding over her mass of cheeping hatchlings, chirruped with pride and joy, half-spreading her wings. The rest of the flock crowed with congratulations and pleasure, and Blaze craned over Elina's shoulder for a better look. She reached up to scratch his neck affectionately. His wing had completely healed by now, but he still spent much of his time with her.

Elina contemplated the hatchlings happily, bumbling around their nest. How adorable they were! This was turning into a delightful summer. The weather was perfect, sunny and warm every day, and the dragons flew home stuffed with fish every evening. There were hundreds of whales now, puffing water into the sky from the deeps, and the seabird colonies along the cliffs teemed with activity, thousands of bird parents tending to shrieking youngsters. Dolphins leaped offshore, and mother bears led their cubs down to the beach to dig for clams. The forest too was lush with life, fat deer slipping through the trees, birds singing in the trees, and Elina delighted in how verdant her garden had grown.

Yes, she thought with great contentment, life had gone well since they'd dispatched the marauders. Not a single intrusion since. She sighed a little in irritation, remembering the unholy mess there'd been to clean up after the massacre. All those corpses, and not even a good meal to be had off them—the dragons' teeth were made to deal with fish, not flesh. Elina had had to toss the bodies off the tower—though the dragons had helped, licking up the blood. And then there had been the chaos downstairs, where the men had marauded through the castle. She'd discovered the beach path door with its hinges removed, the huge slab thrown aside. It had taken her a while to figure out how to rehang it, but she'd managed.

Now, though, things were finally back to normal. Elina smiled at the hatchlings again. No—things were *better* than normal.

Regina crawled around the nest into Elina's arms, and she felt the pulse of the connection between them, as steady as the beat of their hearts, as natural as breathing, as inevitable as love. She looked around at the dragons, each one unique, each one precious, and she knew this was her family and this was her home. Just as she had known that first day, washed up on the beach after the shipwreck, when Regina had flown down from the sky to stare into her eyes and into her mind and forge the unbreakable bond between her and the flock of dragons.

"Forevermore together," she whispered, and around her, her family all broke into singing cries.

~ * ~ * ~

Rose Strickman is a speculative fiction writer living in Seattle, Washington. Her work has appeared in several anthologies, including *Swashbuckling Cats* and *Sword and Sorceress 32*. She has also been published in several online e-zines, and self-published several novellas on Amazon.

Please connect with her at facebook.com/rose.strickman.3 or see her Amazon page at amazon.com/author/rosestrickman.

A Squeaky-Clean Reunion

Mary Jo Rabe

Maq B. Dragon stared grimly at the muddy rivulets of water that ran down their stubborn paths on the dreary gray walls of the spacious Dancehall Cave. This particular bowel of the Earth was spread out over at least two hectares. Flooding in the Dancehall Cave not only threatened his plans for the dragon family reunion; it even threatened the well-being of his home caves located deeper underground.

Maq B.'s sturdy, chameleonic skin itched and tiny rolls of blisters rose up on his dark, gray-green, muscular forearms, creating the same pattern on his hide as the water on the walls. The uncertainty was getting to him.

An optimist at heart, and that over more than a million human-calculated years, Maq B. still felt apprehensive as he looked around. For centuries the Dancehall Cave's gleaming, shiny-white, limestone stalactites and stalagmites had glistened tastefully in the glow of the occasional burst of dragonfire from Maq B.'s snout.

However, today everything in the cave was dingy, dank, and dark. The walls were dirty; the floor was muddy. Unknown life forms, definitely not of animal origin, sprouted their way out of the cracks in the clammy cave walls.

And the whole cave smelled rotten, putrid. This was not right. A dragon's cave should exude the zesty fragrance of smoke, charred animals, and scorched plant tissue. Flames from a dragon's snout should light up shiny, clean walls where dramatic shadows of Maq B.'s two-and-a-half-meter tall physique could play.

Occasionally there had been times in the distant past when this cave got slightly damp for a few days, but these six months of downpour up on the ground were atypical. A few more months of this nonsense and his home cave, though even deeper in the depths of the Maquoketa Caves State Parks system, might start to stink.

Maq B., in top form as always, sporting optimal weight and muscle tone for a dragon in his prime, was also a patient dragon, but some things could not be tolerated. He had another family reunion to organize, and this time he wanted it to take place in the Dancehall Cave, its traditional location for centuries.

True, he had invited the dragon relatives to celebrate on the empty factory farm north of Zwingle some years ago, and his efforts had resulted in rave reviews, but he didn't want to risk a repeat performance. It wouldn't be possible anyway. The factory farm was crammed full of the poor, maltreated, bovine creatures.

Besides, Maq B. had a reputation and a tradition to protect. He was the dragon who put on extraordinary dragon family gatherings in the Dancehall Cave deep down in the Maquoketa Caves State Park, reunions that were the talk of decades, if not centuries. Every dragon on this planet had heard of Maq B. and his reunion bashes.

Maq B. took a deep breath, exhaled a toasty but not incendiary blast of air, thereby calming himself. The ancient biofeedback exercises began to work from deep inside his spacious stomach out to his skin, claws, and esophageal dragonfire combustion cells. His hide gradually took on the calming, light gray-green hue the cave walls used to have. The skin cells undulated rhythmically, and the blisters receded.

Maq B. simply had to stop obsessing about the months of non-stop downpours. He couldn't stop the rain; he had to deal with it. The weather would affect his suppliers, though, and he was looking at ordering huge amounts of edibles and potables for the reunion. He needed to get in touch with Curtis, his human supplier, but first he had to get the numbers together.

Time to retreat to the underground collection of caves he referred to as his home cave. Located many convenient meters beneath the Dancehall Cave, they contained all the technology Maq B.'s engineering skills had put together over the past decades. Dragons who liked to survive had to keep up with the times, and Maq B. planned to live for several million more years.

He flew out of one of the many entrances to the Dancehall Cave, all but one of which were unknown to the human population. Before dawn there was no danger of being seen by the human population. A few brief flaps of his wings and he landed at the expertly camouflaged entrance to the home cave he shared with the bats. Amazing what a few proficient horticultural and telepathic tricks could accomplish.

He walked down the stairs carefully—his dragon feet being a little too large for the steps—and as soon as he was in the first of his home caves, he sank into his favorite soft, leather recliner, custom-made for his dragon form. Here the pristine walls and pleasant, dry ambiance gave him the peace of mind he needed to plan the reunion.

Dry cave or wet, his guests needed to eat and drink. He felt a little overwhelmed at the prospect of organizing everything under these new, wet circumstances, but the bats would be returning soon, and they always put him in a good mood.

The bats in the Maquoketa Caves were all his friends. Their individual brainpower was limited, but telepathically linked together they often surprised him with their savvy. In addition, they were quite amiable creatures. He and the bats enjoyed many pleasant get-togethers at twilight and dawn in his home caves.

They had their own names in bat language, but Maq B. allowed himself the indulgence of giving many of them nicknames in the local lingo.

Before he could force himself to begin his precise calculations for reunion provisions, the swarm of his cave bats floated down the hidden entrance. *It must be morning already*, Maq B. thought. That's when the bats generally returned from their feeding frenzy.

Frenzy, however, this time didn't seem to be the most accurate description. Overindulgence would be more precise. His bats sank down through the air, one after another, their stomachs bulging.

His population of bats continued to increase. Ever since the white-nose fungus spread throughout the Midwest, however, the population of bats outside the Maquoketa Caves had decreased dramatically.

Maq B. had been able to protect his bats. After some creative trial and error experimentation, his dragon relatives were able to help him find a way to neutralize the fungus. It turned out that if Maq B. ingested a bale of roadside hemp and then almost ignited the digestive gas as his stomach expelled it, this singed gas killed the fungus and left the bats immune to further infection. The bats just had to fly through the smoky belches, unfortunately an odoriferous business the bats found unpleasant.

With the help of Bat-Out-Of-Hell, Maq B. had been able to persuade the bats in his caves to accept this therapy. Protection from the fungus meant the bats could go wherever they wanted to and stay alive.

Even though eating and heating all the hemp made Maq B. feel queasy, he offered to treat any bat that wanted his help, not just the inhabitants of his caves. After digesting one bale of hemp, he could treat about a hundred bats.

But the nonresident bats weren't interested. Either they found the stench unbearable or they didn't believe they were in danger or it sounded like too much effort. Regrettably this meant large populations of bats along the Mississippi River perished.

That loss did result in more food for Maq B.'s bats. "Man," Bat-Out-Of-Hell said as he sank to the ground. "The shadflies came out tonight. There were millions of them. You didn't have to chase them, just open your mouth, and they flew in. We are all completely stuffed."

"I can see that," Maq B. said. "You guys will need more hours than usual to sleep off this gluttonous night."

"On our way," Batshit-Crazy mumbled. "Slumber beckons." He bounced up and down a few times and then managed to hang onto the ceiling.

"Tomorrow after you have slept off your annual shadfly binge, I could use your help," Maq B. said. "I have no idea how to fix the conditions in the Dancehall Cave for my dragon family reunion, but maybe your group mind can come up with something."

"Will do," Bat-Masterson said and sprang up to the ceiling.

Maq B. smiled. Bats and dragons had a great deal in common. They were all creatures of flight, even if, technically, bats no longer flew.

Enthusiastic breeding over time had resulted in dragons who made good use of their mammalian and reptilian genetic heritage. Lately, of course, they utilized genetic engineering to maximize their capabilities and longevity, for example breeding for flexible digits on their claws so they could make use of electrical communication devices.

Bats, on the other hand, had chosen to remain content with their original structures, choosing only to evolve some intelligence and appreciation of the finer things in life, like food, food, and more food.

As scientists, dragons lacked perhaps a certain creativity, but they were geniuses at adapting ideas from others, especially humans. With strong legs, flexible wings, and arms boasting of paws with multi-digit claws, dragons quickly excelled at everything they were interested in, especially technology.

Due to Maq B.'s telepathic proficiency, honed over hundreds of thousands of years of practice, none of the human beings in the area noticed the existence of the deepest caves in the Maquoketa Caves Parks system except those Maq B. chose to communicate with. Not only good fences, but sometimes ignorance of existence made for good neighbors.

He never used his telepathic talents to control the lesser creatures directly—that would be morally ambiguous—but rather just to encourage certain emotions already in existence. His favorite distributor Curtis and other associates considered Maq B. to be just another neighbor, his dragon physiology not worth commenting on.

Now it sounded like all the bats were snoring contentedly, hanging down from the ceiling. Maq B. tapped at the appropriate device and called his reliable human supplier. A sunburned, male, human face somewhat hidden by a bushy, unkempt, grayish beard illuminated a side wall. Chewing a blade of vegetation, the man mumbled something or other.

"Good to see you, Curtis," Maquoketa said, leaning toward the cave wall. "What's new? And please take that foliage out of your mouth. I didn't understand a word you said."

Curtis nodded and smiled. "Just wanted to know how many cattle and pigs I should plan to deliver for your festivities. And how about some poultry this time?"

Maq B. reflected. A young chicken, freshly toasted in midair dragonfire, made for an excellent appetizer. He could almost taste it. Some ideologues in the family said it was cannibalism for flying creatures to consume life forms with similar talents, but Maq B. was tired of kowtowing to every new dogma. If dragons didn't want to eat poultry, they should eat something else.

"Yes, add the poultry to my usual reunion order," Maq B. said. "Is there any upper limit to the numbers of animals you can bring me? I plan to do some hunting myself, but that's never enough for the number of guests I expect."

"Naw," Curtis said. "I can get you as many animals as you need. There might be a problem with vegetables. No one was able to plant much this year due to the rain and flooding. I'll do what I can. Same delivery location as usual?"

"Yes, at the official entrance to the Maquoketa Caves State Park," Maq B. said. "Two weeks from today."

"Then I'll call you tomorrow to confirm the numbers," Curtis said, and the wall darkened.

Maq B. preferred to have everything catered except for his own home-made corn whiskey. He had a certain pride in his whiskey which he distilled in one of the back caves. The bats always praised it, even though they never drank much. They said it induced a state of torpor much faster than natural weariness.

Maq B. moved his recliner over to his calculating devices. Making lists of facts often helped him discover solutions to problems. Fact: Water in the Dancehall Cave was dripping down all the walls. Fact: The ground was squishy in the Dancehall Cave, and the air was uncomfortably humid and malodorous. Fact: This was all a result of the constant rainfall of the past six months and therefore could only get worse with time.

Also fact: There was plenty of space in the Dancehall Cave for the number of dragon relatives he could expect to come. Also fact: The relatives always enjoyed celebrating in the Dancehall Cave. Also fact: Combined telepathic powers of enough dragons kept the human population away from the Maquoketa Caves during the festivities.

So what did he need for a successful party and how could he get it under these circumstances? Well, food to begin with.

Foraging had always been sufficient for Maq B.'s personal culinary needs, and when the mood struck him, he still traveled in search of new treats. He was an excellent hunter. At first instinctively, later with precise knowledge of anatomy, Maq B. always bit his prey in the correct location to force a flow of endorphins so they died happy. Maq B. felt they deserved that much consideration.

Currently there was an oversupply of deer and wild turkeys in Iowa, many of which he had already hunted, collected, and preserved for the upcoming reunion feast. He could look for them first.

Dragons in his family came in many sizes. They weren't nearly as hefty as humans assumed—indeed how could they fly in that case? However, the Finnish branch of the dragon family did have a height of some three meters and a wingspan of almost ten. When the dancing and carousing began, the venue had to provide enough space for dragons to interact without damaging each other.

The room had to be clean, attractive, and dry. How was he supposed to dry out a cave when the ground above, below, and surrounding it was saturated with water? And even if he could, the weather forecasts claimed the rain would continue.

Maq B. needed new ideas. It was early morning, and the bats were sleeping. If he flew high enough, none of the farmers would see him. Much as he loved his caves, sometimes he also needed a bird's-eye view of skies, fields, and rivers to get his inventive blood flowing. He flew slowly up and down the Mississippi, waiting for his creative brain to kick in.

It didn't, and so he soared up into the thinner regions of the atmosphere. Evolution had made dragonhide more than capable of withstanding near-vacuum conditions. Up at the edge of outer space he thought he sensed an inkling of an idea. His brain twitched pleasantly.

Now feeling optimistic again, Maq B. flew back. He spent the rest of the day shuffling around in the huge Dancehall Cave, but not accomplishing anything other than getting his claws muddy. Then he gave up and retired to his home cave. Despite not having done much, he felt tired.

Just as Maq B. was ready to let his scaly lids cover his eyes, Bat-Out-Of-Hell stirred and swooped down from the ceiling. "I am so full," he moaned. "I've never eaten that much before in my life."

"Then I don't have to ask how it went for you last night," Maq B. said.

"Well, it's a little lonely along the river now," Bat-Out-Of-Hell admitted. "We used to meet up with hundreds of bats in every little river town. Now we don't see anyone. There's more food, but less entertainment."

It occurred to Maq B. that in the long run the genetic diversity of the bats was endangered, but that was one more problem he had no idea how to solve at the moment. "Too bad," Maq B. said. "I tried to save your riverside friends from the fungus."

"Don't blame yourself," Bat-Out-Of-Hell said. "There's nothing you can do about stupid, and it was stupid of them to refuse your offer. What kind of help did you want from us?"

Maq B. said, "It's dragon family reunion time again. I wanted to have it in the Dancehall Cave, but it's a flooded sauna up there and I don't know how to get rid of the water."

"Hmm," Bat-Out-Of-Hell said. "Beats me. I'll pass this on to our group mind. As soon as more of us wake up, we might be able to come up with an idea." And he swooped back up to the ceiling.

Maq B. closed his eyes and dozed, dreaming about previous climate states of the planet, the solid ice ball, the tropical jungle with palm trees at the South Pole, the volcanic outbursts with the lava first heating up the atmosphere and then the soot in the air cooling it down.

Just as he was about to transition into a deep REM sleep, screeching bats woke him up.

"The solution to your problem is obvious," Bat-Out-Of-Hell said. "You can't get rid of the water. So your best bet is to turn the Dancehall Cave into a water world for your party. Take the water out of the saturated ground around the cave and dump it into the cave. Turn the cave into one gigantic swimming pool."

"Dragons aren't big on water sports," Maq B. began.

"Maybe not yet, but they can splash around," Bat-Out-Of-Hell said. "My guess is that swimming is an acquired taste. A water world theme makes your party something completely new and unexpected. Dragons will talk about it forever; no one will be able to top this."

That got Maq B. thinking. The bats had something there, definitely better than his non-solution. He would have to seal off the Dancehall Cave; he didn't want water dripping into his home caves. And the weight—water and dragons—how could he keep that from collapsing the ground and breaking into his home caves? His engineer brain kicked in and started twitching.

"Thank you," he said to Bat-Out-Of-Hell. "I owe you guys."

"Great," Bat-Masterson said. "And we'll collect. But first we're out to see if there are any shadflies left. Sometimes they live a little more than twenty-four hours."

At that all the bats swarmed out of the cave and Maq B. got busy. Now that he had an idea of what to do, the details emerged by themselves. Huge, thick, impermeable rubber sheets, steel planks and bolts, pumps, riveters, fortunately everything available online. Online sales of his corn whiskey always gave him more than enough credit to pay for same-day delivery.

Once the construction supplies arrived, Maq B. enlisted the help of nearby relatives, Savanna B. Dragon, Galena B. Dragon, Princeton B. Dragon, and Fulton B. Dragon. They were glad to help and brought along their quite skilled offspring. Maq B. set up a telepathic barrier to keep human creatures away from the caves so they could all work day and night.

After only a few days, the Dancehall Cave was transformed into a gigantic swimming pool with thick, rubberized walls and base. They pumped the water out of the earth surrounding the cave into the newly created swimming pool. Blasts from dragon snouts dried out the ground surrounding the cave, but this did take some time.

After consultation with the helpful nearby relatives, Maq B. chose a lightly diluted chemical solution to rid the water of its unfortunate stench. His first try didn't succeed; fortunately some quick blasts of dragonfire prevented damage from the poisonous gases. More experimentation in one of his chemistry caves gave him the formula he needed to give the water a refreshing, waterfall fragrance.

The younger relatives had good ideas about slides, and other dragon-sized pool equipment. Galena B. came up with the idea of anchored floating tables for food and drink. With the tables spread around the perimeter, there would be sufficient space in the center for dragonplay, dancing, gymnastics, and the like.

Emboldened by his success, Maq B. sent off telepathic invitations to all the relatives he was in contact with for the upcoming dragon family reunion.

"Nice looking pool," Bat-Out-Of-Hell commented on his way back from another night of feeding frenzy. "What will you do for entertainment?"

"No idea yet," Maq B. admitted. "I'm still in my just-in-time mode. I fixed the water problem, the food and drinks are ordered, and now I guess you're right. It's time to figure out how to keep my relatives amused and happy. Do you guys have any suggestions?"

"You will have loud music, right?" Bat-Masterson asked.

"Yes, the media equipment is embedded in the ceiling," Maq B. said.

"And your guests will be inebriated fairly quickly?" Batshit-Crazy asked.

"I think we can assume that," Maq B. said. "Generally everyone has been quite fond of my corn whiskey, which will be available in bottles on floating trays."

"Then you need drinking games and dancing contests," Bat-Out-Of-Hell said firmly. "You're afraid the dragons might not take to water, and so you have to distract them. I really think you could be onto something big here."

Maq B. remembered previous family reunions. "You're right," he said. "Guests have to be distracted and kept busy while being tempted with more food and drink than they possibly can consume. This ensures their memories of the event will be pleasant but vague on details they might complain about."

"And how do you want to end the bash?" Bat-Out-Of-Hell asked. "Do you have to get them out of the water at the end? Can dragons drown?"

"No," Maq B. said. "Our instinct for self-preservation always kicks in when we're threatened with minimized brain function. Sleepy or unconscious dragons would float. But I have come up with a useful solution for the end of the party, hundreds of rubber bags with capacities of at least a thousand liters each."

"I wondered why you had them stashed outside the Dancehall Cave," Bat-Masterson said. "What are you doing to do with them?"

"Wait and see," Maq B. said. "The party begins tomorrow night at dusk and ends at dawn. You can watch the departure on your way back in from your nightly tour."

The reunion proceeded just as Maq B. hoped. A moderate telepathic shield kept the human neighbors from noticing the approach of hundreds of dragons.

The first guests were very skeptical. "We dragons are not fish," was one frequent comment. However, after consuming enough corn whiskey, all the guests began splashing around and praising food and drink. Loud music—Maq B.'s relatives preferred pop music of the 1960's—encouraged dragonplay in the water as did the dancing games and the various contests involving comparison of physical prowess. Brute force didn't produce the same success in water as it did on land, and so outcomes of contests were never predictable.

One unexpected advantage to the water-world theme was the absence of fire damage to the cave or to the guests. Arguments that used to end with blasts of dragonfire going off in all directions now ended with snouts being dunked, loud coughing, and subsequent increased consumption of corn whiskey.

Cavorting in deep water turned out to be quite exhausting, straining dragon muscles that otherwise didn't get as much exercise. Maq B. noted the increased consumption of food. The deer and wild turkeys disappeared within the first two hours. Curtis hadn't been able to deliver as many vegetable-based munchables, but the extra portions of beef, pork, mutton, and poultry more than made up for that lack.

By dawn everyone agreed a good time had been had by all. Dragons had already stopped complaining about the watery venue around midnight. Due to higher than usual intake of meat products, the general level of inebriation slowly receded to a soft haze. As the bats flew into the cave, safely out of reach of the guests, Maq B. used the most powerful ceiling amplifier to get his guests' attention.

"There is one last contest before we call it a night," he said. "Everyone can take one of the rubber bags outside. Fill it with water from this pool here. Then fly up quickly past the ionosphere and dump the water at the edge of the atmosphere. Come back here and fill up the next bag. A team of judges will keep track of how many bags each dragon carries up. Whoever transports the most water will win and receive an appropriate prize."

The judges were Maq B.'s neighbor relatives, and the prize was a case of corn whiskey, but no one asked for this information. Instead the now squeaky-clean dragons began to scoop water out of the cave and fly up to the edges of the atmosphere. There was some spillage at first, which Maq B. didn't see as a problem. The human neighbors would surely regard it as yet another strange weather phenomenon. With each trip, dragons became less intoxicated and more accurate. The cave emptied rapidly.

"Neat trick," Bat-Out-Of-Hell said as he floated around. "You get your guests to do the clean-up."

"That's one benefit," Maq B. admitted. "But if things go as I calculate, the ice crystals that form at the edge of the exosphere from these bags of water could reflect sunlight and thereby have a cooling influence on the planet's increase in temperature. In the long run this could moderate the weather and possibly even return it to conditions previous to global warming. It's only a hypothesis at this point, but perhaps worthy of being tested."

"Worth a try," Bat-Out-Of-Hell agreed. "But isn't that only a temporary solution?"

"Probably," Maq B. sighed. "If I want things to continue to improve long term, I may have to get involved in politics. But that's a worst-case scenario. Having dragons carry water away from the planet at regular intervals seems easier."

"Cool," Bat-Out-Of-Hell said. "But what are you going to do for the next family reunion?"

"Hmm," Maq B. said. "No idea. My guess is that I will need your help again."

~ * ~ * ~

Mary Jo Rabe grew up on a farm in eastern Iowa, got degrees from Michigan State University (German and math) and University of Wisconsin-Milwaukee (library science) where she became a late-blooming science fiction reader and writer. She worked in the library of the chancery office of the Archdiocese of Freiburg, Germany for 41 years, and lives with her husband in Titisee-Neustadt, Germany.

She has published "Blue Sunset", inspired by Spoon River Anthology and The Martian Chronicles, electronically and has had poems and stories published in Fiction River, Pulphouse, Space Opera Mashup, Rocketpack Adventures, Whispers from the Universe, Future Earth Tech, Blaze Ward Presents Issue 4—Cloak and Dagger, Blaze Ward Presents Issue 5—Crime and..., Alternate Hilarities, Pandora, Stygian Articles, The Martian Wave, Astropoetica, The Sword Review, Raven Electrick, Mindflights, Star*Line, and Space and Time.

Visit her blog at: https://maryjorabe.wordpress.com/

.

Dragon in Distress

Gustasp Irani

The fair maidens of the kingdom were out on the streets celebrating the birth of the baby dragon. It had been years, almost a decade, since the Damsel in Distress beauty pageant had been held. Many feared the time-honored tradition of knights in shining armor rescuing maidens from the lairs of fire-breathing beasts would soon be a thing of the past: alive only in stories of valor and happily-ever-afters passed down over generations. Now, with the arrival of the baby, there was hope the noble sport of dragon slaying would be revived.

The meeting of the Knights of the Round Table was in disarray. News of the addition of one more member to the population of dragons in the kingdom was received with much cheering and table thumping. Even before the commotion had subsided, some of those gathered around the table were steering the discussion to the rules that would govern the Knight in Shining Armor tournament.

The king who had called the meeting was alarmed. The situation was spiraling out of control. If saner counsel did not prevail, the kingdom would descend into an orgy of celebration—beauty pageants and jousting tournaments. Yes, he missed presiding over these gala events which were once the highlight of the kingdom's social calendar but, as of now, the birth of the dragon called for restraint.

There was a time when dragons roamed the kingdom freely: a time when dragons were a menace, especially after they developed a taste for roasted human flesh. At some point in their evolutionary history, these dastardly creatures realized the male of the human race had this strange affliction that compelled them to set off on the foolhardy task of trying to rescue maidens the dragons kept in their food larder.

It did not take these fire-breathing beasts long to realize they no longer had to go hunting for humans. All they had to do was capture one member of the fair sex and use it as bait and these tasty little bite-size treats came willingly to their dens. They particularly developed a taste for those who came in metal armor casings. One blast of their fiery breath and they roasted over evenly. All they had to do was crack open the metal casing and indulge their palate.

It was not uncommon for these winged beasts to swoop down from the sky and pluck young girls from fields and rooftops and carry them off to their lair. Public messaging about the perils of rescuing stranded maidens proved to be of no avail. Men from all walks of life, from princes and knights to cooks and farmhands with dreams of fame, glory and happy fairy-tale endings, sallied forth to do battle with dragons only to end up as dragon snacks.

One day, the king's surgeon who had lost his only son to the dream of rescuing a hapless damsel accidently stumbled on the Achilles Heel of the dragon. Driven by grief, the medic carved up a dragon that had died of old age and discovered the heart of the beast lay below a thin membrane of skin at the base of its neck.

It did not take long for the Knights of the Round Table to figure out how to slay the beast. Soon the slay-the-dragon maneuver, as it came to be known, was common knowledge. Now even lowly farmhands would engage dragons in mortal combat and emerge victorious. Maidens, fair and not so fair, young and not so young, started to seek out dragons and offer themselves as hostages knowing full well they would be rescued.

One day, a stable hand donned his master's shining armor and set off to rescue a stranded lass. It proved to be more challenging than he had imagined. The first three caves he entered had already been visited by dragon slayers and the maidens who had been held captive there had been whisked off to safety. He got lucky at the fourth cave. It had a living dragon and a not- too- distressed damsel who cheered him on as he danced away from the fiery blasts of the beast's breath and got close enough to plunge his trusty sword into its vulnerable heart.

The rescued lass skipped joyfully to meet her hero…and stopped abruptly. Her knight in shining armor smelled of horse poop. No way was she going to spend her happily-ever-after with a stable hand. She had to find another dragon. Sadly, the first one she approached already had a hostage and saw no benefit in keeping two. So, he indulged himself and popped the second one in his mouth.

The wanton slaying of dragons had pushed the species to the

brink of extinction. Serious action needed to be taken before these now noble beasts were reduced to footnotes in history books. The king decreed the dragon was a protected species. But that did not stop lovelorn maidens from seeking them out and encouraging wannabe knights to poach them. Dragon numbers fell even further. A compromise had to be made.

A delegation of fair maidens sat down with the Knights of the Round Table and struck a deal. The kingdom would hold two events every weekend—a beauty pageant to select a Damsel in Distress and a jousting tournament to select a Knight in Shining Armor. The winners would then set out to slay a dragon in front of a paying audience. The funds collected—both entrance fees and donations—would be invested in a dragon-breeding program.

However, dragons breed slowly and despite the best efforts of all concerned, the population of the species continued to fall. It was not long before the Damsel in Distress pageant and jousting tournament became fortnightly, monthly, bimonthly and annual events. Finally, there were just three adolescent dragons—two females and one male—left in the kingdom. Dragon slaying had come to a standstill.

Now that knights in shining armor had lost their luster, starry-eyed maidens started to woo minstrels. It was the golden age of music in the kingdom. Love songs: odes to rosy complexions, hypnotic eyes and cascading tresses filled the air and floated through romantic night skies. However, these musicians were fickle lovers. There was no knowing when they would up and out of a relationship and move to the neighboring town and village. The tribe soon got to be known as the wandering minstrels.

Then there was light at the end of the proverbial tunnel. One of the female dragons had given birth to a baby—a male. The following year, the other mothered a female dragon. Citizens of the kingdom rejoiced and celebrated. After almost a decade, there was going to be a gala dragon slaying event. The king's protests were overruled. The people of the kingdom had waited in anticipation for so long and they were not going to be denied the revival of their traditional sport. The king was given the choice of either abdicating or choosing the adult female dragon to be pitted against the winner of the Knight in Shining Armor tournament in mortal combat.

Seamstresses across the kingdom were in great demand as

contestants of the Damsel in Distress beauty pageant sought them out. Dresses with puffed sleeves and tiaras were in vogue as they hinted at the possibility that one might be a princess.

Knights spent endless hours applying spit and polish to rusted armor.

The arena built outside the dragon's lair was packed to overflowing on the day the Slay the Dragon event was slated to take place. The Damsel in Distress (chosen after a bitter contest of charges and counter charges of nepotism) played her part to the hilt: screaming for help and pleading with the heavens to send a gallant brave heart to rescue her.

Enter the Knight in Shining Armor. The audience cheers. The dragon fires a tongue of flame. The crowd is on its feet as the knight sidesteps the shaft by skipping to the right. Damsel in Distress gasps in relief. Knight in Shining Armor feigns a move to the left but skips to the right. Feign, skip, skip, skip, feign, skip…. It is a well-rehearsed routine documented in the Handbook of the Dragon Slayer and the more widely distributed Dragon Slaying for Idiots. Though the crowd anticipates every move, they are enraptured as this dance of death plays out. Knight in Shining Armor's performance is near perfect. It suggests he is not going through the routine but improvising each move as the moment demands.

Gasp! Is Knight in Shining Armor showboating or…? Zap! The crowd watches in shocked silence as the dragon cracks open the armor and pops a roasted knight in its mouth. Damsel in Distress is the first to recover and lets out a terrifying wail. It's been a while since the dragon has had a human snack and the roasted knight has whetted its appetite. It picks up the damsel and pops her in its mouth.

As the audience looks on in disbelief, the dragon throws back it head and lets out a fiery burp. The silence that has enveloped the arena ruptures as the crowd explodes into wild cheering.

The king decrees that from this day on Slaying the Dragon will be replaced with a gala annual event: Feed the Dragon.

~ * ~ * ~

Mumbai-based **Gustasp Irani** is part of a husband-and-wife travel writers/photographers team (www.gustaspandjeroo.com). Between foot-slogging across the world and India to research travel stories, he has made time to indulge in a little creative writing. His first novel

Once Upon a Raj was published in 1992. Since then, he has written four more novels, a play and a collection of short stories. He and his wife have created guides (including text and photographs) on South Africa and the Republic of Fiji for the Indian market which were commissioned by the national tourism boards of the two countries in India.

Our Last Battle

Birgit K. Gaiser

I landed carefully. The muddy plain was covered in humans, alive, dead and everything in between. They didn't appreciate us landing on top of them, not even on the dead ones who were beyond feeling or caring. Something or other about dignity, apparently, though one might argue lying dead in a field was not exactly dignified to start with. Whatever; it was a job.

D'Eyn, my mate, briefly circled above, then landed next to me. We rubbed necks, my silver against his red, and gently clashed our horns together. We both cherished this physical contact after the recent battle. While it's true we do not care all that much for humans, it is nonetheless rather unpleasant to kill so many of them.

The servitors ran towards us carrying ladders, towels and bowls of ointments, the flame symbol on their armbands glowing in the setting sun. As soon as they reached us, they started pulling spears, harpoons and arrows from our scaly bodies, then mopped up our blood and rubbed salves on our wounds.

D'Eyn looked at me contentedly and gently purred under the servitors' ministrations. I was glad we had sacrificed some gold to get them. Each individual wound was no more than the equivalent of a scratch, but scratches add up, and it had been a long and draining fight.

We were both eager to take our gold and servants, fly home to our volcano, check in on our young and rest. We might even try for another egg or two while we still could. It was time for a break from the humans' fighting. After today's clear victory, this war was decided.

One of the servitors massaged some salve into a particularly irritating nick on my belly, left by a harpoon that had found its way between two of my scales. I, too, purred with pleasure. This servitor was good. I would request him as one of my quota. We mostly take farmers who can tend our livestock and increase the size of the herds, but there is a little leeway for luxury.

Our alliance with the Midilans was a useful one: without it, we would have to steal cattle and sheep from the humans to feed, and they would try to kill us like they had centuries ago, using armies, magic or guile. I did not want to imagine what would happen if they ever stopped fighting amongst themselves and no longer needed us. Based on my experience over the last century and a half, however, the chances of that happening were slim.

A rumble in D'Eyn's chest brought my mind back to the present. The human general was riding up towards us. Even on horseback, she had to crane her neck to look us in the eye, which she hated as much as I enjoyed it. It was petty, I knew. There was no need for me to prove my superiority given our size difference and that small matter of being able to breathe fire. Technically she is our superior while we are under contract, but it is good to remind them of who is the superior creature every now and then.

"Mey'Ra. D'Eyn."

"General."

We nodded at each other, just the right amount to satisfy protocol in this temporary relationship of convenience.

"I have news."

"Don't tell me," I said. "The Tyrenians are ready to capitulate."

If humans could read draconic expressions, they would have described mine as "smug".

She hesitated and avoided my gaze, staring instead into the empty space between mine and D'Eyn's heads. She ran her hand through her dark curls, visibly uneasy about what she was about to tell us, then cleared her throat.

"I…no, actually, I'm afraid I've come to tell you the opposite. We've had some worrying news about the Tyrenians."

"Yes?" I asked. This sounded ominous. The Tyrenians had looked as good as finished days ago. It had certainly looked like reinforcements were meager and too far away to make a difference at this stage, and after today's battles they could not possibly have enough bodies left to continue putting up a fight.

"We've had words from one of our spies that their queen has hired a wizard", the general said, still not looking straight at either of us

"A wizard."

"Yes."

I took a moment to consider. It had been a while since any

wizards worth the title had let themselves become involved in human wars. There were not many of them left these days, but Tyrenia was a very rich country, and it was not unthinkable that they had managed to convince one to go into battle.

Humans were unlikely to harm us, but magic could. Wizards could.

"Our contract has a clause about this," I reminded the general. "We do not fight wizards."

D'Eyn blew a little smoke to drive the point home.

"I understand. But we didn't know there was a wizard involved when we drafted the contract."

"That sounds very much like it is your problem."

Again, smoke emerged from D'Eyn's nostrils, this time accompanied by a soft but clearly audible growl.

The general's expression changed. I could not read humans that well, but I think it might have been embarrassment. Worry, maybe.

"It most certainly is, and I won't claim otherwise. But I was wondering—seeing as the war is nearly won now, and it's only the one…"

"The one *wizard,*" I corrected her. I was feeling a bit irritated now. She could not possibly hope to convince us by outsmarting us, nor by appealing to our non-existing humanity. The fact she was trying felt rather insulting.

"Yes, of course. One wizard. I was wondering if you might consider, despite the terms of the contract, to help us win this war, once and for all."

"Why would we want to do this?" I asked. "Please explain. And don't try to outsmart us, it's not going to work."

"Well, for one, there is the loss of life. If the war doesn't end, thousands more might perish," she started.

"Irrelevant. Wars kill. You've hired *us* to kill. *Now* you're worried about lives lost?"

"Secondly," she continued—I had to give her credit for standing up to me like this— "secondly, wouldn't it feel like unfinished business to you?"

Ah, the professional pride angle. Once more, I had to disappoint her. "It would, but this, too, is irrelevant. There is nothing shameful about a business unfinished if finishing the business is unwise."

She raised her eyebrows, but nodded. "I understand. Our kinds differ."

"Anything else?" My patience was really running thin now.

"Just the obvious reason," she said. "If they do indeed have a wizard in their ranks, I expect the queen will send him after you sooner or later to avenge the damage you've done and prevent you from doing more in future."

This, I am embarrassed to admit, had not yet occurred to me while annoyance dominated my reaction, but it was a possibility. A very realistic one at that. A wizard would be able to trace us to our mountain home, and if one human knew, more might follow.

My irritation grew. Why could those humans not research their enemies before committing themselves to battle? Before committing *us* to battle? I gently nudged D'Eyn, asking him to take over while I tried to calm down.

"I take it you would like to review the terms of our contract," he stated in his low, booming voice, buying some time and making it clear it would be more complicated than just a quick verbal agreement.

He was the quieter, more contemplative one of us. If he spoke up and considered the contract change, then he must have come to the conclusion there might be an advantage in addressing this problem now. There might be merit in pulling it out by its roots rather than letting it fester and risk having it come back to us in weeks, months or years and living in uncertainty till then.

"Yes," the general confirmed.

"You will of course appreciate," he continued, "that our payment will have to be increased appropriately. This new development will add a great deal of risk, and work, for us. We had expected to rest tonight, then fly home."

The general inclined her head. "Naturally. I have been authorized to offer twice the payment we originally agreed."

I caught myself before inhaling sharply and giving away my surprise. That wizard had to be good. And, therefore, dangerous.

"Thank you. We will take it under consideration."

The general took the hint. "Thank you. I will return in the morning."

~ * ~

In the end, it took several rounds of negotiation, interspersed by small skirmishes—wizard-free, for the time being, Tyrenia was a week's ride away—until we had agreed on an amount of gold and servants we could both live with.

I was still extremely uneasy about the situation. We had not fought a wizard in some time. The odds were about even: we would not have accepted the contract if we did not think we could beat him. But then, the same was presumably true for him.

The sheer amount of gold and servants offered up by the Midilans through the general had made the decision for us. We had insisted on advance payment. If we lost our lives, our young would have plenty of food and gold to see them through their adolescence, and the Midilans, after losing the war, would scarcely miss the gold and a few farmers.

Twice a day, we took to the air to monitor the approach of the Tyrenian reinforcements while wreaking as much havoc as we could possibly fit into the reconnaissance missions.

When we finally saw the wizard, I was surprised, almost a bit disappointed. He did not look like much. In fact, he looked like he had only just figured out how to do magic, a young human with limp, yellow hair, his starred robe hanging awkwardly off his lanky frame. He looked like discomfort personified on his war horse, and from what I could tell from the beast's movements, the horse was not enjoying the experience, either.

We were flying too high for the humans' inferior eyes to make us out, but I was still nervous. Who knew what detection magic the wizard might have deployed?

Overall, there were maybe 500 people in the small army marching towards the battlefield. On their own, they were harmless. With the assistance of the wizard, they could have poisoned harpoons, spears that exploded upon impact, unbreakable arrows, super-strength crossbows, fire protection, impenetrable armor—and we would not know which of these or dozens of other enchantments until it might be too late.

Or maybe that's what the wizard wanted us to believe. Maybe he wanted us to be wary of the humans and focus our energy on carefully eliminating them while he launched an offensive. Maybe the young man on the horse was a decoy and the wizard was riding or even marching among the soldiers, preparing for a surprise attack. The magicking bastards had a reputation for being sly.

We decided to use our night vision to our advantage. A little bit of chaos would soon reveal the wizard, and soldiers woken up from sleep by an emergency were less likely to remember the battle plans conveyed to them in a daytime briefing.

D'Eyn and I slept during the daytime, then spent the first part of the night together, our long necks entwined, keeping each other warm and whispering words of love and reassurance. We did not want to be there, wanted instead to be home, in the mountains, done with fighting. This would be the last time, we promised each other, and just like all the previous times, we would see it through together.

Two hours before dawn we spread our wings and ascended. It was a cloudy night without a moon or stars, making it even harder for the humans to see anything in the sky. We were going alone; the Midilans would be as useless and panicked as the Tyrenians and more likely than not to get themselves killed, whether by accident or the wizard's design.

Once above the camp, we briefly touched wings, then parted to attack from opposite ends. The oiled cloth of the tents caught our fire beautifully and illuminated the ground for us, at the same time blinding the humans to anything in the dark above them. The only way to hit us would be a lucky shot in the dark.

The noise and smell of fire and burning flesh startled the horses, creating another diversion. We swooped up and down without a pattern, burning tents and bodies alike.

Within minutes, the camp was devastated. Some of the humans were grouping together in an effort to respond, either saving injured comrades or firing arrows at us when we were swooping in. Others had chosen escape over potential incineration, and were running as fast as their legs and limited vision could support. They quickly learned incineration was still an option, even if they ran.

Amidst the carnage, a small area of tranquility established itself as we had hoped it would. The wizard's tent, no doubt. I stooped down, breathing fire, first gently, then vigorously, but the flames disappeared before they hit the canvas. D'Eyn tried, too, even stooping low enough to try and grab the tent, but whatever blocked the fire also stopped his claws from penetrating.

We swooped upwards again, keen to put some distance

between us and the wizard. "Did you hurt yourself?" I asked worriedly. My mate's leg did not look injured, but wizards can do invisible damage.

"No," he said. "I'm fine."

"He can't stay in his tent forever," I remarked. It was true—sooner or later he would have to come out and fight us, or risk having the Midilan army find a way through the magic, maybe by digging a tunnel or by slowly wearing it down. And he was only human; he would need sleep eventually. It was in his best interest to make a move.

We tucked in our wings and dived towards the campsite again for our next round of attacks on soldiers, structures and the wizard. Just as we were done and about to lift, D'Eyn screamed in pain. It was a high-pitched, piercing noise, one I had never heard from him. My heart skipped a beat.

I gained a little more height, then looked around me. D'Eyn's beautiful, crimson body was surrounded by light blue lines of light that pulsated gently. Two trails of the same blue light led back to the ground, to where the wizard now stood outside his tent, arms raised to the sky, his lips moving in an incantation I could not make out this high up.

D'Eyn continued his piercing shriek and flapped his wings. I could see the big muscles on his back moving and straining, but the wings hardly moved enough to keep him in place, never mind allow him to gain height and move away from the wizard.

My fear turned into anger, into hatred as red and hot as the scales on my mate's body. Something in me managed to think logically. The wizard was using both his hands for the spell, so he could not also attack me, not without D'Eyn breaking free. He could send something our way, so we must be able to send something back.

Something.

My one choice.

Fire.

I breathed fire, but I was still too high up to aim with much accuracy. His tent went up in flames. I hoped it had been full of scrolls and potions. The gangly wizard, one sleeve of his ill-fitting robe now singed, took a few steps away from the tent, the incantation becoming louder. The blue light became stronger and, slowly but surely, D'Eyn sank to the ground.

He was still fighting, shrieking, now thrashing in the air. I, too, shrieked, too pained by the sight of him to keep calm. I watched as he lost altitude and hit the ground. I gasped, inhaled, waited for my fire to swell up again, to fill me, to be launched at the wizard who had hurt my mate. But I was too late.

The wizard moved his hands in a new pattern. The beams of blue light from his hands tied themselves into a knot which moved towards D'Eyn, tying off the energy that restrained him and bound him to the ground.

D'Eyn's head shifted. It was a small, almost indiscernible movement, but it was enough for me to know he was still alive, still fighting, although the tightening net of blue light around him was visibly weakening him.

I roared with fury and released the flames in short, vicious staccato bursts, forcing the wizard to react. He extinguished one, jumped out of the way of the second, then raised his hands to reflect the third one right back at me. But by then, I had already flown another five lengths towards him, and the reflected fireball narrowly missed me, shooting into the night sky.

My fourth blast hit right in front of his feet, creating a crater and sending pebbles and rocks flying. He started singing and weaving his hands again. The few soldiers who had not run away before did now, aware that getting involved in this showdown was unlikely to end well for them.

The fifth blast went just above his shoulder.

The wizard jumped to the side, his incantation finished, and disappeared.

Invisibility. The coward!

My sixth, seventh and eighth blast aimed where I thought he might have jumped to, but I could only guess. I had to act fast—he could not have gone far, but with every second, he was gaining advantage on me.

It was time to dispense with any semblance of style and elegance and use crude force.

I circled beyond the end of the camp, performed a tight turn and gathered speed. Spreading my wings, I sank down to glide just above the ground, ignoring small impacts of water buckets, flying embers and the limbs of dead soldiers. I thought I might have missed my opportunity when something, no someone, invisible hit my right wing, hard.

The wizard.

The impact broke his concentration, and he tumbled to the ground just under my wing, his body was once more visible.

The sun came up over the horizon, and I saw the torched camp was covered in humans, alive, dead and everything in between. I landed carefully, lowering my body on top of the wizard's. Humans don't appreciate us landing on top of them, but today I was beyond caring about their dignity.

I placed my front legs on his arms and dug my claws in, keeping him from weaving new magic. My head, as large as his entire body, loomed just in front of his, my cold, silver eyes staring into his, daring him to try a spell.

In the end, I decided to make it quick for both of us and simply bit off his head. It was probably more dignified for him than being slowly crushed by my weight, or torched, or waiting for the general and her soldiers to arrive and finish him off. Though one might argue that, one way or another, lying dead in a field is rarely dignified.

The moment he died, I heard D'Eyn roar triumphantly. The blue light around him had dissipated, the wizard's life energy no longer fueling it. He waddled over towards me, weak and disoriented, and we rubbed our necks against each other's and gently clashed our horns, like we always did after battle.

"Can you fly?", I asked.

"Yes."

"Let's go then."

We made our way back to our mountains, not even finishing off the remaining Tyrenian soldiers we encountered on the way. Some jobs did not need to be finished, and now it was time to retire.

~ * ~ * ~

Birgit K. Gaiser's day job is managing the development of software to help look after historic monuments across Scotland, from castles to industrial heritage sites to stone circles. She reads and writes fiction (sci-fi, fantasy, urban, crime) in her spare time and enjoys quirky stories and prompts.

Blacktooth 500

Gwen C. Katz

The air is filled with screams and trills as two hundred dragons strain against their harnesses. Beaked jaws snap in frustration. Scythed claws scrape the ground. Two big males break free of their traces and attack each other, putting down their heads to rake each other's bellies with their horns until their drivers tear them apart.

It's punishingly hot and the sunlight reflects off the black volcanic rock in waves of shimmering heat. Yet thousands have gathered to watch the start of the Blacktooth 500.

Amid the chaos, I examine our team's harnesses while Amelia looks the dragons over and coos gently to calm them. They nuzzle her arms. At fifteen, Amelia already has a way with the beasts. If only she had more discipline, she would be the finest up-and-coming driver in the league.

And I'm not just saying that because she's my daughter.

I check our cart's brakes and each of its six wheels. It's blue with "Angel Peaks Rookery" blazoned on the side in big yellow letters. I give the name one last polish. I want everyone to be able to read it as we blaze across the finish line.

All the best racing teams in the country are here. Ray Freedman, my old rival, is hitching up his team next to me. He beat me on our last sprint, and he won't let me forget it. Across the valley I spot Sanjay Singh with his famous team of hexapods. Quiet and methodical, he's never failed to complete a race.

And there's Arianna Cross. Last year's champion. She stands perched on her deep red cart, her smile a slash across her face. The other teams give her wide berth. Rumors about her dirty tricks and brutal training methods follow her everywhere. But she wins races.

The nervousness prickling in my stomach makes me feel like a rookie. I've driven many races, but this is Amelia's first. What if there's an accident? What if there's an eruption? What if a dragon gets hurt? What if Amelia gets hurt?

I glance at Amelia to see how she's holding up. But, minutes away from the start, I find her sitting with her back against the cart, holding a backpack against her chest and apparently not thinking about the race at all.

"Go put that backpack in the truck. It's time to get in position," I tell her.

"Oh, um, I was going to bring this with me," Amelia says.

"Don't be silly," I say. "It'll throw off your balance, and there's no room in the cart."

She tightens her grip on the backpack and glares at me.

I want to tell her to stop being ridiculous, but there isn't time for an argument.

"All right, you can keep it in the cart," I tell her. "But you can't wear it during the race. I don't want it snagging on something."

She carefully tucks the backpack into the corner of the cart. Then she takes Goldface by the harness and we lead the team to the starting line. Her mind still seems to be elsewhere. I look at her, wondering what she's thinking about. We used to understand each other so well.

I hold out the reins to Amelia. "Would you like to drive the start?"

Her eyes widen. "Really?"

"Why not?" I say, as though giving her complete control of the team is no big deal. "It's your race as well as mine."

She takes the reins and grins.

Ray Freedman queues up his team of guirs next to us. He smirks at our team. "Weavers? That's adorable."

Amelia bristles. "I can't wait to see your guirs flat on their butts," she says.

"Amelia!" I say sharply, though I've wanted to say the same thing to Freedman many times.

Freedman isn't the only driver looking askance at our mis-matched team. While most rookeries specialize in one or two types of dragon, Angel Peaks Rookery breeds all four of the major dragon lineages, and today we're running them all.

Closest to the cart are our two hexapods. Big, muscular dragons with six legs and no wings at all, hexapods are the slowest, but the strongest and most reliable, and a favorite on long races.

Next come our pair of guirs. Guirs, two-legged dragons capable of fluttering short distances, are the most popular type of racing dragon thanks to their sprinting speed.

Ahead of the guirs we're running two weavers, Sylph and Spark. Weavers are long, lithe dragons with webbed back ridges. Most teams shun them in favor of faster breeds, but I stand by our choice. Weavers excel at navigating difficult terrain, and the Blacktooth 500 is exceptionally difficult. Sylph is a pearly white dragon with bright blue eyes. Spark is our smallest dragon, but she's tough for her size and agile on the tricky parts of the course.

In front of them all run our lead pair of drakes, Goldface and Thunder. Drakes are spiny quadrupeds with small vestigial wings. They were once prized for their intelligence and heat vision, but the trend now is to breed them for size and speed instead. Nowadays many drakes have lost their heat vision altogether. But not ours. Thunder is gray and stocky and never loses focus. Goldface, with her bright yellow mask, is sharp-eyed and clever.

There was a fifth lineage once, the true fliers. When I was a child you could still spot their trainers releasing them into the sky on fine days. But they were small and couldn't pull carts so few rookeries bothered to raise them, and fewer dragon fanciers kept them. They dwindled, and then disappeared. Every so often a rumor goes around that someone has found true fliers on some little farm in the tundra. But it always turns out to be baseless gossip.

Ahead of us, a barren salt flat stretches as far as the eye can see. Mindless of the forbidding landscape, the dragons strain against their harnesses, held back only by their carts' claw brakes.

The race marshal fires his pistol with a resounding crack.

Twenty drivers release the brakes.

Forty lead dragons leap ahead and surge across the starting line.

The crowd jumps to their feet, cheering us on.

Cross's team takes a quick lead, with Freedman right on her tail. The rest of the pack, our team among them, runs nearly neck to neck.

"Let's go, let's go!" Amelia calls, flicking the whip over the dragons' heads. Goldface and Thunder scream with delight, happy to be in motion. The cart's wheels clatter over the cracked ground. Wind lashes our faces.

The 500-mile racecourse follows the treacherous volcanic Blacktooth Range. The first leg of the journey passes through the salt flats that run beside the mountains. This is the easiest stretch.

Every team will be running flat-out, trying to gain time to make up for anything that might slow them down later in the race.

The second leg of the race covers the foothills and the plateau. Lava flows turn this part of the course into a treacherous maze, but they're nothing compared to the threat posed by the ignipedes that make their dens in the crags.

On the last leg, the teams have to traverse the mountains and then make it all the way back down to the finish line in the valley. It's tempting to put on a burst of speed on the downhill, but the slopes are crisscrossed with crevices and drop-offs. Whole teams have been lost on the descent.

But there's no use worrying about any of that just yet. For now, we just have to keep pace and make it to the first checkpoint.

Amelia's face glows as she clutches the whip. Her exhilaration lifts my spirits. The world rushing past in a blur, the thunder of the dragons' feet. I fell in love with this feeling when I first raced as a child. I want so badly to pass my love of dragons on to her, and yet for years I've worried she doesn't feel as I do.

The pack spreads out and we begin to fall behind. Amelia's forehead creases and she cracks the whip again. "Come on, Goldface! We can do better than that!"

"Don't push them too hard," I warn her. "Here on the straightaway, we can't beat the guir-heavy teams. But we'll show our strength in the third leg."

She slacks off the whip, but I can tell she doesn't want to.

By the time we reach the first camp, the sky is deep purple and everyone except Singh is already there. Amelia jumps off the cart and stretches gratefully.

"Go into the station and get the dragons some straw to sleep on," I tell her. "I'll mix up their food."

I unpack the kerosene stove and mix up some gruel from water, meat, and kibble. The dragons greedily shove their muzzles into their dishes, splashing gruel all over the salty ground in their eagerness. Soon they're licking the bowls clean. But there's no bedding.

"Amelia, where's that straw?" I call.

Amelia pops her head out of the cart. She's holding her backpack. "Oh—I'll get it in a minute."

"Get it now. The more time we waste, the more tired the

dragons will be tomorrow."

She sighs and trudges into the station.

When the dragons are bedded down and we're drinking our soup, I tell her, "This is a real race, not a joyride. Every minute could be the difference between winning and losing."

Amelia sighs and rolls her eyes. "I'm sorry I'm not perfect."

I try to keep the frustration out of my voice. "I don't expect you to be perfect. But you do want to win, don't you?"

"Sure I do," Amelia says. But her voice is distracted.

My heart aches at the distance that has grown between us. When she was a toddler, she rolled around on the floor with the new hatchlings. At six, she was dressing up our guirs and bringing them to show and tell. By twelve she was breeding her own clutch of dragons.

She threw herself into the project, memorizing family trees and poring over books of dragon biology. But when they hatched, I discovered she'd done the unthinkable and crossed two different lineages, allowing dangerous recessive genes to come to the surface. The hatchlings came out too small, top-heavy, burdened with over-large wings that got in their way but couldn't carry them aloft. I yelled at Amelia when I saw what she'd done. I shouldn't have, but those were real living creatures she'd condemned to suffer.

The kind thing would have been to euthanize them on the spot, but Amelia begged me not to. They still live at the far end of the stable. Amelia visits them every day.

The dragon-breeding incident opened a rift between us that has never closed. Amelia used to tell me everything, but now she's cagey and spends all her time by herself. And it's only getting worse. Even now, in the middle of her first race, all she can pay attention to is that backpack. She has it on her lap.

"What's in there, anyway?" I ask.

Amelia's face colors a little. Reluctantly she pulls out a battered, once-white teddy bear.

I smile. "Johnny Bear! I haven't seen him in a while."

"I just wanted to bring him. For luck or whatever."

I chuckle. "You'll fit right in with the other drivers. I hear Freedman won't race without his lucky underwear."

That gets a snicker out of her.

It's a warm night, and the dragons snuffle soothingly in their sleep around us. As we crawl into our sleeping bags, I feel I've made the right choice in bringing Amelia along.

~ * ~

The next day, the sun comes out in force. Heat shimmers over the sparkling surface of the salt flat and our shirts stick to our backs. Only the dragons are delighted. Their blood running hot, they charge ahead, kicking up clumps of salt.

By now the teams are so spread out I can't see any more than a faint trail of white dust far in the distance. All around us is still. The sharp basalt peaks of the Blacktooth Range jut up to our left while to our right, the crystalline plain seems to extend forever. The team needs no direction and I fall into a trance, listening to the clack of the wheels and the jingle of the harnesses.

A piercing whistle cuts through the air.

I stiffen and look around. "Did you hear that?"

Amelia nods. The whistle is how dragon drivers let each other know there's danger. It isn't reliable; plenty of drivers will happily let another team drive into a sinkhole or lava flow, so if the team ahead is warning us, something must be really wrong.

I put up a hand to shield my eyes from the glare and squint at the dust cloud ahead of us. There's something funny about it. After a moment I realize it's going the wrong way. Someone's team is coming back towards us. Farther off, I spot a second dust cloud, a larger one. There's something on the course. Something that isn't a cart.

"Stop the team," I say abruptly.

"What? No!" Amelia says.

"Stop the team. Now. There's an ignipede ahead."

She slams the brake. The claw digs into the salt. The dragons come skidding to a halt, huffing in annoyance.

"I thought they only lived in the mountains!" Amelia says.

"They come down into the lowlands to hunt. Now keep your voice down. They have very sharp hearing. Hush, Sylph! There's a good dragon."

We hunker down in the cart and watch the dust cloud. Amelia is biting her lip, her eyes wide. She's never encountered an ignipede before, but she's heard the stories.

I recognize Ray Freedman's guirs by their blue backs. They're headed toward us at full tilt. And behind them, undulating through the salt, is the ignipede.

Its scales are glossy black, the skin between them fiery orange. It slithers on dozens of tiny legs, its head perched on top of a long, curved neck. Rapier-sharp teeth line its open jaws.

Ray Freedman plies his whip and shouts at his team. Foolish man. Not even guirs can hope to outrun an ignipede. If you're unlucky enough to attract its attention, common wisdom says to cut the traces of your lead dragon and release it as a decoy. Better to lose one dragon than your whole team and yourself as well. But Freedman is clearly not willing to do that.

The ignipede tilts its head this way and that, sizing up whether a human or a guir would make a better first bite. Then it lunges. It catches the cart by one wheel and flips it on its side, sending Freedman flying out onto the rough salt and his team plowing to a halt in a tangle of harnesses.

Sylph trills.

"Amelia, keep her quiet!" I whisper.

Amelia jumps off the cart and slips forward to stroke Sylph's neck. "Shh, shh, girl. Easy."

But it's too late. The ignipede's head jerks up. It stares straight at us.

"Amelia!" I hiss. "Shut her up or we both die!"

"I can't! She's trying to help!" Amelia whispers back.

The ignipede swerves away from Freedman and slithers towards us. Sylph is still trilling. If I cut her traces now, we might still survive. I flick open my pocketknife and leap from the cart.

I reach Sylph and grab hold of the trace. As I'm about to cut, Amelia grabs my hand.

"No!" she says. "Sylph's the only one who can protect us."

The ignipede is upon us. I can smell the charred-meat smell of its breath. I can see the claws on each of the countless rippling legs.

Sylph rises on her hind legs and trills again.

The ignipede trills back.

It slows and bends its head toward the weaver, blinking its tiny half-blind eyes. It's barely five feet away from Amelia. I can hardly suppress my urge to throw myself between her and it, even though that would be a death sentence for both of us. Amelia is trembling, but she stays still.

Sylph and the ignipede sniff each other. Then the ignipede raises its head again and slithers away, leaving a shallow channel through the salt in its wake.

We stay frozen in place, not daring to breathe, until it's out of sight. Then I throw my arms around Amelia. "Are you alright? Did it hurt you?"

"N…no, I'm fine," she says in a shaky voice. Slowly she rises to her feet.

"I'm not sure what just happened," I admit.

"She's a weaver," Amelia says, stroking Sylph's head. "That lineage—they have ignipede blood in them. When she started trilling…I think she was calling to it. Telling it not to attack."

I look at Amelia in astonishment. "How do you know that?"

She shrugs. "It was in a book, I guess. I've read a lot about dragon lineages."

Pride and surprise mingle within me. When I try to teach Amelia about our dragons, she always seems like she's not paying attention. But somehow she knows more about weavers than I do.

We drive over to Freedman, who lies sprawled on the ground beside his overturned cart. Amelia checks on his dragons while I kneel beside him, trying to size up his injuries. The coarse salt crystals ripped his forearms and the side of his face raw.

"Are you alright? Anything broken?" I ask.

"Just bruised, I think," he says, wincing as he tries to get up.

"His dragons are fine," Amelia says, coming to my side.

"Should we get the medical team?" We'd have to give up the race, but it would be low to leave an injured driver stranded out here.

He shakes his head. "We can make it back to camp. You've done enough. Whatever you did back there…it saved my life."

"I didn't do anything," I say truthfully, putting my hand on my daughter's shoulder. "It was Amelia."

~ * ~

The foothills rise around us, black and rugged. The dragons put their heads down to haul the cart up the rocky slope. One step, then another. Our hexapods huff and strain. Amelia and I get off the cart to lighten its load.

The encounter with the ignipede left us dead last, but we pass one or two teams during the ascent. Drakes and guirs skid and stumble while our weavers confidently navigate the steep trail.

At last the trail levels out as we reach the plateau. But as soon as we crest the ridge, we find half the teams bunched up ahead of us, the dragons huffing and screaming in frustration.

As I crane my neck to try to spot the source of the disturbance, a smell like hot asphalt hits me. Lava.

I call a halt and our dragons flop onto their bellies to rest. Leaving the team with Amelia, I thread through the crowd. An expanse of ripply, corded black rock greets me. A few patches still glow reddish-orange. A fresh lava flow.

"It happened an hour ago," one of the drivers says. "Covers half the plateau. No one can get across."

"Wait—Singh's going for it!" someone else calls.

Everyone swings around to look. There he is, slowly driving his hexapods onto the still-hot flow. I tense up. Hexapods are tough, but even they can't step directly onto lava. If he gets lucky and manages to stick to the patches where the crust is coolest and thickest, he might make it, but one false step and that dragon will never race again.

"Haw, Kamala!" he calls, steering his team to the left. "Whoa—slower, slower. Now gee!"

"He's insane," Arianna Cross says with a laugh. She's standing on her cart with her arms crossed. "He'll never make it."

Singh's lead dragon picks her way forward step by step. Then, a crack. Her leg breaks through the crust. There's a hiss and an agonized squeal as her scaly skin contacts molten rock. Singh runs forward to pull her free and release her from the traces. Eventually seven dragons pull the cart back to safety while the eighth—the wounded hexapod—whimpers in the cart.

The rest of the drivers decide to wait.

A spiny head rubs against my leg. Goldface is next to me, dragging her traces. The rest of the team meanders aimlessly behind her, threatening to get tangled. Behind them they pull the unattended cart. There's no sign of Amelia.

"We've got a loose team," someone calls.

Arianna smirks. "You need to keep better control of your dragons."

Letting your dragons wander off while stopped is a beginner mistake. Cheeks burning with embarrassment, I take Goldface by her harness and lead the team away, muttering apologies to the other drivers.

I stake down the team—more securely than Amelia did, hopefully—and go to look for her. Some of the other drivers have unpacked their stoves to heat up a snack while they wait, but Amelia isn't among them. Could she be lost? The mountains can be treacherous. Echoes bounce from one cliff face to the other, leading the unwary astray. There are cliffs and unstable slopes.

I pick up my pace. The mountains suddenly seem unfathomably vast. Every rock taunts me. What was I thinking, bringing a fifteen-year-old out here?

At last I come around a bend and find her in a secluded cleft in the rocks. She's sitting on the ground, her backpack open beside her, holding something in her hands. Johnny Bear lies abandoned on the ground beside her.

"Amelia!" I cry, rushing up to her. "You can't just wander off like that! You scared me! I thought something had happened to you!"

"I'm fine," she says.

"Well, the team wasn't. They got loose while you weren't watching them," I say, my nervousness bubbling over into frustration.

Then I spy what's in her hands. It's a smooth, oblong object speckled with green. A dragon egg.

"What are you doing with that egg?" I demand.

"I wanted to keep an eye on them," says Amelia quietly.

I look at the open backpack. There are two more eggs inside, carefully swaddled in rags.

"You stole eggs out of the hatchery and brought them on the race?" I say incredulously. "What were you thinking? They'll get broken!"

"They won't! I'm being careful!" Amelia insists, cradling the egg to her chest.

"Wait a minute." I pick up one of the other eggs from the backpack and study the pattern of speckles. "This egg isn't from any of the purebred lineages. You've been crossbreeding dragons behind my back!"

"I had to keep it a secret!" says Amelia. "You wouldn't have let me if I'd asked."

"There's a good reason for that! Don't you remember what happened last time? Those poor beasts in the stable?"

"They're not poor! They're...special."

In the distance, Goldface screams.

"We'll discuss this later," I say. "Pack up those eggs and get back to the team. We've got a bigger problem right now."

Our dragons are fluttering their wings and pulling against their harnesses. Amelia moves from one dragon to the next, making soothing noises.

"They'll eat each other alive at this rate," I say. "And the worst part is that half the course is probably safe. If we could only tell which part!"

"Goldface could," Amelia says.

"What?"

"Goldface could tell which path is safe. With her heat vision. Remember those obstacle courses we used to do where she had to find the hot objects?"

In a flash I see she's right. Goldface can see the temperature of the ground ahead, and she'll instinctively pick the safest path. The weavers will keep the other dragons following her trail.

It's astoundingly risky. But if we can pull it off, we could gain hours of advantage while the other teams wait for the lava to cool.

It's one thing to risk my own safety. Putting Amelia's life on the line is something else entirely. She's never raced before. She's never seen someone's flesh melted by molten rock. She has no idea what she's risking.

I can't tell Amelia that, of course. She'd roll her eyes and tell me to stop treating her like a baby.

But then it strikes me: Trying to protect her is what's driving her away. If I want her to respect me, I have to show I'm willing to let her take risks.

"Let's do it," I say.

Amelia grins.

I make a path through the crowd and lead our team to the edge of the lava. Goldface and Thunder sniff the fresh black rock experimentally.

"Another contender!" Cross says. "This should be fun."

"Ignore her," I whisper to Amelia as I take my place in the cart. "She likes to get under your skin."

Amelia gives Cross a withering look. Few looks are as withering as Amelia's.

"All right now, Goldface, slowly," I say. The drake sets one forefoot onto the hardened lava, then the other. She sniffs. She looks this way and that, peering into the distance with her large black eyes. Then she begins to cross the flow.

The rest of the team is unsure. I can feel their fear as they begin to move. The traces pull taut. With a bump, the cart rides up onto the surface of the lava. My muscles tense as I wait for the heavy cart to break through, but the surface holds.

"She's doing it," one of the other drivers whispers.

Painfully, slowly we creep across the lava flow. The wheels rattle and jolt over the bumpy surface. Heat rises off it, making sweat drip down our faces and plaster our hair to our foreheads. Beside me, Amelia grips the edge of the cart, her knuckles white.

Goldface steps, looks around, steps again. Sometimes she changes direction for no apparent reason. The other dragons huff in confusion. They want to run straight ahead and get off the lava flow as soon as possible. But Thunder and the weavers keep them in line.

Behind us comes the crunch of another set of wheels. I look over my shoulder. Cross is driving her team onto the lava, following our trail. Where our team jagged to the left, so does hers. Where we swerved to the right, so does she. And she's gaining on us.

"Get lost!" Amelia says. "Find your own way across."

"This is a race, you know," Cross says.

As the plateau stretches on, Goldface grows more confident. She's up to a regular walking pace, though she still carefully scopes out the path in front of her. Cross is right on our tail by now. Her drake screams and snaps his teeth at the back of our cart. It's an extra level of pressure we don't need right now.

The edge of the lava flow comes into sight. Goldface perks up when she spies the cool ground ahead. The last few steps go quickly, and then, at last, the cart trundles over the edge of the flow and we're back on safe ground. Amelia and I both let out a sigh of relief.

From behind us comes the crack of a whip. "On your left!"

Cross shouts as she beats her team into a full gallop and surges past us, throwing a cocky grin over her shoulder.

"I'm beginning to hate her," Amelia says.

"You're not the only one," I reply through clenched teeth. I hand the whip over to Amelia. "Want to drive this next bit?"

She nods, glaring at Cross's cart vanishing into the distance. Amelia cracks our whip and our team is off.

~ * ~

It's the last night of the race and I'm trying to keep Amelia from noticing how keyed up I am. Angel Peaks Rookery has never won the Blacktooth 500. There's prize money on the line, but that's not what I care about. I want to prove we can do it. That our dragons can do it. That being like Arianna Cross is not the only way.

Amelia is sitting up with her arms wrapped around her knees. In training they always tell you the importance of getting enough sleep. They don't tell you how on earth you're supposed to do that while adrenaline courses through your veins.

A movement makes me look up, startled. Arianna Cross is sitting on the edge of our cart, her legs hanging over the side.

"Nice stunt with the lava," she says. "Looking forward to tomorrow?"

"We are, actually," I say tartly.

"As am I. It promises to be a most exciting day." Before either Amelia or I can think of a retort, Cross slips off the cart and disappears into the darkness.

~ * ~

The air itself is betraying us. We gasp, desperately seeking oxygen in the thin alpine atmosphere, which is tainted by the sulfurous fumes that pour out of vents in the mountainside. Our heads pound. Our limbs are heavy. The dragons are feeling the same effects, but they trudge on, pulling the cart step after agonizing step up the steep trail through Blacktooth Pass.

Spires of stone jut up nearly vertical on either side of us. True fliers once roosted on these peaks hundreds of years ago when they were still found in the wild. Or anywhere.

We're ahead of most of the other teams, but Cross is still in the lead. I'd hoped our hexapods' strength would give us an advantage on the climb, but every time we come around a bend, she's farther ahead. Her dragons run like they fear for their lives and, not for the first time, I wonder what she does to them.

We reach the crest and look around, surveying the view from the top of the world.

"Wow," is all Amelia can say.

Though the air is hazy with volcanic gases, we can see for miles. The world spreads out around us on every side, the Blacktooth Range running north and south, the plateau with its fresh layer of lava, the salt flats spreading out clean and white to the east. It's harsh and stark and breathtakingly beautiful.

Behind us, the other teams zigzag slowly up the ridge, but there's only one spot of movement amid the still landscape ahead. Cross.

I say, "Let's get her."

Amelia nods, a big smile on her face.

"Whoa, whoa, slowly now, Thunder," I call as we begin down the slope. The dragons, happy to be on the downhill, want to gallop. They don't know how quickly the cart could get out of control. But they trust me and allow me to hold them back.

We pass truck-sized boulders and wide cracks threatening to swallow us into the fiery bowels of the mountain range. Our guirs skid several times and even Goldface loses her footing once, but Slyph and Spark keep the team steady.

Cross is still putting more distance between us, letting her team run with reckless disregard for either their lives or her own. Goldface screams. She doesn't like seeing Cross in the lead any more than I do.

We're past the hardest part of the descent. So I ease up and let the team go a little faster. Now we're matching pace with Cross, but it's not enough. She'll outstrip us again in the final sprint.

I let the dragons pick up just a little more speed. Cross's bright red cart grows larger ahead of us. We're doing it. We're really doing it. We're going to catch her.

And then I notice the traces going slack. The dragons are still gleefully galloping down the hillside when the prow of the cart nudges the hexapods' tails. Then it bumps the back of their legs. The cart is no longer being pulled. It's rolling on its own, and it's picking up speed.

"We're jackknifing. Set the brake!" I call to Amelia.

She lowers the claw brake, only to watch in horror as it snaps off and tumbles away.

Someone must have loosened the screws. Cross. She was on our cart last night. But there's no time to dwell on that. The cart is still gathering speed. If I call the dragons to a halt, it will ram into them and drag them after it. The only thing to do is ride it out and try to steer onto flatter ground where we can slow down.

The cart goes over a bump, throwing me and Amelia around and scattering our gear. Amelia's backpack goes flying and lands on the mountainside.

"The eggs!" she cries, grabbing the edge of the cart and vaulting over.

"Wait, stop!" I call in a panic. But before I can move, Amelia is leaping from the careening cart.

"Amelia!" I scream.

She hits the ground. I flinch at the crunch of the sharp lava rocks. She rolls, then scrambles to her feet and grabs for the backpack. Is she all right? Or, in the heat of the moment, is she just not feeling her injuries?

I look around for a way to stop. There's a narrow crevice in the ground beside me, not wide enough for the cart to fall into but wide enough to catch the wheel. It'll be a hard crash, but it'll stop the cart.

"Thunder, Goldface, haw!" I call.

The dragons swerve, jerking the cart off its runaway course. As the wheel lodges in the crack, the cart comes to a stop with a neck-wrenching jerk that nearly throws me onto the ground. I slam into the side of the cart, wrenching my shoulder. Stars burst across my vision. The wheel snaps off and the dragons are yanked to a sudden halt, yelping and screeching.

Mindless of my throbbing shoulder, I jump from the cart and rush to Amelia's side. She's got bits of gravel lodged in both arms and a bleeding cut on her cheek, but she doesn't even notice. She opens the backpack and checks the eggs for damage.

"Amelia, how could you do something like that?" I ask. "You could have died, and you just lost us the race!"

Amelia picks up the largest egg. She whispers, "It's hatching."

The egg trembles in her hands. A tiny crack forms at one end, then another. The web of cracks bulges as the baby dragon tries to push its way out. Then, all at once, the shell splits in two and the hatchling lies in Amelia's arms, wet and sticky with albumen.

I brace myself for a twisted body and misshapen limbs, but the creature in front of me is nothing like that. It's small and sleek, with two delicate clawed feet, a long tail, and two broad, membranous wings that it stretches and folds as it lies there on its back, trilling at us.

I know this dragon. I saw them soaring and wheeling across the sky when I was a little girl.

"A true flier," I whisper.

Amelia nods. She cleans off the hatchling with the edge of her shirt.

"How?"

"I read about it when I was studying dragon lineages. All those recessive genes: They're true flier genes. They're not gone, just hidden. All I had to do was crossbreed the right dragons."

"Amelia," I say in awe, "You're a genius."

The hatchling sits up on Amelia's hand and flaps its wings experimentally.

"I think she's ready to fly," Amelia says. She offers the baby dragon to me. I'm filled with awe for the delicate creature in my hands and for the brilliant, amazing girl beside me who saw what I couldn't see even when it was right in front of me.

The dragon is so light. I can feel it trembling as it looks around at this strange new world. I raise it on one hand and release it.

Far below, Arianna Cross drives across the finish line. And the baby dragon takes off into the sky.

~ * ~ * ~

Gwen C. Katz is a writer, artist, game designer, and retired mad scientist who lives in Altadena, California with her husband and a revolving door of transient animals. Her first YA novel, "Among the Red Stars", follows the adventures of the all-female WWII bomber regiment known as the Night Witches. Her short fiction has appeared in venues such as Glittership, the PRISM Award-winning Dates 2, and We're Here: The Best Queer Speculative Fiction 2020.

When she's not making up stories about dragon racing, she can be found hiking, gardening, and teaching kids about wildlife at the local nature center.

Here by Choice

Gerri Leen

Tien Shen watched as Kuan Yin lounged by the waterfall, trailing her hand back and forth through the water as she stared up at the clouds overhead. A subtle odor of lotus surrounded her, reaching him where he sat. She gleamed like an emperor's pearl, if a distressed pearl—she cocked her head, listening for some sound and frowning deeply.

"What do you hear?" he asked. He heard nothing, not even with his dragon-keen ears.

She didn't answer him, so he tried to assess her mood. Her eyes glinted and for a moment, he thought he saw tears, but then she seemed to force a smile as she laid her head back onto the hard ground. But he could tell she was still listening, that not even the waterfall could drown out whatever it was that called to her.

"What is it you hear?" he asked again.

She finally looked over. "Everyone." This was how she was. This was how she answered. As if she could not spare the breath she no longer needed. She had achieved enlightenment; Nirvana waited. Why was she wasting time lying by this river not answering him?

"You don't have to stay, dragon." She sounded as if she wished he'd go.

"It is my honor to guard those who will enter Nirvana." Although in this case, it was rather a pain as well.

She lifted her head and gave him a look that could only be considered amused—at his expense. Then she lay back again and closed her eyes.

He made sure no one would threaten her before settling down some distance away, and she glanced at him, as if checking that he hadn't gotten too close. He seemed to make her unhappy—had since he'd told her he was her guide to paradise's door, but he didn't know why that distressed her. So many were striving for Nirvana; she'd achieved it, but no joy lit her face.

Letting his head come to rest on the softer scales of his side,

Tien Shen listened to the water. The roaring sound of the river crashing over the rocks lulled him into sleep.

He woke slowly, blinking to clear his eyes. Then he blinked again, not believing what he saw—or didn't see: the woman he was supposed to protect was gone.

He closed his eyes, trying to find a trace of her with his inside-eyes. Nothing.

He listened, heard only the cry of the hawk, the grunt of the tiger, and the swish-snap of a squirrel in the underbrush.

He sniffed, breathing in the scent of evergreen; of hard, sandy soil; the blue smell of water; the hot, red odor of the pepper flowers he loved to eat. But no scent of pearls and lotus, no trace of the woman who had ridden the wheel of life until she'd earned paradise.

Taking to the air through force of will, he soared, annoyed by an eagle that flew near and peered at him, as if unsure how an un-winged thing like Tien Shen could live in its world. He roared at the bird, and the eagle flew away, but not without a defiant cry.

"Kuan Yin?" He formed the words slowly, sending them out into the world. They fell to the earth as rain, the drops merging to form the symbol for her name.

She didn't appear. She didn't call out. He still couldn't smell her. And the earth didn't give her up, didn't whisper to him that she'd been there. So he flew on.

He called for her over and over. Frogs echoed her name, but they were just playing. A deer bolted from a thicket as Tien Shen's calls grew more frantic.

One woman, ready for paradise, and he had lost her.

"Dragon," he heard in his inside-ears, and then he saw her with his inside-eyes. She was with a group of women who were studying a writing of a kind he'd never seen before. Curious, he settled on the ground just beyond them.

One of the women let out a little squeak, but the rest went on writing, not even looking over. The first woman stared at him, as if she could not believe what she was seeing.

"Chao Ma, pay attention to the lesson," Kuan Yin said softly, and the woman bowed and went back to creating the simple letters, so long and angular compared to traditional writing.

Tien Shen inched toward Kuan Yin, until he was right next

to her, and she turned to look at him. He found he couldn't meet her eyes. But what did he have to feel guilty for? He was only trying to do what he'd been told. To see her safely to her rightful reward.

"I worried you, dragon?" The lotus smell changed, grew spicy, and he imagined it was regret that caused it.

"You did." He sighed and wished he could tell what she was thinking.

"I'm sorry. I don't wish to cause pain, even to you."

He accepted her apology—weak as it was—with a nod of his head. "It's time to go, my lady."

"Do you know why they're here?" She glanced down at the feet of one woman. They were bound, and Tien Shen knew the woman would hobble a little as she walked.

"They're bored?"

"Hardly." Kuan Yin laughed, and her laughter was cold and hard and full of pain he didn't expect. She glanced again at the feet of the woman. "I think it's less cruel to simply cut them off."

To his shock, he felt her hand on his back. "The language is called Nushu." She rubbed his neck softly, her fingers hitting spots he hadn't even realized were itching. "It's a language only for women."

He knew women were denied education. "You taught them this?"

"As I was taught."

"Who first handed you the brush?"

"I don't remember. So many lives. So many first lessons."

But he suspected she remembered every one of those lessons. His look must have told her he didn't believe her, because she laughed, and this time her laughter was like a brook as it bubbled over smooth stones or like the sound the sun made as the clouds tickled it.

The sounds of paradise—why was she waiting? She leaned against him, her fingers still working their magic on his scales.

"Why are we here?" he asked her.

"I'm here because I want to be. Why are you here, dragon?"

"To serve you."

She looked displeased. "That's the wrong answer." And like that, she was gone.

He sighed, and Chao Ma left her writing and walked over to

him. She reached out, then jerked her hand back.

"It's all right."

"You don't bite?"

"Well, I won't. This time." He let out a little rumble of pleasure as she traced the pattern of his scales. Her touch moved him almost as much as Kuan Yin's. He was used to spirit creatures, insubstantial and fey, with touches just as light, not this more substantial rubbing.

"Why do you study the language?" he asked her.

She swallowed hard. "Because it gives us some measure of freedom. It allows us to have secrets. No man can read it."

"Why do you need secrets?" Secrets were never a good thing among dragons. They usually meant something bad was going to happen.

"My husband is cruel to me. Tan Lao's husband cheats on her. Mei Ling's brother sold her to an old man she doesn't love."

"How is your husband cruel?" Tien Shen did not care about the others. But this woman who was scratching his back deserved better.

"He yells. Hits, sometimes. Not all the time. Just…when he's angry."

Tien Shen sensed Kuan Yin reaching for him, the sound of her voice loud in his inside-ears. He heard the creak of the door between the worlds being opened, the rustle of a beaded curtain being pulled back. "I have to go."

"All right." But Chao Ma held on to him.

He rested his snout on her arm for a moment, was surprised to see tears in her eyes. She pulled away, but one of her tears fell onto his leg, and it burned as it sank into his scales.

Kuan Yin called again, and he forced himself away from Chao Ma and appeared where he felt his charge calling from.

Kuan Yin stood in front of the brightest light imaginable. It was so beautiful—Tien Shen never tired of seeing the sight, but then it wasn't one he saw very often. Those who attained Nirvana were few.

Soft breezes blew out of the light. A subtle smell of flowers and spices wafted over to him; Kuan Yin's scent seemed to grow in reaction, sweet and strong and still distinct even among such glory.

"Dragon?" Her voice was so small.

"You must go." But then he heard it: a small sob. And another. And another. His leg where Chao Ma's tear had fallen began to burn again.

Kuan Yin turned and stared out at the world, her back to Nirvana. Her eyes welled up, then she blinked, and the tears ran freely down her cheeks. He moved closer, lifted his leg and let her see the scales where the woman's tear had fallen were turning silver.

"I hear them all, Tien Shen," she whispered. "The cries of the whole world."

He nodded. "I hear them now, too." He looked past her, at the beauty that was Nirvana. At the peace it promised. It was everything this remarkable woman had worked for.

It was what Tien Shen wanted for her.

And yet…

"I can't go just now." She took a deep breath. "I'm needed here."

The beaded curtain fell back, dimming the light. The breeze died, and the smell of Nirvana's flowers became fainter and fainter, as the scent of Kuan Yin grew.

Compassion. This was what compassion smelled like.

She turned to look at the door. "I'm needed here."

It slammed shut.

But the light remained. Growing brighter and brighter, and Tien Shen realized it was coming from her.

"My Goddess," he murmured, bowing his head. As he looked down, he realized the silver patch on his leg was reflecting her glow.

"There's much to do," she said, pulling the light around her like a cloak. It finally dimmed, drawn inside her. But he knew she could call it back if she wanted to.

He studied his leg; it still shone just a little. Even with no light to reflect.

She began to walk back into the world.

He hurried to get in front of her, and her eyes flashed with annoyance. Then he knelt, and said, "You should ride. I can be of help to you."

She touched his head before hugging him hard, her face pressed against his. Then, without a word, she jumped on his back and waited.

He listened and heard the loudest cries to the east. Without asking her, he flew for the rising sun.

Her hand tightened on his neck, and she sang a song he didn't know, her voice beautiful in its rawness.

"You gave up paradise," he said softly.

"How could I go there when even one person suffers?"

He had no answer to that. Only, he'd seen others do it. Perhaps Nirvana wasn't for the perfect. Maybe it was for the almost perfect. And someday they'd be back again to find perfection by helping those who still strove—and hurt.

"But it was beautiful, wasn't it?" she murmured. "And it smelled good."

He knew it was the last she'd ever say about it.

~ * ~ * ~

Gerri Leen lives in Northern Virginia and originally hails from Seattle. In addition to being an avid reader, she's passionate about horse racing, tea, and collecting encaustic art and raku pottery. She has work appearing in Nature, Strange Horizons, Galaxy's Edge, Deep Magic, Daily Science Fiction, and others. She's edited several anthologies for independent presses, is finishing some longer projects, and is a member of SFWA and HWA.

See more at gerrileen.com.

The Fool's Fiddle

Austin Charles Roberts

"Look, it's not that big of a deal," Guy says, stretching his arms out to the side in a show of false contrition. His right leg slips back in a courtly bow.

The chair is big. Like castle big. He has to look up to see his audience.

"But you are here." The voice is full of menace.

"Yeah," Guy says, "but it isn't like that. You want the story you have to stop interrupting. It is what it is. Got me?"

"Yes. I have you. That is the point of all of this, is it not? I. Have. You."

"Tomato tom-mah-to." Guy smiles. Not just a smile—The Smile. Teeth sparkle, eyes shine, an unruly breeze blows his bangs away from his face, and somewhere off in the night a bodice unlaces itself. "Am I telling the story, or am I telling the story?"

"Yes, you are telling the story."

"Good. So let me tell it," Guy says and begins to pace. "It all begins a moon ago when Allen Two-Finger tried to pull a Fiddler's Fool down at The Crooked Way.

"What's a Fiddler's Fool, you may ask?"

"I didn't."

"Well, it goes like this. Some bum with a fiddle sits at the bar. He eats, drinks, whatever. When the tab comes, he's got no coin. Got sticky-fingered or forgot, whatever. What matters is he don't got it. What he does got is his fiddle."

"His fiddle?"

"Nah, his grandfather's fiddle," Guy says. "Passed down three generations."

"Great-grandfather."

"What?"

"His great-grandfather's fiddle."

"Look, it doesn't matter whose fiddle it is, it don't even matter whose fiddle he says it is," Guy says. "That's not his part."

"Part?"

"Yeah, slow Joe in the back row, his part. He's the setter. Sets it up. Bartender takes the fiddle as collateral and Two-Finger limps away to get the money to pay his tab." Guy pauses, looks at the chair, makes sure his points are being followed. "The moment Two-Finger is out the door, Allen Oh steps up to the bar and says, 'Hey, let me look at that fiddle' and the bartender he says—"

"Allen Oh?"

"Allen Oh," Guy confirms.

"Both of the confidence men are named Allen?"

"I'll call'm Daisy if it helps."

"But his name is not Daisy?"

"His name ain't Allen Oh either," Guy says, "that's just what the right folk call him. So the bartender, he says, 'Aint my fiddle.' And Daisy says, 'That's a Starlinky.' 'A Starlinky' the bartender says, 'A Starlinky' repeats Daisy."

"Is his name Daisy or Allen Oh?"

"It doesn't matter. It really doesn't," Guy says, wiping the frustration out of his eyes. "What matter's is that someone in that bar thinks the Fiddle's worth a load of money. When Two-Finger comes back to pay the tab and collect the fiddle, that someone offers him a generous amount of money for it—"

"For his great-grandfathers fiddle?"

"The fiddle Two-Finger bought off Poor John Seconds for half a shiny copper moments before he walked into The Crooked Way. That fiddle. He butters it up. Sob story. My grandfather's fiddle. Cry, cry. Tears, tears." Guy wipes a pretend tear from his cheek.

"Great-grandfather."

"Great-grandfather's fiddle, sure," Guy says. "And Two Finger walks out The Crooked Way with ten solid gold clenched 'tween thumb and pointer. And someone just paid ten solid for a half shiny fiddle."

"That is not very honest."

"Neither is offering ten gold for a Starlinky. That's the short con, it only works on folk trying to cheat other folk." Guy runs his fingers through his hair. "Two-Finger took what was offered."

"And what do the two Allens and a Starlinky have to do with you being here?" The temperature in room rises with the last. Coins fall off the pile of gold beyond the chair and bounce across the floor, rolling just past Guy's feet.

"Nothing," Guy says, "they've got nothin' to do with it. But the guy who bought the fiddle does. He's connected, see. Royalty. Second cousin of a second cousin of someone's mistress twice removed, you know how it is. Anyway, he learns the true value of his fiddle and is not well pleased. Decides to make an example of Two-Finger. Teach Allen a lesson he'd failed to learn eight times before—if you know what I mean. Being a crook with two fingers is hard, but no fingers?"

Guy pauses and takes a breath. Lets it all sink in deep. Timing is important.

"That's when Shay comes to me," Guy says.

"Shay?"

"Yeah, Shay. Two-Finger's sister," Guy says.

"Why would she come to you?"

"She's my shadow. My main squeeze. You know, my damsel in dis-dress." Guy waits for a reaction. Anything. Nothing. Tough crowd. He continues. "Shay tells me there won't be any more dis-dress if folks start calling 'Two-Finger' 'Nub' and I had to do something about it. So I did. I went to the guy who had a lesson to teach and made him an offer."

"He's the one who hired you to steal my gold?"

"Nah, no-one hired me to steal your gold, that's just a perk of the job." Guy smiles, reaches up behind his head and scratches his neck. Then he says it a little too casual, trying to slip it by, "he just wanted your head."

~ * ~

The roar is deafening. It echoes off distant walls, shatters piles of gold. Forces Guy to his knees, blood dripping from his nose, ears clenched between hands. The silence that follows the roar is just as profound. And in that silence a shadow lifts away from the chair, the gigantic chair, and slowly lowers down to Guy's level. The closer it comes the more substance it gathers. Long. Vivid green. Lined with teeth. And two eyes staring right at Guy.

"He sent you to kill me?" The dragon laughs. "Something as small, and stringy, and fragile as you?"

"No." Guy cowers. "He sent someone *with* me to kill you."

"Which one?" the dragon asks.

"Brent, Sir Brent," Guy says. "He was in the service of the

man who hired me. A game hunter of renown and—"

~ * ~

Sir Brent stands victorious on a battlefield. His armor gleams with light and splashed blood. Banners fly out behind him in a stiff breeze, blocking out thousands of enemy corpses. One foot propped on the skull of a gigantic furred—

~ * ~

"Don't tell me." The dragon interrupts the start of another story. "Show me. Which one?"

Guy drags himself ten paces across the hot stone floor, avoiding shred limbs and pools of blood, to the three corpses. They lay raggedly strewn across the stone in mismatched states of whole.

"This one." Guy points to the larger of the three, the most complete. Sir Brent's armor was punctured in countless places, bent and twisted where it had been impaled by the dragon's tail before Brent even had the chance to draw his sword. The armor did not protect Sir Brent, but it certainly held him together.

"Disappointing," the dragon says. "Are we so forgotten in the world of men that you think we can be defeated by a single man?"

"Yeah," Guy says. "Forgotten total, actually. You're a story so old, even children don't believe."

The dragon grunts, then looks at the man. "Forgotten by all, it would seem, but you."

Guy pulls himself to his feet and does not look at the other two corpses. Does not look at the gristle that is left of them. Does not look at their faces frozen in terror and pain and the accusation that he alone caused their deaths.

"Give me your word to honor our deal." Guy forces his eyes to focus on the dragon, "before I continue. Give me your word."

"Yes, yes," the dragon says, "I give you my word. If I can't figure out how you were going to get the gold out of my vault after my untimely demise, you may go free. Unsoiled. Alive."

"It wasn't just for me," Guy says.

The dragon looks at Guy and grins, "I cannot turn back time. But very well. You and your team may leave here freely and live in peace all of your days—the very little good it will do them."

Guy nods his thanks.

"A dragon must keep its word once a bargain is made," Guy says, "and may not lie."

"True," the dragon says. "Now tell me your story, so I can tell you your plan, and then eat you."

Guy takes a deep breath and begins to pace once more.

"The first step was finding you. There ain't no way all the dragons could've been killed off, and there are enough bones around to show you did live at some point. What I needed was a scholar. A very special kind of scholar..."

~ * ~

Guy stands half-lit at the intersection of two tunnels. Torch held high. Knee deep in human waste. There may be more comfortable hideouts. There may be more efficient hideouts. But nothing stops unwanted visitors like a dark tunnel full of shit.

"Randal," Guy calls. "Come out, come out, wherever you are!"

His voice echoes down the tunnel until it is so distant it converts to whispers calling his own name back at him. The city has miles of these tunnels. These tunnels have miles of their own tunnels underneath, and those tunnels probably have tunnels. Entire civilizations of heebie jeebies have grown and died in tunnels like these without ever knowing the light of day.

"Ridiculous," Guy mutters, as he sloshes to the next intersection. "Mountain tops. Abandoned temples. Unpassable forests. The list is endless. But Randal has to play it like this." Guy calls out again. Again, nothing. And moves on to the next intersection.

The next intersection is the same as the last intersection. Dark. Damp. Reeking of shit—

~ * ~

"I get it," the dragon says. "It was unpleasant. You do not have to bore me with the repetition of describing every single intersection you searched."

"Unpleasant? Unpleasant is constantly being interrupted while trying to tell a story. I had to burn my shoes—my pants. And 'cause Two-Finger was that much closer to being called Nub, Shay started the fires before I'd even taken 'em off—"

Guy stops. The dragon had climbed off its throne during the telling, and now lay sprawled out on the floor. Its head casually resting on forelegs not two swords' lengths from him. It stares at him lazily, their eyes level.

"Get to the important part." The dragon blows a smoke ring in Guy's direction. "I am getting hungry."

"Right," Guy stutters. "Ah. Well. Sewers. Muck. Rats. Where was I?"

"The scholar," the dragon says.

"Got it," Guy says. "I needed a special kind of scholar. A mage in the guild wouldn't look twice at a guy like me. So I needed someone unguilded. But anyone not powerful enough to enter the guild stays as deep underground as they can on account of The Sniffers."

"The Sniffers?"

"The Sniffers," Guy says. "They hunt out the unguilded. The weak. The untrained. Steal their magic. The Sniffer gets a power bump, the unguilded gets—"

"Dead," the dragon says.

Guy nods.

"Randal," Guy says, "he don't play by their rules. He's got this special doorway…"

~ * ~

Guy's last torch begins to sputter when he finds it. On the tunnel wall, just above the waterline, a door. Not just any door, The Door. Its gilded wood frame reflects the fire. Each intricate carving coming to life under the scrutiny of Guy's eyes. He reaches to knock. The door opens first. Sunlight beams through, along with a light breeze and the sound of distant waves.

The room on the other side is comfortable. Pillows and throws line the floor. Books line the walls. And at the center of the room is a desk. A desk and Randal.

Randal is neither tall nor short. Fat nor thin. Handsome nor ugly. He is, in fact, perfectly forgettable. So much so that even the least trained of minds would know immediately they were under the power of an enchantment in his presence. Not that the knowledge helps them remember him any.

"Randal," Guy says, "long time no see."

"A purposeful gesture, I assure you," Randal says. "I don't generally accept uninvited guests, Guy."

"I wrote."

"I didn't respond."

"Tell me about the dragons."

And Randal does. He tells Guy all about the dragons. Where they like to hide. How much gold they have. That they can't lie or break their oath. That they love riddles. Everything.

~ * ~

"It was that easy?" the dragon asks.

"Easy?" Guy asks.

"Yes. Easy?"

"Nah," Guys says. "You're bored and hungry. Figured I'd keep it short for ya. Randal took some convincing. Then—he helped."

"After all the tunnel searching and the buildup of that special door, I just thought the story of Randal would be more interesting," the dragon says. "That is all."

"That's all? You want me to tell you I know where his sister lives? His mother? Or, that his kid brother calls himself Nichols and runs fast cards in Market Town for sight seekers? That I know things nobody but Randal should know? I could tell you these things, or I could get to the good part."

"Of course," the dragon says.

"You want more detail? I'll give more detail. It's not like I'm dinner or nothing if I don't. Other than studying all the time without blowing his top, Randal only gots two tricks. That door of his, he can open it up where'n when he damn well please. And illusion. Even when you go through that door, who knows where you is."

"He makes illusions that convincing?" the dragon asks.

"Convincing?" Guy pauses. "He could be living in my place. Sleeping next to me all night like, and Shay or I wouldn't know the difference. That convincing."

"Very well then. Do get to the good part," the dragon says. "But, first, did you learn anything else interesting from Randal?"

"Yeah. Only that no one really knows how we know what we knows about dragons. Like it all just popped up one day. Like poof. Pop. Pow. Know what I mean?"

"Yes, actually." The dragon smiles at Guy appearing all too pleased with itself. "I do. Now get to the good part."

Guy studies the dragon a moment. Nods his head while sucking his lower lip. There is something else going on here, and they both know it.

"Alright," Guy says after a moment. "Alright, alright. So, I had me my knowledge and a hedge-wizard. Got me a knight with kill'n skills. What I don't got is someone to get us where we go'n. I needed a rogue, a trickster, someone who could loose a lock as easy as spot a trap. Only person I trust in that category, because let's be honest, you can't trust anybody in that category, is Raxel Woodworm."

"Wormwood, you mean. It has medicinal properties," the dragon says proud of its knowledge of lesser species. "Ancient human naming traditions used professions as surnames. Your friend Raxel's ancestors had been healers of renown I would guess."

"Nah," Guy says with a laugh. "It's Woodworm, on account of all the places his wood worms, if ya know what I mean."

The dragon sighs.

"In fact," Guy says. "Rax got the name at the same time he got hard to find. See, Rax was never really quite a thief, per se. He didn't steal gold or jewels. Nah, he didn't really steal nothing. Rax had a different soft spot. Something he liked being given—the virtue of married women…"

~ * ~

The manor stands tall in the dark. Silhouetted on the edge of a cliff by clouds and the moon glinting off the not-so-distant sea. A barbed wall contains the cliff and the house. Stretched between the wall and the manor stand gardens lit by torches and patrolled by guards. And with the guards, and the gardens, and the moonlight is Rax.

He counts to himself each footstep of each guard. Timing their movements with his own. He is just another shadow to them, a lump in the night. Flitting tree to tree, bush to bush, until he reaches the brick sides of the great manor house. If anyone thought the guards would be a problem, the manor was far less of one. His lutest's fingers slip easily into the cracks between masonry and stone, and his assent up the house is faster even than his passage through the garden. A rose in his lips, a lute on his back, and Rax is prepared for the evening.

At the very top of the house, a single candle waits lit in a lone window. This is the signal. Tonight is the night. Her husband is away.

Rax reaches the window and draws his second-story dagger, slipping its thin flexible blade between the window and sill, disengaging the clasp. And like that, Rax is in the house.

The room he enters is lavish. A fire roars in the fireplace, a four-posted bed waits with feathered pillows and down throws. On the bed, his love of the night, The Lady Baroness De Silva.

"I have come, my love," Rax says. "Let me play my lute for you, and then let me play you like my lute."

He pulls the instrument from his back and sings a long laudy ballad filled with the promise of the rest of their night. He throws the rose onto the pillow and pulls the lips of The Lady Baroness De Silva to his own, kissing her passionately.

"Why don't you kiss me, my love?" Rax implores, looking down at the woman of tonight's dreams. And it is then, and only then, he realizes he holds her head in his hands but her body remains on the bed.

"You fool, Woodworm," The Baron screams from his hiding place in the closet. "Look what you made me do!"

~ * ~

"The Baron cut off his own wife's head?" the dragon asks.

"Truly told."

"Before he knew she was sneaking around in the night with Raxel," the dragon says. "This is not a man to be reckoned with."

"He is not."

"Then why would Raxel do it?"

"For the very reason you said, The Baron is not a man to be reckoned with. That is Rax's love. It isn't the women, though he would never admit it himself—it's the challenge. The getting away."

"But he did not get away," the dragon says smugly. "Did he."

"No. His fate was worse than The Baroness's. He was caught and captured. Taken to the mages. They used his love of traps and tricks against him. Against his mind."

"They did not." The dragon recoils slightly.

"They did," Guy nods. "Mind-maze. So powerful it ends only when he does. Then set him on a corner, in the mud and filth, with only enough of himself left to eat and shit."

Silence fills the cavern as both Guy and the dragon pause.

"That is a terrible fate," the dragon finally says. "I would wish it on no one."

"Yeah," Guy says.

"But if that is the case; how could you get him to join your crew of misfits?"

"Hmmm," Guy says, "that was easier than anticipated…"

~ * ~

Guy embraces Rax. Holding him close. Lovingly as a child would hold an injured bird found in the garden. Shay holds Rax's hand. She says words of love and affection. She kisses Rax's forehead. And then together, Guy and Shay, push his head into a full rain bucket until the bubbles stop.

~ * ~

"You didn't!" the dragon gasps.

~ * ~

Rax's corpse flops onto the floor where Guy, Shay, and Randal take turns smashing his chest with a large, padded mallet. Thwack. Thwack. Thwack. They play tattoo until Rax's heart beats again and water fountains from his mouth.

"Why you bunch of no-good, mother wenching—" Rax shouts.

~ * ~

"And the spell was broken," Guy says.

"Until death," the dragon says. "Very clever."

Guy only shrugs. "We all have talents."

"Yes, I suppose we do." The dragon flips over onto its back, wiggling to scratch an itch. "Now finish your story."

"So, I had my team," Guy says. "The four of 'em came to my place to plan. Randal's knowledge. Brent's strength. Rax's stealth. My brains. We figured the best way to do the job was—"

"That is only three. You said, 'the four of them came to my place.' That implies four people came to your place to plan. Randal, Brent, Raxel. That is only three."

"It's a four-man team," Guy says. "That's all there is. Four men. Anyway, you know most of the plan from there. The sneak gets us down here, the hedge-wizard and me distract you, Sir Brent takes your head."

"Tell me anyway." The dragon purrs.

~ * ~

Rax disables the last trap on the last door before the dragon's horde.

"Is everyone ready?" Guy asks. "You know your parts?"

They know what they're doing. They've worked together before.

"Then let's do it," Guy says.

The door swings open, letting in the heat of the dragon's cavern and the unmistakable scent of an uncountable number of coins. Each member of the team goes about their business. Randal and Guy slip through the door. Sir Brent—

~ * ~

"Rushes into my chamber and shouts, 'Death to you ye foul beast of the night!'" the dragon says with a laugh. "And then he falls to his knees to pray. To pray! Rather than slaying me, he prays. He had me at the disadvantage. I had no idea you were even there—"

The dragon laughs so hard it can no longer speak. It rolls across the floor, tail smashing piles of gold and valuables beyond measure.

"This story will never get old," the dragon says. "I will tell it to my young when it hatches from the egg, and they to their young for centuries to come. Oh the laughs we will have."

Guy leans against the column. "You done?" he asks. "Can we get this over with?"

"Of course. Show me your gear and I will tell you your plan."

There is only one bag. About as long as a man and twice as wide. Guy undoes the lacing and pulls out four identical objects—bags. But not just any bags. Each made from heavy cloth. Leather straps triple-stitched onto them. Each with a handle as thick as a man's leg. Big enough for ten men to stand inside.

"That is all you brought?"

Guy nods.

The dragon looks at the bags, looks at Guy. Thinks. "I honestly have no idea how you were going to get my gold out of here," the dragon finally says.

"It's good knowing you then." Guy wipes sweat off his brow. "Deal's a deal, oaths and promises and such. I'll never be seeing you later. Ta ta."

Guys turns to walk away. Towards the entrance. Towards safety.

"But," the dragon says.

Guy stops.

"I have changed my mind."

The dragon's tail swipes through the air blocking off Guy's retreat. "It would be a shame to waste such a meal as you." The dragon pauses for a moment. "Can I tell you a secret?"

Guy turns back to face the dragon. "You gave me your word," he says.

"That is the secret I do so wish to tell you," the dragon says. "You know how your friend Randal does not know where all your dragon knowledge comes from? Well, it comes from us. We wrote it down. We gave it to you, just for delicious moments like these."

"You're tell'n me it's all a long con?" Guy asks, deflated. "A hustle?"

"Yes." The dragon claps its forearms, mouth smiling wide with glee. "You humans are so much easier to deal with when you think we cannot lie, and that we must keep our word as if by some magical decree. You are all just. So. Stupid."

Guy is speechless, for once.

"Do you know how long it has been since I have had a knight in my cave?" the dragon asks, "There was a time when it was one or two a week. They would come for wisdom, or wishes, or thinking to slay. Lured in by promises of honesty or gold or magical cures— like I am some sort of genie—and when they disappeared no one questioned it. No one said, 'Oh, look, Sir Steve went to the dragon and now he is gone, he must have been eaten.' No. No, instead it was all, 'Sir Steve's wishes must have come true, we should all go to the dragon now. Come on everybody.'"

The dragon walks his talons across the floor, pantomiming villagers walking to his cave, up his neck, and into his mouth.

"Those," the dragon says, "were the good old days."

Guy backs up slowly, inching his way towards the door. An appropriately delivered monologue is often the best time to escape

—just not today.

The dragon's tale smashes into the ground in front of Guy.

"I am trying to decide if I should eat you raw or rare. It is such a difficult choice."

Guy lets the dragon have its moment. He watches as it rolls and giggles. As it playfully flings handfuls of gold into the air. When it is done gloating, the dragon turns back to Guy.

"I have decided," the dragon says. "I am going to eat you well done."

The dragon's head rears back, sucking in air to fan the fire in its belly.

"That's what I thought," Guy says.

The dragon stops. Its glee gone. Smoke pours out of its nostrils. "What did you say?"

"It's a shame really," Guy says. "But, that's what I thought. Shay didn't believe me. See, the idea of a creature that can't lie? It's great. A monument to truth. Something to stand for. Regal. Elegant. Honest. Too good to be true."

The dragon sinks down to Guy's height once more.

"Continue," it says.

"There were actually two plans for your gold," Guy says. "So you were partially right. If you kept your word, I was gonna walk out'a here empty handed. With hope for the future, yes. But gold? None of it. I don't steal nothin' from the honest, not my way. We'd a just put the egg right back, no one the wiser."

"The egg?" the dragon asks.

"Yeah," Guy says. "Walk away clean if you was honest. But, if you was what I thought you was, the plan's you carrying it to the surface for us. In the bags. If you lied. And you did. So…"

"Tell me about the egg," the dragon demands.

"I don't have to tell you. You already know." As Guy says this, the bodies of Sir Brent, Randal, and Rax slowly fade into nothing. The blood and dismembered body parts go with them.

"Randal is an illusionist." Smoke escapes from the dragon's clenched teeth.

"Yeah." Guy unfolds the four bags, laying them out next to each other. "I want them all full; they can carry the weight—I've already checked."

"Without my head you won't save Two-Finger," the dragon

says.

"Who finger?"

"Two-Finger," the dragon says. "He is the reason you are here in the first place."

Guy puts his finger to his chin, thinking. "Ya know. Nope—I don't know anybody by that name," he says. "Why don't you check on that egg."

The dragon climbs over its throne, through its piles of gold, until it is out of sight. Guy covers his ears before the roar comes, and it comes full of anger and hatred and the promise of vengeance. When the dragon returns it is different. Older. Tired. Broken.

"Where is it?" the dragon demands.

"Shay grabbed it while we were talk'n. Would've put it right back if you kept your word, if you let me walk, but...." Guy shrugs.

"So," Guy says, "why don't you fill these bags nice and full and bring'm topside for me like a good little dragon. Do good, and your egg will be back before you know it."

"I will find you," the dragon says. "I will hunt your families until not a single drop of your cursed blood runs in the veins of man. You. Randal. Shay. Raxel. Brent. I will kill them. I will kill their friends. I will kill—"

"But," Guy interrupts, "who are you look'n for exactly?"

Guy's features shift. His skin gets darker and then lighter. He grows taller, then shorter. His nose bulbous, then cute.

"Who have you seen but me? And given the time I've been here, let's be honest with each other for once, I bet that enchantment is start'n to work—even on you."

The dragon tries to focus on Guy's face, to picture it in its mind, just a single feature to hold on to, but can't. It roars and screams in frustration. Smashes its throne. Topples its piles of gold. Then turns on Guy.

"Careful." Guy wags a finger. "You just keep think'n 'bout that egg."

A door appears in the air behind Guy. Its gilded wood frame reflects the hatred in the dragon's eyes. Each intricate carving coming to life under scrutiny. It opens before Guy can knock.

"Why?" the dragon asks. "If you were willing to walk away empty handed, why come here at all?"

Guy stops halfway through the door. He turns to face the

dragon.

"I believed in you since I was a kid. I wanted to meet a creature who couldn't lie. A creature bound to truth in ways I am not. I wanted to see—well—I wanted to see a dragon."

They stand a moment in silence.

"And?" the dragon asks.

"And what?"

"Was it worth it?"

Guy looks the dragon in the eye one last time.

"Honestly," he says. "Feels liking payin' ten solid for a half shiny fiddle."

And the door closes. Cutting off the sunlight. Stopping the breeze. The sound of distant waves fade slowly into the dark. And the dragon stares for just a moment, then begins filling four bags with its most precious of gold.

~ * ~ * ~

Austin Charles Roberts is a creative coach, story doctor, and developmental editor. He holds an MFA with a focus on The Unreliable Narrator in Fiction and Film from Goddard College, as well as an MBA with a focus on Talent Acquisition and Development for Creative Teams. When not doing writerly things or playing with his children, Austin hides in his workshop and builds anything that fits his fancy; predominantly hand-forged knives and axes, jewelry, custom firearms, skin-on-frame boats, and musical instruments.

You can follow his exploits at AustinCharlesRoberts.com.

The Dragon's Choice

Annie Percik

"Time to go, Marta!" her mother called up the stairs, strain clear in her voice. "The others are starting to gather in the square!"

Marta double-knotted her boots and stood up, smoothing down her tunic. She took a deep breath, squared her shoulders and glanced round her room one last time. The objects of her childhood threatened to undermine her resolve, sending her back in time to when she still needed the comfort of a stuffed bear at bedtime. She reached out to stroke its soft fur, thinking that time wasn't really so long ago. She had celebrated her sixteenth birthday two months before, which made her eligible for The Dragon's Choice, and that meant her place was in the town square with the others. Once she left this room, she might not see it again for a long time, if ever. Her breath stuck in her throat on the intake and a sense of tightness spread across her chest.

Squeezing her feelings into a tiny box in the back of her mind and closing the lid tightly over them, Marta turned her back on her childhood and made her way down the stairs. Her mother stood at the bottom, gazing up at her, moisture glinting at the corners of her eyes. Marta gently brushed the tears away, knowing if her mother cried it would undo her.

"None of that, mam," she said, her voice steadier than she felt. "I might well be home in time for tea."

It might take the dragon a few days to make its decision, but eventually all but one of the candidates would return home, none the worse for wear. Until the time for the next Choice came around in ten years, of course. Nobody knew what criteria the dragon used, so it was impossible to prepare. Marta would just have to travel up the mountain with the rest and deal with whatever happened once she got there. For now, she kissed her mother's cheek and walked out of the house.

A quavering call of, "Good luck," followed her out but she didn't look back.

Nervous energy propelled Marta into a jog as she made her

way to the square. Most of the others were there before her but she was glad to see she wasn't the last to arrive. All youngsters of the town aged sixteen had to present themselves on the day the trial of the Dragon's Choice began. Marta joined the group, exchanging glances with one or two of her friends. Nobody spoke. Movement at the edge of the square caught her eye and she looked over to see Gavan lurking in an alleyway. He met her gaze and gave her a helpless shrug. His seventeenth birthday had been two days ago, so he wouldn't be joining the others on their journey. Marta ached to feel his arms around her one more time, but she just averted her eyes and pretended she hadn't seen him. They had said their goodbyes the night before and that would have to do. A hand slipped into hers, squeezing her fingers, and she looked up to see her best friend, Elise, next to her.

Elise nodded in Gavan's direction. "He try to persuade you to stay?" she whispered.

Marta managed a smile. "He knows I don't have a choice. I'm not sure if he's relieved, guilty or annoyed he's not coming with us."

Elise rolled her eyes. "Boys..." she muttered.

They both turned at the sound of someone clearing their throat. The mayor had climbed up on a small dais at one side of the square to address the candidates. The group shuffled towards him, now nearly thirty-strong.

"The whole town stands with you," he said, though Marta noted the rest of the townsfolk were conspicuously absent. It was tradition nobody came to see the candidates off. "We wish you all the best of luck and will see most of you here again before you know it," the mayor continued. Then he nodded once and walked away.

"That was it?" Marta hissed.

Elise rolled her eyes again. "Old people..."

The candidates looked around at each other, seemingly not sure what was supposed to happen next. Marta took Elise's hand again and strode in the direction of the path out of town towards the mountain, carefully not looking over at where Gavan may or may not still be lurking. They had a long walk ahead of them and there was no point putting it off. Whatever was going to happen when they reached the dragon's lair was going to happen, whether or not they dawdled on the journey. They might as well get on with it. But, as the ground ahead started to slope upwards, Marta was glad to have a friend at her side.

~ * ~

A stab of sunlight slipped round the edges of the curtain that hung over the small window, making Jerris clench her eyes more tightly shut. She couldn't ignore the daylight for long, however. It was an important day, after all.

Reluctantly, she rolled out of bed, shoved her feet into her thick slippers and staggered over to the cabinet at one side of the room. She poured some water from the waiting pitcher into a dish and splashed it over her face, gasping at the chill. She looked around the stone chamber with its rich tapestries and ridiculous four-poster bed. It wouldn't be hers for much longer. Jerris shook her dripping fringe out of her eyes, trying to send her melancholy thoughts with it. She might as well make the most out of her last few days up on the mountain.

Before she was replaced.

She pulled a thick robe on over her nightshirt and made her way out of her room and down the underground passageway to the main chamber of the complex.

"Up and at 'em, Kay-Kay!" she called out. "Big day!"

A huge shape shifted in the back corner of the chamber, a low growl accompanying the movement. A gravelly voice sounded in Jerris' mind, heavy with sleep and annoyance.

Why must you be so cheerful about it?

Jerris kept a false smile on her face, hoping it would help her voice to sound happy. "Why shouldn't I be cheerful about getting out of this place? Ten years is a long time to be your servant, old girl. Aren't you looking forward to having a new, fresh young thing bouncing around here with youthful energy and the excitement of a new challenge?"

The long, scaled snout of the dragon, Kayda, emerged from the darkness, her glowing eyes seeking out Jerris' slender form.

But you know exactly where I like to be scratched.

Jerris took the hint and reached out to find the spot, just under Kayda's chin. The dragon closed her eyes and actually purred.

And you know how to prepare my snacks properly. And how to keep the saddle leather supple so it doesn't rub. And where all the best mud pools are for bathing. And…

"Enough!" Jerris said, giving Kayda a playful slap on the nose. "The new kid will learn. It's time for me to go home and get on with my life."

Though what was there left for her down in the town? Her uncle and aunt had packed up and left the valley when Jerris was elected The Dragon's Choice ten years before, glad to be relieved of the burden of her care. And what few friends she'd had would have little in common with her now she'd spent the intervening time as servant to a dragon. What could she possibly have to talk to them about? And, even though her duties were mostly menial, how could life in the town compare to the life she'd built here with Kayda? Where could she live that would compare with her luxurious room here? And how would she cope without access to Kayda's marvelous library? Not to mention the guarantee of plentiful food and excellent companionship. Jerris had no idea what she was going to do. She was twenty-six and had no skills that were of use in a normal job.

The dragon blinked at her.

Are you really so eager to leave me?

Jerris leaned forwards and kissed the scaly skin where she'd slapped it. "It's been fun. And you know I love you. But the candidates will be arriving soon, and they expect you to choose one of them to replace me. The whole town expects it."

It was how the valley had been run for generations. Kayda offered protection from bandits, wild animals, invasion and bad weather, making the valley a safe and prosperous place to live. And, in return, the town provided her with a companion and helper, who served her every need for ten years. It was a position of high honor, bringing prestige and status to the Choice's family, not to mention a generous stipend to compensate them for the loss of potential income from the youngster.

Jerris had been glad enough to leave the town behind when Kayda chose her ten years ago, and would be very sad to leave. But she wasn't about to suggest upending a century-old tradition, just to be able to stay in her comfy bed and continue serving Kayda past her allotted tenure.

"Come on," she said. "Let's get you outside. There's enough time for me to give you a good scrub before the children get here. You want to make a good impression, don't you?"

~ * ~

The sun rose higher in the sky as the group toiled up the mountain. Marta kept having to push her damp hair out of her face, cursing her mother's insistence on curling it overnight. By now, she was sure, it would be reduced to a frizzy mess, straggling down her back. She would have been much better off with sensible braids like most of the other girls, or even hacking it off altogether to demonstrate a lack of interest in spending time on her own appearance.

But how did you make a good first impression on a dragon? Would The Great One want practicality? Pride in personal presentation? A willingness to subsume oneself in dedication to the dragon's needs? Nobody knew. Marta had only been six years old when the last group of candidates made this journey, and all but Jerris came back within a few days. She couldn't remember what Jerris had been like before, and only knew her as a tall young woman who was very occasionally seen in town, ordering supplies or making requests on the dragon's behalf.

Marta was still at the front of the group as they turned a sharp bend in the path and an almost blinding glow appeared above and before them. On a wide, flat platform of rock in front of a vast cave entrance, the dragon was stretched out in all her glory, sun glinting off her golden scales. Marta had only ever seen her high in the sky, flying to combat some threat to the harmony of the valley. Up close, she was huge, her head drooping over the edge of the platform at one end, and her tail disappearing from view over the side at the other end. And there was Jerris, reaching up to scrub the scales of the dragon's back with a long-handled brush, soap suds frothing.

There was a squeal of surprise from someone behind Marta. Jerris spun round, spraying soapy water all over herself, and the dragon's great head swung up, nostrils flaring.

"Oh!" Jerris exclaimed, dropping the brush with a clatter and trying to smooth her rumpled and now damp tunic. "You're earlier than I expected. Um, welcome, I guess? You've caught us a bit unprepared."

She cocked her head to one side as if listening to something Marta couldn't hear, then stepped forwards, beckoning them to join her on the edge of the platform. Marta and Elise strode up and stopped a few feet away from the dragon's large bulk, with most of the other kids following behind them.

Jerris kept beckoning. "Come on, there's nothing to be scared of. Kay-Kay here is really just a big pussycat at heart. She's not going to eat any of you."

Marta reflected that she'd known more than a few pretty vicious cats in her time, but she didn't quibble. She glanced over her shoulder to see three or four of the group dragging their feet, their expressions wary. Eventually, though, they were gathered in a ragged cluster, just off the path. Marta looked between the dragon and Jerris, waiting for someone to tell them what to do. When the instruction came, it took her completely by surprise. A low, silky voice spoke to her, but not aloud, directly into her mind.

If you can hear me, step forwards away from the others.

The words echoed between Marta's ears for a moment before fading away. She looked at Elise, who met her gaze with wide-eyed astonishment. Elise had heard the voice too. They both took a couple of steps further forwards. Eight or nine of the other kids moved with them, leaving the rest hesitant and confused where they were.

"Right," Jerris said in a decisive tone, clapping her hands together. "That's the first test done. I'm afraid if you can't hear Kayda speaking, you're eliminated from the Choice." She waved at the group who hadn't moved. "I'm sorry, but you can go home again now."

Most of them reacted with surprise or obvious disappointment. One of the boys burst into tears, though Marta couldn't tell if it was because he was upset or relieved. A girl took a step forward and raised one finger, her eyebrows drawn down and her lips stretched into a thin line.

"I'm sorry!" Jerris said again, cutting her off before she could object. "There's really no point in trying to argue with me. If you can't hear the dragon, you can't serve her. It's as simple as that."

There were a couple of grumbles near the back of the group, but the twenty or so rejected candidates did now turn and start shuffling back down the path, one of the other girls taking hold of the objector's arm and pulling her along.

As Jerris turned to the remaining ten or so, Marta found herself bouncing on the balls of her feet and forced herself to still.

"Well, that's a more manageable number, at least," Jerris said with a wry smile. "I guess the next thing to do is—"

The remaining candidates never got to find out what the next step of the selection process might be, because Jerris broke off as the dragon—Kayda, Marta reminded herself—snorted violently and craned her neck off towards the woodland in the distance. Jerris stood motionless for a few seconds, presumably listening to the dragon speaking. Marta assumed Kayda must be able to restrict her vocal broadcast just to Jerris if she wanted.

Then Jerris threw a startled glance in the candidates' direction before turning on her heel and pelting back into the cave system. Elise and Marta exchanged confused looks, while the others shuffled and whispered to each other around them. Kayda heaved herself to her feet and the kids backed away from her, just in case. Within a couple of minutes, Jerris was back, carrying what looked like a weird saddle, a bulging canvas bag of something hooked over her shoulder.

"Sorry, folks!" she called as she started strapping the saddle onto Kayda's back. "We've got to go and deal with something." She gestured to the cave. "You can go inside if you want to get out of the sun. But don't wander off and don't touch anything!"

As Marta watched in wonder, Jerris scrambled up to take her place on the saddle pad at the base of the dragon's neck. Once she was settled and holding on securely, Kayda lumbered into a run and launched herself off the platform and into the sky.

~ * ~

The wind whipped through Jerris' hair as Kayda made a beeline for the forest along the border of the valley. She focused her mind so she could convey her words directly to the dragon through their mental connection. It had taken months to make the bond strong enough for her to do this, and it was still a strain, so she only spoke to Kayda this way when she wouldn't be able to hear the words aloud.

What are we looking at?

Kayda's muscles rippled beneath the saddle as she banked and turned in the air. Jerris felt the saddle straps cutting into her thighs and clutched the pommel more tightly.

There are armed men in the woods. One of them tastes strange.

The ways in which Kayda sensed things that were out of physical range were still a mystery to Jerris, even after ten years. But the dragon had developed a vocabulary to describe what she sensed and the best analogy she'd been able to find was eating. Jerris wasn't sure she wanted to know what would make a person taste strange to a dragon's mind, but she guessed she was about to find out.

Want some coal?

In response, Kayda craned her neck around while still flying, until her snout was as close to Jerris as she could get it. Jerris fumbled in the bag she was carrying, pulled out several lumps of coal and tossed them one by one into Kayda's open mouth. The dragon had a pouch in the back of her throat where she could generate super-heated air. With coal as a fuel source, swallowed back into the pouch, she could create streams of fire. They had used the technique to keep farmland clear of encroaching underbrush, and to scare off a manticore that had stumbled into the valley that one time, but never against human enemies. The lords of the neighboring territories knew well enough not to bother the valley, not with a dragon providing protection. Who would be so stupid as to bring armed forces across the border?

As the edge of the woodland came into view, Jerris could see men on horses with armor and lances just emerging from the trees onto the open grassland beyond. There were about fifty knights but amongst them rode one man in robes, who didn't seem to be wearing any protection or carrying a weapon. Not that armor and lances would do them much good against a dragon, but still, it was odd. One of the knights shouted and pointed up, his horse snorting and prancing as Kayda got closer. Jerris gritted her teeth as the dragon's maneuvering threw her against the harness straps again. Kayda swung on a low pass in front of the advancing troops, scorching a line across the earth with her flame as she went. Jerris twisted her head to look behind them and saw the horses all rearing and scrambling away from the heat. All except the one ridden by the robed man, which remained stock still.

The man raised his arms, his mouth moving in what looked like shouted commands, though Jerris couldn't hear him. A blast of white air shot out of his fingers and hit Kayda and Jerris broadside. The pain of intense cold exploded up Jerris' leg and she looked down to see ice forming on her leggings. Kayda swung away with a bellow, crystals frosting on her scales all along one side. Jerris tossed her some more coal as they came back around to lay another line of fire across the path of the men, trying to stay out of range of the ice blasts at the same time.

The battle continued in this vein for some time, maintaining a stalemate as Kayda couldn't get close enough to drive the knights back without risking more ice damage and the ice-flinger was unable to press his attack because of the burning lines of grass blocking his way. Jerris reached into the bag of coal and found only a few more handfuls remaining.

Looks like we'll run out of coal before he runs out of ice.

Kayda snorted, smoke pouring out of her nostrils.

I could make a more direct run and send the next bout of flame right at him.

It was certainly an option, though a risky one. It would put them in range for a more full-on attack themselves, and Jerris also wasn't keen on the idea of actually trying to burn the man alive, even if he and his companions were the aggressors. But what else could they do at that point?

She didn't need to find an answer to that question, as the men removed the necessity of deciding. As Kayda swung round for her next run, the robed man gave some kind of signal and all the horses wheeled and started galloping back into the forest and away. Before Kayda had to decide where to direct her next burst of flame, they had all disappeared. The dragon circled overhead a couple of times, watching the disturbance of their progress back through the trees, until they were sure the invasion attempt was over.

Jerris was baffled.

What was that all about?

Kayda's shoulders rocked backwards in an approximation of a shrug, tipping Jerris back with them.

I do not know. It does not seem like a tactic designed to achieve much more than drawing us out here to waste our time.

The dragon's mental voice fell silent for a moment, then she bellowed, all her muscles tensing.

We must get back to the mountain. Immediately.

Kayda pivoted in midair, then shot back the way they had come, as if her tail was on fire, Jerris hanging on as best she could.

~ * ~

Back on the platform outside the dragon's cave system, it was

Marta who led the remaining candidates inside, Elise at her side. She strode inside with confidence and curiosity as the others hung back, apparently unsure about venturing in. The cavern closest to the outside was huge, stretching back into shadow so it was impossible to see where it ended. The ceiling vaulted high above, making it feel less cramped and claustrophobic than Marta had expected. She kept going, wanting to see more. Elise tugged at her sleeve.

"Don't you think we should stay out here?"

Marta shrugged. "For one of us, this might be our home for the next ten years. I want to see what it's like."

"But Jerris said —"

Marta didn't wait to hear the rest, instead moving further into the space. Elise followed shortly after, sticking close to Marta's shoulder, one hand clutching the bottom of her shirt. When they finally reached the back of the main cavern, there was a hallway cut into the stone that led deeper into the mountain. It was lit by torches in regularly spaced sconces along the wall and Marta wandered through, looking into rooms on either side. There was a pantry and kitchen, and an impressively large library.

"But how does the dragon turn the pages?" Elise wanted to know.

One chamber had a solid-looking door with an iron latch, so they decided not to try and open that one. But Marta was drawn further and further, until they reached a staircase at the end of the corridor, leading downwards. A breath of warmer air caressed Marta's cheek as she leaned in to see how far down it went.

"Maybe we should go back," Elise said. "This feels like we're trespassing."

"You can go back if you want," Marta said. "But I want to see where this goes."

She grabbed one of the torches from a nearby sconce and started down the stairs. After a few seconds, she heard Elise hurrying to catch her up. The staircase wound round in a spiral, deeper and deeper into the mountain. The air grew warmer as they descended, until it was almost uncomfortable to breathe. But Marta was determined to see where it led, so she continued on. Eventually, the stairs ended in a much more roughly hewn cavern than the ones above. There were stalagmites growing up towards the roof and some places where they had met stalactites reaching down and formed stone columns. A red glow emanated from off to one side and day-light filtered in from the other side, where a large opening looked out across the valley. Despite being open to the sky, the air was thick and hot.

Marta looked round to grin at Elise. This was by far the most interesting place they'd found in the cavern system so far. Her excitement was immediately brought up short by a scuffling sound and a man's voice cursing. Elise's eyes widened and Marta put a finger to her lips. She was pretty sure nobody but the candidates was sup-posed to be on the mountain, and certain this area wasn't meant to be accessed by the townsfolk. They crept forwards until they were up against one of the stone pillars and Marta risked a glance round to see where the sound had come from. She saw a soldier in armor bearing the livery of the next-door land, whose lord only main-tained peace with the people of the valley because it was impossible to do otherwise with the dragon protecting them. The man was wearing thick gloves and wielding what looked like a pair of large tongs. He was leaning over a depression in the rock where the red glow was coming from and Marta could see sweat pouring down his face. She couldn't tell what he was doing but he definitely wasn't supposed to be there.

Marta looked around and spotted a fist-sized rock a short distance from her feet. She crouched down and scooped it up.

"What are you doing?" Elise hissed in her ear, but Marta just waved her off.

Trying to stop her feet from scuffing too much in the dust of the cavern floor, Marta left the cover of the stone pillar and crept out into the open. She edged towards the soldier, feeling moisture start to prickle across her scalp and forehead as the heat from what-ever was causing the red glow began to intensify. When she was right behind him, she reached up with one hand to tip his helmet forwards over his eyes, simultaneously exposing the back of his head so she could swing her other hand up and bash him with the rock.

The shock of the impact reverberated up her arm and the man gave a loud cry of both shock and pain. He stumbled, drop-ping his tongs and almost pitching into what looked like a lake of molten lava. Marta grabbed the back of his jerkin and yanked him away from it. He crashed to the floor and she threw herself on top of him.

"Elise!" she cried. "Help me!"

Within seconds, her friend was by her side, and, between them, they managed to pin his arms and legs, sitting on him to prevent him from getting up. He struggled feebly but he was impaired by not being able to see and whimpered pathetically at his predicament.

"What do we do now?" Elise asked.

Marta hadn't thought that far ahead, but she was saved from having to come up with a plan, as the sound of great wings came to them from outside and she looked up to see the dragon swooping in from the opening in the side of the cavern.

~ * ~

Jerris was still completely at a loss as to why Kayda was hurrying back to the mountain and was even more surprised when the dragon flew around to the entrance to the lava pit, rather than landing in the usual way on the platform outside the main cave. Things got even more confusing when Kayda set down in the cavern right next to two of the candidates, who seemed to be grappling on the floor with a man. Kayda roared a question.

What is going on here?

Jerris released herself from her straps and scrambled down to the floor, striding up to the group huddled on the floor.

"I'd quite like to know that myself."

The girl with the mass of curly hair, who had been at the front of the candidate group at every opportunity, gazed up at her, looking like she might be sick any minute. She pulled herself together, though, and started to explain.

"We were just exploring, and we found this guy, doing something over there I figured he wasn't supposed to, so we captured him."

"Captured him?" Jerris gave them a wry smile. "Looks more like you're trying to suffocate him. But you're right, He definitely shouldn't be here."

Let him up. He has explaining to do.

So do you, Kayda, Jerris thought. But there would be time for her questions later, once whatever situation this was had been resolved.

The two girls scrabbled around and managed to get to their

feet in a fairly undignified manner. Once released from their weight, the soldier pushed himself up into a sitting position and reached up to slide his helmet back onto his head properly. He immediately looked as if he'd rather go back to not being able to see, as he found himself facing an angry dragon.

Jerris decided to take pity on him. "You can explain yourself to me, or I can just leave you to Kayda."

The soldier dragged his gaze across to her, then shuffled a few feet further away from the dragon. "I—I was sent to steal the egg."

"Egg?" Jerris said, shock jarring down her spine. "What egg?"

Words came pouring out of him then, tumbling over each other in his eagerness to get them out. "A wizard came to see the king. He said he could help us combat the dragon. He can cast his mind into birds and had been spying on the mountain. He said he'd seen the dragon laying an egg and knew where she had hidden it. He led a force across the border to draw you away and my job was to scale the path to this cavern and steal the egg."

Jerris turned to Kayda. "You laid an egg and didn't tell me?"

I was waiting for the right time. Based on today's events, that time should have been before now. I'm sorry.

"Well, never mind that now, Kay-Kay," Jerris said, though she was still reeling inside from the revelation. "What are we going to do with him?"

Tell him to go back to his king to report his failure. He can take the message that I know the flavor of their wizard now and will be able to sense if either he or his mind encroaches on our territory again. And, soon, we will have two dragons to protect the valley.

Jerris relayed the message and sent the soldier on his way. He all but ran to the opening and flung himself down the steep path down the mountain, grateful to have escaped with his life. As soon as he was gone, Kayda shuffled over to the lava pit and started making a weird cooing noise Jerris had never heard from her before.

The curly-haired girl spoke up. "Is the egg safe?"

Kayda swung her head around.

Thanks to you, yes. If that man had succeeded in extracting it from the lava and taken it outside, the embryo would have perished. You have my eternal gratitude for saving my child. What is your name?

"Marta. And you're very welcome."

Marta, would you agree to stay here with us and become guardian and companion to my child when she is born?

Jerris watched as Marta opened and closed her mouth a couple of times. She understood how the girl felt. Everything that had happened in the last few minutes was making her feel a bit weak at the knees herself. She was impressed by how quickly the girl managed a coherent response.

"Yes. Oh, yes! I'd be honored!"

The other girl looked back and forth between the dragon and her friend. "What about Gavan?" she said.

Marta gestured with one hand towards the cave opening and with the other towards the lava pit. "Teenage boys versus baby dragon? Come on, Elise, that's not a real choice! He'll get over it."

Elise turned her attention to Kayda. "But what about The Dragon's Choice? I mean, the town are expecting all but one of us to come home. If Marta stays to look after the egg, won't you have to choose someone else from the group to serve you? I'm not sure how they'd react if you take two of us. And Jerris' time is up."

A thought popped into Jerris' head and a surge of hope swelled up in her chest. "But does it have to be? Who says I have to go back after ten years?"

It is the way it is done.

"But why?" Jerris caught and held Kayda's gaze. "If I want to stay, why can't I?"

A humming bounced around her mind as Kayda considered.

Ten years was agreed as the town did not want to lose their children for longer and always before my companions have been glad to be reunited with their families after that time. But, there is nothing to say you can't stay. If it's what you really want?

Jerris threw her arms around Kayda's neck. "Yes, it's what I really want. I love you, Kay-Kay. I can't imagine my life without you and it's not as if I have anywhere else to go." She glanced over at Marta. "So, what about it, kid? Happy to share?"

Marta grinned. "Absolutely!"

Elise looked crestfallen. "But I'll hardly ever see you. For ten whole years."

"Says who?" Jerris asked.

"You only come down to town when it's essential. And you

never stay long or really talk to anyone. What people can remember of the other chosen is similar too. We assumed the dragon had some kind of rules about it."

Jerris laughed. "Not at all! I'm just not that fond of people. I don't have any family left in town and Kayda here provides all the companionship I need." She realized how this sounded and hurried on. "Not that I object to you coming to live with us, Marta. But you can visit in town whenever you like, as long as it doesn't interfere with your duties." Sharing the space with another human would take some getting used to, but Jerris was sure she would adjust.

Marta's eyes widened. "Really?"

"Of course! I'm pretty sure you'll like it up here, though. It's a nice place to live, which is why I think most of the chosen preferred to stay put."

I don't choose a candidate who would be sad to be separated from their family.

Jerris smirked. "See? Kayda may be a dragon, but she's not draconian."

It was a weak joke, but they all laughed anyway.

The Dragon's Choice was made.

~ * ~ * ~

Annie Percik lives in London, where she writes novels and short stories, whilst working as a freelance editor and proofreader (https://alobear.co.uk/?page_id=778). She writes a blog about writing on her website (www.alobear.co.uk), which is where all her current publications are listed, including her debut fantasy novel, The Defiant Spark (http://getbook.at/DefiantSpark). She also makes a media review podcast with her husband, Dave (https://stillloveit.libsyn.com/), and publishes a photo-story blog, recording the adventures of her teddy bear (https://aloysius-bear.dreamwidth.org/). He is much more popular online than she is.

Domain of the Dragon

L.H. Davis

Lunar Orbit (2060 AD)

A gleaming trail of ice, eroded from the comet, curled down toward the lunar surface. The cratered landscape, passing slowly beneath my boots, seemed much closer than a hundred kilometers. On the surface of the comet, a mere twenty meters away, the six guidance thrusters fired short, stabilizing bursts, seemingly at random. Evenly spaced around the icy sphere, all but one had found solid purchase. *T5* again teetered. Correcting with a burst of lateral jets, it then fired its primary engine to reseat its LDI. The Load Distribution Interface, a mesh covered ring, flexed under the load, conforming to an odd depression in the ice. Black splinters spun away from the ring as its graphite composite backbone snapped.

"*T5*'s coming apart." Unclipping my safety tether from the capsule, I propelled myself toward the damaged thruster. "I'll back it off manually and set down ten meters to port."

"Nadia," Duncan screamed. "Are you insane?"

"I can save *T5*."

I'd done enough spacewalks to know I could make the crossing, but I hadn't considered the random bucking of the thruster until after pushing off. Poor timing and any number of struts could have ventilated my suit, or one of its huge fuel tanks might have simply booted me out into deep space. Estimating my point of impact, I searched for a suitable feature to attach my safety tether, which I still held in my hand. Spotting the steel hydraulic line feeding the nearest deployment strut, I thumbed open the clip of my tether. The floods of my helmet bathed the surface of the comet beneath *T5*. The depressed area was fractured, as if it had collapsed under the thrust loads of deceleration. The bottom, however, was smooth and featureless as if the crater had partially refilled with a dark liquid, which had since refrozen. Under my lights, the surface shone dark red.

"Duncan, you're the comet expert. Why is this one red on the inside?"

"Red?"

"Never mind," I said as plumes of vapor spewed from *T5*'s retrorockets. I reached out to attach my tether as *T5* lurched. The deployment boom struck my face shield, reversing my direction of travel. I tumbled backward, head over heels, but only once. Reaching the limit of my tether, the cable snapped taut. Arching downward at the full extent of my tether, I focused on the mesh of *T5*'s LDI and managed to penetrate the large weave with my arms. Locking my wrist, I recoiled and groaned, more out of concern than strain.

"You okay?" Duncan said.

"Affirmative." Glancing back, I checked my tether attachment. The hydraulic tubing had kinked, but it had held and didn't appear to be leaking. "But we'll need to make a few repairs," I said. A curlicue of plastic wavered before my right eye. I brushed the debris from my visor, but a deep crevice with spider cracks remained. "I gouged the crap out of my visor. I'll need to switch to my backup helmet."

"You're a lunatic," Duncan said.

I laughed but wondered if he might not be right. *Not the smartest thing I've ever done.* Pushing off, I floated toward *T5*'s manual control console centered over the mesh. I swung up, over the handrail, snapping my boots into the restraints. Releasing the control shield, I palmed the emergency override, shutting down the thruster. The mesh, compressed taut over the broken ice, relaxed, gently launching the spacecraft. Taking the joystick, I backed *T5* away, shifting laterally until the LDI cleared the depression. I then settled *T5* back onto the surface and reactivated the autonomous controls. Purely as a habit, I said, "It's all yours, *T5.*" The six thrusters had never been programmed to accept voice commands, but I'd worked with them for so long I'd begun to think of them as people. Scanning the surface of the small alien world, I mumbled, "This is one ugly comet."

Two years earlier, I had led the team of NASA engineers that tested and debugged the thrusters on orbit. Their original mission had been to capture asteroid 2340 Hathor, three years after launch; however, Caesar's Comet, C/-43K1, showed up unexpectedly on a more favorable trajectory, which shortened the mission by two years. The team of six thrusters autonomously captured the small comet by landing in opposing pairs. Each thruster had then cycled through a phase of leading and slowing the comet as they turned it toward Earth. Caesar's Comet, the brightest comet ever observed from Earth, was thought to have left the solar system in 44 BC.

"Congratulations," Duncan said.

"For what?" I asked. "Not being dead?"

"Okay, for that too," he said. "I meant for being the first person to set foot on a comet."

"Sorry, I didn't mean to cut in line. But I haven't actually touched this thing yet, so when you come over just put your foot on it…then *you* can be the first. Besides, I don't think I really want to touch this thing. This is one strange looking comet."

"How many comets have you seen up close like this?"

"Good point," I said, "but it still doesn't look right."

The comet had been in lunar orbit for eight months. Over the first few months, it shed some kind of slushy outer layer. What remained appeared to be solid, nearly spherical, but it was covered with several dozen strange looking lumps, although they were irregular enough in size and spacing to be natural formations of the ice.

But something about them still looks too…familiar? Pointing at the red depression, I said, "What is that stuff?"

"Not sure," Duncan said. "I guess it could be a layer of oxidized iron dust, but I've never seen any…blood red before. Could it be hydraulic fluid?"

"There's nothing that color aboard these thrusters. What about a fungus or some other kind of biological growth?"

"If it is," Duncan said, "it'll be the first extraterrestrial life ever discovered. So no, it's not biological. We're not *that* lucky."

"You're the expert. My job is just to put you on the surface of this thing, which I can't do from over here. I'd fly back over, but I'm not sure this face shield could survive another landing like my last one. Send over the arm."

Transferring to the foot restraints on the remote manipulator, I rode the arm back to the bent hydraulic tubing and unfastened my safety tether. "*T5*'s LDI snapped," I said as Duncan brought me back to the capsule, "but it should be fine." Reaching inside the open hatch, I secured my tether. I palmed the release of my foot restraints but remained firmly attached. Pushing off the safety latch, I smacked it again. "You're up," I said, drifting in through the hatch. "You riding over or flying like me?"

"Unlike you, I'm not crazy," Duncan said dryly.

Strapping in at the console, I repositioned the arm to a more favorable angle. Duncan attached his drilling tools aft of the foot restraints, as I read the checklist aloud.

"Is that everything?" he said.

"Everything on the list, but don't forget that drill lanyard." While training in low Earth orbit, Duncan had lost one of his drills, which burned up in Earth's the atmosphere.

Stepping out on the arm, he said, "Are you ever going to let that go?"

I chuckled. "Just trying to help. There's no atmosphere below us, so anything we drop will go all the way down to the surface. I'd hate to find out we punched a hole in that brand new emergency shelter." I pointed through the open hatch toward the moon, where the glow of the rising sun backlit the horizon. "The sun's just coming up. That gives us two hours of daylight."

"Let's go," Duncan said. "That red ice will have to wait. Core samples first. Let's start with that mound to starboard."

"Which one?" I asked. "They're all over the place."

"Surprise me," he said.

Using the fixed camera on the arm, I position Duncan over the nearest mound, applying a countering thrust as we made contact. The additional load from the capsule nudged the comet into a slightly lower orbit, awaking the six autonomous thrusters. As a team, they nudged their payload back to its programmed altitude of one hundred kilometers.

That's my good boys. I knew the little quirks of each, and, in a way, thought of them as my children, the ones I'd never found the time—or husband—to have.

Splitting the screen, I displayed both of Duncan's helmet cameras. His forward cam showed nothing but deep space, but his rear cam had focused on me in the capsule. *Even more boring.* "No wonder I can't get a date," I mumbled. "How come the chicks in space flicks always look so sexy?"

"Maybe it's because they *are* sexy," Duncan said.

"It's not fair," I said. "I can look sexy, too…in high heels and a skirt."

"I'll believe that when I see it," he said. "Do you even own a pair of heels?"

"I have a pair." *Somewhere.* "What are you doing, now? I can't see anything."

"I'm drilling a pilot hole."

"Lean over a little more so I can see the bit." He did and the drill came into view. "Good. How deep are you?"

"Just over three hundred millimeters."

"What do you see?"

"Ice," Duncan said. "I did see a layer of dark gray, which might be interstellar dust, but— Whoa. Can you see this?"

"Yep, it's that same nasty red stuff."

"I've never seen—" Duncan stopped drilling. "What was that? Did you feel something?"

"I'm not su—" The capsule lurched.

"Get me out of here!"

"Hang on," I said, retracting the arm. As it settled, the arm-mounted camera focused on a fissure at the base of the mound. "What the hell did you do?"

"It's coming apart," Duncan said. "The thrust load from the capsule must have sheared a plug out of the ice."

"That's a big plug," I said. "It's bigger than this capsule."

"Yeah, back me up a little more. If it floats free, we'll get a good look inside."

The sheared face of the plug revealed multiple layers of dark gray strata, probably deposited while passing through clouds of interstellar dust. The red inner layer, the last one visible, was thicker than the width of Duncan's gloved hand.

"That red layer gives me the creeps," I said.

"Maybe *it is* bacteria," he said. "In some parts of the solar system comets collect dust, while in other areas they collect more water ice. At some point in the past, maybe thousands of years ago, it could have picked up bacteria or fungi that propagated over the surface before being buried under more ice. It's likely dead, but we still need to be careful."

"The plug has stopped moving," I said. "Must be hung up. Give it a kick."

"Use the arm. Wedge the end of this platform against the sheared face and rock it a little. But go easy."

"Pull the slack out of your tether," I said, repositioning the arm. "If something goes wrong, release your foot restraints and pull your ass back inside."

"Roger that. Ready when you are."

"Hang on." I flicked the joystick forward. Fist-sized chunks of ice launched outward as the plug broke free. It drifted upward in a lazy spiral.

Duncan peered down into the dark void beneath the rising plug. After it cleared Duncan's head, the spotlights of the capsule illuminated the vacant chamber. "That's odd. It's hollow…like a bubble. The entire thing is lined with that red stuff."

Unbuckling my safety belts, I pushed away from the console. Grabbing a spotlight, I floated toward the open hatch. The beam of my light cast Duncan's shadow deep into the red wound. Its smooth inner surface, unmarred by fractures, now seemed more egg-shaped than round. "What could have made that?"

"Methane," Duncan said, "or maybe some other gas released by the fungus, which is what I'm starting to think it might actually be."

"Then the other half should have the same contour. Right?"

"Yes…if it is a gas bubble."

Shining my beam on the plug overhead, I shook my head. "Not a gas bubble." Something, roughly the size of the hollow in the comet, protruded from the bottom of the ice plug. A network of veins, or possibly a membrane, covered its smooth undulating contours, which glinted in my light with silvery hues of blue. A tubular, tapered structure wrapped entirely around its outer perimeter.

Duncan said, "Maybe it was made by—"

"Duncan," I yelled as the plug drifted into the light of the sun. "Look up!"

"Um," Duncan said. "That *thing*…is in the fetal position." Looking back down into the depression, he said, "This is an egg."

"Then those are too," I said, shining my light over the other mounds.

"Do you realize what this means? How long before we can talk with Mission Control?"

"Another twelve minutes," I said. "Should we go after it? Could it be alive?"

"There's no way it could be alive. It's been frozen solid for thousands of years, if not millions. The last time this comet passed Earth was in fourty-four BC, which was over twenty-one hundred years ago. That might have been its first pass, we don't know, but the odds are it's been in space a lot longer than that. Most comets have been around for billions of years. They don't just pop up out of the ocean and start flying around. That thing can't be alive."

"Could it be from Earth?" I asked. "I mean, we know an asteroid strike can launch debris back into space. That's why we find meteors from Mars on Earth. Maybe it's a—I don't know."

"A what?" Duncan asked. "You have a theory. Let's hear it. A what?"

"A dinosaur? It looks like a petrified fetus."

"That *is* a theory, but—"

"Think about it. The current theory is that an asteroid strike wiped out the dinosaurs. So isn't it possible the same impact launched debris back into space?"

"I'm certain it did," Duncan said.

"Then maybe these are dinosaur eggs that went along for the ride."

"Unbroken?"

"Maybe they were already frozen solid…*before* the impact. Or maybe they were launched by another impact millions of years later during the ice age."

"They're awfully big…but I guess it is possible," Duncan said. "Let's get a sample and then go after that thing. We can at least tether it to one of the thrusters until NASA can get a ship out here to bring it home. It's too big for us to tackle."

"It's too big to fit inside this capsule," I said, moving back to the console. I strapped in and peered out the porthole behind me. The creature, bathed in sunlight, cast a rainbow of colors. Although it continued to drift away from us, it seemed larger and less organized. *It's breaking up.* "There might not be anything left of it by the time we catch up with it."

"Why do you say that?" Duncan said.

"It's baking in the sun. I think it's falling apart."

"That's too bad. Hopefully, there are others…still inside."

"And you still want to drill holes in it?"

"No, I don't. And I won't unless NASA orders me to. I'm not sure this thing's even a comet, but I do want a sample of that red ice. Drop me down inside…the depression."

"Can't say egg?"

"Not when I'm getting ready to climb into one."

"Hang on. Up and over," I said, lowering him inside.

Duncan attached a larger cutting head and then reengages the drill motor. Chips of red ice swirled around the spinning bit. "You're kicking up debris," I said as a chunk of ice careened off the open hatch.

"Negative. The chips are clinging to the surface, like they're wet or something. Maybe friction is warming them up. See if you can get a temperature reading of the ice near my bit."

Floating to the storage rack, I retrieved the hand-held infrared scanner. I powered it up, sighted on the depression, and took a reading. "Two point five degrees. Just above freezing."

"That's not possible," Duncan said.

"Apparently it is," I said. Another chunk of red ice floated past my gouged face shield. Leaning out, I peered above the capsule —and groaned. *That can't be real.*

The creature's huge wings shimmered in the warming rays of the sun. Its wide rear feet and glinting talons, hung motionless from its stout, muscular legs, but its front feet, smaller and dexterous, gripped the remains of its shell. Icy fragments, like glittering bees, swarmed around its head as it bit down on the shell with spiked teeth, longer than my fingers. After consuming the last of the red ice, the creature stretched, flexed its wings, and uncurled its slender, silvery neck and tail. Green vapors wafted from its nostrils and two opposing orifices at the base of its skull.

"You better get in here, Duncan. I think my air mixture is contaminated. Do you feel okay? I'm hallucinating."

A small flame shot from the back of the creature's head, pushing it nearer.

"What are you talking about?" Duncan stood and stared back at me over the crest of the shell.

"That just can't be real," I said, pointing up. "You don't see it...do you?"

Duncan leaned back and peered up. Abandoning his drill, he hammered on the foot restraint release mechanism.

"Release the safety," I yelled, as a wave of flame consumed the comet. Duncan, engulfed by the inferno, wailed.

Dual streams of fire trailed back to the creature's snout. Opposing flames, much smaller, blazed from the back of its head.

Its eyes, large crystal spheres, roiled with fire. As the flames receded, Duncan's air tank exploded, launching shards of debris against the capsule. Duncan's comm fell silent.

The flames dissipated as quickly as they'd appeared. Reaching Duncan's tether, I pulled in the slack and then tugged. His charred body swayed at the end of the arm, his boots melted around the restraints. The creature's eyes, now clear and blue, met mine. Flames burst from the back of its head, nudging the beast closer.

"No!" I pushed back, away from the hatch. Reaching the console, I twisted the joystick, swinging the arm toward the monster. Pieces of Duncan drifted away, although the bulk of him remained attached to the manipulator. I groaned and murmured, "I will not puke in my helmet."

Arming the hatch controls, I palmed the button. It flashed red. Safety interlocks had sensed Duncan's tether in the opening. As I scrambled back toward the open hatch, an eye, the size of a tennis ball, peered inside. Snagging the communication console, I pulled back, out of sight.

A snout, with nostrils as large as my fist, slowly entered the capsule. Gleaming scales covered its face. The creature nosed inward until its eyes crossed the threshold. Green vapors curled from its nostrils. As if sensing a trap, it backed out.

I peered out the porthole. The bulk of Caesar's Comet had disintegrated. A dozen massive eggs floated freely in space. The thrusters had recaptured what remained of the icy mass, now less than a quarter of the size it had been only minutes earlier. Small flames flickered at the base of the creature's skull. For a moment, it stared at the capsule as if puzzled or curious, but then it reared back its head as its eyes again filled with fire.

It's going to burn the capsule. I released my tether from my suit. Coasting through the hatch, I placed my boots on the hull and propelled myself toward *T5*. Its polished steel tanks flickered with the reddish-orange glow of the burning capsule. A white light flared behind me as a blast of heat engulfed my legs. I cringed as the capsule's hatch spun past, impacting and deforming *T5*'s fuel tank. I held my breath anticipating vapors, flames, and death. My heart drummed in my ears as Duncan and the arm spiraled past, bound for the lunar surface.

The colliding hatch rolled *T5*, lifting the near side of the LDI from the ice. I slammed into the mesh as *T5* settled back onto the surface, pinning my fingers between the mesh and the ice. I screamed. Spun by inertia, my helmet slammed into the base of the operator console. I floated inverted above the mesh—dazed— tethered by my ensnared fingers. As awareness returned, my eyes focused on the flickering heads-up display in my face shield—and then on the gouge, which had grown twofold in length. The hiss of leaking air sent a chill down my spine.

"Mission Control," I said. "Do you read?" The delay should have been less than three seconds, but no one replied. *Shit! No capsule, no antenna.* I glanced up as *T5*'s high-gain antenna rotated toward Earth. "Yes." Rolling onto my stomach, I groaned, "Turn… me…loose," and yanked on my trapped fingers. "Aah!" They didn't budge, although they did start throbbing.

Rolling again onto my back, I stared up at the console. The safety cover hung from its hinges, off to one side. Raising my body from the mesh, I pivoted my wrist until my boots reached the console. Twisting, I hooked the toe of my boot over the lip. Taking a few deep breaths, I visualized the placement of the joystick from where I normally stood at the console. *Back and to the left.* Clipping the joystick with the tip of my boot, *T5*'s autonomous controls disengaged. As the thruster shut down, the mesh relaxed, gently launching the spacecraft from the ice. "Good boy," I said, pulling my fingers free. Sensing no further input on the joystick, the autonomous routine resumed, reengaging *T5* with the ice. I slipped into the foot restraints at the console and then patched my headset into *T5*'s comm—with sore but functional fingers. The creature now basked in the sun, apparently content. Several of the eggs were fractured, although no others had fully hatched. "Mission Control, do you read?"

As if hearing my transmission, the beast turned to face me.

"Welcome back, Nadia," Mission Control replied. "You had us worried. It appears we've lost your data downlink. Since we still have comm, it must be a glitch on this end. How was the dark side of the moon?"

"It sucked," I said, backing *T5* away from what remained of the comet. The monster, its eyes again aflame, arched its neck as it retracted its head. "No. Please."

"What's going on?" Mission Control said.

I closed my eyes as the heat engulfed me. But then the glare in my eyelids began to fade, so I twisted the joystick, spinning *T5* on axis. Pushing the stick forward, I glanced back. Unburdened of all ice, nine additional eggs floated in the void between the remaining thrusters.

"Nadia, do you read? Talk to us. Tell us what you need."

"I need directions to that emergency shelter at Tranquility Base," I said, dropping toward the lunar surface.

"There are maps in the capsule's database," Mission Control said, "but we can put one on your monitor if that helps."

"I don't have a monitor…or a capsule. Patch into my helmet cam."

"Nadia! Where are you? Where's Duncan?"

"He's dead. I'm flying *T5* down to the surface. Find someone who can give me verbal directions from the video feed of my helmet cam."

I looked back, expecting to find the beast on top of me. The creature wasn't chasing me, although the other thrusters were—and closing. "Not good," I said as they flashed past. *T6* turned, aligning its LDI with *T5*'s, precisely as programmed. I backed off the throttle as the other four moved into their assigned positions at three, six, nine and twelve o'clock. *This will never work. To land on the lunar surface, I'll need to set down on the LDI, which the others are programmed to oppose. If I back down with them hovering overhead, I could climb down the hull and jump, but I'd land in the exhaust plume of T5's primary engine. Dead either way.*

"Mission Control, kill the autonomous routine," I said. "I'm flying the stick, which prioritizes *T5*, so the others are following my lead, regrouping in front of me. It's going to be a train wreck when I try to land. Kill the routine!" *But then what? Crap!* "Wait. Mission Control, DO NOT kill the routine. That'll shut me down, too. Initiate follow-the-leader subroutine six…zero…eight."

"Understood, Nadia," Mission Control said. "Initiating subroutine six…zero…eight. *T5* has the lead."

The thrusters backed away. *T1* fell into position behind *T5*, and the others followed in numerical order with *T6* bringing up the rear, far enough back for *T5* to slip in line should the lead change.

"Good boys," I said, throttling up. Glancing back, the glint of blue chrome caught my eye, although it remained well behind

T6. "Mission Control, what about that navigator?"

"Jack Simpson is on his way. Tranquility Base is roughly five hundred kilometers ahead of you. Correct five degrees to starboard. You'll fly right over it."

T5's console was designed for basic line of sight navigation. Lacking instrumentation, I estimated the correction. "How's that?"

After the three second delay, Mission Control said, "That's close enough to get a visual. What's going on up there?"

An orange light flickered in my peripheral vision. I froze but cut my eyes. Flames billowed from the back of the creature's elongated skull. Slowly, it pulled ahead of *T5*. Snorting a small burst from its snout, it matched my speed. With its unmoving wings fully extended, the beast coasted, flameless and graceful. The tip of its long tail spiraled, circumscribing a small circle. Articulating its long, slender neck, it scanned the lunar surface below.

"Nadia! Speak to us. We've lost all telemetry from the capsule. What happened?"

I turned my shoulders, capturing the image of the beast with my helmet cam. "He happened."

Much more than three seconds later, Mission Control said, "He?"

"Well," I said, "I'm pretty sure that's...*he* stuff back there."

"No consensus on this end," Mission Control said, "but we all do agree you need to lose that thing before you reach Tranquility Base. The hull of that emergency shelter is made of very thin aluminum. It was designed to keep air in, not dragons out."

"Dragon? That's a dragon?" I asked.

"Call it whatever you want, just lose it."

"Roger that. I wonder how well that thing can maneuver its big body with that scrawny neck. Find me a twisty canyon through that mountain range ahead. Let's see how it likes the taste of moon rock."

"Nadia, this is Jack...Jack Simpson. I've studied this terrain in detail but don't trust my assumptions when it comes to elevation. I could be off by several meters. Correct your heading fifteen degrees to starboard. You should see a mountain pass dead ahead."

I made the correction as I dropped toward the flat expanse of the small desert like mare. "Talk to me, Jack. What's my altitude?"

One. Two. Thre—

"Just under two kilometers."

I dove toward the surface.

"Pull up," Jack said. "Hold it there. You're just above one kilometer. Remember your speed. You're pushing five hundred meters per second. Two seconds is all the margin of error you have."

"Which means he has that much time, too." I dove lower.

"Easy," Jack said. "The surface will come up fast."

"That's what I'm counting on."

"Level off," he said. "The canyon narrows beyond those peaks. At your current velocity, after about five seconds you'll need to make a sharp turn to starboard. Then a turn to port after three seconds, followed by another to starboard almost instantly."

"Starboard, port, starboard. Got it. I just hope his brakes are as bad as mine."

The canyon was wider than I'd hoped. Banking into the first turn, I easily cleared the outer wall. Halfway into the second turn the passage narrowed. With my eyes focused on the encroaching rock wall, I failed to notice the steep incline of the canyon floor. Banking again to starboard, I saw nothing but rock and pulled back hard on the stick. Climbing, I tweaked my trajectory toward a dip in the outer wall—which I almost cleared.

The drooping quadrant of the broken LDI clipped the rim of the canyon, cartwheeling *T5*. My chest slammed into the console, pinning the joystick at full throttle. The added thrust buckled my knees as it launched *T5* out over the open expanse of Mare Tranquillitatis. Supported only by my foot restraints, I fell backward, folding at the knees. *T5* tumbled out of control. Upside down, I groped for the mesh of the flailing LDI, which now dangled from only two of its four deployment actuators. Lacking input on the joystick, the autonomous control reassumed command, arresting the fall of the gyrating spacecraft. With *T5* hovering fifty meters above the lunar surface, I pulled back up to the console. Although light, gravity had again become a part of my world. Once on my feet, I found *T1*, *T2*, and *T3* hovering nearby. *T4*, also with a broken LDI, still wobbled from a similar spill. "Where's *T6*?" I said, but then it cartwheeled over the rise. Before *T6* fully stabilized, flames appeared above the rim of the canyon.

The dragon slowed, blazing first from his nostrils and then from the vents in the back of his head. The flames pulsed as he hovered and then settled onto the rocks. Articulating his long neck, he scanned the horizon. After a final snort of green vapor, he turned his attention to the formation of battered thrusters hovering above the mare.

"What are you waiting for?" I screamed. "Get it over with."

"Nadia," Jack said. "Are you alright?"

"No. That bastard is just toying with me. I'll never lose him."

"Relax, we have a plan. You're only a few minutes away from the shelter so just keep going, one eighty from your current orientation."

I pivoted and accelerated.

"Slow it down by half. We need about five minutes to patch into your controls."

"Roger that," I said, backing off the throttle. "What's the plan?"

"We're going to fly *T5* remotely. We won't assume command until after you're over the target, so the three second delay won't be a problem. There's a small crater near the shelter. We want you to hover inside, just above the floor. That should position you out of sight, below ground level. After we take command, we want you to jump and hide in the crater. With a little luck, he won't see you leave the spacecraft. But if he does, we think you should play dead. We'll fly all the thrusters out across the mare. He should follow them. *T5* has the least amount of fuel, but we can still fly them all for another fifteen minutes, which should give you enough time to make the short walk to the shelter. After that, we'll have to set them down to conserve fuel, so we can put you on orbit when a rescue ship arrives. Hopefully by then, he'll have moved on."

"I like it. *T4* and *T5* both have damaged LDIs, so they won't survive the landing."

"Understood."

"How much further?" I asked.

"Two minutes," Jack said. "Is he still following you?"

I crabbed the thruster and glanced back down the line. Copying my maneuver, the other five also crabbed, revealing a distant glint of blue chrome. "Affirmative."

"The Apollo Eleven landing site is coming up. Adjust your heading by five degrees to port as you pass over the old base. You should then have a visual on the shelter and crater. How's your air supply? We're seeing an off-nominal reading. You should have almost three hours left, but we're not seeing anywhere near that amount."

"I cracked my face shield...so yeah, I'm low."

"You can refill your tank and repair your helmet with the supplies in the shelter, but you'll need every drop of air in your tank to get inside, so don't waste any time."

"Understood," I said, slowing above the crater. "You guys ready to take over? I'm settling into the crater now."

The dangling LDI touched down first. The ring slid sideways until striking the rebound mass in the center of the crater. The broken outer ring flexed under the weight of the thruster. "Crap." *If that thing snaps* T5 *will drop like a rock on top of me.* I estimated my current elevation at twice my height. "Okay, Jack, T5's all yours."

"Taking command," he said. "We transferred your comm to the high gain antenna on the shelter. Good luck."

Patting the console, I said, "Thanks T5. You did good. Take care of yourself." Releasing my foot restraints, I stepped off, pushing away to ensure my backpack cleared the deck. "Nice and easy," I said, feeling the gentle acceleration of the moon's gravity. Landing on the steep inner wall of the crater, I pushed off. Bounding downhill, I toed a small boulder and stumbled. Unable to find purchase in the flowing rubble, I fell forward, slamming my face shield into the rocky debris. Stones clattered against my helmet, but even they didn't mask the deafening hiss.

"It worked," Jack said. "He's following the thrusters."

"I'm in trouble. Cracked face shield. Loosing air."

"Cover the crack with your glove and get moving. The Apollo crews found bouncing highly effective."

Pushing up, I stood. Pain flared in my right knee." Damn it. I screwed up my knee."

"Hop," Jack said. "It's just as fast."

Balancing on my left leg, I leaned forward, bent at the knee, and pushed off. Landing more than halfway up the slope, I pushed off a second time, clearing the crater. On the curvature of the horizon, I spotted the gleaming shelter. "That's a very long short walk," I mumbled. My chest burned after only a dozen hops. "I don't have ...enough air...to make it."

"Yes, you do. There's still air in your tank. The crack is bleeding off the pressure in your suit. It's the same as loosing cabin pressure in an aircraft."

"I can't...catch...my breath." Stumbling facedown into the lunar dust, I huffed into the blackness of my face shield. My breathing eased. "Jack! Compressing the crack into the dust slowed the leak. I don't hear the hiss anymore."

"Don't move," Jack said. "He's back. Check your rear helmet cam."

"My heads-up display's not working. What's he doing?"

"He seems to be...thinking? He looks down at you and then stares off at something...probably the shelter. He just keeps looking back and forth, as if he's trying to make sense of what you're doing. I'll try rebooting your video cards."

Several seconds later, the dragon's giant blue eye appeared in my heads-up display. His face grew small as his head reared back, revealing a mouth overflowing with teeth.

"No!" I screamed, pushing up. With bounding leaps, I moved toward the shelter, gasping harder with each jump. "Swimming...in syrup. I...can't...bre—"

~ * ~

"Nadia! Wake up! Nadia!"

"What?" I said, opening my eyes. Facedown in the dust, only stars were now visible in my heads-up display. "Jack?"

"Get inside," he said. "Now! You're technically out of air. Move!"

"It's too far. I just want to sleep."

"It's not too far. You're already there. Nadia! Wake up!"

"What?"

"Reach out...above your head. Pull yourself up on the hatch. Do it!"

"But—" I said, finding the structure within reach. I glanced up, got my bearings, and then reburied my face shield in the dust. Taking a deep breath, I pushed up, palmed the entry button, and tumbled inside. Standing, I fisted the "CLOSE" button and staggered back. I slid down the wall, gasping for air. The weight of my helmet seemed to double with each wheezing breath. Spotting the pressure indicator above the hatch, I yelled, "Come on!" I then pawed at the release of my helmet, knowing I'd soon blackout.

"The pressure's close enough," Jack said.

My helmet fell into my lap as the light above the hatch turned green. I huffed. "It…stinks…in here." Sprawling out on the deck, I mumbled, "Need…a minute."

~ * ~

I awoke, starring into my helmet cam.

"Welcome back," Jack said over the shelter's intercom.

"Hope I didn't snore," I said. "How long was I out?"

"Just over an hour," Jack said. "How do you feel?"

"Alive. And hungry."

"That's a good thing."

"Thanks, Jack. I would have died out there if not for you. I remember falling, but I *don't* remember getting up and hopping the rest of the way."

"That's because you didn't," Jack said. "Your boyfriend carried you…in his teeth."

I laughed. "Yeah, right."

"I'm not kidding," Jack said. "Take a look. He's right outside."

Rolling onto my belly, I crawled to the wall beneath the porthole. Slowly, I stood. My bluish-chrome dragon seemed to be grazing on the lunar landscape. Beyond him, twenty-one others of various metallic colors, nosed the dust and rocks as if searching for snacks.

"Are they…feeding?"

"Like cows in clover," Jack said. "We've yet to see any signs of aggression."

"I certainly saw some. That blue one fried Duncan."

"Might that have been an accident?"

"I don't see how. Duncan was standing right there, plan as day, in its…nest. Crap!"

"That's our theory, too. Your buddy thought he was protecting his siblings."

"*T5* had already crushed one of them," I said. "One of the eggs had collapsed, which was why *T5* was unstable. But why'd he burn our capsule?"

"Do you mean the capsule that might have looked like a hungry monster…with an enormous gaping mouth…and a claw, which happened to be stuffed inside one of their eggs?"

"That's the one," I mumbled. "And that's why he didn't torch me when I transferred to *T5*. He wasn't trying to hurt me. He was thawing out the rest of his brood."

"That's also what we pieced together from the videos we downloaded from the thrusters. By the way, the boss wants to talk with you when you get back. Something about that stunt you pulled the first time you transferred to *T5*."

"I knew I'd get spanked for that one. What's my big blue friend eating out there? Dust?"

"They seem to be eating select rocks. It's hard to tell for certain from here, but spectrometers on Earth are detecting an increase in free olivine, so we think they might be foraging for that. If that's what they need, they went to the right place. The moon's full of it."

My dragon nuzzled a small boulder out of the lunar dust. Scooping it up with thin dexterous lips, he crushed the stone in his jaws. Errant bits of debris clattered against the shelter's hull.

"Easy, big boy," I said.

The dragon turned, stared at the shelter. Seeing me in the window, he snorted. Green vapors curled from his nostrils. He shook his head and resumed foraging.

"Nadia, meet Julius," Jack said. "We named him while you were asleep. But he's your boyfriend, so feel free to give him any name you'd like."

I couldn't take my eyes off him. "Julius is perfect," I said. "Jack, where do you think these guys came from? I mean…what are they doing way out here?"

"*That* we'll never know," Jack said.

"Oh…I don't know about that. I have a few months to kill. Maybe Julius can teach me how to speak…dragonese or something. He seems intelligent enough."

"Good luck with that."

"I'm serious. Did you notice how he reacted to my first transmission from *T5*?"

"We did. He seemed to hear you. The comm team is reviewing those videos now. They'll need a few days to generate some theories, but I suspect they'll want you to run some tests."

"That's what I was thinking. Is there a spare transmitter up here? One I can tinker with?"

"Several," Jack said. "But even if you do figure out how to talk to those creatures, they're newborns. They won't know where they came from."

"I guess that's true…if they *are* newborns. But maybe those *weren't* eggs. Maybe they were a form of spaceship or capsule. Or…maybe they're newborns that retain the memories of their parents. Anything's possible. Hell, I'm still alive…on the moon…with dragons. I guess it's just my lucky day," I mumbled.

"Maybe so, but apparently just on the moon," Jack said. "Someone trashed your front lawn last night."

I laughed. "And how would you know that?"

"I live three doors down from you."

"No shit? You're the guy that drives that silver Porsche?"

"I *was* the guy," Jack said. "Now my ex-wife's boyfriend drives it. She got it last week in the divorce."

"Sorry to hear that," I said. "I really liked that car. It would've looked good on me."

Jack laughed. "It certainly would have. I guess I'll have to look around for another one. What's your favorite color?"

Julius raised his head, gazed at me. I smiled and said, "Metallic blue."

The Yellow Sea (44 BC

An arrow found the last male's heart. The young man's aim had been true and his arrowhead keen, but only fate could have guided the tip to the old wound where the scale had not fully regrown. Thinking of the female and their unborn brood, the male returned to the depths where their kind had prospered for thousands of years. But they were the last and could no longer survive on Earth. The journey would be treacherous, and she might not survive, yet the male urged the female to return to the home of their ancestors. In the cold embrace of deep space, their unborn could endure all but eternity. So as she rose in flames from the Bohai Sea, the male spread his wings and lay back in the gently rolling waters. With tears in his eyes, he watched her blaze skyward, until his pierced and broken heart fell silent.

~ * ~

"The heavens themselves blaze forth the death of princes."

William Shakespeare, *Julius Caesar* (1599 AD)

~ * ~ * ~

Laurance H. Davis is the author of two science-fiction novels, *Outpost Earth* and *Planet Nine*, which were published by Double Dragon Publishing in the spring of 2017. Laurance's third novel, *The Race,* a women's historical fiction, was published by Hoffman & Hoffman in the summer of 2017. *The Race* is the second novel in the *That Boyce Girl* series, the first having been written in 1939 by his great uncle, R. H. Davis. Laurance self-published the third novel in the series, the *Murder of Miss Shelby Putnam,* which is a sleuth-style mystery. His post-apocalyptic short story, *Shoot Him Daddy*, was published in Metasaga's anthology, *Futuristica Vol. 1* in 2016.

He won the 2018 *Teleport Science Fiction Contest* with his short story *Domain of the Dragon.* His short story, *Girl Meets Robot*, was published in 2019 in Dreaming Robot's *Young Explorer's Adventure Guide, Volume 6.*

Before becoming a writer, Laurance worked as a mechanical engineer specializing in robotics. He holds multiple U.S. patents.

Meal Ticket

Gregg Chamberlain

"Tell me again," the Dragon said, "how this is going to work?"

"Fine," the Princess said with a sigh. "I'll explain it again just once more. It's very simple, really."

Hmph! the Dragon thought, reaching back with a forepaw to rub at one of her hindlegs. *Simple, my arthritic wing and hip joints!*

"I stay with you as your captive princess." The Princess began counting off well-manicured fingers one by one. "Heroes come to rescue me. They fight you. The winner proves he is my one real true love. We ride off to live happily ever after."

"Mmmhmm." The Dragon scratched an itchy patch of scale and hoped it wasn't a sign of senility shedding. *Oh, please,* she thought, *not at my age.*

The Princess stared. One velvet-slippered foot tapped with undisguised impatience. The Dragon ceased her scratching and grunted as she flexed her wings slightly. "And I get to eat the losers, right?"

"Well, I suppose, yes, they would be losers after all, wouldn't they?" An index finger, glossy with crimson nail lacquer, tapped lightly against a pouting lower lip. "Not really worthy of a princess after all, wouldn't you agree?"

The Dragon considered. *I'm getting too old,* she thought, *to go hunting and then having to risk my neck, or at least my tail, arguing over a kill with some younger, and stronger, dragon hothead poacher. And what are the odds a real champion will show up right away? And, best-case scenario, if nobody shows up any time soon to claim Miss-Look-At-Me-I-Am-A-Troll-Stupid-Princess, I can always eat her. Worst case, I give her a week to get on my last nerve and then I still get to eat her. It's a win-win, either way as far as I'm concerned.*

"Alright," the Dragon said. Thick smoke gushed from her nostrils. "I agree."

The Princess coughed. "Wonderful!" She waved away the smoke with both hands. "Do you always do that?"

"I'm a dragon." The Dragon snorted smoke again. "It's what

we do."

"Yes, well." The Princess crossed her arms over her silk-and-satin-clad breast. "We'll just need to set some living condition guide-lines then, won't we, for while we're staying together."

The Dragon sighed. *The things I have to put up with*, she thought, *just to have something to eat. If I was just five or six decades younger now, oh, wouldn't things be different then.*

The Princess brushed past the Dragon, heading towards the other's cave. The Dragon watched her march along, the round bottom of her peach-blossom gown swinging imperiously from side to side.

Hmmm, the Dragon mused. *As lunatic ideas go, this mad scheme might be just crazy enough to work. The best thing about it is that just about any princess would work as bait.*

Slitted eyes sized up the oblivious Princess. *Wouldn't even need to be a real princess*, the Dragon pondered. *Any human female able to fit into those clothes would do. A knight who is stupid enough to go hunting dragons isn't likely to think too hard about the pedigree of the damsel in distress he's trying to rescue.*

"Oh. My. Lord!" The Princess stumbled back out of the cave, one hand waving frantically in front of her face. "It reeks in there! I expected a dragon's cave to be smoky. But—phee-ew—that stench is just absolutely foul!" She crossed both arms over her breast. "I'm not staying in there until you've aired the place out."

The Dragon heaved a sigh. "Might not even last a week," she muttered to herself, turning about and making her way to her cave. "Maybe I should get started on a candidates list now?"

"What was that?" A regal foot tapped again with unrestrained impatience as the Princess watched the Dragon's slow approach.

"Nothing," the Dragon said with a huff. "I was just thinking out loud."

"Hmmph! Well, don't dawdle! I'd like to get settled before nightfall." She glanced down at her folded hands, frowning as she noticed a slight smudging on her fingertips. "And I'll need hot and cold water for bathing."

The Dragon glanced aside at the Princess as she slithered past the other and slid inside the cave.

May not even last until tomorrow morning, the Dragon mused. *Wonder how she'd taste lightly smoked?*

~ * ~ * ~

Gregg Chamberlain lives in rural Ontario, Canada, with his missus, Anne, and their two cats, who regard all dragons as wuss-pusses. He writes speculative fiction for fun and has several dozen examples of his fun in venues that include Daily Science Fiction, Mythic, Weirdbook and other magazines, and various anthologies.

Dragon Life

or

How Fajrigulo Avoided Having a Wife

Barbara G. Tarn

It is a truth universally acknowledged, that a single dragon in possession of a good hoard must be in want of a wife. At least for his mother, nothing is accomplished until he settles in his own lair with a female. Not alone, since that's a disgraceful state. He's supposed to find a wife as soon as possible.

Fajrigulo didn't want a wife. He didn't want to share his hoard with anyone. His mother still bemoaned the fact he was the only one of her hatchlings who hadn't "settled" yet. He'd been called "greedy beast" or "grumpy male", but he didn't care. As long as nobody touched his treasure, neatly stashed in his lair.

It had taken him time to find the right cavern of the right size where he had started to gather his collection. He loved how the sun came in from the entrance and brushed the raw earth, never reaching the corners where he put his treasures.

When he wasn't out feeding, he spent the time polishing his hoard—gems, jewels, weapons (magic or not), books big and small—and methodically putting everything back afterward. He was a very neat dragon and didn't like having a messy lair.

He certainly didn't need a female dragon to keep his hoard clean. He actually thought she would be a hindrance to his method of stashing. She'd want to move things around and be in charge… no, no, he was better off by himself.

And just imagine if she happened to lay some eggs! All those hatchlings toying with his hoard? The simple thought made him growl low in his throat. He really didn't need or want company. Unless he found a female with a hoard bigger than his, of course. But in his two centuries of life, it hadn't happened yet.

And then one day his glorious solitude was disturbed by a querulous human voice at the entrance of his lair.

"Hello? Anybody home?"

Fajrigulo raised his horned head and turned his pointed ears, trying to catch more sounds. A slight tingle, as if someone was wearing heavy metal clothes. The voice was young but definitely male. Not another young knight in search of adventure!

Fajrigulo grumbled and turned so he faced the entrance. He glanced at the fourteen human skeletons amassed in a heap on the side and wondered if he'd have to add to that. Although before killing the stupid human, he could probably add things to his collection.

He opened his bat-like wings so he'd cover the sight of his treasure from the newcomer. He noticed his pale belly was getting plumper, but he didn't really care. He still had the most glorious emerald-green scales on the rest of his body.

He towered inside the cave and crossed his short front limbs on his belly as he sat on his hind legs. Keeping the wings spread wasn't hard, but he better not lay on them or it would become painful.

The long shadow of the human became a small young man who barely reached his knee and gaped at the sight of him.

Fajrigulo snorted, white smoke coming out of his nostrils.

"Well?" he asked, showing his fangs.

"I-I'm sorry," the young knight stammered, dropping his sword and his shield that clanged to the ground. "I wasn't expecting someone so big!"

"What were you expecting?" he asked, amused.

"Well…" The knight huffed and took off his helm. He was very young indeed, with no trace of facial hair and bright blue eyes. He seemed to be sweating a lot in his silvery armor. "I don't know," he admitted frustrated. "You know when they tell you *just go* and don't bother explaining anything? Just go and slay a dragon! Just go and conquer a princess! Just go and do it! I mean, I would have appreciated some advice, you know?"

"So who sends you?" Fajrigulo asked, feeling sympathy for the young man who clearly didn't want to follow tradition any more than he did.

"My father." The knight rolled his eyes and shook his head. "He said I'm twenty-five and should go looking for a bride. And King Richard said he'd give me his daughter's hand only if I bring him a dragon head."

Fajrigulo sniggered.

"What?" the knight protested, outraged.

"I know of a king who does give his daughter's hand—just the hand—to prospective sons-in-law. Unless you want a one-handed princess, you better give up any king's daughter."

The knight gaped at him, then realized what it meant.

"You mean?"

"Yes."

"Oh, that's gross!"

"Yes."

And then both burst out laughing.

The knight sat on the raw earth and Fajrigulo relaxed, closing his wings and crouching to see his visitor from up close.

"I didn't know dragons could talk," the knight said, taking off his armor piece by piece.

Fajrigulo snorted. "You don't seem to know much about dragons, young man!"

"True." The knight grinned. "I'm Prince Leonard, by the way. Do you have a name?"

"Fajrigulo. So you're looking for a bride?"

"Actually, my father kicked me out of the castle and told me to go looking for a bride. But now that I found you, I could just stay here and never come back. He'll assume I'm dead and won't bother me again." He stared hopefully at Fajrigulo.

"Why would you want to stay here?" Fajrigulo showed his fangs again.

"Because I don't want to get married," Prince Leonard answered. "Do you dragons have to get married?"

"Actually, we do. I'm supposed to find a wife and settle with a family of little dragons. No way I'm ever going to do it, though."

"Me neither! But I don't have a place where I can live, can I stay here with you? You can have my horse for dinner if you want!"

"I don't eat horses. I'm quite fond of them."

"Good, because so am I! I could tell you plenty of jokes and make you laugh…"

"I don't want company!" Fajrigulo roared, exasperated. "Get out of here, puny human!"

"Please? Fajrigulo?"

The prince was on his knees with his hands clasped in prayer and didn't look scared anymore. He even managed to say the dragon's name without stammering or mispronouncing it. Fajrigulo paused, studying the human.

Prince Leonard wasn't a common human. He was different from those haughty knights who had tried to get his head and his hoard to earn some stupid princess's hand.

Fajrigulo narrowed his eyes and almost bumped the young man's shoulder.

"I'm not too fond of humans. How about I eat you?"

"If you must. But you'd miss on something. Why don't you try my companionship?"

Fajrigulo pulled his head away, arching his long neck.

"You can read, I assume?"

"Yes, of course."

"Then you can read me this, one tale a day, and then you must leave." He pushed a very large book towards Prince Leonard who gasped at the sight.

The knight jumped to his feet and grabbed the heavy leather cover, managing to open the book. He had to climb on it to get to the first page and to stand to be able to read the big words under his feet.

"This will take some effort, but it's worth it," he said after reading the title aloud. "So, where can I put my armor and weapons?"

~ * ~

Fajrigulo could read as well as Prince Leonard, but he didn't mind listening to his guest while he kept polishing his treasure. The prince went hunting and insisted on having cooked meat, so Fajrigulo breathed fire and burned his meager dinner while the knight was still trying to start a fire.

"You're mean!" Prince Leonard protested while he chuckled. "Not everyone can eat raw meat!"

"Sorry, sorry!" Fajrigulo composed himself. "Get more wood and you can cook some of mine."

He pushed what was left of his deer and Prince Leonard scowled but nodded.

Night fell on them and Fajrigulo felt the human toss and turn until late. Naturally Prince Leonard was asleep when the sun came up, so Fajrigulo went to feed, then curled up outside the cave until he heard movement inside.

When the prince came out, Fajrigulo smelled his things on

the young man. "And where are you going, Prince Leonard?" he asked, his yellow eyes staring intently at the young man.

He heard the prince's horse neigh in panic. It was tied to a tree nearby, out of sight of its owner.

"I guess I should probably go back," Prince Leonard answered with a shrug. "You don't like company and I miss my bed. I'm a spoiled prince and sleeping on the ground was tougher than I expected."

"Mm, I see. Aren't you taking something with you, you weren't supposed to touch?" The dragon's muzzle touched the prince's chest and his nostrils inhaled. "Are you stealing from my hoard, Prince Leonard?"

"No, I mean, not stealing, asking!" Prince Leonard pulled out a piece of jewelry—a medallion very similar to the one around his neck—and a small pale blue ring. "These belong to my brother, Brandon. He's the heir. If I go back with these, my father will make me the heir."

"And won't he ask you for the head of the dragon who killed your brother?" Fajrigulo asked with a fanged smirk.

"I'll make sure he won't. Unless he wants to lose his last heir, that is. Come on, Fajrigulo, you can't use them and it would really help me!"

The dragon's long neck pulled back. The huge body didn't move, trapping the prince at the cave entrance.

"So, you don't want to get married, but you want to inherit your father's castle?" Fajrigulo asked.

Prince Leonard blushed.

"Actually, I do want to marry…my brother's betrothed. So thank you for killing him, now can I go back with the proof of his death and take his place by my father and Isabel's side?"

Fajrigulo erupted in a roaring laughter, then bared his fangs again.

"And what will you give me in return? You're taking away two things; you should leave four in payment."

"Four? That's outrageous!"

"Then you're not leaving alive."

"All right, all right, let me see…" Prince Leonard checked his purse. "I have four gold coins, would that do?"

"You have more than four." Fajrigulo could count by the

sound of the jingling purse. "Leave your purse and you can go."

"Fine." Leonard sighed and threw his purse in front of the dragon. "May I leave now?"

Fajrigulo took the purse in his teeth and rose. He majestically headed for the cave on all four, closing his bat-like wings. He put down the purse and turned around.

There was the stupid prince thinking he had made it. Fajrigulo had thought Prince Leonard was different, but obviously he was just like the other knights who either wanted to rob him or kill him.

Fajrigulo smirked. He watched the human mount his horse and head for the forest. He wouldn't go far. Not with the loot.

Fajrigulo exited the cave and flapped his wings. He took off and flew over the forest, looking for last night's guest.

There he was. Fajrigulo plunged and his talons grabbed Prince Leonard by the shoulders. The knight screamed in fear and he dumped the human on a rocky slope unceremoniously.

"Oops. You fell from your horse..." Fajrigulo sniggered as the horse neighed and galloped away.

He glided near Prince Leonard and took whatever he could from the bloodied corpse.

"Pity, you were kind of nice," he muttered as the blue eyes of the prince stared into space, wide open in death.

He took off again and went back to the cave to put back the loot. He entered the cool cave and sat down, watching his beloved hoard. He opened the huge book that was actually *his* Book of Tales and took a large eagle feather that still looked very small in his claws. He wished he could find someone to make him a stylus that wouldn't break, so he could write more.

He made his own ink with blood and lemon juice to make it more liquid. The blood usually came from his victims or his food— he primarily fed on boars, but smaller animals also filled his belly when he wasn't starving—and he had found a lemon tree in an orchard at the limits of the forest.

He usually went there after sunset and was back in his lair before dawn. The farmers never seemed to notice the missing lemons and he never ran out of ink. His book of tales had brown writing on the thick parchment pages, but Prince Leonard had probably attributed it to being an old manuscript.

Which it was. He dipped the tip of the feather in the ink-pot he had made out of a small pottery and spread the parchment with a clawed hand. He had only four fingers, but one could be used like a human thumb to hold the feather and write.

He added the entry of the latest visit as if it were an adventure story told by the point of view of a human, like the one Prince Leonard had read the night before. He was still quite proud of that first story he'd written a century ago, adding demons and mercenaries to a real story.

He liked writing stories, putting in them whatever he had heard or read somewhere during his long life. He wondered what people would think when they found his Book of Tales. But then, considering what people thought of dragons in general...

His peers themselves couldn't appreciate a good book, even though they all loved stories. But dragons were more into oral tradition than writing and reading. When he'd been younger, Fajrigulo had even composed poetry, but after a female dragon he fancied had laughed in his face, he had stopped showing it or telling anyone about his hobby.

He put the eagle feather back in the ink-pot and closed the leather cover with a sigh and lay down with his muzzle facing the cave entrance, inhaling the scents of the forest. Soon it would be autumn and maybe the she-bear would come back to hibernate in a corner of his cave.

He didn't mind the company of bears, since they weren't interested in his hoard and they had behaviors very similar to dragons. Not to mention the fact they sought shelter in his cavern during winter, when they were mostly fast asleep. Excellent companions indeed, although the females ended up with a cub or two in the spring.

But the lively little buggers weren't as bad as a litter of dragon cubs. And they soon left with their mother for the forest, leaving him to his solitary existence. If only humans were as smart!

A solitary deer passed in the clearing and stared fearful at him, but he didn't move. Those antlers looked quite fearsome and he didn't want to scratch his belly on them—his scaly hide wouldn't be hurt, but his belly was another story.

A sun ray caressed his muzzle and he dozed off in the warmth of the cave.

~ * ~

Fajrigulo glided over the small mountain lake and landed on the shore. Time for a bath and a good drink. He could have dived from the air, but he preferred walking slowly into the water. He wasn't a water dragon and his wings didn't allow him to swim that much.

When he felt clean and had drunk his fill, he headed back for the shore, shaking off the water from his glittering green scales. He liked how the sun reflected on them, making him look quite handsome.

Heh. He was a good breeding male, pity he had better things to do than mating! Why dragons had decided to copy humans by marrying was beyond him. They weren't monogamous like wolves, they were like bears, for Fire's sake!

Fajrigulo took flight again and headed back for his lair. He stopped to grab a fat boar and took it to his cave, where he quickly disposed of it, eating it raw and throwing the bones out into the clearing. Smaller scavengers would take care of them.

He opened the Book of Tales and started pondering about a new story—maybe a nymph or a mermaid? —when he heard some-one exclaim in disgust at the remnants of the boar in the clearing. Sighing, Fajrigulo put away the book and rose to check.

Another human. Drat. But this one didn't seem to want in. Fajrigulo pushed his long neck towards the entrance and saw a brown-clothed, tonsured old man who gasped when he saw him.

The newcomer wasn't a knight, but a religious man from his looks. With a walking stick and a big leather bag that contained books.

"Saint George protect me!" the man said, making a sign of a cross in the air.

"What's with this Saint George people keep invoking?" Fajrigulo snapped.

"Don't you know?" the man sounded indignant. "He's the dragon-slayer of legends!"

Fajrigulo snorted. "Never heard of him. And you are?"

"Friar Matthew." The man frowned. "How come you speak?"

"Because dragons are not just dumb animals?" he answered, not bothering to hide his sarcasm. "What's in those books you carry?"

The friar looked surprised and put a hand on his bag as if to protect it.

"Ah, uh…well…I have my book of prayers and some…um …less canon books from non-religious people…I'm a copyist and sometimes when I find something I like, I copy it for myself."

"Nice! Come on in, let's share stories!"

Fajrigulo couldn't believe he had just invited a puny human inside his lair. But then, Friar Matthew was a man of religion, not of war. He may be armed, but only with a tiny knife he probably used to cut food. And his beliefs probably didn't allow him to own anything precious, therefore he wouldn't try to steal anything.

"So you are a member of which congregation?" he asked, crouching in his usual corner as the man hesitantly stepped in the cavern, looking around warily. "Do you need to get married? What does your god teach?"

Surprise crossed the man's face again. "Well, I'll be damned! I guess I will jump at this occasion of bringing a fiery dragon to the one true God!"

He sat on the raw earth like Prince Leonard had done and started taking out books and parchment from his travel bag, readying for his lesson.

Fajrigulo smirked. He wasn't going to convert to any human religion that called him an animal and praised knights who hunted and killed his kind. But Friar Matthew was quite nice. He spoke much better than Prince Leonard and knew a lot more tales.

While the friar drank from his flask after talking for a long time almost without a pause, Fajrigulo pulled out his book again. He needed to take notes. Some concepts were really fascinating.

He took the feather and the ink and started jotting down things, then realized the friar had come closer and was watching him with eyes wide in wonder.

"You…can write?" Friar Matthew asked, amazed.

"I can read also," he retorted. "Keep telling, I'm noting down the most interesting things."

"Is that your own notebook?" Friar Matthew asked, excited. "We could compare notes!"

"Why? You'd listen to a dragon's story?" Suddenly he was so nervous he broke the feather. Darn. It had taken him so long to find one that worked for him!

"You broke your pen!" Friar Matthew dropped his book and took the broken feather, looking distraught. "I'll make you another stylus!" he promised then, beaming again. "Just wait until I find something that fits that big hand of yours!"

He rushed outside quite fast for a man not in his prime anymore. Puzzled, Fajrigulo waited, flipping through the pages of the book the friar had dropped. Strange ancient language. He thought humans didn't use that anymore!

Friar Matthew rushed back in with a small, straight branch in his hand and gave it to Fajrigulo.

"There you go! I'll make more if this works properly!"

Fajrigulo took it and looked at it closely. The friar had worked one side of the branch so it had some kind of point, like a quill or the broken feather. Fajrigulo dipped it into his ink-pot and tried to write.

"It actually works better than the feather!" he said, delighted. "And it's even more comfortable to hold! Thank you, Friar Matthew! I was reading your book and…"

"You read Latin?" the friar marveled.

"I thought humans had stopped using that language, but I was obviously mistaken." Fajrigulo shrugged.

Friar Matthew gaped at him, then snapped back to reality. "Well, let's continue our most interesting discussion, then," he said, sitting down again and taking the small book. "Did you have any questions?"

~ * ~

Time flies when you're in good company. The old friar was still very curious about the world and Fajrigulo was amazed at his knowledge. They spent hours talking, sometimes forgetting to eat and comparing notes and stories on their personal booklets.

Friar Matthew had left his monastery because he'd felt confined among those walls. He'd been traveling for a good part of ten years and was tired now. Climbing the mountains where Fajrigulo lived had been particularly painful.

"I don't think I'll ever see another human again, my friend," he said one night, huddling by the fire Fajrigulo had lit for him. He seemed to be always cold and kept shivering in his brown vestment.

"But then, it was an honor to meet you."

"Is there anything I can do to ease your discomfort?" Fajrigulo asked, worried for the first time in his long life.

"Alas, my friend, there's no cure for old age." Friar Matthew sighed. "When I set out on my quest, I didn't know what I was actually looking for, but I think I found it. A nice place to die in peace with a good friend by my side."

"Don't talk about death in front of me." Fajrigulo growled. "You know the stories of those fourteen skeletons!"

"And I know I won't be killed by you, but if my time comes, please reduce me to ashes and let me fly in the wind," Friar Matthew replied. "Don't let me lie next to them."

Fajrigulo looked away, unhappy. He didn't want to lose the only person who seemed to think like him. A human who hadn't married and collected knowledge instead of treasures or adventures.

He thought Friar Matthew ate too little. Only herbs and berries and no meat. No wonder one day the friar didn't wake up.

Fajrigulo screamed in frustration, a roar that echoed through the peaks, then muttered to himself, "Reduce him to ashes and let him fly into the wind. How am I going to do that?"

He decided to take his human friend outside of the cave. It was a windy day and if he wasn't careful, he'd set the whole forest on fire, losing his cover.

He delicately grabbed the friar with his powerful jaws and dropped him at the cave entrance. He stepped over him and turned around in the cleaning, staring one last time at the peaceful eternal sleep of Friar Matthew.

Then he took in a deep breath and shot fire that engulfed the man's body. It was quickly consumed and Fajrigulo used his tail to move the stash of cinder out of the way. The simple movement made the ashes fly off and soon all traces of Friar Matthew were gone.

"Murderer!" The high-pitched scream startled him. "You killed an innocent friar!"

"Actually, he was already dead," he grumbled, looking around through the trees. "I granted his last wish. Where are you, child?"

"I'm not a child!" From behind a large oak emerged a tall blonde with a pink dress and a little crown on her head. She stomped towards him and scowled at him. "I'm Princess Isabel and

I saw you burn the poor man!"

"He was dead." Fajrigulo rolled his eyes. "He was old and died in his sleep! Why would I kill my only human friend?"

"The friar was your friend?" she asked, staring suspiciously at him.

"Yes, as a matter of fact we enjoyed each other's company quite a lot," he retorted. "Now what do *you* want?"

"I've come to look for two valiant brothers. The younger's horse came back alone, so I took it and was brought here." She crossed her arms over her bosom and challenged him with her chin high.

"Oh, my." He sniggered. "Would that be Prince Leonard and his brother Brandon?"

"Yes! Them! What did you do to them, you ugly beast?"

"Hey, lady, will you tone down the insults? They came here to kill me, what was I supposed to do? I call it self-defense!"

"I call it murder!" she screamed. "And you shall pay for it!" She stormed off.

"Yeah, yeah, whatever…" he muttered.

He headed back inside the cavern and curled up in his usual corner, saddened by the loss of Friar Matthew. Pieces of their lively conversations came back to him, and he closed his eyes, dozing off.

~ * ~

Soaring pain awoke him. He couldn't open his right eye, since something had stabbed it deeply. He roared and broke whatever was planted in his poor eye on the cave wall, then focused his left eye on the little blonde princess who was laughing madly.

"You will die, you bastard dragon, my dragon lance pierced your tiny brain, and I will take your head back in triumph!"

"And where is the mighty sword that will allow you to cut it off?" he replied, trying to shake out what was left of the lance that had indeed sunk into his eye, but definitely not touched his brain.

"Ha! I'll find something! As soon as you crumble lifeless…"

"After you, my lady," he roared.

He took a deep breath and shot his fiery breath at her. Her screams as her pink dress and hair took fire were deafening. She turned to run out of the cave, and he blocked her, pinning her to the ground with his front paw.

"No, you're not going to burn the whole forest, you stupid princess," he growled, watching her burn to death.

When she was finally still, he pushed her charred remains to keep company with the skeletons and tried again to take the piece of lance out of his eye. It came out, but his eye was damaged for good.

He slowly went out and with his impaired vision tried to find herbs that could ease his pain. Walking shakily through the trees, he reached a stream where he washed his wound and finally found some moss that would help healing.

He returned to his lair and sat down, sniffling, as he put the moss over his ruined eyeball and eyelid. The pain was slowly subsiding. He wondered what Friar Matthew would have said of Princess Isabel's attack.

~ * ~

A few days later, while he was still adjusting to the new, impaired eyesight, his mother decided to pay him a visit. Mostly because with Friar Matthew he'd forgotten to go and see her, so she was worried.

Her scales were of a darker green because she was so much older, and her huge form barely passed through the entrance opening.

"Faj, what happened to you?" she asked, shocked, seeing his dead eye. "One of those pesky humans took out your eye?"

"Actually, it was a female," he answered with a shrug.

"A female! My oh my, what's becoming of us if females start hurting males?" his mother complained.

Fajrigulo was about to correct her but stopped. It was his mother who had assumed he was talking about a female dragon. Let her think that way. Maybe she'd relent with her marriage suggestions.

"And a handsome male like you! Who is that bitch?" She bared her teeth, ready to punish whoever had dared hurt her boy.

"I already punished her, Mother," he answered, looking away. "But now you know why I don't want females in my life. Too much trouble."

His mother's eyes narrowed. "Would that include me?" she asked.

"Let's just say; if you hadn't been pressing me into finding a suitable bride to share my hoard with, maybe I'd still have two eyes," he answered. "Not every single dragon in possession of a good hoard is in want of a wife."

His mother looked daggers at him. "Fine. I see I'm not welcome anymore. I shall leave you to your own devices. Try to not lose the other eye!"

"I won't let another female near me," he promised as she turned around and left with as much dignity as she could muster.

He waited until he saw her shadow leave the clearing, then sniggered. Finally. Maybe now he'd be able to enjoy his hoard alone.

Whistling to himself, he went back to polish Princess Isabel's golden crown before putting it back on the stash.

~ * ~ * ~

Barbara G. Tarn had an intense life in the Middle Ages that stuck to her through the centuries. She prefers swords to guns, long gowns to mini-skirts, and even though she buried the warrior woman, she deplores the death of knights in shining chainmail. She likes to think her condo apartment is a medieval castle, unfortunately lacking a dungeon to throw noisy neighbors and naughty colleagues in. Also known as the Lady with the Unicorns, these days she prefers to add a touch of fantasy to all her stories, past and present—when she's not wandering on her fantasy world of Silvery Earth or in her science fantasy Star Minds Universe. She dabbles into historical fantasy with her Vampires Through the Centuries series and post-apocalyptic/steampunk in the series called Future Earth Chronicles.

She's a writer, sometimes artist, mostly a world-creator and story-teller. She writes, draws, ignores her day job and blogs at: https://creativebarbwire.wordpress.com.

A Thread of Adventure

Sally Jo

Sheila Fairspotter's mother had told her a million and one times to fix the loose thread at the bottom of her jacket. Sheila had thought nothing of it—after all, it was the job of mothers (or parents in general, it was just that Sheila only had the one and she happened to be a mother) to nag their daughters (or children in general, it was just that Sheila had realized many a year ago she was a girl) to fix their clothing. And it was the job of daughters (or maybe not all daughters, but certainly this one) to ignore their mother's warnings and go about forever (or at least until they were fully grown) dressed in straggly clothing.

Besides, Sheila thought, it was a cute little loose thread—what harm could it do?

Now, as she blinked at the enormous piles of treasure surrounding her, and she heard the bone-rattling roar of a very, very angry dragon, she realized exactly how much harm that little thread had caused. And in the blink of an eye, no less. She was meant to be at her grandma's aunt's nephew's half-sister's adopted daughter's fourteenth birthday party, not in the cavernous (yet sauna-like) home of a raging dragon.

That morning, Sheila had dressed in her finest party clothes—a blue and silver skirt-of-many-pieces over black leggings with a powdery green wrap-around top. The outfit made her feel extremely fairy-like, and she was ready to dance the next few days away. It was a little chilly outside though, so she'd shrugged on her battered old coat (with the seemingly innocuous loose thread at the bottom) and skipped off to the nearest 7-League Boot Booth.

Her mother had offered to bring Sheila along in the transport spell that would carry the entire family along to Welling's Hallow, where the party was being held, but Sheila (who was obsessed with all the latest magical inventions and was the proud owner of a subscription to Magi-U Weekly, the hottest teen-magic-magazine around) wanted to go via Boot Booth. So she told her mother transport spells had been making her feel sick lately. It was a flimsy excuse, but her mother (who had been obsessed with all the latest magical inventions when *she* was young) accepted it.

So off Sheila had skipped.

To be honest, Sheila hadn't been much impressed when she arrived at the nearest 7-League Boot Booth. Tall, thin, and made of some sort of black material, it sat on a nondescript roadside on the edge of town, looking nothing like the glamorous, glittering booths she'd seen in the two-page, color spread last week that included closeups of celebrities like Muncher the Vampire and Three-Howl Fendin (the werewolf, not the selkie) posing playfully within and around the boxes. The sleepy troll sitting next to the booth was also a far-cry from the sparkling uni-fey attendants shown in the magazine spread.

Still, Sheila had put on a smile and told herself that at least if it didn't *look* like the magazine, it would still do what it was supposed to.

When Sheila explained she wanted to go to Welling's Hallow and produced a silver drop, the troll grunted, scratched its scraggly ear, and pulled a contraption from beneath its seat. Sheila knew from the magazine this was a new tech-wiz gizmo, created specifi- cally for the booth operators to calculate which direction a traveler should face within the booth, and how much Essence of Boot to paint on the bottom of the traveler's foot.

After a few quick button punches, the troll grunted again, scratched its other ear, and took what looked like a paint can and brush from behind its chair. Sheila was motioned through the front flap of the booth. There wasn't enough space inside for both her and the troll to fit, so the troll directed her with flicks of its stubby fingers, positioning her exactly above two glowing footprints on the ground then rotating her two clicks to the right.

Then came a few grunted instructions—Sheila was to lift her right foot for a moment. The troll would paint the bottom of her foot with the Essence of Boot it held in the paint can (the company behind the 7-League Boot Booths was adamant that no 7-League Boots had been harmed in the making of the Essence; they had merely been thoroughly examined, studied, and released back to the wild). Then, Sheila was to take one normal step forward. She would find herself in the 7-League Boot Booth just outside Welling's Hallow.

As Sheila raised her foot, she wondered what would happen

if another of her relatives (for there were Fairspotters in most corners of the world) decided to use a boot booth to get to the party. She opened her mouth to ask, but the troll had already painted her foot and shut the door flap, leaving Sheila in darkness that was softly illuminated by the footprints beneath her. Hoping for the best, she went to step forward and instead found herself tugged back and to the side by a pressure from the bottom of her coat. In the second before her foot landed (in a spot that was definitely not where she was supposed to have stepped), she glanced back and saw, with much chagrin, the loose thread from the bottom of her coat had gotten caught in the front flap of the booth.

Then a blink, a brief popping sensation, and Sheila found herself on the side of a crumbling cliff overlooking the sea. She stumbled to the side, her right foot taking half a step. Either the Essence of Boot was stronger than expected, or the troll had painted too much on her foot, because she felt that brief popping sensation once more, and thus found herself in a dragon's lair. She did try to take another step, thinking to at least escape the cavern, but apparently the Essence of Boot was now fully gone, worn away with the last fateful half step that had brought her here, among gold and jewels and trophies that gleamed in the torchlight and sweated in the humidity.

Another jaw-popping roar echoed throughout the cavern, and now Sheila felt the ground trembling beneath her. She did think to hide, but there was really nowhere to go. She only slipped and slid when she tried to climb around one of the piles. So instead she stood in place, disappointed but accepting that this was how her short life would end.

The pile in front of her burst apart, Sheila's raised hand doing nothing to stop the coins from peppering her as a behemoth of a dragon reared up before her. The dragon's scales were the most beautiful shades of deep green and blue, fading into black around its joints. The majestic creature flared wings of shimmering ruby (which, not that it particularly mattered in these last few moments before her death, told Sheila this was a male dragon—everyone knew the females had gold-drenched wings) before dropping to its forelegs and snapping its jaw in front of Sheila, who reasoned that as she was going to die, at least it would be for the sake of feeding such a gorgeous being. She closed her eyes, clasped her hands in front of her, and—

"Fairspotter?"

Sheila cracked an eye open. The dragon had retreated onto his hind quarters, his slimmer forelegs now crossed in front of his chest. If Sheila had been more familiar with draconic expressions, she would have recognized the annoyance held in the snarling face. But she wasn't, so she didn't. Instead, she saw only gleaming white teeth and flashing black eyes and wondered why she hadn't been eaten yet.

"You're a Fairspotter, aren't you?" the rumbling voice came again, and now Sheila opened her other eye.

"Oh, aye, I mean, yes, yes I am." Sheila didn't have to ask how he knew—the Fairspotters (who lived, as mentioned before, in most of the corners of the world) all shared three distinctive features: hair that looked like waves in the moonlight, a nose that curled into a spiral, and one ear that was far too short for the size of their heads (though exactly which ear was a topic fiercely debated at nearly every family dinner). Sheila, of course, shared those features. If the dragon had recognized her as a Fairspotter, at least one of her relatives must have crossed his path before.

Now, the dragon growled. "Would that you weren't a Fairspotter—I haven't eaten in a week because of a bad case of the firegrumbles. I was just about to go hunting when you showed up." He leaned forward, the scales on his bulbous snout reflecting the dancing torches. "How did you manage to show up in the middle of my caves, anyway?"

"I...I mis-stepped from a 7-League Boot Booth."

He snarled. "I knew no good would come from those winds-cursed contraptions. I thought my strongly worded letter to the business council would have put a stop to such tomfoolery, but I see my advice was ignored."

"If you please," Sheila rubbed her ear (her right ear, which she was certain was the smaller of the two, but which her step-brother swore was the biggest), her brow scrunched in confusion. "Why is it that you can't eat me?"

The dragon gave her a considering look. "I'd say it was probably one of your great-great-great ancestors who stumbled upon me when I was a young, century-old-dragonling. I had been trapped—I won't tell you how, it's too embarrassing to admit one was captured by a trap meant to stop coyotes from stealing chickens —and your great-great-great whoever they were released me and gave me three chickens so I might heal well enough to fly back to my cave. That young creature—your ancestor—made me promise not to eat any of their family I might come across in the future. So alas, here we are."

Sheila, feeling extremely grateful to her unknown ancestor, felt a smile break across her face. She was not going to be eaten today! But then she remembered where she was supposed to be at that exact moment, and her smile fell. "Oh dear," she said, plopping onto a lumpy gold chair that sat nearby. "I'm afraid this day is not going at all as it should."

The dragon snorted, curling his long tail around himself as he lay down beside Sheila. "I should say not. Where in the world were you meant to be going when you so ridiculously stumbled?"

"My grandma's aunt's nephew's half-sister's adopted daughter's fourteenth birthday party in Welling's Hallow."

"That's a far cry from my caverns."

"I know," she said glumly. But Sheila Fairspotter was not one to be down long. In fact, even as she sat, sulking, her mind was racing. Perhaps there was a 7-League Boot Booth nearby. If she could get there quickly, she might even make it to the party before anyone noticed she was late. But when she inquired, the dragon sniffed and said he had allowed none of those "ill-advised poppy-cock boxes" to be built on his private island.

Well. That certainly threw things into perspective. If they were on a private island, that meant the only way off the island was…. Sheila looked at the fiery visage above her. "Is there any chance you would be willing to—"

"Stop right there." The dragon held up an elegant claw. "There is no way I would stoop to playing delivery dragon at my age. You'll have to find a different way to get home."

"But—"

"No."

Sheila settled back into the lumpy (rather uncomfortable, really) golden chair, arms crossed. She pouted. If the dragon was unwilling, there was no way she was going to make it back to the party. On top of arriving without a gift (sometime during her second half-step with the Essence of Boot painted on her foot, she had lost the bouquet of copper brambles she'd spent the last few weeks cultivating) she would probably be so late the four-day party would be over. If only there were something she could bargain with that would convince the dragon it was worth his time to—

"That's it!" she cried, leaping out of the lumpy (and ridiculously uncomfortable, to tell the truth) golden chair.

The dragon shifted in what Sheila would have thought was surprise, but she knew so regal a creature would never feel such paltry emotions.

"Good dragon, I invoke the right of worth by trial. Set me any three tests, and if I pass them, fly me to Welling's Hallow."

"What!" The roar rattled the piles around them, setting off miniature avalanches of gold.

"I invoke the right of—"

"I heard you, I heard you!" he snapped. He sat up, rustling his wings in a perturbed manner. Sheila could have sworn she heard a grumbled *I told those fools in the draconic council not to accept that bargain with the sentient creatures' representative,* but she wasn't entirely sure.

"Very well," the dragon said, tail lashing, "I accept your invocation. Your first trial starts now!" He snatched Sheila up with his strong forelegs and swept her over the countless treasure piles and out the mouth of the cavern. The bright sunlight blinded Sheila for a moment, so she didn't see where the dragon dropped her. With a strangled yelp, she found herself plunging first through the air, then through salty water. When she managed to struggle to the surface, she discovered she was floating in the sea, the waves gently pulling her back and forth. There was no land in sight, but the dragon hovered in the sky a few hundred yards away.

"Your first test is to survive in these waters for seven by seven minutes. If you're still alive when I get back, I'll set you another test. And I'll give you hint—your real worry isn't the waves, it's the flesh-eating gulls who roam these waters." The dragon pointed to his right, and Sheila saw what looked to be a flock of the red gulls circling over the waves. The birds were disturbingly close to where she now bobbed, a tender morsel should the gulls notice her.

The dragon had flown off, leaving Sheila to float and fret about the flock to her left. She hoped they wouldn't see her. She could swim, but not very fast. And she was *not* good at holding her breath. If the gulls noticed her, she had no doubt *they* would have no qualms over eating a Fairspotter. So she floated, and waited, and hoped.

Her face was starting to feel a little sunburned when the flock of gulls started shifting closer. With horror, she watched as they dipped and wheeled, their raucous cries growing louder. Her mind raced, jumping from point to point, considering things from every angle when—

Sheila laughed. Of course! Her hair! It was perfect camouflage in the sea! All she had to do was let out her braid, cover her face with her hair, and she would look like just another wave splashing around the sea.

She had just released her hair when a particularly violent shriek split the air—the gulls had spotted her. Breathlessly, Sheila spread her hair around her, over her face, and watched with mounting confusion and terror as the gulls wheeled as one and sped directly toward her.

But...her hair. She should have been hidden, should have been—

Sheila groaned. Of course! Her hair! It looked like waves in moonlight, but right now the sun was beaming down happily from above, oblivious to its part in completely and utterly ruining the one trick Sheila had for hiding from the gulls.

As the birds drew closer at frightening speeds, Sheila began to hyperventilate. She was trying to prepare her woefully inadequate lungs to take the deepest breath they could. She'd have to try to swim far enough underwater so when she surfaced, the birds wouldn't see her.

But just as she was about to take her biggest gulp, something yanked her under the waves. The last thing she saw before the world turned blue was an angry red face snapping an enormous black beak.

Beneath the waves, Sheila's first thought was she hadn't taken a deep enough breath. But then she realized she could breath—in fact, she seemed to be sitting in a bubble of air.

"What—"

"Hello there."

Sheila yelped. She would have scrambled backward, but there wasn't much room in the bubble. The reason for her yelp—and the source of the greeting—was a disembodied face floating in the side of the bubble. Though now that she'd had a moment to process, she could see the face wasn't sitting there on its own—a sleek, half-human half-fish body extended into the waters outside the bubble.

"How, how do you do?" Sheila said shakily, falling back on the good manners her mother had drilled into her (no, not literally drilled, obviously—the Fairspotters weren't a family of sadistic dentists, after all; they traded in normal, respectable love potions and joint ointments, things everyone needs once in a while). She stuck out her hand, then felt silly for having done so seeing as only the mermaid's face was in the bubble.

But then shoulders, a small bosom, and two scaly arms pushed their way into the bubble. The mermaid grinned and took Sheila's hand. "I'm quite well. It looked like you were in a spot of trouble up there. And I must say I've fallen quite in love with your hair. I would have hated see it ripped up or covered in blood had those gulls gotten hold of you."

"Oh, well, thank you." Sheila had never spoken with a mermaid before. She found the tinkling tones of the female's voice to be quite pretty as well, if a little difficult to understand.

The mermaid settled her elbows on the bottom of the bubble, rested her chin on her hands. "I've decided to make you an offer."

Sheila glanced at the top of the bubble, through the waters above. She could just make out the shadowed, blurry forms of swooping gulls. It would be great if she could stay in this bubble until the gulls had flown away. "What offer?"

"I've decided your hair is so lovely that you simply must come live in Atlantis. Then I can visit you and see your hair any time I like." She reached out to Sheila, running her slick fingers through the hair in question, which had fallen into stringy waves around Sheila's face and wasn't—Sheila thought—looking its prettiest. But the mermaid's blue pupils were wide with fascination.

Reluctantly, Sheila cleared her throat. "I'm sorry, but I can't go to Atlantis. I'm trying to get to my grandma's aunt's nephew's…well, my relative's fourteenth birthday party in Welling's Hallow. I'm trying to survive for seven by seven minutes while the gulls above—" she jerked a thumb upward, "—try to eat me. Would you mind terribly if I just stayed in this bubble for a bit?"

The mermaid's face fell. "You don't want to live in Atlantis?"

"I'm sorry, but no."

"Then I'm afraid I can't help you."

"Can't I just stay here for a while?"

The mermaid gnawed on a slimy nail. "I'm not allowed to save people on a whim. The mer-society has had some bad experiences with that. You're sure you won't join me at the bottom of the sea?"

Sheila confirmed she could not, though she couldn't say so without regret. As much as she wanted to find her way to the birthday party, she had to admit it would have been wonderfully magical to be taken to Atlantis.

"That's really too bad." The mermaid pouted and began to retreat. Water started rushing into the bottom of the bubble.

Yelping, Sheila tried to stand, but found herself sinking into the water instead. "Wait, wait!"

The water calmed in an instant, settling against her knees. Her skirt-of-many-pieces floated lazily on the surface like slim tentacles.

"You've changed your mind?" The hope in the mermaid's voice was difficult to bear. There was no way Sheila could spend the rest of her life in Atlantis. But she couldn't just go back up to the surface on her own, either. She could still see the hazy shapes of the gulls above.

"I…I…" she stared at her skirts, swirling about her legs. Like tentacles…like seaweed…like…hair…

"I'll *give* you my hair if you'll let me stay in this bubble until the seven by seven minutes are up!"

Slowly, the water began draining from the bubble. The mermaid's face was speculative. "You'll give me your hair?"

"Yes. Do you have anything sharp? I'll cut it off for you— you can put it in Atlantis and see it whenever you want. Or—or whatever."

The mermaid clapped her hands in delight, then produced a razor-sharp clamshell (presumably from somewhere on her person, but then Sheila wasn't one to presume).

A quick slice was all it took to separate Sheila from her hair. The mermaid wriggled with joy as she accepted the soggy bundle. "The bubble will last however long you need. Just swim out the side when you're done." And with that, she vanished into the depths.

Sheila wasn't sure how long it took for the gulls to disperse (her family wasn't a big fan of time-telling devices, hence her current lack of a means for counting down the minutes until the dragon would return). But eventually the shadows of the gulls disappeared.

She opted to stay in the bubble a while longer though—she wasn't sure it would remain if she needed to come back to it at some point. Instead, she waited until a giant shadow began circling up above. Hoping it was her dragon (not *her* dragon, of course, just the one specific dragon she was hoping the shadow belonged to, rather than a different dragon who might be inclined to eat her after all) she swam out the side of the bubble and up to the surface.

It was indeed her dragon (not *her* dragon, of cour—well, you know already) circling the waves, so she shouted a greeting, waved her arms about.

The dragon scooped her from the sea with nary a struggle.

"I see you've survived," he grumbled, in a fashion Sheila might have called begrudging coming from a less fantastical beast. "But lost your hair in the process, have you?"

She explained about her trade with the mermaid.

"But that's...that's cheating!"

"You never said I couldn't use my hair."

A few grumbles reverberated from the dragon through Sheila, but he only said, "Fine. On to your next test then."

In no time at all (even Sheila with her lack of a time-telling device could tell that), the dragon dropped her (rather unceremoniously, she had to say) into the middle of what seemed to be an enormous hedge.

"Your second test," the dragon called, though she couldn't see through the brambles above her to where he hovered in the sky, "is to find your way out of this never-ending hedge. If you reach the edge, call my name seven times, and I will find you."

"But I don't know your name!"

"Grindestal!"

The roar reverberated through the bramble, and Sheila covered her head with her arms as twigs and leaves rained on her. When the echoes stopped, she was fairly certain the dragon—*Grindestal*—had gone.

At first, she tried to determine the direction of the sun. It was still mid-morning after all—surely it had only been a few hours since she had stepped into the Boot Booth. But though the sun slanted nicely into the hedge, it bounced off branches and leaves and left her entirely confused as to its original direction.

Her next thought was to draw a line on the ground behind her. If she could keep the line straight, she reasoned, she would eventually come to an edge. Of the hedge. She chortled at the rhyme as she climbed through the thicket, stepping over low-growing branches, ducking under others. After a few feet she looked back at the line she'd been drawing with a thin, fallen branch.

The line was not straight.

In fact, the line looked much like her nose—all twisted and spiraling. And though it was a lovely characteristic for a nose to have, it was not at all how she'd hoped her line would end up.

Out of ideas for how to go about the test in a logical way, Sheila walked. She still stepped over and ducked under branches, but she went whichever way was easiest. After what seemed like hours (but what she would have known was about fifteen minutes had she possessed a time-telling device of any sort), she stumbled upon the curly-cue line she'd drawn on the ground earlier.

With a groan, Sheila plopped onto the ground. How was she ever supposed to find her way out of this thicket? She had no idea even of how big the thing was—maybe it would take days of walking, even in a straight line, to reach the edge of the brambles. Perhaps she should just accept she wasn't ever going to reach the party; perhaps she should start learning to live in here.

As Sheila was taking stock of the various scratches and bruises she'd earned in her initial foray through the branches, her nose started twitching. Was that...roasting meat?

With a mighty inhale (the force of which drew her to her feet), Sheila smiled. That was definitely a roasting meat kind of smell threading its way through the foliage. Perhaps she wouldn't have to live alone in here—surely the owner of the fire and game producing that delectable smell wouldn't mind company.

So off she went, her nose guiding her more surely through the thicket that anything else could have. And when she finally pushed aside the last branch before the fire, she couldn't help but laugh.

There, on the edge of the hedge (for yes, that's where she found herself), was Grindestal, facing away from her, roasting some enormous beast over an even more enormous fire.

He was humming to himself.

Sheila cleared her throat. A lesser creature might have jumped in surprise. The dragon, of course, did not (though she did think he had maybe, just ever so slightly, flinched).

"*Who dares—*" Grindestal cut off when he saw Sheila standing behind him. "You! How did you escape the hedge so quickly?"

"I followed my nose," she said, tapping the wonderfully curled appendage and winking.

The dragon's powerful jaw dropped. "But that's cheating!"

"You never said I couldn't use my nose." She dropped to the ground beside the fire (though not too close, it was *hot*). "Besides, you're the one who decided to roast a beast right next to the brambles. May I have some, by the way?"

"Oh very well," the dragon snapped, rolling his shoulders irritably. But now Sheila thought she saw a gleam of amusement in his eye.

When they'd finished the roast (Grindelstal, of course, ate the majority of the thing, right down to the bones and tendons and fat), the dragon stretched his wings and gave Sheila a considering stare. "You may have beaten the first two tests, but I guarantee you won't beat the third!"

With that, she was in his arms once more, being flown through the air. By now, Sheila was starting to suspect Grindelstal might not be quite as fearsome as she'd first thought him. She also thought it silly he hadn't just flown her to the party in the first place—surely that would have been faster than flying her all over and waiting for her to try each test? But, well, she was two thirds of the way done already. Nothing for it but to buckle down and pass the last, ultimate test. And yet—

"By the moon's spit, what is that?"

Sheila stood before a hill that seemed to writhe and surge as she looked at it. The surface undulated, flashing black and yellow, black and yellow. But it was the sounds that overwhelmed—sibilant shushing, like millions of wings rustling, and a droning buzz that vibrated the air, causing a poor westerly wind to come quite undone before it had even summited the hill. It was the sounds that made Sheila realize—

"It's a mountain of bees! But…what in the seven tiers of hell—" (normally, Sheila would never have sworn in front of an elder, but she'd begun to feel quite irreverent around the dragon she'd started thinking of as a true companion despite their only having met that morning) "—am I supposed to do with that?" She gestured wildly at the swarming insects then turned, finding an entirely draconic smirk on Grindestal's giant mug—he was clearly feeling quite smug (even Sheila, who was not familiar with draconic expressions, could tell).

"Well," he said, lips curling with satisfaction, "since you seem so fond of using your...unique attributes...I've decided on this test specifically. You won't be able to use any of those pesky attributes to pass! This hill, beneath the bees of course, is covered with white flowers. There is but one of them that is red—red as the cleanest blood. Your third test is to find that red flower and pluck it from the ground. When you do, say my name seven times, and I will find you. Now go on, get on with it." And so saying, he turned three times in a circle and curled up on the bee-less grass. Within moments, he'd transformed into a slumbering mound whose snoring rivaled the bees' buzzing in strength.

With a slightly exasperated shake of her head (of course she could never be *truly* exasperated with such a great being as a dragon), Sheila began gingerly wading into the sea of bees. She murmured gently as she went, "There now, we're all friends here, I won't hurt any of you so no reason to hurt me either, there now, we'll all just stay as calm as pie..."

And the bees were calm—they rose a few feet in the air in reaction to Sheila's nearness, letting her catch a glimpse of the flower colors beneath them before they settled back down. But as it was only the bees she was closest to who moved, she couldn't see very far around her at any point. At this rate, she was looking for a needle in a haystack (a test she'd read about in one of the fairytale collections her mother had given her when she was younger; it seemed like a more boring test than the one she was currently undertaking, though perhaps a bit safer).

She looked around, trying to see how far she'd traveled from the edge of the bees, but all around her was only the swarming mass, no edge in sight. She couldn't see the dragon either.

Coming to a stop, Sheila crossed her arms crossly (the similarity of the words made her smile though, so she couldn't stay cross for long). She tapped a finger on her arm. What she needed was a plan. She couldn't just go wandering about haphazardly—she'd seen how well that worked in the hedge. Perhaps she should find her way back to the edge of the bees, and work her way around the hill in ever smaller circles until she reached the top? Perhaps she should go straight to the top and work her way down in ever bigger circles?

As she stood thinking, the bees grew bolder. She first noticed their gentle touch on her legs, as they settled on her skirts and leggings and began working their way around her, trying to figure out exactly what manner of creature had stumbled into their domain. Their limbs felt like fairy kisses along her arms. When they got to her neck, she giggled. They reached her chin, and she laughed. Then they found her left ear, and started humming in appreciation.

Oh, they whispered, their feet scritch-scratching on and mandibles tickling in her ear, *what a small, lovely ear. We've never seen an ear so perfectly sized.*

"Thank you." Sheila, who, never having been complimented by a bee before, fairly buzzed with pleasure. Her ear *was* perfectly sized, wasn't it? Though she would never admit to her step-brother that he'd been right about which one was smaller.

Their tiny voices sighed together, *What are you doing on our hill, oh lovely-ear owner?*

Sheila explained about her grandma's aunt's… (she sighed) her *relative's* fourteenth birthday party in Welling's Hallow, the unfortunate incident with the Boot Booth, and her three tests, ending with her current task on their hill.

Ah, rasped the bees, *we know of this flower. We do not sip from it for it was made poisonous to bees by an evil wizard long ago—she was trying to kill our queen. We will show you where it is so you can remove it from our hill once and for all.*

With that, a small group of bees flew into a tight grouping in front of Sheila, and set off toward her right at a leisurely pace.

She wasn't sure how long they walked (that pesky business about no time-telling device again), but sometime both sooner and later than she expected, the buzzing group in front of her dispersed, taking with them all the bees that had been crawling on the flowers in the area. A cluster of white flowers bobbed together, swaying from the departure of the bees. And there, slightly beneath the curving white petals, hid a single red bloom.

Carefully, Sheila pushed the white flowers apart, grasped the red flower near the base of its stem, and tugged it from the ground. She had a brief moment of panic thinking she'd touched a poisoned flower, then remembered the bees had said it was poisonous to *them*. But why would a wizard have wanted to poison their queen in the first place? She would have asked, but it seemed the insects dared not approach her now that she held the bee-poisoning flower in her hands, so instead she straightened, clasping the flower close to her chest, and called Grindestal's name seven times.

Almost instantly, a shadow fell over her. The poor bees were batted this way and that in the powerful gusts from the dragon's wings as he swooped low enough to pluck Sheila from the hill. He grumbled about having his nap interrupted so soon, but she ignored him (imagine that—her, Sheila Fairspotter, having the audacity to ignore a *dragon!*).

As they soared through the air, she couldn't help but laugh. She'd done it—she'd completed three tests and earned a ride from the dragon. She wouldn't miss the entire party after all!

They said nothing as they flew (for Grindestal set an even more grueling pace this time, and it's rather difficult to hear anything with the winds rushing by so quickly), but the trip passed in less time than a nose wrinkle. Sheila was especially delighted to see so many types of landscape flow beneath them—forests, plains, rocky outcroppings, crashing seas. Grindestal's arms were warm, so she didn't mind the bite of wind against her face.

Dusk had just begun to show her lovely gown when Sheila arrived at her grandma's aunt—her relative's birthday party, born through the skies by her new friend (because yes, she had decided to count the dragon as a friend, even if he was a prickly one). She was overjoyed to see the dancing was in full swing, though many bodies paused as faces turned to the skies to track the arrival of the mighty dragon.

Grindestal dropped Sheila at the edge of the giant dance floor, where hundreds of Fairspotters grooved under bouncing strings of lights (they bounced, of course, not because of the wind from the dragon's mighty wings, but because the Fairspotters are rather exuberant dancers, one and all, and together created a force strong enough to shake several trees nearby in addition to the strings of lights, which stood no chance at all of remaining elegantly in place while there were dancing Fairspotters beneath them).

The guests seemed rather more aloof in the presence of a dragon than Sheila might have expected (wasn't anyone worried about being eaten?), but then the family had always loved to party so much she couldn't blame them for continuing the festivities even at possible risk to their lives.

Though many of her family members did send a few curious looks her way (and the dragon's way), only a few came running up to Sheila when she landed—her mother, her step-brother, and the night's most celebrated personage herself of course, Sheila's grandma's aunt's nephew's half-sister's adopted daughter (and Sheila thought she should really learn the girl's name, because listing their relationship was getting entirely too taxing). The three of them shouted their questions at her all at once and over the top of each other, including *how did you get a dragon to bring you to the party?*

With a laugh and a promise to explain everything later, Sheila produced the red blossom and handed it to the birthday girl. "I'm sorry," she said, "this is the only present I managed to bring with me."

At that, Grindestal stepped forward, clearing his throat with a jaw-shaking rumble that caused a few anxious glances to be shot his way (the sound still wasn't enough to stop the dancing though). "I believe I can be of some assistance here." He opened his mouth, and out spilled enough gold and jewels to buy a life-time subscription to Magi-U Weekly, among other things. The birthday girl squealed in delight, and ran off to find a basket or some other such container to put her new treasure in.

Sheila turned to the dragon, her friend, and thanked him warmly.

"Oh tut," he grumbled, shifting his wings, though by now Sheila could tell the draconic expression on his face was an embarrassed pleasure. "You earned it with how cleverly and quickly you solved the tests today. And here—" He opened his mouth once more, and this time the lumpy gold chair (the uncomfortable one she'd so happily left behind in the cave) tumbled out. "I noticed you seemed to especially like this while we were in my caverns. You deserve something nice for yourself, too, so here you are."

Though she wasn't especially happy about the gift, Sheila found herself smiling. She couldn't fault Grindelstal's intent or generosity, so she thanked him profusely.

Besides, she could have the chair melted down when she got home.

Despite multiple invitations to stay, the dragon said his good-byes and left. And Sheila joined her family in the dance.

After the requisite four days of partying, the Fairspotters prepared to return to their own homes. There were many tearful farewells and declarations that they couldn't wait for the next birthday party (which was, of course, only the next week, as could be expected in a family of such incredible size).

Sheila and her family (her immediate family, not her entire family, that would have been ridiculous), returned home via her mother's transport spell (the lumpy golden chair joined them). And finally the story of Sheila's three tests was told. Her family was appropriately awed by the tale, laughing and gasping and crying in all the right places.

Sheila's mother vowed to never again nag her daughter to fix her clothing (as might be expected of a mother whose daughter had completed such a wonderful quest), but Sheila said the experience she'd had was quite enough for a lifetime; she vowed to never again allow loose threads to remain on her clothes (as might be expected of a daughter who'd learned the consequences of not following her mother's advice). And both were quite content and confident about Sheila's prospects—or lack thereof—for future escapades (as might be expected of those who know not the myriad ways adventure calls).

~ * ~ * ~

Sally Jo is a technical writer by day and a creative writer at all times. She publishes shorter works on Instagram, under @sallyjopoetry. Her poetry has been published in 'Rise! An Anthology of Change,' 'Variant Literature,' the 'Mad Swirl' poetry forum, and the upcoming 'Frost Fire Worlds 2021 Edition.' Her first collection of poetry, 'Droplets: Of Four Sisters,' is available on Amazon. Two of her short stories will be included in upcoming anthologies: 'A Quiet Afternoon 2' and 'Crunchy with Chocolate.'

Domestic Dispute

Fred Phillips

Feirefiz cracked an eyelid and groaned when the shadow fell over the mouth of the cavern. He knew what was to come next. It was the same thing every evening. A shame, too, he'd been enjoying his afternoon nap.

A pair of plump sheep hit the cavern floor in front of him, and he opened his eyes, knowing it would do no good to feign sleep.

"Prepare those for supper, you lazy lizard," the smaller purple dragon who had entered the cave said. "It's the least you could do. I don't know why I put up with you, laying here and sleeping the day away while I do all the work."

Feirefiz looked up at Maledysaunte. The evening sun shone off her deep violet scales, creating small rivers of iridescent color all over her body and cloaking her with a many-colored glow. It was one of numerous things Fiz loved about her. Mal was still as beautiful as the day he'd married her. She answered his long, loving gaze with a snort and stalked off into the depths of their not-so-happy home.

Fiz turned his attention back to the two sheep, carefully removing the wool and other inedible parts. He blew a thin line of flame out of one nostril, roasting his meat, but Mal's he left alone. He'd developed a taste for cooked meat over the years, but she, of course, still preferred hers raw, "as a dragon should." Fiz had only recently gotten her to let him remove the wool before she ate, but cooking was a step too far.

He'd return the wool to the farmer's house tomorrow while Mal was out. He felt a great deal of guilt about stealing sheep and saw no reason the farmer shouldn't at least get something from his efforts to raise the animals. Mal would disapprove, of course. She disapproved of most of the things he did these days.

His family had tried to warn him about marrying her. Purple dragons were notoriously willful and impossible to live with, his mother had said. His father said he should marry another red, "as was proper," while his brother suggested a meek and submissive white. He wouldn't listen. He had been madly and deeply in love with the fiery Maledysaunte. He still was, in truth, but sometimes she made it tough to remember that.

He supposed the situation was at least partially of his making, though. She often accused him of becoming complacent and toothless. Mal wanted him to hunt among the villages and make himself seen and feared again. Fiz would far rather take human form, walk among those villages and learn. Sure, terrorizing the countryside had been great fun 100 years ago, but now his passion was knowledge. Mal thought all he did was sleep all day. Of course, if she ever found out what he was actually doing during the day, she'd leave him and likely burn down every town in a 100-mile radius in her rage. He couldn't have that on his conscience, so he'd let her continue to think he had turned into a lazy good-for-nothing oaf.

She would disapprove, but she would stay. As much as he disagreed with many of her beliefs about what a dragon should be, he couldn't bear the thought of losing her.

Mal returned to the main cavern, shaking water from her scales after a bath in the small underground pool farther back in the caves. Without even glancing his way, she stretched out and began to feed with great gusto, noise and mess. Feirefiz watched her briefly, then turned slightly away from the gruesome spectacle. Maybe he was inching closer to the humans he spent his days with, but he didn't have the stomach for such things anymore.

After she was sated, Mal stretched out on her back, trying a different tactic. She shot him a playful glance.

"Fiz. Why don't you join me on the hunt tomorrow, dear?" she asked. "We could do a fly-by of all the villages, then pick up a few cattle and have lunch by the lake like we used to. After that, we could find a spot higher in the mountains to spend the night under the stars…doing other things we used to. Perhaps this time even…"

She let the words hang in the air, and Feirefiz was sorely tempted by the offer. This was something new for Mal, and he had to admit the possibilities were enticing. It would be nice to spend a romantic evening with her again, and even though he knew she was only teasing him, he had always wanted young ones around the cave. Unfortunately, she didn't, so it wasn't possible. As much as he'd like to believe she could change her mind, he knew her too well.

Oh, he'd definitely enjoy a meal by the lake and what might

come later, but the hunt itself wasn't what it used to be for him. He'd found a new passion and just didn't have the heart for old school dragon things. Besides that, Feirefiz had other obligations. He had an appointment to keep. One Mal could never know about.

"I'm sorry, dear. I'm afraid I don't feel up to it tomorrow," he said, with no small amount of real regret in the words.

Maledysaunte rolled over and got to her feet with a snort.

"Father told me reds were weak," she said. "He told me you'd be no good for me, and I wish I had listened. But instead, I'm married to a weak, lazy, good-for-nothing loafer. I'm going to bed, don't bother to join me."

Each word drove a spike into his heart. When she stormed off into the deepest reaches of the cavern, Fiz wanted to go after her, to apologize, to tell her he would join her tomorrow. But it was too late now. She wouldn't hear anything else he had to say tonight. With a deep sigh, he curled up near the cavern entrance and fell into a troubled sleep.

Mal awoke him with a kick the next morning on her way out. He opened one eye to look at her, and she sniffed and kicked him again.

"You're not sleeping all day. If you don't intend to help me get your supper, I at least expect this mess cleaned up when I get home."

"Yes, dear," he mumbled, closing his eyes again.

With a huff, Mal spread her wings and took flight. As soon as she was away, he crept to the mouth of the cavern. He watched until she disappeared into the distance. Then, taking the two sheepskins from last night's meal into a claw, he stretched his own wings and took flight.

Trying to keep a low profile, Fiz glided down the slopes toward a certain farmhouse at the foot of the mountains. He swooped over the house, letting the wool fall in the yard near the door, then turned quickly and headed toward his appointment.

As he neared the small town in the valley, he dropped into a stand of firs and pines. When he emerged again, he wore the guise of a human scholar. Ruddy brown robes hung from a thin frame, and he carried a sheaf of parchments, though he couldn't use them. Fiz was still learning to write the human language, and he longed to one day write the story of his life for humans to read, and just perhaps, to understand what it was to be dragon the way he was learning what it was to be human.

He strolled casually into town, looking for the man he was to meet, a traveling priest by the name of Samuel. He'd been fascinated with the man when they met the day before, so Feirefiz had set up an appointment to have lunch with the man at the town's small inn before he left. The priest had traveled the world, and Feirefiz, who had never been out of these mountains, despite his ability to fly, longed to know more of those places. He even dared to hope to see them one day.

Samuel greeted him warmly as he entered the common room, despite having just met him. Even before their meals arrived, they were already in deep conversation which lasted long into the afternoon—much longer than Fiz had planned. The dragon was fascinated by the tales of faraway places and people, and even by the man's religion and its idea of treating even the least among his people with kindness. They seemed to be kindred spirits.

"Do you mind if I ask a personal question?" Samuel said, turning the conversation back to the dragon.

"Not at all."

"It's just that Feirefiz is a strange name. It seems out of place here."

"It's a family name," Fiz answered. "I was born in the mountains, a few miles to the east, but I've lived here most of my life."

After a few moments of thoughtful silence, Samuel spoke again.

"Well, you seem to have a great interest in the world. Would you like to see it? I could use a companion on the road, and possibly even an apprentice at some point."

Fiz immediately brightened at the offer. Here was the thing he'd only daydreamed about—traveling the world, seeing new places, learning new things. His heart soared, but fell just as quickly, along with the smile on his face.

"I'd love to join you, but sadly, I fear I cannot."

"Family?"

"Only a wife who despises what I've become. She'd prefer a stronger man to a scholar, but I still love her dearly."

Samuel placed a comforting hand on his shoulder.

"I understand, my friend. If it's any consolation, I think

you're one of the stronger men I've met on my road," he said with a couple of taps to his temple. "I've enjoyed our conversation this afternoon more thoroughly than I've enjoyed one in ages outside the monastery. It's rare to find a deep thinker these days.

"Perhaps I'll pass through again one day. If so, I'll be sure to find you."

As they rose and clasped hands, a scream went up outside. Both men rushed to the door. People milled in the streets pointing to the eastern sky. Feirefiz followed their gestures and emitted a low, rumbling growl. Maledysaunte soared toward the village. Diving, Mal tore the thatch roof off a nearby house and threw it down to crash among the people in the road. He saw at least one person go down underneath the wreckage, and chaos erupted. She passed low, waves of terror emanating from her and heightening the panic below. Fiz watched in horror as she took pleasure in tormenting the people he called friends.

"Excuse me," Feirefiz said politely to his companion, stepping away a short distance and letting his human guise drop. Shouts rose from all around as his full form materialized among the already frightened people. Ignoring the screams, he spread his wings and launched himself into the air.

"MALEDYSAUNTE! Stop this at once!" he roared.

She paused and turned to regard him.

"So this is how you've been spending your days? Disgraceful."

Then, Mal smiled and looked to the ground where the villagers ran about, shouting and pointing toward the spectacle in the sky.

"Feel their awe and their fear, Feirefiz," she said. "Feel it and remember what it's like to be a dragon. Remember the ecstasy of the kill. Come back to me, my dear Feirefiz."

As she said it, he experienced for the first time in many years the feelings emanating from the panicked people on the ground. He felt the rush of their fear, mingled with a sweeter taste of admiration and some primal instinct from his past took him. The adrenaline surged through his veins, intoxicating him. Feirefiz shrieked and shot higher into the air. Turning at height, he fell into a dive toward the people below, intent on showing his true power, feeding on their fear, reveling in what it was to be a dragon.

His gaze focused on one target, the priest Samuel. A man who had almost taken this power and fury away from him. As he hurtled downward, teeth bared, villagers pushed and shoved trying to reach the false safety of the surrounding buildings. He could burn them to the ground with a breath, and would when this was done. The priest, though, stood his ground serenely in the middle of the road. He locked eyes with the oncoming dragon, blood-thirsty and crazed dragon eyes meeting the resolute eyes of a man of faith. As they locked gazes, Fiz saw in those eyes fear of neither dragons nor death. In that moment, Feirefiz faltered. He pulled up a few feet short of Samuel, soaring back to the sky, the wind from his descent knocking the priest to the ground.

He turned just in time to see Maledysaunte, shrieking in rage, bearing down on the inn. He threw himself in front of her onslaught, taking a gash down his flanks from her claw, but managing to save the building and the people inside, at least for the moment.

The purple dragon rose into the air and turned a hate-filled gaze on her mate. Feirefiz returned it with a steady stare.

"Weakling," she spat. "You are no dragon. You're a lowly worm.

"What will you do now that your pets know your secret? Will you return to your little cave and spend the rest of your days hidden away like the coward you are?"

Instead of taking the bait, Feirefiz hovered, regarding her calmly, and smiled in the face of her rage. He'd made a decision; one he knew he was going to have to make sooner or later. He replied with deep sadness but full resolve.

"Why, no, my dear," he replied. "In fact, I'm going to do what you've wanted me to do for years. I'm going to let my presence be known in the world, that is if my friend will still have me along on the journey after I've almost killed him."

He turned to cast his gaze on Samuel, who was just pulling himself up from the ground and dusting his robes off. Just as he had during Feirefiz' attack, the priest stood serene, staring at a massive and fearsome beast who had just called him friend. After a moment, Samuel smiled and nodded.

Mal sneered.

"Have your little pets, then. But in doing so, you lose me."

"My love, they're not my pets. They're my friends. I wish you would travel with us, see the world…"

"Pah. I'll not associate with these creatures. They are beneath us. We are dragons. Look at me, and show me the human who is my equal," she shouted, spreading her wings wide and gliding above her mate.

He felt a deep twinge in his heart staring up at her. She was truly marvelous, and he still loved her deeply. But he couldn't live the life she longed for. He could no longer take pleasure in instilling fear in the people of these mountains or destroying just for the sake of destruction. If this was the way it had to be, perhaps it was better for both of them.

"I'm sorry," he said. "Truly."

Maledysaunte faltered in her flight, looking stunned. It was the first time in a long time Fiz had seen any uncertainty in his mate. She knew the power she wielded over him and had fully expected Fiz to grovel for forgiveness. He wouldn't this time, and he could see his refusal struck her like a hammer blow. She hovered for a moment, unable to find the voice to speak her outrage. Instead, she screamed again, a sound that sent a shiver through every creature for miles. She spun and sped off into the evening sky. Feirefiz heaved a great sigh and floated gently to the ground beside the priest. He lowered a wing and helped the man onto his back.

"We should probably go now," Fiz said, seeing a few of the villagers already beginning to wander out of cover.

"What about her?" Samuel asked hesitantly. "Won't she come back?"

"No," Feirefiz answered, staring after his departing mate. "She is a creature certain of her power, and I've thrown some doubt into her mind, shown a weakness to the world she didn't think she had. It's something I should have done long ago. It might have saved what we had. I think she'll move on and not return to this place. There are too many memories here, for both of us. If I know Mal, she'll want to leave them behind, just as I do, go somewhere she can be the dragon she desires to be."

The priest reached up and stroked the dragon's neck in sympathy. Feirefiz shook his great head and gently launched himself into the air with Samuel on his back. He let the memories fall behind him as he glided away in the opposite direction of Maledysaunte. He had much to see.

~ * ~ * ~

Fred Phillips has been writing stories since elementary school, when they were pecked out with two fingers on a manual typewriter found in a closet and the heroes of the stories were thinly veiled versions of him and his friends. He spent nearly 20 years telling true stories as an award-winning writer and editor in the newspaper business before he finally escaped. Fred now works in communications for a Fortune 500 company. He has also written book and music reviews and stories for various publications, websites and a national wire service.

Fred was born and raised in Louisiana, where he still resides. When he's not exploring fantasy worlds, he's usually exploring the woods and waters of his home state with his son.

Madras

Mabel Ginest

"You want me to *what?*" Madras stared in disbelief at the young knight before him, and swept his tail into a nearby tree, nearly shattering it with the force. "No. Absolutely not."

"But Madras," the knight protested, sidestepping Madras' tail as it came back the other way, "You're a dragon; dragons kidnap beautiful girls all the time, especially if they're princesses!"

"First of all," Madras said icily, "Dragons do not 'kidnap beautiful girls'. We carry them off. Second of all, I have been retired for years. I haven't been in the business since before your father's grandfather was born, and I have no desire to bestir myself now. I'm quite comfortable as I am."

"Please?" the knight pleaded. "It's just one little favor, Madras."

Madras gave the young knight a dark look and grumbled something under his breath. "No. You're not dragging me into your mad schemes, Tyrone, and that's final. If you want to marry this princess of yours, why don't you do what normal people do? Go to her father and *ask*."

"I was only knighted last year," Tyrone protested. "I haven't had time to make a name for myself; there's no way the king would even let me *see* Penelope, let alone actually consider letting me marry her. I'd be out on my ear before I could finish asking. But if I rescue her from a dragon...well, the king would *have* to listen to me then!"

Madras snorted, smoke trickling from his nostrils, but he had to admit the knight had a point. Humans, he thought derisively. They were constantly trying to outperform each other; it was the sole means by which they judged each other. They were always trying to prove they were the most impressive of their species, when really, the whole lot of them were pathetic. Dragons, now, dragons didn't have that problem; dragons were unarguably impressive, and didn't feel the need to prove it with idiotic feats of bravery.

"Come on, Madras," Tyrone begged. "Won't you help me out, just this once?"

Madras eyed the young knight, taking in the dusty armor, and Tyrone's earnest dark eyes. In spite of himself, the dragon found himself reconsidering Tyrone's proposition. It was a ridiculous idea, of course, and totally typical of humans, but Tyrone did seem set on the project.

Come to think about it, Madras didn't want the knight unhappily in love—he'd been quite bad enough while *happily* in love. No, the dragon decided, it would be much better to keep the knight from sinking into the despair of unrequited love; a horror of human emotion he had witnessed all too often. Besides, Tyrone was a likeable enough little tyke, once one got past the annoying chatter and endless optimism, and he'd hate for the fellow to be unhappy. Tyrone wanted to rescue the princess? Fine. Madras would see to it he could rescue the princess.

"Oh, very well then," Madras grumbled. "Have it your way."

Tyrone's whole face lit up. "You'll do it? Really?"

Madras growled in annoyance, both at himself and the knight, but sighed and said, "Yes, yes, I'll do it."

Tyrone gave a shout and flung his arms around a surprised Madras. "Thank you, Madras! You're the best!"

"Tyrone, really," Madras protested, shaking free of the knight's surprisingly firm grip.

Tyrone looked up at the dragon eagerly. "When's the soonest you can carry Penelope off? Could you do it tomorrow?"

Madras opened his mouth, about to firmly put an end to the ridiculous notion—carry off a princess with less than twenty-four hours' notice, the very idea! —but at Tyrone's pleading expression, the dragon grumblingly acquiesced. "Oh, very well. Tomorrow."

"Perfect!" Tyrone exclaimed. "You kidnap her—sorry, carry her off I mean—first thing tomorrow morning, and then I can come by in an hour or so, and—"

"Don't even think about it," Madras interrupted, glowering at him. "You'll keep a wide berth of this place all day tomorrow. I don't want to catch even a *scent* of you until just before sunset, understand?"

"But Madras," Tyrone protested.

"Don't 'but' me, you little shrimp," the dragon told him tartly. "If we're going to go through with this idiotic scheme of yours, we're going to do it properly; that means we do battle at sunset, and not a moment before. There are *rules* to rescuing princesses, and if you think I'm going to let you waltz in here and haphazardly do as you please, you have another thought coming. You want to impress this girl's father by rescuing her? Then it has to look authentic." Madras pulled his lips back in a pointed, gleaming smile, and added, "Besides, I'm a ferocious dragon, and I have a reputation to uphold."

Tyrone considered this a moment, then nodded. "All right," he said. "That's fair enough. I'll be here at sunset then." His excitement burst forth again and he hugged Madras' neck once more. "Madras, you are a king among dragons!"

Madras swatted at the knight irritably with his front foot. "Get off me," he demanded, and glared at Tyrone. "You've gotten what you wanted...now why don't you go away, so I can get things ready for tomorrow? There's a lot to prepare, and not much time to do it in, and I certainly can't do anything if you're underfoot."

Tyrone immediately began gathering his things, excitedly making plans for the morrow while he did so. Then, with a final thanks and farewell, he bounded cheerfully down the hill, turning to wave and shout, "I'll see you tomorrow, at sunset!"

Madras watched the knight turn and disappear from view, his expression softened tolerantly. As far as the old dragon was concerned, Tyrone hadn't changed much from the first time he had stumbled across Madras' cave; he was only a little taller and broader. Madras clearly recalled the first time he'd met the knight, back when the latter was a gangly, freckled-face child who had, for some inexplicable reason, taken a shine to him. After their first meeting, Tyrone had returned to the dragon's cave again and again, until Madras gave up trying to chase him off, and allowed the boy to keep him company.

Madras had assumed that, with time, the child would lose interest in him, and had steeled himself for the moment; but years passed, and Tyrone had continued to visit him daily, until he had become a regular fixture in the dragon's life. Madras had been there as Tyrone grew up; when he had decided to become a knight; and all during Tyrone's training. And now the inevitable had happened: Tyrone had met a pretty girl and fallen in love.

The dragon shook himself back to the present with a puff of smoke that trailed up from his snout, lingering a moment in the afternoon air before dissipating in the breeze. Then, briskly, he turned and entered his cave; it had been a long time since he had carried off any maidens, and as he had told Tyrone, there was much he needed to ready.

~ * ~

At noon the next day, Madras carefully polished his green-and-gold scales, turned matte in his old age, until they gleamed. Then, after checking his appearance in the gold-framed mirror (part of his hoard) that leaned against one wall of his cave, Madras nodded in satisfaction and exited the cave.

Once outside, the dragon pushed himself into the air with three powerful pumps of his wings, and took off. He coasted through the air effortlessly towards the slender stone castle, a short flight of perhaps eight minutes.

After circling the castle at a distance in order to get his bearings, Madras swooped towards the tallest tower where, as the dragon knew from his many hundreds of years of experience, the sought-after princess was sure to be found. Sure enough, leaning out the narrow window was a slender, feminine figure. Madras shook his head over the unoriginality of human beings; kings in particular. When, he wondered, would they learn that merely sticking their daughters in a high tower was not enough to ensure the girls' safety?

The princess had not noticed him yet. She was leaning far out of the window, watching something on the ground below her, and while her attention was still diverted, Madras seized his opportunity. With a sudden burst of speed, he swooped towards the girl, who looked up just in time to see him. She screamed as Madras plucked her out of the tower room, but Madras was already flying away, and anyone who came to the aid of the princess would be too late.

~ * ~

When he got back to his cave, Madras carefully set the princess on the ground, and backed away, steeling himself for the hysterics that inevitably followed upon a maiden's being carried off. The princess slowly sat up and glanced around, pushing back clouds of fluffy brown hair partially obscuring her face.

Curious, if only for the sake of Tyrone's interest in her, Madras studied the girl. After a moment, he judged her to be pretty by human standards, if not extraordinarily beautiful. Her face, with a scattering of impudent freckles across her upturned nose, was a little too small, and her large brown eyes were a trifle too far apart for true beauty; but she was by no means unpleasant to look at.

At the moment, she didn't appear to be about to go into hysterics. As a matter of fact, she was looking around his cave, quite calmly, with a curious expression on her face. Her gaze encountered Madras, and she popped to her feet. "You must be the dragon," she said, and extended one hand. "Pleased to meet you!"

Madras regarded her hand for a few minutes in silence, then looked up at the girl's face. Misreading his blank expression, she winced, and withdrew her hand. "Of course, dragons don't shake hands, do they? I'm very sorry, I didn't mean to offend you; only I've never met a dragon before, and I don't know the proper things to do."

While Madras watched in growing disbelief and horror, the girl pulled out a small bag she had with her, and began rummaging in it. She pulled out a hairbrush in one hand and a bottle of perfume in the other, then glanced up and met Madras' gaze. "When do you think I'll be rescued?"

It took a minute for the words to work themselves out of Madras' mouth, and when they finally did, the dragon's voice was a little too squeaky to be a proper, fear-inspiring dragon's rumble. He harrumphed and tried again, with better results. "Sunset is the traditional hour."

"Right," Penelope said thoughtfully, "Not much time to waste, then. I'd better get ready now." She drenched herself with the perfume, making Madras sneeze, and then crammed the bottle back into the bag and began attacking her hair with the brush, with the ruthlessness of long practice. "I admit," she said, walking over to Madras' mirror to study her appearance, "I was worried when you didn't show up last night, but I suppose in the long run, it's actually better you waited until now. More witnesses to my being carried off, you know."

"You were *expecting* me?" Madras demanded, slamming his tail into the floor at the unexpectedness of this statement.

"Well, of course I was," Penelope said, as if it was the most ordinary thing in the world. "Why do you think I conned Daddy into letting me sleep in the old tower tonight?"

Madras stared at the princess. "You mean to tell me you wanted me to carry you off?" He blew out a small spurt of fire and eyed her irritably. "What kind of a self-respecting princess are you, anyway?"

"But don't you see," the girl said pleadingly, "I *had* to let you capture me. Otherwise, Tyrone wouldn't feel like he could ask Daddy to marry me."

There was a lengthy silence in which Madras gaped at the girl. Finally, he closed his jaw with a snap. "…What?"

"Tyrone," the girl explained. "He's this absolutely *wonderful* young knight I met the other day; I'm absolutely mad about him. We want to get married, but the silly idiot thinks he has to do something impressive before Daddy'll let him. I tried telling him Daddy would let me marry whoever I wanted, but he wouldn't listen." Penelope shrugged, and tossed her hairbrush aside. "Then, when he mentioned a dragon lived nearby, I decided to stay up in that old tower. I thought it might induce you to carry me off; and then Tyrone could rescue me, and feel better about asking Daddy to marry me."

"You didn't tell him you were going to do this, did you?" Madras asked dryly.

"Of course not," the girl scoffed. "That would take away the point! No, Tyrone doesn't know I planned it."

Madras considered the princess in front of him in silence for a few minutes. Finally, he sat back on his haunches, and said, "You humans are a ridiculous breed. You're worse when you're in love," he added grumpily, smoke trickling out of his nostrils.

"I dare say we are," the princess laughed. "What particular ridiculousness are you referring to right now?"

"You and Tyrone," Madras told her. The princess looked at him inquiringly, and he continued, "Your gallant knight is an old acquaintance of mine. He was up here yesterday, begging me to carry off the princess he had fallen in love with, so he could rescue her and impress her father."

"He *what?*"

"I'm not sure how he talked me into it, but he did," Madras said. He stared at the princess for a moment, considering her, and added, "And now you tell me that *you* arranged things to get me to carry you off, so Tyrone could rescue you." He shook his head and added in disgust, "Humans."

"You mean…" Penelope's mouth worked indignantly for a few moments. "You mean I went through all that work to set things up so you could carry me off, and all the while you were going to do it anyway?"

"That's right."

Penelope fell silent. Amusement and indignation warred on her face for a few moments, but at last amusement won out, and she gave vent to a rueful laugh. "Well, at least I made things easier for you. You won't tell Tyrone, will you? He's gone through such trouble to arrange things with you, I'd hate for him to feel like I wasn't properly impressed by it all."

Madras flashed her a white, pointed smile. "Don't worry. Tyrone won't find out. You just make sure you play your part of a terrified, captive maiden."

Penelope smiled sunnily up at him. "I can do that," she agreed. "Now that we've gotten all that taken care of, don't you think you ought to tie me up? Outside, if it's possible."

Madras glowered at this request. "You're not acting properly terrified of me," he grumbled. "You're far too eager to be tied up."

A sheepish smile crossed the girl's face. "Well, it wouldn't matter normally, but you see, I arranged it so James—one of our servants, you know—would follow after you carried me off, so there could be a witness to Tyrone rescuing me." Her cheeks reddened. "I thought it would help lend credibility to things."

Madras resigned himself to the madness with a sigh, and lumbered out of his cave. "Follow me," he told the princess, who eagerly leapt to her feet and scampered after him.

He led the girl across the clearing in front of his cave, to a large oak that was conveniently situated nearby. "Right over here, your highness," he said.

"What's your name, anyway?" the princess asked, trailing after him.

Madras glanced over his shoulder at the girl. "Madras," he said. "I was Madras the Malevolent when I was a young thing, but it's just plain Madras now." They reached the tree, and Madras nodded to it. "Stand right there."

The girl positioned herself artistically, and the dragon scooped up a coil of rope with one claw and began tying the princess to the tree. He was careful to keep the girl from any real discomfort, although managing to give the impression that she was tightly bound. The dragon stepped back to admire his handiwork and nodded in satisfaction. "Tyrone will be here at sunset," he told the princess. "In the meantime, at least try and look like you're frightened."

"I will," Penelope promised; altogether too excited at the thought of seeing Tyrone so soon, Madras thought, turning away. Humans in love were all the same; absolutely disgusting. At least it would all be over with soon; and then Madras could go back to his regular routine. Or, not *quite* his old routine; Tyrone, after he rescued the princess and they got married, would no longer come to see the old dragon every day. He'd be far too busy with his new life to spare time for that. Which, Madras told himself sternly, was perfectly fine with *him*; he always did think Tyrone talked too much. Suddenly and unaccountably irritable, Madras stomped off away from the princess to wait for the knight in his cave.

~ * ~

Promptly at sunset, Tyrone came tramping up the hill, dressed only in light armor and carrying no weapon but his sword. Madras nodded approvingly, then took a deep breath, shoved aside all thoughts except those concerning the business before him, and rushed out of his cave. He reared up on his hind legs and roared, crashing back to earth with a spurt of flames; determined to give the princess' watching servant plenty to witness.

The mock battle lasted a little over a quarter of an hour, and ended with a dramatic final clash, and Madras, defeated, dramatically collapsed to the ground and lay still. He waited there until he was sure Penelope's servant had gone, and when he could no longer bear listening to the lovers' raptures towards each other.

He clambered to his feet and walked over to the couple, who were clinging tightly to each other and whispering nauseatingly sweet nothings to each other. Humans, Madras thought derisively. Thank heavens dragons weren't sentimental. "You'll make me sick," the dragon told Tyrone, lumbering past the pair and plopping on the ground in front of the entrance to his cave. "Honestly, you humans."

"Madras!" Tyrone exclaimed. "You're all right, aren't you? I didn't hurt you? You were wonderful! Quite authentic!"

Madras snorted in indignation, and a trickle of smoke went up. "You couldn't hurt me if you tried, you little runt. And I should hope it *did* look authentic. This isn't the first fight I've had you know."

"Oh, you've offended him!" Penelope cried laughingly, leaving Tyrone's side and going over to Madras. "Don't listen to him, Madras. Tyrone is a numbskull."

Tyrone was staring at them. "Wait, you aren't frightened of Madras?"

"Of course not," Penelope said warmly. "He was very gentle and kind."

"Really," Madras said irritably. "I'm supposed to be a terrifying, fire-breathing dragon; calling me gentle and kind is the worst insult you could offer me!"

"Sorry," Penelope said, not sounding at all contrite, and patting the top of his head.

Madras shook her hand off and shot her a sour glare. "When are you two leaving? Shouldn't you be heading back to the castle?"

"Yes," Penelope said. "I wanted to give James a bit of a head start," she said in a low voice. In a normal tone, she added, "I just wanted to say goodbye to you first," she smiled at him sweetly. "Thanks for everything; you've been a perfect dear." She turned to Tyrone. "Come on, Tyrone; let's go tell Daddy."

"You think rescuing you will be enough to convince him I'm worthy of you?" Tyrone asked, his forehead creasing in concern.

"Positive," Penelope assured him. "Daddy will love you, don't worry. He has to, because *I* love you." She flung her arms around Tyrone and added, "We'll be married as soon as possible. And you're going to come to the wedding too, of course," she added over her shoulder to Madras. "I insist on it."

Madras snorted. "Ridiculous idea. What would people say if you had an old dragon as a guest at the wedding of the princess?"

Penelope smiled. "Nothing," she said sweetly, "Because I am the apple of my father's eye, in addition to being the crown princess; and if I want to invite a dragon as my special guest, I will, and nobody can say anything about it."

~ * ~

The princess made good on her threat. She delivered his

official invitation herself, by hand; and three weeks later, Madras found himself in the front row of the beautiful outdoor wedding of Princess Penelope and Sir Tyrone. To his own surprise, Madras enjoyed himself thoroughly, in spite of the occasional side looks he received from the other guests.

At the celebration following the wedding, the couple, resplendent in their wedding finery, preformed the first dance as the official start of the festivities. Watching the pair, Madras grudgingly had to admit that they made a fine couple; and it was clear from the way that they looked at each other that no amount of affection would be lacking in their marriage. Still, as the night progressed, Madras no longer felt like celebrating, especially after the newlywed couple announced they would be leaving for their two-week honeymoon on the following day, and shortly after that, he returned to his cave, alone.

The next day, as two o' clock in the afternoon—the hour Tyrone usually visited the dragon—passed without remark, Madras found himself growing more and more unaccountably irritable. After trying unsuccessfully to amuse himself with reorganizing his hoard, an activity he normally enjoyed, the dragon gave up and stalked outside. It was a beautiful spring day, but he was in no mood to enjoy it.

He was being an idiot, the dragon told himself fiercely. He was glad to be rid of Tyrone's incessant chatter; he could go back to enjoying his afternoon in peace and quiet, something he hadn't had for over twenty years. Besides, it wasn't as if Tyrone was going to stay young forever; he was bound to have fallen in love and married sooner or later. Still, in spite of all that, Madras was achingly aware of the silence, in a way he had never been before.

There was a fortnight until the newly married couple returned from their honeymoon, but even once they had, Madras knew he couldn't expect to see Tyrone regularly again. The knight would be busy with his new duties as prince consort, and once he and Penelope became parents…Madras sighed and lay his snout across his front paws. No matter what he told himself, Madras couldn't get around the fact he *missed* the young knight.

Suddenly, the dragon lifted his head as he caught an unmistakable whiff of Tyrone's scent, and the princess too. Madras quickly sat up, and waited for the pair, who came into sight a few moments later.

"What are you doing here?" Madras growled, unwilling to admit even to himself how glad he was to see them. "Aren't you two supposed to be on your honeymoon?"

"Well, you didn't think we were going to leave without saying goodbye to you, did you?" Penelope demanded, hands on her hips. "After all, we wouldn't even be *going* on our honeymoon if it wasn't for you."

"You humans," Madras sniffed. "So sentimental." He glowered at the couple, who were wearing matching expressions of smugness, and added, "Well, you've said your goodbyes; now go away."

"Not yet," Penelope said slyly. "Not until you've promised us something. Tyrone told me how important a dragon considers his word to be, and I know if you promise us, you won't go back on your word."

Madras glanced from her to Tyrone, then back to the girl. "I'm too old a dragon for you to hoodwink me so easily," he warned her. "What exactly is it you want me to promise you?"

"After Penelope and I get back," Tyrone said, "You have to promise you'll still let us come and visit you every day."

"Every day," Madras repeated stonily.

"Yes," Penelope said, nodding defiantly. "*And* we want you to be godfather to our children."

Madras, who was idly letting smoke curl up into the air, choked on it. "You want me to be *what?*"

"Godfather to our children," Penelope said again. "When we have them, of course, which may not be for a while yet." She grinned at the speechless dragon. "You have no choice in the matter, Madras. You're going to be a part of the royal family whether you want to be or not."

Madras looked helplessly from Penelope to Tyrone. Finally, with a puff of smoke, he grumbled, "Oh, very well. Since you have everything so tidily figured out. I'd hate to mess up your plans."

Penelope squealed and threw herself around his neck. "I *knew* you'd say yes!"

Madras pulled away from her, and demanded in disgust, "What *is* it with you humans and the hugging thing?" He dislodged the princess, more gently than his gruff voice would have led one to believe, and added, "Now that you two have gotten what you wanted, why don't you leave an old dragon to what remains of his peace and quiet, and go off on your honeymoon? I'll still be here when you get back."

"I suppose we should be going," Penelope said regretfully. "We're late already. But we'll visit you as soon as we get back. Goodbye Madras!"

"Goodbye," Madras said warily, watching the couple until they were out of sight. He had the feeling Penelope was a hard-headed young woman, and would make good on her promise—threat? —to make him a part of the royal family, whether he wanted it or not. Tyrone he already knew to be hopelessly stubborn; it seemed that, for better or worse, he had been accepted into the young couple's lives permanently. It would mean giving up his peaceful, quiet afternoons again, of course; but he had done without them for twenty-odd years already, and Madras felt he could manage just fine without them a little longer. He settled himself comfortably in front of his cave, feeling more warmed than the afternoon sun alone could account for, and drifted off to sleep.

~ * ~ * ~

Writing has always been an important part of **Mabel Ginest's** life, and she knew at a very young age she wanted to be an author. One of her earliest attempts at creating the next best seller was at seven years old, when she wrote an amalgamation of Shakespeare's *A Midsummer Night's Dream,* and the Greek myth of the Minotaur. Since that time, she has greatly enjoyed using her fertile imagination to craft innumerable stories, all with a quirky, fantastical bent to them—she still hopes to hit the best seller list someday, but as long as she can write she's happy. During the summer months, Mabel works in a local greenhouse, and has amassed quite a bit of information about a variety of plants...which she often uses to her advantage in her writing. She currently lives on her family's farm with her cat, Polly, and far more books than she has bookshelves.

The Princess and the Dragon

Karen G. McCullough

Suppose that, like Cyndrith, you happen to be the child of an ambitious mother joined to an insolvent father, a young lady of high birth, better than average looks, and broad but unorthodox education. As fate twists—only slightly assisted by your own and Aunt Vellie's peculiar talents—you catch the eye of a handsome prince at a time when he's under pressure from the relatives to consider his duties. Your problems are solved. Right?

But further suppose you do the obvious and necessary, you snag your man, and then you wake up the next day or week or month to discover your handsome, charming husband is a terrific dancer but an incompetent prince. And worse yet, your father-in-law, overjoyed junior is finally settling down to business, and having just enough *mens sanus* left to realize he's losing it, decides to retire to Bath to take the waters, leaving the kingdom in the hands of your sweet but unqualified husband.

Cyndrith found the literature dealing with her particular problem scarce. The old legends insisted everyone tended to live happily ever after, but her story looked likely to be a short, brutal tale—a leader who is hazy on the difference between cavalry and chivalry can generally expect an early and traumatic retirement.

Cyndrith learned the extent of the problem on a glorious spring morning shortly after the campaign season opened. The spies and lookouts her father-in-law had posted throughout the off-season returned with the news their wily neighbor, King Josef of Borgary-Cambara, was mustering a force of more than four hundred cavalry, and everyone knew he'd been lusting after the fertile valley of the Rimborne River and might just be inclined to go after the whole ball of wax while he was at it, namely, Cyndrith's home kingdom of Bradenveld.

She had come along to the strategy session simply to be near her husband. She listened with him to the reports and waited while the captains and generals conferred. The Prince's serious look and intense concentration fooled everyone into believing he was conceiving deep thoughts and brilliant plans. Until they actually got down to the business of talking strategy, when it became evident from word one her beloved hadn't a clue.

His first suggestion, that they invite their enemies over for a dinner party, was received with the mirth his captains no doubt thought he intended; but his second great idea, that they go charging out to invade the superior enemy on their own ground, killed the laughter and spread tactfully concealed dismay around the room. The generals and commanders beat a strategic retreat to do some planning of their own and figure out how to manipulate the Prince into agreeing to whatever scheme they concocted.

Cyndrith also withdrew, to consider her options. Living happily ever after, it appeared, might not be a simple matter of sitting on her throne, admiring her jewels, and letting a bunch of well-fed peasants wait on her hand and foot. She sighed and twirled her hair around her finger in an unregal manner. If she expected to have any future at all, she'd better get to work on securing it.

General Dietrich Von Kamden received her with the courtesy due her position as Princess, shadowed by doubt about her intentions. She put him at ease in fair order. "We have a problem," she said after the appropriate formalities had been observed, getting to the heart of the dilemma at once. "My husband is perhaps not the best tactician and that creates an awkward situation. I'd like to offer a solution. At least, a partial solution."

The General nodded his handsome blond head without committing himself and listened to her proposal. By the time she finished speaking, he looked cautiously enthusiastic but dubious about one point. "An interesting idea, but where are we going to get a sorcerer to provide the invisibility cloak?" he asked.

Cyndrith picked up the jeweled metal dragon figure from Von Kamden's desk and held it up and out on the end of her fingers. As she stared at it, the heavy statue began to rise from her hand. It drifted slowly across the space between them, circled once around the General's shoulders and returned to her, settling lightly back onto her palm. "I come from a rather eccentric family," she explained, placing the figurine back on the desk. "But if any hint— any whisper! —of this gets around the court, I'll turn you into a wild pig, and no amount of kissing—beautiful maiden or no—will restore you."

"I see," General Von Kamden said, while a huge grin spread across his face. It faded again as another doubt reared. "A cloak of invisibility for twelve men is a bit more involved than levitating a metal dragon."

"Trust me. You find the back door to the castle, and I'll provide the invisibility."

The smile broke out again on his face. "And the Prince?"

"It was his idea to beard the lion in his den," Cyndrith pointed out. "With a little…care I think I can convince him the rest of it figured in his plan also."

"The invisibility spell?"

"He needn't know about it." She pulled herself up to her full height of five-foot-three and gathered regality about her like a robe. "And the men involved shall not know the source."

"Indeed, Your Highness."

The scheme worked like the proverbial charm. Cyndrith rode out with the men, disguised under cloak and helm, while her maid spread the word at the castle she was ill and had taken to her bed. General Von Kamden's scouts found a back entrance to the enemies' fortress, she provided the invisibility spell, the castle gate was opened before King Josef knew what was happening, and her Prince's troops took the place and its army by surprise. Moreover, the Prince believed they owed their success entirely to his brilliant planning.

When the General's men secured the castle that day, they found themselves holding some interesting prisoners. King Josef provided a handsome payment for the release of himself, his sons, his daughter-in-law, and a couple of nobles he happened to like. He would have ransomed one particular concubine as well, but General Von Kamden decided he didn't want to let her go. And the prisoner herself didn't seem particularly upset about relocating.

Cyndrith soon began to wish the courtesan would escape, or leave, or just disappear, however. She didn't object to the General having a mistress at court; and Dhrealglina didn't interfere with or intrude on their periodic strategy sessions. But shortly after her arrival, the woman served notice she didn't intend to limit her attention to her supposed captor.

Cyndrith had enough problems already and didn't need any competition for the Prince's affection to add to them. The kingdom's situation was far from stable. King Josef might be tamed for the moment, but there were plenty of other nobles in the neighborhood waiting for the right opportunity to strike.

The most serious difficulty lay in finding out where danger would materialize next. She and General Von Kamden had already put together a package that maintained the old King's system of spies and informants, but Cyndrith never felt confident about the security or reliability of their data. A spy who could be bought by one prince might well sell out to a higher bidder.

She could use the spell of far-seeing, of course, but that one really took it out of her. When she tried it twice in the same week, she ended up sleeping for thirty straight hours and miffed the entire court by missing a state dinner.

Worse yet, while she was snoozing, the gorgeous, buxom, red-headed Dhrealglina was snuggling up to the Prince, consoling him on his wife's unfortunate indisposition, and batting her big green eyes at him. Several of the court gossips flocked to Cyndrith's bedside before she was barely awake to regale her with the stories.

Two weeks later, over the hot but futile objections of General Von Kamden, the woman was installed in the purple suite, the set of rooms traditionally reserved for the King's mistress. Cyndrith decided not to open a rift with her husband but to bide her time and opportunity.

She found herself hoping none of their enemies would choose the next few weeks to try some fancy new maneuver. She was going to be occupied with a private war, fought close to home but, nevertheless, on unfamiliar turf. The enemy was a beautiful but baffling stranger.

Cyndrith agreed with the wisdom of whoever had or would coin the phrase about the best defense being a good offense. If they didn't practice that bit of wisdom at the kingdom level, the reasons owed more to suspect offense than philosophy. She opened her private war with a frontal assault that should at the least provide a clue to the nature of the threat.

Dhrealglina was in the spacious, airy, purple suite when Cyndrith knocked and entered. A maid groomed the woman's gorgeous, waist-length red hair with a ruby-encrusted silver comb. The mistress of General and Prince stood when Cyndrith entered. "Your Highness," she said, bowing in the required courtesy, performing the rite with the merest hint of satire.

Dhrealglina was tall, taller than Cyndrith, slim where a concubine should be slim, and rounded where a…you get the idea. A white dress covered her voluptuous figure without concealing a thing. The woman waved the Princess to a chair, then resumed her seat on the bench, signaling the maid to continue service on her hair.

"I'm honored you should choose to visit me, Your Highness," the woman said after studying the Princess with keen interest. Her voice was surprisingly low, deep and rough, almost hoarse.

"We have a common interest." Cyndrith looked pointedly at the maid.

Dhrealglina smiled narrowly and dismissed the servant with a toss of her head. A strange yellow spark flared deep in the woman's green eyes. "A certain handsome Prince?" she said when the door was again shut.

"Quite." Cyndrith attempted to make her spine even straighter than it was. "And that presents me with a problem. The situation in the kingdom is unstable, and I can't afford distractions at the moment. Therefore, I'm offering you the opportunity to retire from the field gracefully. You may keep the General if he suits you, but I can't concede the Prince."

The woman's tawny brows rose as another reflection flamed up in her eyes. "No offense intended, Your Highness, but is the Prince yours to concede?"

"He was, and will be again once you're gone from the scene." Cyndrith stood up and quietly summoned an illusion. The Princess' slim form wavered, then rose and stretched, elongating to a height close to ten feet, glowing with a sun-bright beauty and majesty. Her arms rose in a graceful whirl and her shape wrapped itself in a swirling blue miasma of power and terror. People unused to the effects of sorcery tended to shrink in awe of that display.

Dhrealglina watched and permitted herself to be openly unimpressed. "Does the Prince know he's married to a sorceress?" she asked.

Cyndrith canceled the illusion, seating herself again in a manner that refused to concede she was cursing inwardly. "No more than he knows his mistress is one also," she answered.

"But she's not," Dhrealglina said with perfect calm, staring at her reflection in the mirror. Her tiny smile showed she knew that statement would discomfort the Princess even more. And damn the woman, she was right.

"Had you no magic, you wouldn't still be sitting there," Cyndrith countered.

"I made no such claim. I said only I'm not a Sorceress." The woman's slim fingers, tipped with long, pointed nails, caressed a strand of red hair.

Cyndrith summoned a smile as sly and devastating—she hoped—as the other woman's. "You think you have power enough to challenge mine? I'd remind you it was by my efforts King Josef was defeated."

Dhrealglina laughed. "King Josef! Pompous little man." She shook her head, waving reflected ripples of light from the candles down the length of her hair. "He wasn't worth the lifting of a... hand in his defense." She fondled a huge stone, set in a ring on her left hand, which collected the glow in the room and shone in a blood-red fire.

So much for a civil request. Time to find out if Dhrealglina could put her power where her mouth was. Cyndrith cupped her hand and muttered, "*Sulium Vocularo Ignis.*" From the tip of her finger a sharp, quiet, indigo flame gathered and erupted, pushed itself out, and crawled across the room, lengthening like a stretched bit of gut, until it finally jerked free of the umbilical attachment to her hand and raced toward the red-haired woman in front of the mirror. The blue flare reflected back from the glass behind her.

The woman laughed, but her defense shocked the Princess even more. Making no move to counter the flaring brand speeding in her direction, the woman instead opened her mouth, sucked in a large breath, and inhaled the air around her, flame and all. With a swish and a hiss, the blazing missile disappeared down her throat. Dhrealglina didn't even hiccup as she closed her mouth and let the smile spread across her features. "So much for playing games, Your Highness," she said, in a voice just marginally hoarser than before.

Cyndrith refused to allow any dismay to show. "What the hell are you?" she asked.

The smile faded slowly as every inch of the woman's form convulsed, wavered, misted over, stretched, shifted, and reshaped itself into something quite different: a giant lizard, nearly dwarfing the immense chamber, glittering with scales that reflected the candle-light in red-tinted rainbows. The creature's long sinewy neck bent forward to prevent the head from scraping the roof of the chamber; the snout protruded under the gleaming brow ridges in a surprisingly graceful arc. Wings of gossamer fine web folded up against the creature's body. But the eyes…

Cyndrith summoned a spell of clear-seeing. It worked, she could feel the drain of the power, but the report her brain received from her eyes failed to change. Something other than sheer sorcery, then. The woman was the truth, and the dragon was, also, reality. So… "I thought were-dragons existed only in legend and story."

The shape wavered and changed again in a blur of mist hiding the melting form. "Those revisionist historians refuse to believe anything they can't find documented in their records," Dhrealglina answered. "If you have nothing better in your arsenal than cheap fire tricks, Your Highness, I suggest you consider retiring from the field. You may keep your title and your chamber if you wish, I have no need of them." She picked up the jewel-set comb and pressed its encrusted side against her cheek.

"Generous, Madame, and if I could do only parlor tricks, I might consider the offer. As it is, though…" Cyndrith collected her power, concentrated it into her hand. If the dragon could swallow heat without harm, then how would it handle the opposite? She imagined cold, forming the icicles in a mental picture that gradually materialized as frost in her hand. When the force reached an appropriate level, she tossed it toward her adversary, watching daggers of ice shimmer around the other woman.

Noises sounded outside the chamber, more movement than normal through the castle halls, and a chatter of voices rose. Cyndrith ignored them, to concentrate on maintaining the icicle shower in the room. Dhrealglina's form again wavered and misted over, and her skin became a gleaming armored hide of scale around the shape of the woman. She held that partial transformation and sat impervious while the treacherous shards of ice fell onto and around her.

A pounding sounded on the door while they continued their battle. Dhrealglina twisted suddenly and an arm—or was it a wing?—shot out toward the princess, reaching for her neck with long, clawed talons. Cyndrith abandoned the icicles and imagined a rock, smashing down on the tip of the wing.

The summoning took shape, and the dragon yelped as its claws were squashed by the stone. It reared back and huffed in a deep breath. Cyndrith formed an ice shield around her in preparation for a wave of flame.

It didn't happen. As Dhrealglina prepared to exhale, a great bell rang and voices yelled. "Under attack! The castle is under attack!"

"Attack!" Cyndrith shook her head and waved an arm at the other woman, forming a quick order. "Hold!"

A sulfur-tinged breath came from the dragon, but no flame sparked as she exhaled. The claw withdrew and Dhrealglina resumed her normal shape, while Cyndrith dispersed her ice shield. She made a small motion of her hand, and the bolt on the door released. Three men tumbled into the room.

"Your Highness, your presence is requested by General Von Kamden," one of the men managed to spit out. His companions seemed too awed in the company of the women to do more than stare. "An army approaches, will arrive within the day. A siege party. Sizable."

"How many precisely?" she asked.

The man shook his head. "They approached through the forest. We don't know how many."

"Whose troops are they?"

"The standard belongs to the Archduke Bergeril."

"Bergeril, that snake," Cyndrith said. "I might have known. But why did the spies not warn us?"

Dhrealglina snorted "Spies can be bought by the highest bidder. And Bergeril has deep pockets."

"Too true. Tell the General we'll attend him presently," Cyndrith directed the soldier. The man bowed and left, taking his tongue-tied companions with him.

"You talk to Dietrich," Dhrealglina suggested. "I believe I can learn how many of the enemy there are."

"Or you could warn Bergeril we're scarce prepared to meet his attack," Cyndrith replied. "You abandoned King Josef's cause readily enough."

The woman turned to face the Princess, slinging red hair back from her face. "Josef never asked for or received my loyalty. It happens this place suits me, and I wish to preserve it. For the moment our interests run parallel, Princess. Take what aid I can give, and we'll settle our differences later." Her eyes challenged Cyndrith.

The Princess weighed the other woman's offer. To take her gift was a risk certainly, but one Cyndrith thought she couldn't afford to refuse. "Well enough," she agreed.

Dietrich Von Kamden was in the front part of the main keep, directing the mustering of troops. Because they'd been making an effort to improve Bradenveld's standing army, the situation wasn't quite so hopeless as it might have been a few months ago. Still, they were likely to find themselves overmatched.

"How much time do we have?" Cyndrith asked him.

The General shrugged and stroked his clipped blond beard. "A day or two at most I should guess. I wish I knew how many we faced."

"We will shortly," Cyndrith assured him. A soldier came up to request urgent assistance from the General, and Cyndrith departed to find her husband. The Prince was dealing with the crisis in his usual calm manner. His only real concern seemed to be that the third string on his lute refused to hold tune.

Cyndrith explained the situation to him and wasn't surprised when he assured her there was nothing to worry about. "I rely on Dietrich to have the problem under control," the Prince soothed. She cuddled up to him for a while and let him calm her fears and dismiss her doubts.

Sometime later she met Dhrealglina in the passage leading to the purple suite. "Three hundred foot troops," the were-dragon reported. "Perhaps a hundred mounted, three siege engines. They're about a league hence and camped for the evening already."

"Does Dietrich know about you yet?" Cyndrith asked.

"No." The woman hesitated, tossing her hair repeatedly. "He doesn't know…and I would prefer it to stay that way for now. It would upset him."

Well, well. "I'll take the report," Cyndrith offered. "He knows I'm a sorceress. He'll think I used a spell of far-seeing."

"How many do we have to meet them?" the dragon asked.

Cyndrith sighed. "Perhaps eight score trained. Two to three score more untrained but willing to help."

"Including a sorceress and a dragon," Dhrealglina pointed out. "It can be done. But they have a sorcerer in their ranks, too. Perhaps not of your power, Princess, but strong enough to see through most illusions, or create a few."

Dhrealglina's expression softened as she looked over the Princess' shoulder. Cyndrith turned to follow the direction of her gaze. General Dietrich von Kamden approached them. So... The woman's emotions were engaged, then. This did help the cause. If only she could find out what Dhrealglina really wanted most.

In the meantime, though... "Could you take out the sorcerer?" Cyndrith whispered to her. "If not kill him, disable him for a while?"

"Can you provide me with a cloak of invisibility? Such as you managed at the castle, when I was 'captured'?" the woman asked. "Just for a little while?"

"Long enough, I think," Cyndrith agreed as the General joined them. He briefed them on the Castle's state of readiness. The Princess in turn told him part of her plan; her words eased the lines of strain that seamed his face.

Cyndrith maintained the invisibility shield; under its cloak Dhrealglina knocked the Sorcerer cold, sweeping him from his horse with a wave of her powerful wings before he realized any threat approached. With the only person who could undo her work removed from the picture, Cyndrith was free to call up all the advantages her talent could provide.

She gathered her own energy and drew upon a series of runes of power she'd prepared earlier for an emergency. After some thought on how best to spend her capital, she summoned the forces of wind, water, and fire to produce a storm—a real humdinger of a storm—complete with thunder and lightning, lashing rain, hail, and raging wind.

The downpour soaked the enemy's encampment as well as the troops, particularly after the wind had blown away their tents and lean-to shelters. A bolt of lightning exploded two of the siege engines into a roaring blaze which in turn panicked the horses.

Six hours later, with no loss of life on either side, save one horse that stumbled and broke a leg rushing to escape the flames, a bedraggled and demoralized force of the Archduke Bergeril decided to await a more auspicious time to attack the Kingdom of Bradenveld. At Cyndrith's insistence, the army was allowed to return home unhindered, nursing their runny noses and stuffy heads as best they could.

Late the next day, after a long sleep had restored the Princess to a functioning condition, she sought out Dhrealglina in her chambers to finish the battle they'd begun earlier, the one that would really decide the fate of the kingdom.

Cyndrith watched as the Were-Dragon began to take shape from the form of the woman again, and the clawed hand reached out toward her throat. The Princess had decided on a change of strategy and was working on a giant knife when another realization intruded into her brain. Some balance in the contest had subtly shifted. Dhrealglina's underlying attitude had changed; some of the deep confidence had drained from her. It had started when Cyndrith threatened to tell Dietrich about his concubine. The dragon didn't want him to know, possibly because she really did care for him. And that suggested a chance to find a different sort of solution.

"Hold a moment!" Cyndrith suggested, facing the dragon. "I would ask— What is it you really want? What do we battle for?"

"Want?" The claw paused an arm's length from the Princess' throat. "The kingdom, of course," Dhrealglina returned, in the harsh growl of the lizard.

Bravado, Cyndrith decided. "All to yourself? What about the Prince?"

The dragon's brow ridges twitched. "The kingdom goes with the Prince."

"Do you want the man, or just his power?" Cyndrith asked.

The booming noise was half laugh, half dragon-grunt. "The man? Prince Karl-Erich von Bradenveld? I should want that spineless wimp? You've got to be kidding."

"You want Dietrich, though," Cyndrith said. "I saw the way you looked at him."

"He's three times the man your Prince is." The woman was intrigued enough by the direction of the questions to abandon the dragon form and resume her human shape.

"You would put him on the throne and be his Queen?"

This time her laugh was entirely human. "Stones, no. All those boring state dinners and tiresome ambassadors. I can't abide ambassadors. They don't even taste good." She wrinkled her nose in disgust.

"You don't want the official position, but you want to rule the kingdom?" Cyndrith asked.

"More or less."

"Is that why you tried to seduce the Prince?"

"Succeeded, Your Highness." An angled red brow rose in challenge.

Cyndrith controlled her reaction and waited, secure in her assessment of the situation now. "Why then?"

The woman glared at her and finally shrugged. "These rooms, for one thing."

The Princess tried to keep her utter astonishment out of her voice and face. "Rooms?"

"The apartment Dietrich offered me was too confining. It had only one small door and an even narrower window. I need space and large openings for access."

Of course. Cyndrith should have figured that out herself. "You seduced the Prince to get the royal mistress's apartments?"

"That. And some say in how the kingdom is run," the woman added. "I told you I liked it here. I'm ready to settle down in a secure home. I watched how your Prince dealt with a crisis, and, I must say, I wasn't impressed. You, on the other hand…I think perhaps I needn't worry so much about security as I thought." Dhrealglina measured her opponent with a look and appeared to be doing some mental calculations.

Cyndrith paused a moment to add weight to her next words. "Perhaps we can reach an accommodation," she suggested. "The rooms are yours, as well as the General." Indeed, Cyndrith hoped the woman would keep Dietrich happy for a long time; a General of his ability was worth a few sacrifices. "The Prince I cannot concede or share, however," she added. "There will be no rivals to challenge the claim of my children to the throne."

Dhrealglina stared into the mirror, then looked back over her shoulder. "Are you proposing a deal, Your Highness? The rooms and the General if I'll leave the Prince alone?" She looked more closely at the Princess, a cunning smile playing around her lips. "But I already have the rooms and the General, and the Prince I could probably take, too." It was her last card, and she knew, even as she played it, how little it was worth.

"Perhaps," Cyndrith agreed. "But you couldn't hold him, and you'd lose Dietrich in the process. I guarantee it." She paused to let the threat sink in, then baited the hook. "In any case, I'm willing to offer more. I notice you've a fondness for jewels. I presume you like gold and other precious metals, as well?"

Dhrealglina nodded slowly, eyes narrowed.

"I happen to know the locations of a few forgotten caches of treasure. I could find others. Indeed, it's a trivial exercise for a sorceress."

The woman didn't answer and appeared to consider the offer, but Cyndrith had seen the gleam of greed light her face. "You really do love that deceptive hunk of a Prince, don't you?" Dhrealglina asked finally.

Cyndrith drew a breath. "He may not be much of a military commander, but he's very good at entertaining ambassadors. He's sweet-natured, charming, a wonderful dancer. And he'll make a fine and royal father for my children."

Dhrealglina nodded and offered a long-nailed hand to the Princess. "Dietrich is still three times the man. I hope I can rely on your discretion concerning my nature. In return, your own secret remains safe with me, Sorceress."

"Quite," Cyndrith agreed, taking her fingers. "I believe we'll deal well together. Who knows? We might even manage to live happily ever after. But I'm not betting the kingdom on it."

~ * ~ * ~

Karen McCullough sold her first novel to Avalon Books in 1989 and has since written more than two dozen published novels and novellas in the mystery, romance, suspense, and fantasy genres, including the **Market Center Mysteries** Series and two books in the **No Brides Club** series of romance novels. She has won numerous awards, including an Eppie Award for fantasy, and has also been a finalist in the Daphne, Prism, Dream Realm, Rising Star, Lories, and Vixen Award contests as well as a semifinalist in the Writers of the Future contest. Her shorter fiction has appeared in several anthologies and small press publications.

Karen is a member of Mystery Writers of America and its local Southeast chapter; Sisters in Crime and its local chapters, Murder We Write (Greensboro, Winston-Salem, High Point, NC area) and Triangle Sisters in Crime (Raleigh Durham area); and the Piedmont Authors Network. She's a past president of the Southeast Chapter of Mystery Writers of America and has served on the national MWA board and been a judge for its annual Edgar Awards.

She is currently treasurer of the Piedmont Authors Network.

She lives in Greensboro, NC, with her husband of many years.

Website: http://www.kmccullough.com
Blog: http://www.kmccullough/kblog
Facebook: https://www.facebook.com/KarenMcCulloughAuthor

The Beggar Prince

Mark Bruce

"I'm tired of trying to see the good in people," my dragon wife sighed, a puff of smoke escaping from her lips.

"My sweet," I replied, "you married a thief. You are constantly battling and barbecuing foolish knights who come to our cave thinking they will make their reputation by skinning your scales. I can't think as to how you would ever have seen the good in any of the people you have to deal with. And I humbly include myself in that menagerie."

She gave me a sideways look from her kaleidoscopic eyes. She sat on a tree branch in her human form, a melancholy expression on her cute chubby face.

"Nonetheless," she said, now looking off into the distance, "I can be a trusting soul. I want people to be good. Every once in a while, a human will surprise me by actually having good qualities and doing me a good turn."

"When you are in womanly form," I said.

"Yes," she said dismissively. "No one is inclined to do a good turn when I am in full dragon regalia. They are too terrified."

I sat down on the branch. I put my arm around her and kissed her on the neck.

"My wife," I said, "I know you too well to think this is some passing fancy. Tell your husband what ails you."

She shook her head.

"You will think me foolish."

"Everyone knows dragons are wise from their thousands of years of living," I said. In fact, sometimes my wife did foolish things. She would rouse herself in anger at some local town over some slight insult—the last incident was a puppet show in Middleton, in which a dragon did not fare well in the script—and she would fly over and set fire to portions of the town. Then she would return to me, sheepishly admitting her indiscretion.

"No," she said, "this time you will truly think me a silly old female."

"Ah," I said. "It involves some beautiful young man."

She nodded silently.

I am not a beautiful young man. I am a middle-aged thief tending toward fat. I have a rubbery face and salt and pepper hair. She loves me because I know who and what she is and nonetheless love her madly, even when she is in dragon mode. Dragons are not easily fooled—except by youth and beauty.

"Tell me about this young fraud," I said.

She sighed again, another little puff of smoke escaping from her.

"When you went to St. Bartholomew's Fair to lift a few purses," she said, "I found him at the mouth of the cave. He was bruised and scratched and had a few sword wounds. He looked to be nearly dead."

"And he was young and blond and beautiful," I said. My wife has a weakness for blondes of either sex.

"He was moaning softly, so softly I did not hear him at first," she continued, saying nothing about my guess as to the appearance of the young man, and thus confirming it. "I was sleeping."

My Dragon Wife is a heavy sleeper. I doubted the young man's moans were soft.

"I went out of the cave in my woman's dress. He sprawled on the ground as if someone had cast him there. My heart melted. He seemed so innocent and lost."

And beautiful, I said to myself.

"I brought him some water and he gratefully drank. Then he looked at me with the most glittering green eyes you've ever seen." My Dragon Wife is partial to green eyes, as they most closely resemble a gemstone. "He thanked me, called me 'his good woman,' told me I was an angel and I was the loveliest maiden he'd ever seen."

"Did you bother to tell him you were married? And a dragon?" I asked sharply.

She shook her head.

"I told you I was foolish," she said in a low voice.

"Well, it can't be helped now," I said. "What happened next?"

Actually, I knew what happened next, being a thief and wise in the many ways a man can make a woman part with gold and jewels and whatever else she has.

"He told me he was a prince, a crown prince whose evil

cousin had kidnapped him and had taken him to the woods to kill him. But as his cousin and his mercenaries neared the cave, they decided they would not bloody their hands with him. They beat him senseless so he wouldn't cry out. They left him unconscious in front of the cave to let the dragon have him."

The old Lost Prince dodge, I thought. I'd done it once or twice in my own youth, though I was never so bold and brassy as to try it on a dragon.

"I took him into the cave. I fed him some of that hare you cooked before you left. He revived at that, then regaled me with tales of his life in the castle. He had a Princess to whom he was betrothed, he said. If he didn't get back to the castle soon, his wicked cousin would marry her and become a false king."

And in order to raise an army, I thought to myself, he would need gold and jewels and other precious things to recruit good men to rally to the cause. Yes, I've done this dodge a few times. I was now too old and fat to pose as a young, beautiful prince.

She told me she gave him a hundred pieces of gold to raise an army. I nodded sagely.

"He promised to come back to show me his grand army before he went to claim his birthright," she said. "That was weeks ago. And he never came back."

She sighed again, this time a small lick of flame escaping her nostrils.

"I don't know if he's been captured or killed or whether I have given my money to a thief," she said. "In a way, I rather hope he's been killed. It would restore my faith in humanity."

I pulled her closer to me and whispered in her ear, "Then, my love, we will believe he died a bloody and excruciating death, whispering your name on his tongue as he died."

My wife is known as Lady Eloise. As are all dragons, she is of noble blood.

"Did he happen to mention which kingdom he was heir to?" I asked. She surprised me with her answer.

"Of course he did. I am not *that* foolish. It was Stargard."

This did not fit the pattern. It was important, when playing the Lost Prince Dodge, to be vague about the kingdom from which you came. Stargard was a very real kingdom, some hundreds of miles from our cave.

She jumped down from the tree.

"I will go to Stargard," she said. "I will see if he has died a brave and horrible death; and is therefore honorable—or whether he's spending my gold in a tavern on barmaids."

"In which case," I said, "he will likely still suffer a horrible death, if not nearly so brave."

She smiled at me and transformed herself.

~ * ~

I insisted on coming with her, riding on her neck as she flew. I doubted whether her young blond, green-eyed beauty was within a thousand miles of Stargard. If I had conned a dragon out of a hundred pieces of gold, I'd go as far and as fast the other way as I could.

Within an hour we were nearing Stargard. I suggested it might not be a good idea for her to fly into town in her fearsome true form. She agreed and set us down in the hills behind the kingdom. We emerged from the woods and onto the main road, two middle aged people out for a stroll.

We found him in the third tavern we tried. We heard laughter and jeering and cries of "Your Majesty" sung in a sarcastic tone. Lady Eloise looked at me, her eyebrow cocked. We went in.

There, standing on a table, was a beautiful blond youth, his green eyes flashing, his clothes ragged and dirty. The crowd around him threw ale and chicken bones at him.

"You know your rightful king has been usurped!" he cried. "You know Prince Halbert has dark designs on the Princess Aurora and this kingdom. If you do not assist me, you will be taxed to death and your homes will never be safe!"

The landlord pulled the young man off the table and took him by the seat of his pants. He unceremoniously threw the lad out of the tavern, to the cheers of the crowd.

The young man sprawled on the street and lay still for a long moment. I looked to my wife and saw her eyes soften.

So this young idiot wasn't a con man after all. Still, I doubted he was the Crown Prince. He looked more like a mad beggar.

My wife went to the boy and lifted him up. He seemed groggy at first, but then looked at her and began to cry.

"Oh, my Lady Eloise," he sobbed. "I am unworthy of your

tenderness. I have failed and failed and failed again. No one will follow me."

"Poor dear," she said.

"My Prince," I said, deciding to play along with the madman's game, "have you been trying to recruit your army in taverns?"

He hung his head.

"I've tried everywhere. Farms. Inns. Churches. But they all laugh and call me 'The Beggar Prince.'"

I looked at his ragged blouse, his dirty pantaloons. His blond hair was smeared with dirt. His face was scratched and bruised.

"I have to admit, sire, you certainly look the part," I said.

"I know, I know," he said. "Sometimes I wonder if I am not the victim of some crazed demon who makes me believe I am a Prince." He looked down.

"Poor dear," my wife said again. "We need to clean you up. Get you some better clothes. Then perhaps you will have better luck."

He smiled a sad smile but shook his head. Then he jumped up and walked over to the alley behind the tavern. He returned with a burlap sack.

"I hid this before I went into that tavern. At least, my lady, I can return this to you intact," he said. I heard the jingle of coin.

My wife reached out for the sack and looked inside. Being a dragon, she knew each coin she owned by its essence and sheen. She did not need to count.

"It's all here," she said in pleased surprise. "Why did you not offer this to your recruits?"

"Because I wanted them to fight for the right reason," he said. "As king I will be a good and fair monarch. That should be enough for a man to fight. Already my subjects are grumbling about my cousin's heavy taxes. He punishes all who speak against him, sends spies out into the world. They are frightened by the disappearance of parish priests who preach against his oppression." He gestured to the bag. "I fully intended to give them their pay. But not before they declared their allegiance. Paid mercenaries are poor soldiers."

In that moment I realized our blond youth was not mad. He might even be a prince. In any event, by returning my wife's gold he had won her heart completely.

"When is the wedding of your cousin and Princess Aurora?"

she asked him.

"Tomorrow at ten o'clock," he said sadly. "So it is too late. I have failed. But I will always be grateful for your assistance, my Lady." Then he chuckled ruefully. "You have the gratitude of the Beggar Prince."

At that moment we felt rough hands seize us and throw us to the ground.

"Ah, so this is the young upstart who impersonates the late Prince Robert!" a voice said. I spotted five men with clubs and swords. They wore dark doublets and were broad chested and unshaven.

One of the swordsmen lifted his blade to kill the youth but another stopped him.

"Remember, we are to take him alive!" the second man said. The first man grunted. Then he gestured at myself and my wife.

"No one said anything about taking these two alive," he said. I reached for the little dagger I kept in my left boot. I had no intention of being skewered without a fight.

But my wife stood defiantly before them.

"You will apologize for laying hands on me," she said. "I am Lady Eloise of the Brook."

"Oh, my Ladyship," said the first rough, a laughing tone in his voice. "I had no idea."

My wife's eyes narrowed as she regarded the man.

"You will apologize," she repeated, "or you will regret it."

The rough looked around him mockingly.

"My Lady seems to have forgotten her bodyguard," he said. "Unless this fat old man and this feckless boy are escorting you."

Her eyes narrowed even further. She approached him and he swung his sword to take off her head.

When in Human form, a dragon's reflexes make lightning look like molasses. She disarmed the man with a swift overhand move, then relieved him of his head with his own sword. She spun and skewered the second one before he could raise his weapon. The other three roughs did not tarry to see what she planned for them.

"Well then," Lady Eloise said. "Perhaps we should look into finding some suitable clothes for your coronation, my Prince."

~ * ~

It wasn't cheap. As if the merchants of Stargard knew they were dealing with a wealthy woman, they charged her three times the true worth of the clothing and armor she purchased for the Beggar Prince. Each time a merchant would demand gold pieces for their wares, my wife would whisper to each coin in anguish that she loved them and would miss them and would somehow devise how to rescue them from the greedy hands of humans who had no idea of their true worth. She told each coin they were being sacrificed for a good cause. Then she would shed a sulfurous tear and hand the coins over.

The result, however, was magnificent. The Beggar Prince, in rich dress and shining armor, looked every inch royal.

When we finally went to the shield maker, he whispered instruction to the man as to the appearance of his family crest. The shield maker paled.

"My lord," he said, "such a herald is illegal in these parts."

My wife sighed.

"How much more?" she asked.

The man's eyes turned from fright to greed.

"At least twenty gold pieces," he said.

"Done," my wife said, not deigning to bargain with the man. It was the last of the hundred pieces of gold.

When we retrieved the shield later that afternoon, Prince Robert took it on his arm with professional acumen. The Lady Eloise looked at the heraldic animal on the shield and her eyes misted over. The Beggar Prince gave her a shy smile.

"Thank you, my Lady," he said. "If my family is to be exterminated tomorrow morning, at least we will go out flying our own colors and our own family crest."

The shield gave me an idea.

"My Prince," I said, "what sort of army does your cousin surround himself with?"

"Mercenaries," he said.

"Ah," I said. "So they are loyal to money, not to the man." I looked over at my wife. "How are you planning on defeating your cousin and his army tomorrow?"

"Defeating?" the young prince laughed. "I cannot defeat an army on my own. But I can die with honor so the world will know what a usurping dog my cousin is."

"So you plan on charging your cousin in the open courtyard," my wife said doubtfully.

"Yes," he said defiantly.

"My Prince, I have a different idea." I nodded to the shield. "Tomorrow go into the courtyard with your ragged beggar's clothes covering your armor. Then, when your cousin appears, toss the rags away and call upon the guardian of your royal line to aid you."

He looked at me doubtfully.

"That is madness," he said.

"No more mad than charging a hundred armed men." I shrugged. "What do you have to lose?"

~ * ~

The next morning the Beggar Prince and I squeezed our-selves into the palace courtyard. The mercenaries had erected a pyre, upon which was tied a priest. The priest's mouth was gagged, and above him was a sign: "Thus to all who preach against Prince Halbert."

Surrounding the priest were at least two hundred knights in various armors and colors. The mercenaries. They all smelled of mead. They were drunk, laughing and shouting bad jokes to the priest about having a "hot time."

It was all I could do to keep Prince Robert from charging the pyre and attempting to free the priest. I reminded him we had a plan and his wicked cousin would likely make an appearance to commence the burning before the wedding.

"I miss the Lady Eloise," he said.

"Alas, she has matters that need tending to elsewhere," I said.

"It would have been noble to die in her presence," he said.

"Isn't it enough I'm going to die with you?" I asked ruefully.

Our conversation was cut short by a blast of off-key trumpets. The mercenaries brought themselves to random order and faced Prince Halbert.

He was a fat, ugly customer, dark haired. I looked into the man's eyes and recognized a fellow thief, a greedy gleam in his eyes. But there was also a cruelty and an arrogance in his face I never allowed to sneak into my own, even when I was running the con of the Lost Prince.

Prince Halbert wore a shiny chest plate, his fat crowding

around it. He looked around the courtyard expectantly. He saw nothing but a crowd of townsmen, a ragged beggar, and a thief in motley. He nodded.

"My subjects," he said in a squeaky voice, "We have business to transact before my wedding to Princess Aurora. This priest has prophesied my late Cousin Robert of the House of Elder will return to claim his throne. As we all know, Prince Robert was devoured by the evil dragon of the North. I cannot have such slander being preached. Look upon his agony and learn, my subjects. I do not wish to be a cruel ruler unless you force it upon me."

He nodded at a mercenary who held a flaming torch. The man nodded back and approached the pyre.

The Beggar then leapt in front of him. He slapped the torch out of the man's hands.

"NO!" he bellowed, pulling a sword from his rags.

"What are you about, villain?" Prince Halbert said.

Prince Robert climbed to the top of the pyre and tossed off his rags, revealing his splendid armor.

"I am Prince Robert and I have come to reclaim my place as ruler of this kingdom!"

I could see the color drain from Prince Halbert's face. He recognized the boy. Nonetheless, he shouted:

"Imposter! Kill him!"

The mercenaries began to charge the Prince. The boy raised his shield to the sky.

"I call upon the guardian of the House of Elder to aid my just cause!"

The mercenaries paused for a moment, confused.

"You idiots," Prince Halbert screamed, "he's bluffing. No beast from a shield is going to come rescue him!"

The mercenaries then laughed and resumed their charge. The boy bravely lowered his shield and held his sword at the ready. I had leapt on the pyre, my little dagger out of my boot.

"This is my fight, thief," he muttered at me. "Go home to your good wife."

"She'd never forgive me for leaving you, my Prince," I said. "Anyway, this is as good a way to die as any."

By this time the mercenaries had regained the torch and decided it was easier to set us on fire than to risk a scratch from our blades.

One of them touched the pyre, which roared up immediately.

"I guess tactical thinking is not your strong suit, my Prince," I said. I used my blade to cut the ropes holding the priest. "Fortunately for you, my tactical skills are excellent. Now raise your shield again and call once more on your guardian."

To the boy's credit he didn't ask questions. He raised his shield so all could see its heraldic beast painted in red and glowing with the reflection of the fire.

"I call upon the guardian of the House of Elder who is no stranger to fire to aid me in my just cause!" he shouted with all the confidence he didn't feel. This time the mercenaries didn't quail. They laughed and called up rude names.

"Once more," I said to the Prince, starting to feel the heat and sweating in my motley. "I don't think she heard you."

"She?"

"Your guardian."

"I call upon…"

He didn't get the rest of it out. A rough wind filled the courtyard—which, unfortunately, fanned the flames higher toward us. I felt my motley singe.

The mercenaries and Prince Halbert put their hands to their eyes. The fierce wind knocked some soldiers down.

Then a tremendous roar scorched the air. From behind the far castle wall, rose a large red dragon—almost the mirror image of the one on Prince Robert's shield. Its massive wings flapped, causing more wind. Its mouth spit fire, first in little balls of flame that blackened the rears of mercenaries, then in a long stream that ran along the far wall of the castle near Prince Halbert.

The mercenaries did what mercenaries do best. They ran.

My Dragon Wife flew over the pyre and grabbed the Prince from the flames in her talons. She deposited him safely on the castle steps, near his fat cousin.

I grabbed the priest and we both leapt off the pyre just as the floor of wood collapsed. I shot a glare at my wife, who didn't notice, as she was gazing lovingly at Prince Robert.

Then my wife's kaleidoscopic eyes hardened toward Robert's cousin. She took Prince Halbert into her talons and flew up high into the heavens. We all thought she was going to drop him into the flames, as well she should have. But after dangling him in the air, she unceremoniously dropped him in the middle of the muddy courtyard.

Prince Halbert rolled and groaned. A fireball from my wife forced him to rise, then to fall on his knees before Prince Robert.

"You are my true liege," Prince Halbert said in a shaky voice, "and I pledge fealty to you."

Prince Robert had the grace not to look surprised. Instead he raised his shield to my wife, who still hovered above him.

"Guardian of the House of Elder," he said, "I will be true to your spirit."

The people in the courtyard cheered.

~ * ~

"Having the Dragon of Elder appear put the people on his side," my wife said as we sat in our cave a few days later, eating a bit of hare stew. She was in her human form again. "Much more effective than an army."

"Your timing was a bit off," I grumbled. "That fire got a bit too close to me and that poor priest. Were you intending to come back for me?"

She shrugged.

"I figured you'd have the sense to jump." She looked dreamily into her stew. "Prince Robert is a beautiful boy," she said. "I'd completely forgotten how I'd helped his great-great grandfather two hundred years ago."

"Who, no doubt," I said, "was also a beautiful green-eyed blond youth."

She looked into the distance, a small smile on her face.

"Yes," she said. "He certainly was." Then she sighed. "My only regret is the loss of my gold to buy the boy's armor." She sighed as if thinking of lost lovers.

"Ah, my dear," I said, pulling out my purse. "This is why you married a thief." I poured the coins into her lap. "After the coronation, I liberated your gold from those greedy merchants. And serves them right for overcharging you."

My wife's kaleidoscopic eyes glowed with surprise and delight. She picked up the coins and held them to her considerable breasts. She whispered happily to them, hot tears in her eyes. The she pulled me closer to her, the pleasing scent of sulfur on her breath.

"Ah, my love," she whispered, "you have restored my faith in humanity."

~ * ~ * ~

Mark Bruce is a Vietnam-Era Disabled Veteran (US Air Force) working as a solo lawyer in San Bernardino, California. He obtained his BA in Journalism from Humboldt State University (magna cum laude) and his JD from UC Berkeley's Boalt Hall School of Law, where he was a finalist in the McBain Oral Advocacy Competition, arguing in front of Justice Antonin Scalia (Scalia's take on Bruce: "You're not a wimp.")

He has published short stories in Alfred Hitchcock Mystery Magazine, Black Cat Mystery Magazine, The Griffin and other publications and anthologies. He won the 2018 Black Orchid Novella Award from the Nero Wolfe Society for his story "Minerva James and the Goddess of Justice." He has also published poems and essays. Some of his comic essays on the lawyer's life have been used by the California State Bar in client relations training.

His son is about to receive a Ph.D in Aerospace Engineering at Michigan University. That's right, his son is a rocket scientist. His son's family recently added "grandpa" to the list of titles Mark Bruce rejoices in when Augusta Bruce came into the world in March 2021.

At present Bruce lives in Hesperia, California with a stuffed mermaid named Mariah and his writing support dragon, Ferdinand.

The Wyvern and the Dragon

Claire Davon

The dragon soared over the ship, its scales glinting green in the sunlight.

Corsud surfaced to breathe, pausing for a moment on top of the waves, and watching the drama. Terrified humans ran along the deck of the craft, pointing to the sky. The dragon belched a gout of flame, leaving smoke trails in its wake. It wheeled on its tail and came back. If there had been any hope it was simply passing by, that was dispelled by the turn.

Corsud's grey hide was drab. Like him, it paled in comparison to his larger cousins. Even if the emerald dragon spotted him, Corsud doubted he would care.

That was how it went with his bigger kin. Wyverns did not need their corresponding element to be whole as the dragons did, but neither did they gleam like the bigger beasts.

Corsud ducked under the water before the dragon could detect him. The dolphin pod that was nearby swarmed the area, chittering to one another. The sailors had been feeding them morsels their entire journey, causing both the pod and Corsud to follow.

Now the ship was doomed.

None of the local sea animals had the ability to take on the scaly, four-legged, fire breathing beast. He had two legs to the dragon's four, and a fish tail where the dragon had a huge, barbed thing. He could barely fly on his meager wings. In addition, he could not be out of his element for long. It was absurd to think he could fight such a monster. He would be defeated in no time.

The dragon shot past, flame drifting behind him as he flew. He turned as soon as he passed and came back. He repeated this, each time the arc growing smaller. On the dragon's next pass it would be close enough to set the masts on fire.

His powerlessness beat at him. He was only one wyvern and could not rescue an entire boat. Perhaps he could get a few to safety, but even that was questionable. More likely they would go into the sea and drown or be eaten by sharks.

The dolphin pod was nowhere in sight. He couldn't blame

them. He should do the same, but something kept him there. These sailors had been kind to him when nobody else had. He was an unneeded wyvern, with no clutch, and no friends to call his own. It was hopeless—but he was the only thing standing between the men and disaster. He was a lone wyvern, and would not be missed if he failed.

Corsud plunged to the bottom, his frills flowing behind him as he went down. When he landed on the ocean floor he began running, using his claws to propel himself forward.

When he had gained sufficient speed, he launched toward the sky, his wings and legs tucked against his body for added aerodynamics. The sun grew brighter as he soared upward.

When he broke the surface, he spread his wings, water streaming off him as he flew. The emerald dragon turned its wedge-shaped head toward Corsud. Its whiskers twitched before it turned away from Corsud and focused once again on the ship. It roared and a gout of flame blasted the mast. Corsud spat the water in his mouth at the dragon's target as he reached the top of his arc and began falling back to the ocean. The blaze guttered and died. The dragon screamed his anger. A small fire persisted on the mast and as he fell, he saw men scrambling up the pole to deal with the damage.

Corsud sensed more than saw the larger emerald dragon streak after him. When he hit the ocean he regained his balance and made his way downward.

The ocean rocked when the emerald dragon slammed into it. Schools of fish darted this way and that, their terrified eyes showing their distress. The water quickly changed from the sunlight zone to the midwater zones, losing the light, as he plummeted down. Sharks lurked in the depths, scanning for food. Eels and turtles swam past him, paying him no attention.

His only chance lay at the bottom of the ocean, and his gills and tail. It wasn't much of an advantage, not when the behemoth was twice his size. The other dragon was right behind him, judging by the underwater waves.

To his shock, out of nowhere dolphins surrounded him. Their leader raised his nose to Corsud in a gesture of greeting before the pod turned to face his attacker.

The other dragon was to Corsud's left, having headed straight down when Corsud feinted to the side. His body glittered in the faint light and would have been remarkable if he were not trying to snap Corsud into wyvern morsels. He doubted the dragon could see in these depths, giving him an advantage.

The dolphins formed a circle around the intruder, nipping at him with their sharp teeth. The emerald dragon flailed in the deep. He headed for the surface, using his great legs to propel himself. Bubbles streamed away and he suspected it wouldn't be long before the dragon needed air. He thought about attack, but then decided it was better to let the monster go. Their point had been made, and it should move on to less-difficult prey. This emerald dragon was not the biggest or the most respected of all the dragons, that was reserved for the gold and silver dragons, but it was a fearsome beast nonetheless. Their elements, the ones they needed to survive, were much more sought after than the one this dragon required, but all metals and gemstones had value to humans. The dragon breached the surface and flew away, becoming a speck in the distance. It remained to be seen if it was gone for good or just for now. In the meantime, the humans had a reprieve.

~ * ~

One of the masts was burned and patchy and the boat now lay idle. He'd seen the men use wooden objects to move when the wind died, but air was their primary method of transportation. Now they would have to employ a different method to get back to land.

Dolphins began surfacing, and some men broke off from their repairs to watch the pod dance. Humans thought of dolphins as friendly, amiable beasts. They had never seen the pod circle schools of fish, forcing them into tight spirals until they gulped down as many small bodies as they could. That was the nature of things. Eat or be eaten. Kill or be killed. It was no different for wyverns. Useless males were cast out of the group to fend for themselves.

Now the entire pod was playing, breaching and coming up, entertaining the humans. Corsud watched their shenanigans, wishing he could participate.

It was only when the shouts grew shrill that Corsud understood the danger. He had ducked underwater himself and surfaced, stretching his wings out in a parody of flight. He glanced over at the humans, expecting them to be applauding, when he noticed they were pointing upward. Corsud followed their attention, and saw the emerald dragon was returning. He had hoped for more time, but that had been foolish.

The dragon went from a speck to a blob to full-sized in a matter of moments. He raced toward them faster than Corsud could have imagined and grabbed a half-grown dolphin in its huge jaws. It tossed its head, snapping the still-writhing creature in half. He swallowed the portion as the other part of the dead creature fell. The remaining dolphins chittered and darted under the surface, moving away.

The dragon roared in triumph, and wheeled around to the ship. The sailors were once again crying out in horror. They had armed themselves with oars and pieces of the mast as well as human implements, such as what Corsud understood was a cooking pot. Humans liked to cook their food, something Corsud did not understand. There was nothing better than raw fish. Except, perhaps, raw dragon.

The emerald dragon descended, belching fire, its multi-faceted eyes trained on a second mast. He could not see the pod, but he did not blame them. They had just watched one of their own get eaten as easily as if they were minnows. He was on his own, despite their brief allegiance earlier. He retreated to shouts of dismay when he disappeared.

Once again Corsud went down far enough and then began a rapid climb upwards, gaining speed as he went. He could not see the beast in the air, but he had marked his location when he went under. Sea life scattered in front of him. He doubted he had the strength to reach the dragon, but he had to try.

When he shot out of the water the dragon was spraying fire over the remaining ship's masts, which were glowing with yellow /orange flames.

Corsud plowed into the dragon, knocking him sideways. He roared in defiance as Corsud opened his wings, trying to use them to pivot as the dragon had.

Corsud raked the other dragon with his claws as his trajectory began to lead downward. His wings were already failing.

"Get the dragon. Get the dragon," the sailors shouted.

He turned with his claws out as the dragon roared at him. There were multiple rows of teeth in his impressive mouth. The fire was spreading near the deck. He still had water from his run. Corsud angled past the other dragon. Fire touched his flank as he dumped his load onto the masts.

He turned around to face the giant maw of the other dragon. It roared at him, emitting a bit of flame. Corsud had no flame, no wingspan, nothing to defend himself against this monster. It was going to be over in a matter of moments.

"Push him toward us," a grizzled old man with a long white beard and only one eye said. The ship, wet on the decks but still burning at the top, looked small and vulnerable in that vast ocean. They, like him, were no match for the dragon. The difference was Corsud could escape to the water, and the men would drown—or be eaten—there.

The other dragon roared and lurched toward him. Corsud managed to dodge just in time. The dragon went past, its tail knocking him off balance. Corsud plummeted, spiraling, flapping his paltry wings to try and get purchase. The wind changed, but it was an artificial breeze. The dragon was following. He dropped past the craft and pulled up, skimming over the top of the waves. The dragon went a few leagues before pivoting and turning back to him.

Grey shapes darted around him. Corsud stared in amazement even as the dragon sped toward them. The dolphins had not fled after all.

In the distance he saw additional mammals, ones that were not of the pod that traveled with him. The new entrants spat at the dragon, who wheeled away as the dolphins came closer. They came in waves, their grey bodies spinning as they launched into the air before falling back to the sea. Corsud banked, using his wings in a way he hadn't imagined he could.

Corsud skimmed along the waves, trying to keep close to the water. The sailors hurled small projectiles at the emerald dragon. One of the dolphin pod spun out of the depths and poked its beak at the dragon. The dragon tried to turn its massive bulk, but it was too slow. More beasts pecked at the dragon and he flapped his mighty wings to escape their forays.

Corsud's wings were weak, straining against his weight, but he could do no less than the others. The emerald dragon turned and Corsud feared he would begin his run again. The masts were still burning, but the flames were being extinguished one at a time.

The dragon roared again. Bits of fire streamed out of its mouth, but much less than before. Corsud waited for a full roasting, but it didn't come. The dragon spat a word in his speech. *Emerald.* Somewhere in that ship's hold was emerald, as Corsud had suspected. That was what the dragon wanted. He chittered his understanding at the pod. One jumped onto the deck and bumped against one of the humans, bobbing its head to the hold. The dolphin chittered at the man, who stared at it in astonishment. Corsud emitted a roar, hoping the man would recognize what he wanted him to do. The dragon did not move from his position. *Emerald*, it said again. The men watched as it circled, its multi-faceted eyes fixed on the belly of the ship beneath the waves. If only he could make the man comprehend. The gems were valuable to men, and perhaps they were not willing to part with it.

Then he saw one of the men was holding a piece of the mineral. In its natural state the emerald was encased in the rock they had chipped it out of. It didn't have the coloring of the dragon, but that wasn't important.

The dolphin nosed the emerald, and then indicated the sky. The captain nodded his approval and the sailor hurled the stone at the dragon. The piece struck the dragon and dissolved into its scales. The scales it touched gleamed brighter. The dragon let out a triumphant roar. The man shouted something to the others. Some scrambled down an opening and vanished. They emerged a minute later holding a burlap sack.

As he watched the original sailor handed chunks of emerald to his fellows. This was their cargo, the reason they were on the sea and yet they were now sacrificing it. Emerald pieces flew at the dragon, each piece sinking in as it struck the beast. This went on for almost a minute, the projectiles making the dragon's hide brighter. The dragon turned this way and that, catching each new missile.

The dragon flew upward, shooting high, and then pivoted, heading back down. Corsud's heart fell. The men hadn't supplied enough of their emerald. This had been a mere appetizer. Now the dragon would dive through the ship, ripping it apart in search of the rest.

Instead, the dragon headed for Corsud. He tried frantically to flap his wings to get away, but he was no match for the monster.

The dragon streaked toward him, the emerald lending it strength as well as color. Corsud waited for the rake of the dragon's claws, but it twitched its whiskers at him and sped off. He watched as it receded into the distance, its newly green hide gleaming in the sun.

Corsud plummeted to the sea, his strength ebbing from him. His puny wings could support him no longer. He was so tired, all he wanted to do was fall to the ocean floor and sleep. Against all odds they had beaten the dragon. He didn't know how the creature had gotten the man to understand. Dolphins tugged at him until he focused on the foundering ship. The danger may be over, but the men were not safe.

Summoning his strength, he struggled to the surface. The fire was out, but the masts were burned, the sails gone. He wanted to rest, but his job was not done. Without his help they were still in trouble. They would drift on the current and die of starvation or thirst. He couldn't allow these men to come to harm.

Corsud rose from the sea again to observe their surroundings. A tiny speck in the distance caught his attention. He hoped that was where the land was. It was very far away. He pointed his body in the direction they needed to go, his aching wings threatening to give out with every flap.

The dolphins flanked the ship and began guiding it. The remaining oars were lowered into the water. Corsud led them, despite his flagging strength, toward land. When he was sure they were going in the right direction he went back to the sea and let exhaustion claim him.

~ * ~

When he woke they had gotten close enough to hope they would be able to make it back. Far in the distance was the tops of what might be the masts of other ships, a sign they were nearing human civilization. It had been almost a day since he collapsed, and he was amazed the pod had carried him for this long. They had not abandoned him.

The men shouted at each other as land came closer. When Corsud poked his nose through the waves they cheered and pointed toward him.

Despite his failing wings, he rose from the sea to come level with the craft. The men gathered on the deck and waved. He stayed one moment longer. They smiled and bowed to him. Then he swam alongside the dolphins as they guided the humans toward land.

When they were close enough he watched as the boat made its slow way toward safety, the men shouting encouragement as they rowed. He would never see those men again. Their story of a dragon and a wyvern would be chalked up to fever dreams. That didn't matter. They knew the truth of what had happened there.

He watched them go, and then turned back to the sea. This was his pod now. Part of him longed for his own kind, but no wyvern had done for him what the dolphins had. These creatures had proven their friendship. They were better than the wyverns because they accepted him for who he was. It would have been easy to swim away, but they had not.

One carried a fish to him in its mouth. Corsud consumed it in one bite, realizing how hungry he was. He located a fish ball in the distance. One was not going to be enough to sate him. He had fought a dragon—a dragon! —and won.

Corsud shook his paltry wings, the ones that had held him when it mattered, and chittered to the dolphins. Then they began swimming, heading for their prey.

~ * ~ * ~

Claire Davon can't remember a time when writing wasn't part of her life. Growing up, she used to write stories with her friends. As a teenager she started out reading fantasy and science fiction, but her diet quickly changed to romance and happily-ever-after's. A native of Massachusetts and cold weather, she left all that behind to move to the sun and fun of California, but has always lived no more than twenty miles from the ocean.

In college she studied acting with a minor in creative writing. In hindsight she should have flipped course studies. Before she was published, she sold books on eBay and discovered some of her favorite authors by sampling the goods, which was the perfect solution. Claire has many book-irons in the fire, most notably her urban fantasy series, The Elementals' Challenge series, but writes contemporary and shifter romances as well as.

While she's not a movie mogul or actor, she does work in the film industry with her office firmly situated in the 90210 district of Hollywood. Prone to break out into song, she is quick on feet and just as quick with snappy dialogue. In addition to writing she does animal rescue, reads, and goes to movies. She loves to hear from fans, so feel free to drop her a line.

Nog, the not so Terrible

Kevin David Anderson

Nog the Terrible felt pretty jubilant these days. Certainly, a lot less terrible and more like a plain old, every day, run of the mill, dragon. At least a month had gone by without a single human, sprite, or even a courage-impaired pixie shrieking away from him in terror. The changes he had made to his life were causing real emotional healing not only within himself but to those around him. He truly was a changed dragon.

But he felt a twinge of that old destructive rage as he returned to his lair after what had been a delightful afternoon, playing with the local village's children. The sudden rush of anger stimulated by his acute senses informed him he had uninvited guests waiting inside. From the smell of them, he could distinguish three intruders; a dwarf, an elf, and a wizard who it seemed had given up bathing as an item on his daily to-do list.

At first, he was tempted to give in to the ferocious fire-breathing rage, an emotion that had sent hundreds to a scorching, painful death. But then he remembered; that wasn't who he was anymore. He put the unneeded emotion into his angry box and mentally transported it to a happier place. With a calm and euphoric sense of tolerance, he took a deep breath. Upon exhaling, he focused his energy on not setting them on fire. He had decided, unwanted guests or not, setting people on fire, at least without a proper conversation, was just rude.

Trying not to appear threatening, the twelve-ton dragon strolled into his lair with a friendly swagger in his spiked-tail. The mass of muscle, claws, and scales colored a deep bleeding red, took up most of the entrance, but it was his smile or at least his attempt at a smile that seemed to draw his guest's unexpected gaze.

"There he is," Peepeeoh shouted, spokesman for the Elf Clan of the Blue Shield. "There is that no good—"

"Silence," Pentagun cried, raising his wizard's staff high over his pointed hat. "We are here to talk, not yell."

Fairy nuts, Nog thought, sighing deeply. It seemed representatives of the Guild of Magical Creatures were lying in wait. He knew his behavior would elicit a response, but he thought they'd at least start with some stern correspondence or perhaps a yelling message delivered by one of the shouting Hamsters of Eczema. The Guild just showing up in person and unannounced felt unnecessarily aggressive. Nog contemplated just eating them all in one big gulp. But no, that was the old Nog. The new Nog would hear them out. And then decide whether or not to eat them.

Before speaking he took in the trio. Peepeeoh dressed in his war uniform. Lots of bright colors, draping silks and jewels, not very practical for war, really. Morgot, The Dwarf King looked as if he had been working in a mine only minutes ago, dust, flecks of gold, copper, and silver glinted in his beard like stars in the night sky. And then there was Pentagun, the Wizard, and sometimes friend. The wizard looked as bad as he smelled, and with zero fashion sense. Wizards are not known for their sense of fashion, but Pentagun seemed to take a lack of balance and style to new heights. Nog wasn't a hundred percent sure, but it looked like the wizard had on two different shoes, one with laces and the other a slip-on. The wizard truly didn't give a sprite's fart about how he looked.

"Well, then," Nog said, continuing to smile and not show too many teeth. "We're all here I see. Can I get anyone anything? Roasted Griffin leg, troll-head stew, tea perhaps?"

"This is not a social call," Peepeeoh said.

Nog sat down on his enormous haunches. "No, I don't suppose it is."

"I'd like some tea," Morgot said, taking a step forward.

"Oh, do shut-up," Peepeeoh snapped.

Morgot folded his arms, "Just thought a spot of tea might make everyone a bit more relaxed. Nothing wrong with that."

"I don't wish to relax." Peepeeoh's pointed ears seemed to become more erect and extra pointy. He turned to Pentagun. "Can we move this along?"

"Fine," Pentagun said. "Nog the Terrible, we of the council have gathered here at your place of business to intervene in what we see as destructive behavior."

Nog raised a scaly eyebrow as big as a serpent. "Destructive behavior? Is this a joke? I haven't destroyed anything in months. Haven't set any crops on fire, eaten any virgin sacrifices—"

"Exactly," Peepeeoh yelled. "What's up with *that*?"

Pentagun stepped in front of Peepeeoh. "Let me, please."

Peepeeoh pointed a finger. "You better talk some sense into your friend here, wizard."

Pentagun took a deep breath. "Nog, witnesses have come forth to say that not a fortnight ago you were spied playing with a group of children. Some kind of game with a ball and stick."

"That's an exaggeration," Nog said. "I wasn't *in* the game."

"Please, explain," Pentagun said.

"Well, it is simple really. The kids divide into two equal teams, and then one after the other they take turns attempting to hit a ball toward the other team. When one hits the ball, they run about and—"

"Not the bloody game!" Peepeeoh was livid. His ears had grown so pointy they looked as if they could cut a diamond. "You insolent beast!"

Nog fought the urge to smirk. He knew exactly what this was about, but he wasn't going to make it easy for these sanctimonious gits.

"Now Nog," Pentagun said. "What were you doing there?"

"They needed a backstop."

"A what?" Margot said leaning forward on his ax.

"Backstop, I lay behind the one with the stick to keep the ball from rolling too far away if they miss," Nog explained. "And also seats."

"Seats!" Peepeeoh shouted.

"Yeah, some of the little ones sit on my tail and watch. I told them to be wary of the spikes. They are sharp as you know, but you can't tell kids anything nowadays, can you? They just have to learn fire is hot the old fashion way, know what I mean?"

The three Guild members stared at Nog, their faces made of confusion. Clearly, they did not know what he meant. Peepeeoh finally broke the silence. "The beast is completely mental."

"Silence," Pentagun said. He took a step toward Nog. "Do you plan to continue this strange interaction with the young humans?"

"Oh yes," Nog said. "They said next time I could try being the umpire. I don't know what that is, but I'm very excited."

Peepeeoh raised his hands. "What is he talking about!"

"Okay." Nog Sighed. "As much fun as it is watching an Elf's skin tone go from green to heart attack crimson, why don't we just cut to the chase. What's this really about?"

"Fine," Peepeeoh said. "Let's get to the charges." He pointed at Nog. "Do you deny that in the past few months you have committed such acts as rescuing drowning sailors at sea?"

Nog shook his head. "I don't deny it."

"That you blatantly prevented famine by diverting streams and other water sources to revive failing crops."

"Yep, did that too."

"Did you guide a nomadic human tribe to new and fertile lands, previously forbidden to them, where they are now thriving, with no fear of attack from dragons."

"Well, it just seemed like the nice thing to do. They'd been following this guy who didn't seem to know where he was going, and they were having a heck of a time wondering about —"

"And worst of all. You've already admitted to it. You have actually befriended the human's larvae!"

Nog felt a twinge of anger. Some of those larvae were his friends. "They are called children and before you say another word, remember the end of your life could be just a really hot burp away."

Peepeeoh seemed to hear the threat and took a step back. When he continued his tone was less angry but slightly more sarcastic. "Do you have any idea what this goody-two-shoe, touchy-feely behavior of yours is doing to my people?"

Nog shrugged. "It just feels nice to be a part of the solution instead of the problem."

"Without burned crops," Peepeeoh said, "there is no famine and disease. Without famine and disease, there is no need for the humans to purchase my clan's Health and Hex protection charms. There is no need for healing potions and elixirs. There is no—"

Nog waved a clawed paw dismissively through the air. "Your health tonics are mostly whiskey, scotch, and ale."

Peepeeoh visibly became unglued. "You lazy sack of scales!"

Morgot put down his ax to help Pentagun restrain the now livid Elf Lord. While Peepeeoh spent the next few minutes yelling obscenities in Elvish, Nog took a moment to ponder the little pointed-eared putz.

Jeez, Elves were wound-up tight. So many issues Nog didn't even know where to begin. Height inferiority, immortality anxiety, and their entire economic structure hung on bogus potions and the health protection racket. Sad really.

Nog tuned back into Peepeeoh's rant. "…and the respect is gone. We used to walk into villages as gods of healing. Now kids throw dog poop at us and chant 'Go back to the North Pole.'"

"North Pole?" Nog cocked his head. "What's that mean?"

"I have no elfin' idea, but it's all your fault." Peepeeoh looked back at the dwarf. "Tell him, Morgot. Tell him what his outrageous behavior is doing to your people."

"Well," Morgot began, seemingly reluctant. "Since you have stopped destroying villages, castles, and other such valuable human real estate, we have suffered a serious decline in our gold lending operations. You see if the humans don't need any capital to rebuild their dwellings, then we can't exactly lend it to them, can we?" Morgot picked up his ax. "No lending, no interest; no interest, no Dwarf Economy."

"Don't you feel any guilt at all about living off the humans like this?" Nog asked. "I mean really. I destroy their homes, so the dwarfs can help rebuild them. I destroy their crops, so Elves can save them from disease and starvation. I terrorize their castles, so the wizards can be called in to vanquish me. I mean where does it all end?"

"That's the point, you dim-witted troglodyte," Peepeeoh said. "It doesn't end!"

"Wait a minute," Morgot said. "You know, I think Nog has something—"

"Oh, go suck a harpy," Peepeeoh snapped.

"Both of you shut-up," Pentagun yelled. The wizard took a long deep breath then looked up at Nog. "That does remind me, old friend—do you know what effect your behavior is having on the subservient magical creatures?"

"Oh yeah, that's right, you malcontent," Peepeeoh said.

"Shut-up, shut-up." The Wizard's fuzzy eyebrows convulsed like two enormous caterpillars having strokes. "If I have to, Peepeeoh, I swear I will invert your ears."

Peepeeoh fell silent and took a step back from the wizard.

"Now Nog," Pentagun began again. "Have you heard the news about the Harpies?"

"What news?"

"They're revolting."

"Of course they're revolting. They're *Harpies*. Ugly flying no good bit—"

"No, no." Pentagun waved his hands in the air like he was erasing something. "The Harpies have rebelled. They all left their posts and flew south for the winter."

"What?" A puff of smoke plumed from the dragon's nostrils.

"The last anyone heard they were all lying on Mediterranean beaches, eating Trojans and chasing Sirens for sport." Pentagun pointed his staff at Nog. "You have disrupted the fragile balance between magical creatures and humans that has lasted almost five millennia."

"Look, I'm sorry about all that, but the whole death and destruction thing…I'm just not about that anymore. I'm a much happier—"

"And the treasure?" Pentagun cut him off. "I heard you're not hoarding treasure anymore."

Nog sighed, feeling he wasn't being heard at all. "Yeah, that's true. The new *me* isn't about material things. I don't need piles of gold to define me."

Pentagun briefly looked around the cave. "So what happened to it all?"

Nog lay down letting his enormous belly lounge around the cave-like a lethargic herd of cows. "I gave it away. Flew over a couple of poor and tired old villages and just redistributed the wealth. I can't tell you what it felt like to finally give back—"

"He's gone crackers!" Peepeeoh said. "I don't give a unicorn's fart if he's your friend, Pentagun. We may have to put him down."

"Nobody is getting put down," Pentagun said. "Look Nog, it's not just the Guild that is upset with you, but the Noble Rich humans as well."

Nog huffed. "Noble Rich. Now there's an oxymoron."

"Never-the-less, the humans of the Noble Rich are not pleased. We are supposed to supply the fear and dread so they can keep their lower-tier citizens in line. Fear is vital in maintaining the status quo, and like it or not, you are a major *fear factor* in this delicate equation."

Nog rolled over on his back like a whiny five-year-old on the verge of a tantrum. "I don't want to be a fear factor."

"There is no talking to this one, Pentagun," the Elf Lord said. "We need to cut our losses before he changes everything. My people are on the verge of boarding our trans-dimensional ships and sailing right out of this world."

"Oh, that would be tragic," Nog said. "A world without alcoholic potions and placebo health charms."

"That's it," Peepeeoh said, lunging at Nog. "It's go-time!"

Morgot swiftly hooked his ax around Peepeeoh's waist and started to pull him outside. But the Elf Lord kicked back with his foot and caught Morgot's groin. The Dwarf released the ax as he fell back and Peepeeoh seized the weapon. Raising it over his head, he charged at Nog who watched the scene with only mild concern.

As the Elf Lord neared, Nog lifted his head slightly and unhooked his jaw, the detachable joints clicking just under Nog's skull. Peepeeoh charged like a rabid sprite foaming with rage. Nog waited until the elf was a few steps away, then opened his mouth creating a cavern that rivaled the cave itself.

The Elf Lord, with ax raised, ran headlong into Nog's open mouth. Nog could feel his angry footfall move over his tongue, past his uvula, and continue to about midway down his esophagus. Nog figured it was at this point the Elf Lord had decided to pause, take a deep breath, and contemplate his enormous error.

"Was that really necessary? You know he is sensitive about their wares," Pentagun said.

Nog reattached his jaw and swallowed. "Do you want me to throw him up?"

Pentagun shook his head. "No, let's see if being born out the backside of a dragon will improve his mood any."

"Doubtful," Morgot said as he stood up, one hand clutched to his groin.

"You all right?" Nog said to the Dwarf King.

"No horseback riding for a while, but I'll live."

"Sorry about your ax." Nog raised a sincere brow. "If you want to wait around, I can get it back for you. You know when it works its way out."

Morgot held up both hands fast as if he were about to fend off an enormous boulder. "No thanks. I was due for another, anyhow."

Pentagun moved toward the dragon and touched the tip of his staff to Nog's nose. The old wizard mumbled something and two floating spheres emerged from the staff. Nog inhaled them quickly knowing that the round spells would travel to where the Elf

Lord was surely now gasping for air. One sphere would keep the elf from suffocating the other would prevent him from being digested.

"Morgot, would you mind giving me a moment with my old friend?" the wizard asked.

The dwarf nodded and hobbled out of the cave leaving Nog and Pentagun alone. The old wizard walked to Nog's other end and sat on the dragon's tail. "So, what is this *really* about?"

Nog took a deep breath. "Are you familiar with the village of Lafayette?"

The Wizard scratched his chin. "Southern Province, I think."

"It used to be," Nog said. "No longer, because two seasons ago I torched it. Torched it to the ground."

"That was you?"

"Yep, that was mine," Nog said. "Nothing was left standing."

"And…"

"And nothing. I mean the governing human nobles did nothing. They didn't hire a wizard, they didn't help the peasants whose lives I just made miserable. They had excuse after excuse as to why they couldn't send help, why they couldn't guarantee the loans from the dwarfs to rebuild. I mean it was sick. The inefficiency of it all."

"So what happened?"

"It gets worse," Nog continued. "Those poor people gathered what meager things they had and paid for the services of six knights to come out and slay me."

"Uh huh," Pentagun said while doodling with his staff in the sand. "And how did that go?"

"Oh, about how it usually does. I played with them a bit, let them think they were doing well, and then I ate them." Nog slapped a clawed paw over his forehead. "Jeez, I had chain-mail stuck in my teeth for a week and contrary to popular opinion, armor does *not* digest well. So a week later I'm sitting in the river, in agony, trying to pass six brave knight's helmets, and I ask myself—what am I doing with my life?"

"You aren't going to tell me this is a mid-life thing are you?"

"Mid-life my scaly butt," Nog scoffed. "I'm past that benchmark. Look Pen, I'm six hundred and twenty-nine."

Pentagun chuckled. "Liar, you're eight hundred and twenty-nine."

"Whatever. The thing is I got one maybe two centuries left,

tops."

"Yeah, so?"

"Well I don't want to be remembered as Nog the Terrible. I want to be Nog the Terrific or Nog the Tremendous."

Pentagun shook his head. "Peepeeoh may be right."

"About what?"

"You're crackers. Have you been snorting pixie dust again?"

"Noooo…a little…not much. But Pen, don't ya' see? It's like that fairytale you told me about the dinosaurs."

Pentagun's brow furrowed. "For the last time that wasn't a fairytale! They really did exists!"

"Yeah, yeah, I know, big thunder lizards. Who cares? The point is Pen, everything changes. The Guild can't stop it. I can't, you can't. Our time is ending. You must've felt it."

Pentagun sighed. "That may be, but the Guild fears change and dammit, so do I. They won't hesitate to put you down."

Nog lowered his snout onto his forearm. "If it came down to it, would you come after me?"

Pentagun cast his eyes toward the dirt. "Just don't put me in that position, Nog. I don't want it to come…" He stood up fast, tears in his eyes. "For both our sakes will you just go out and kill a few people? You'll feel better."

Nog sighed knowing arguing with a two-thousand-year-old wizard made about as much sense as trying to convince the rain to fall up. Once a wizard hits a thousand, they are pretty set in their ways. "Okay, I'll give the matter some thought." Nog smiled warmly. "Now can we just have some tea and a nice visit?"

Pentagun brushed a tear from his wrinkled nose. "Yes of course. Is that troll-head stew warm?"

Nog invited Morgot back inside and the three spent the rest of the evening reminiscing about the days when humans worshiped them as gods and fear and dread flowed like the Nile. Pentagun told the same stories Nog had been listening to for eight hundred years, but the dragon took them in with a smile and a twinge of sadness. Deep down Nog knew he would never hear the old wizard spin tales of heroes, monsters or even those mythical dinosaurs, ever again. For the next time they met it would mean the end of one of them.

The Wizard and the Dwarf King bid Nog farewell with a gloomy finality no one wanted to acknowledge. Magical creatures don't hug, but Nog wished they could.

Less than ten hours later Nog sat in the river, the memory of passing those helmets still painfully fresh in his mind. As the cool water moved around him, he could feel something else moving inside him. He lifted his tail, pushed slightly, and something plopped into the water.

Nog turned around to see the Elf Lord flailing about in the river. Since Elves can walk on water they never bother to learn to swim. *Kind of short-sighted*, Nog thought.

He pondered whether or not to let the elf drown. But then Nog remembered Peepeeoh had seven wives, none of whom liked him, and sixty-two kids. No matter how big a nob the Elf Lord was, Nog wasn't about to create, even through inaction, seven elf widows and sixty-two fatherless elflets. Besides Peepeeoh was only in two feet of water and drowning was unlikely.

With a sigh, Nog reached out and lifted the elf out of the water. He held Peepeeoh up over the river in his scaly clawed hand as the elf gasped for air. Before the elf was even breathing properly the pointed-eared git started cursing in Elvish.

It appeared Morgot had been right. Traveling down the digestive tract of a dragon hadn't improved the elf's mood one bit. And strangely enough, the Elf Lord still had Morgot's ax. Nog saw him grip it in both hands and raise it to strike.

Unbelievable, Nog thought. Talk about your one-track mind. "Take one swing, Peepeeoh, just one, and I swear there won't be enough left of you for your wives to mourn over."

With clenched teeth, Peepeeoh became motionless, obviously contemplating the pitfalls of his predicament.

Seeing the elf was frozen in a storm of indecision, Nog decided to give him a suggestion. "Why, don't you drop the ax? It could use a wash anyway."

Peepeeoh let it fall into the river as his hands fell by his side and his shoulders slumped.

Nog set the elf onshore and brought his snout to within an inch of Peepeeoh's nose. "Now I want you to deliver a message to the Guild. I am no longer a fear factor."

The elf took steps back and shook his head. "This will be the death of you."

Nog smiled. "We all have to die of something."

"What happened to you?"

"It's just change, Peepeeoh. It's coming like a herd of mad centaurs and there isn't pixie spit you can do about it. I may not be around to see it, but that doesn't mean it isn't coming."

The Elf Lord started walking up the beach. "I'll be back, dragon, and I won't be alone."

Nog smirked knowing those who clung to the old world would always be alone, even if they didn't know it. The dragon watched Peepeeoh disappear into the distance and hoped it would be many days before they came for him.

In the meantime, Nog had heard a rumor some kids from the village were starting up a game down by the lake. Maybe, just maybe, they would need an umpire. And if not, they could always use a great big scaly backstop.

Nog flew up into the mid-morning light, soaring headlong into his final days.

~ * ~ * ~

Kevin David Anderson's debut novel is the cult zombie-romp, *Night of the Living Trekkies* and his latest book is the horror-comedy *Midnight Men: The Supernatural Adventures of Earl and Dale*. *Night of the Living Trekkies* was required reading in college courses, most notably the class designed for incoming freshman, *How to Survive Your Freshmen Year by Studying the Zombie Apocalypse*, at Mansfield University in Pennsylvania. Anderson's fiction has appeared more than a hundred times in different publications from anthologies, magazines, podcasts, radio dramas, and award-worthy publications like the British Fantasy Award-winning *Murky Depths*, and the Bram Stoker nominated anthology *The Beauty of Death*. Anderson's stories have been turned into audio productions on Parsec Award-winning podcasts like, Pseudopod, Drabblecast, and on the popular No Sleep and Horror Hill Podcasts.

When not writing horror-comedy, Anderson spends time at the beach with his family, attends horror conventions and book festivals, and writes and tells bad, corny, nerdy jokes. Dad jokes with a geeky twist are his specialty, and under the pen name Giggles A. Lott and Nee Slapper, he has published such works as *JURASSIC JOKES: A Joke Book 65 Million Years in the Making* and *STAR WARS: The Jokes Awaken*. Visit him at: www.KevinDavidAnderson.com.

Tied to The Whim of a Tender Tyrant

S.H. Mansouri

Sepia did not eat the child. She merely perched on the pinnacle of a barren mountaintop, overlooking the seaside town of Tilladune, and considered what to do with the little thing. She wrapped her bronze wings around her chest, sheltering the child from tempest waves that lashed about above the darkening sky, and recollected the morning's hunt.

She found no joy in the yielding of men and women. There were no screams of 'Oh God, help me,' no ducking behind towering trees, no brave souls pulling steel brazenly in the name of some Lord, or King, or Queen. There was not even the faint fragrance of fear that follows the chase, the wounding, and finally, the kill. There was only a human, an infant wrapped in swaddling cloth, abandoned in the middle of a forest clearing.

One swift slash, one slight puncture, and she would have eaten like the dragons of old. The flesh of children was coveted above all delicacies: juicier than a giant's jugular, more savory than a maiden wrapped in sage, and rarer than the innards of a unicorn —plucked one by one and stuffed with the still-beating heart of a bearded wizard.

But Sepia was not like the dragons of old, and over the years she had grown weary of the hunt. She wondered if humans were more than food, more than sacks of meat to grind and gobble.

Mwwaahh, mwwaahh.

Muffled cries crept through crimson-scaled cracks, sealing her wings together into a paunch, leathery bungalow. She pretended not to hear them, swaying her golden, swan-like neck back and forth, as if searching for the origin of the sound somewhere up in the clouds where the Gods clashed and clanged a bitter battle of lightning bolts and heavy rain. Sepia sighed, her nostrils spewing a twisted plume of dense black smoke that rose and disappeared among misty tendrils.

I hear you, little meat sack, she thought.

Sepia hung her horned-head over the top of where she imagined the child would be if she spread her wings to fly. Never had she thought about how to handle a meal with care. Her head protected the infant from the pelting rain as she reached inside, cupped her claws beneath the wailing babe's tender bottom, and flew off. Through the clouds and down the mountainside she soared until she reached a cliff that served as the entrance to her sacred cavern.

~ * ~

Craven, a former guardian of Tilladune who, in his youth, was charged with barring the passage of evil spirits from entering the open windows of children, sparked a bonfire by flicking his stone-gray fingers against a pile of flint rock. Beneath a hooded brow, crouching low with cupped hands, he blew violently at a bunched-up ball of tinder and twig. As Sepia lurched inside the cavern, opal eyes swaying in the darkness like a devil's lullaby approaching, Craven shuddered and fanned his hands nervously above the pyre. It was unbecoming of a gargoyle to move about with such trepidation.

"Good evening, my Lady Dragon," he said, as the firelight grew.

Sepia, with serpentine fingers wrapped tightly around her fleshy prize, smirked as she approached the bonfire, her taloned feet sliding smoothly across the cavern floor.

"Good evening to you, Craven," she said. "A fine evening it is."

As Craven prepared a place to cook whatever tender morsel the dragon had caught, he could not help but wonder why she had such a gentle glow about her. It was not a common thing for her to return home from the hunt so satisfied, let alone for her to greet him in any kind of pleasant manner. And so he steeled himself. He watched her cautiously while stacking short wooden logs around the fire pit.

"Will you need spices this evening? Perhaps a cauldron for stewing?" he said.

"Craven?" she beckoned, ignoring his questions.

He peered up from his work. Thin, flaking fissures ran down the length of his throat as he swallowed.

"Yes, Lady Dragon," he answered shyly.

"What do baby humans eat?"

The question caught Craven off-guard; he nearly laughed.

However, he dare not let such laughter loose. The last time he had mocked Sepia, she ripped his wings clean off. He glanced over his shoulder in a gesture of remembrance. He did not look her in the eyes as he gave his retort.

"They do not eat, my Lady Dragon. They do not yet have teeth to tear and grind. They only drink. They only suckle."

Sepia swept her wings to feed the growing fire. She loosened her grip on the ball in her lap and leered between her fingers at the writhing infant inside. It rolled and banked and tickled her hardened flesh. Her eyes widened. In that moment, she felt the first inkling of a mother's concern for her child.

Mwaaahh…

Craven gawked at the flailing child as Sepia lowered her palms above the blazing fire.

"A bit higher, Lady Dragon," he said. "Unless you plan to roast it alive."

"I plan on no such thing!" she barked, pulling her hands away from the leaping flames. "Do not look upon me with such treachery. I only wish to warm the thing."

He jolted upright and shook his head in urgent denial.

"I would not, my Lady. Please. I only wish to help."

"The child surely cannot suckle from *me,*" she said.

Craven did not answer.

"And what does it drink?" she said. "Curdled blood? Warm bile? The tears of frightened fairies?"

"Milk, my Lady Dragon."

"Then fetch the milk for me," she said.

Craven had spent his youth in the service of the king of Tilladune. He knew the ways of humans; he knew they would come in droves to find the child someday.

~ * ~

Dead milkmaids piled up high inside the cavern. Craven waited patiently each morning near the farms of Tilladune, snatching up the maids as they made their way into town with buckets full of freshly squeezed milk. He took the milk for the child and fed the maids to Sepia, who grew more and more irritated at the time it took him to climb the mountaintop.

"They will soon take notice of the missing maids," said

Craven, as he swept charred bones into a neat pile near the center of the cavern's belly.

"What shall I name him?" Sepia asked, running the claw of her index finger along the crease of her ponderous brow. "It is a male, is it not?"

Craven tossed his broom aside and approached the baby's wicked bassinet. It was made of smooth milk-maid bone and padded at the bottom with hay and frayed braids of human hair in hues of gold and brown and black. He pinched the lower half of a red cotton shawl that covered the child, peeled it back, peeked inside and snapped away.

"It is a male," he said.

Sepia thought long and hard about what name to give her little boy. Names were important to her, important to all dragons, in fact. She was given the name 'Sepia' as a tribute to the deep, royal shades of red and bronze that shimmered from her squamous skin.

"I will name him Peethral Latah," which is to say, 'little pearl' in the dragon tongue. "Will you celebrate with us? Will you mark the naming of this boy with song?"

When Craven looked upon the child, the only thought that crossed his mind was the humans would come to reclaim him. However, he did not wish to anger Sepia with such foreboding thoughts. She was happy, and he would celebrate with her.

He dove into a cove near the back of the cavern and returned with a pair of bear-skinned drums and a tambourine made from the finger bones of mining dwarves. Sepia plucked the little pearl from the bassinet and set him down, snuggled and warmed inside the curvature of her jagged, coiled tail.

Bum-bum-ba-drum, bum-bum-ba-drum.

Craven pounded out a slow, rhythmic cadence as Sepia rattled intermittently.

Chee-chee-ka.

Her pointy ears drooped down beside bulging temples as she closed her eyes and swooned above the firelight.

> *Peethral, the unforgiving sea has pardoned me*
> *and gifted me a pearl.*
> *Latah, the smallest mote of dust*
> *sheds light upon the world.*

Peethral Latah, my little pearl will grow.

I found you in a forest field
filled with moans and cries,
until I took you to the mountaintop
beneath the stormy skies.
Peethral Latah, my little pearl will grow.

They crooned into the night until the fire died down and the moon rose above the placid sea, casting its pale countenance into the cavern's crooked entrance. As mother and son fell fast asleep, Craven crept outside.

He descended the mountain and walked to the tower of Tilladune. As he approached, Craven thought of the many years he had been absent from his post. He yearned to protect the children again, to crouch proudly above the homes of humans and ward off spirits which stole away the innocence of youth. Sepia took him when he was just a budding gargoyle, his nascent wings too weak to aide in his escape. He laughed when she told him she would raise him as her own in the ways of the dragon; and for that, she took his wings. He pitied Peethral Latah, just as he pitied himself.

He climbed the tower and sat idly until his skin hardened into seamless stone. Only his eyes moved. He watched the people congregate. He watched them sharpen their swords and light their torches and point to the cavern on the mountaintop.

~ * ~

Peethral Latah began to crawl. He began to even walk. His first words—well, not so much words as sounds—were the words of fire. He snarled and gnashed his newly protruding teeth. Craven tied a severed braid to a seam on the back of his oversized dress (as maidens' clothes were the only clothes available in the cavern). The little pearl whipped his hips about, mimicking the movements of his mother. He blew into the pyre when Craven set about kindling the fire, as if his baby's breath would someday miraculously transform into dragon's breath. Sepia could not be prouder.

She spent less time hunting and more time teaching Peethral how to carry himself as a dragon would. She let his fingernails grow, sharpening them against the cavern walls, into tiny, spear-like stems. He was strong enough to climb mounds of corral in the cavern now, gashing his fragile flesh against jagged spurs as he made his way to the top. He roared triumphantly, compressed his bowed legs, flapped his chunky arms and leaped. A pile of wet, jerking fish caught his fall. He scowled, plunged his claws into the raw fish, and bit into them with chipped teeth, which had already begun to rot.

"That's it, my little pearl," said Sepia. "Eat your fill and grow into a strong dragon like your mother." She lifted Peethral up and pulled him to her chest, nuzzling her cheek against the top of his black, matted head.

"My Lady Dragon?" Craven mumbled.

She set the child down and turned to him.

"Yes, Craven."

"We have done a great injustice to Peethral Latah. We cannot keep him here."

Sepia lunged at him. Her white eyes flashed with fire. She thrust her neck forward, the inlets of her nostrils flaring and throbbing as the tip of her nose met the top of Craven's bowed, hooded head. Her chest expanded like a sail set loose in a strong southern wind. As she spread her wings across the length of the cavern, Craven lifted his head, met her eyes and inched forward toward impending doom.

"Are you a creature so feared you would boldly incur my wrath with a notion such as this? Peethral is home, this cavern is his home, and I am his mother." Her bulging belly glowed. "Explain yourself, Craven. Explain why I, a powerful queen, loved and revered for centuries, should lend ear to the bumbling banter of a mutilated mascot."

He lifted his arms slowly and spread them out before the Lady Dragon. He no longer feared her, for he could not watch the boy become what he had become: a docile servant, a miserable child chained to the whim of a tyrant, a slave.

"You have taken this boy away from the world in which he belongs, just as you ripped me away from the thatches of homes I was born to protect. You are not his mother. You are his captor. And in your curiosity—your amusement—for all things small and weak, you have crippled him. Look through the fire in your own eyes and see what will become of him. Look no further than the wingless stone sloth I have become if you wish to see what lies in wait for your little pearl."

The embers in her gut waned. The breath she held in anticipation of roasting Craven alive deflated, pushing back his hood,
revealing rows of deeply scarred stone on the top of his hairless
granite head.

Craven calmly closed his eyes and waited for death to fall
upon him.

It did not come.

He then heard a sound that could only be described as the
manifestation of generations of pain, isolation, and exile. He
opened his eyes and saw Sepia crumbled in a tangle of scales and
smoke and tears, fetal upon the cavern's dusty crust. She slid her
cheek across the ground and met Craven's vacant gaze near the spot
where his gnarled feet stood frozen. She moaned a mixture of metal
and wood and rust.

Craven hesitated. He did not trust the sight of a weeping
dragon. He did not trust that his words had penetrated deep enough.

"I am alone," she groaned as she lifted her swollen eyelids,
the fire in her eyes completely extinguished. "I have forced my solitude upon you. I have kept you from your heart's desire, from your
place in the world. I have damaged you beyond repair, my oldest,
dearest friend. I am ashamed," she wept.

Craven exhaled the breath that was to be his last, kneeled
down, and placed his hand inside her open palm.

"I am the spoils of the hunt," he said, "pushed about like
fodder in a pen by the pitchfork of my own toneless voice. I've
feared you from the day I began to wither away inside this god-
forsaken cavern. And yet, I've grown to love you. I know the solitude you speak of all too well, for you have been its harbinger. You
have become the hunted, the prey of time's decay."

Craven pulled her polished claw to his chest. Not that it
would shift her weight, but that it would move her.

"Up with you, my Lady. If the king witnessed you in such a
state, he would surely come for your head."

"I cannot return what I have stolen, Craven. I cannot give
you back your wings, nor heal the wounds on your head. I am useless," she said. She composed herself and trudged to the mounds
of corral to look upon the little pearl.

"Release me. Return Peethral Latah to Tilladune. That, my
Lady dragon, is a start."

~ * ~

The day Peethral Latah was to be unleashed upon the world, Sepia, accompanied by Craven, glided down the mountainside and searched for the forest clearing where she'd first laid eyes on him. When she found the spot, a couple of yards away from the nearest farm, she curled open her claws and Peethral wobbled out like a drunken sailor down the plank of a Spanish galleon.

Craven slid down Sepia's spine and hung a care package on Peethral's shoulder. It was filled with trinkets and toys so that the boy's memory would quicken if he ever forgot his time in the cavern on the mountaintop. Peethral squirmed beneath the weight of the satchel, itching and scratching at the strap as if it were a pet's collar to be escaped from. He was wild beyond any creature Craven had ever seen.

"If you would, Craven, give him the rattle so he does not feel alone. The humans will find him in time, but until then I'd like to know he's comfortable," said Sepia. She could not shift her gaze from the haunting trees swaying dance to the chilling, winter wind. She could not bear to look him in the eyes.

Craven shook a hawk-skull rattle and the teeth inside jangled and clanged about. And Peethral Latah giggled and ran his snub fingers along the length of his neck, signaling for his mother to begin a song. She grabbed him up and tucked him tightly inside the crook of her wing. Peethral Latah felt her heartbeat thrum. He heard the thumping sound and imagined Craven was pounding on his drums. She planted him down and turned to Craven.

"If you do not mind the long walk, my friend, I wish to be alone." Craven nodded. Sepia flew off. The wind from her wings blew Peethral's clumpy locks, and chunks of dry mud showered down upon his blood-stained dress. He looked up and watched his mother disappear beyond the cloud line.

Craven led him out of the forest, across the yellow fields, and to the watering troughs where the horses cooled themselves. He removed his hooded cloak and held it in his right hand while scooping handfuls of water from the trough with his left. The water soaked into Peethral's dense clot of hair, ran down his scuffed cheeks, and pooled at the tip of his scabby chin. He bucked and jerked like a wild stallion. Craven dunked him forcefully to make sure he was at least presentable to his former family. Or whosoever would take him in. As soon as Craven pulled him from the trough, Peethral took flight, sprinting through the fields and lashing his fingers at long stalks of golden wheat. Farmers watched, and then maids, and then soldiers, and finally, the king emerged from the gates of his throne-room, accompanied by a small band of armed guards.

"And what do we have here?" the king asked. "Have you found the courage to return to your post, Craven?"

Craven palmed his head and bowed. Peethral kicked at the posts surrounding the horse stables. He snorted and slid his bare feet across the gravel as he eyed the portly king.

"I have always had the courage, your grace."

"And what of the dragon?" said the king.

"I have come to reclaim my post. Let that which is sleeping remain asleep," he said. "Am I welcome still?"

"Of course you are, old friend. And what *is* that wild thing over by the stables? A friend of yours? Perhaps a child possessed by an evil spirit? Don't tell me you've forgotten how to protect children, Craven?" the king said sarcastically.

"I am charged with him, your grace. He is a child of Tilladune, abandoned as an infant in the middle of the forest."

The king stepped out from the cover of his entourage. He lifted his arms to the sky and pronounced: "Whosoever this child belongs to, step forward."

No one moved. The townsfolk looked vacantly to each other, pointing fingers and murmuring about what an awful thing it was to leave a child alone in the woods. Peethral charged at the king and rammed the top of his head into his gut. The king cringed and forced a smile.

"A lively, sturdy lad he is, indeed," the king said through gritted teeth. "I think it best, since you have spent the most time with him, that you finish what you have started, Craven. Along with the duties of a guardian, you shall keep an eye on the boy. Make sure he understands what is expected of a citizen of Tilladune."

Craven took Peethral by the wrist.

"Of course, your grace," he said.

"The show is over," the king said. "Craven has returned. He shall protect the young and raise the wild. Do not let us down, gargoyle."

Craven bowed and led Peethral back to the watering trough.

~ * ~

It was difficult, at first, for Peethral to assimilate, as he was a child raised in the ways of the dragon. The children of Tilladune tortured him for being different, for wearing a woman's dress and for bursting out in song instead of tears. His teachers and elders scolded him for his unkemptness and inability to speak the language of the humans. They yanked his hair when he refused to comb it, and when he did not wash it, they cut it from his head. His only friend was Craven. But Peethral did not look upon him as a child looks upon its guardian. He knew only the gargoyle had taken him from the cavern on the mountaintop and placed him in a world in which he did not fit. However, Peethral adapted.

He found friendship in the king's daughter, Cymphonee. She was more beautiful and kinder than all the maidens in Tilladune. And as they grew, they fell in love.

When the time came for Peethral to ask the king for his daughter's hand in marriage, he marched into the throne-room and bared his heart for all to see.

"I wish to take the Lady Cymphonee's hand in marriage, my king," he said in perfect human tongue. "We are an exquisite match, like twin stars in the sky that light the pathway lovers yearn to tread. Ours is a fierce love that burns like dragon's fire." The king twitched at the last words Peethral spoke, for he had not forgotten, after many years, the dragon on the mountaintop. His eyes narrowed, keen slits searching for the perfect paradox in which to hurl the humble lamb before him.

"Love is cheap, my lad," the king said. "It is a fickle thing, like luck or foul weather. If you wish to marry my daughter, you must prove yourself worthy. You must prove to me you are capable of holding on to my most precious gift."

"What would you ask of me, my king?"

"I will announce the conditions of the Lady Cymphonee's betrothal come morrow morning. Until that time, my lad, consider my blessing something to be won."

Peethral bowed, his eyes fixed upon the king. He had not forgotten the king's indifference toward him as he grew into a man. His mind whirled and raced. *What will he ask of me?*

~ * ~

The next morning, messengers of the king, adorned in noble robes, pushed open the doors of the king's throne-room, slammed and barred them shut, and began hammering. They nailed an official document to the doors of the throne-room and went on about their day as if the king's announcement was a casual thing.

All able-bodied men and women, if your hearts be stout and your steel is sharp. I will offer up the hand of my daughter in marriage to the first who slays the dragon on the mountaintop. Proof of the beast's demise must be presented to me.

—King Randolph

A crowd gathered around the door. Men and women, young and old, cheered and shook their fists at the challenge. Grinding stones sparked, forges flared, armor shined and vows to never return until the task was complete were taken. One by one, soldiers lined up at the neck of the road that led to the cavern on the mountaintop.

Peethral looked up at the declaration and ripped it down. He walked straight to the tower of Tilladune and climbed the stone steps to where Craven was studying. Upon reading the king's decree, Craven was troubled.

"You cannot enter the cavern, Peethral. The dragon is your mother."

Peethral looked dismally at the baby rattle in his hand. He had not forgotten the Lady Dragon, nor had he failed to let a day pass without remembering the ways of fire in which he was raised.

"Blood is blood," Peethral said. "Such is the way of dragons. Do not follow me Craven. I will win the hand of the Lady Cymphonee at any cost." Craven pleaded with him, but he would not yield. "I will enter when the moon rises once again and take the dragon's head as proof of my victory."

So Craven and Peethral sat upon the tower and watched the soldiers ascend the winding road to Sepia's cavern. Not a single soul returned. The sun set, and the moon shed its frown upon the hour in which Peethral was to climb the mountainside. He carried the satchel holding the remnants of his childhood, along with a dull iron breastplate affixed to the front of a red maiden's dress, and an executioner's axe the length of two men standing head to toe.

~ * ~

Sepia was exhausted. Her hide was marred and punctured with pikes that swayed like a porcupine's backside at every twitch and turn. She had not eaten of the flesh, as she had vowed to keep the little pearl safe by assuaging the king's wrath against the missing citizens of Tilladune. She ate only fish and undergrowth that Craven, secretly, had brought to her on each twilight passed. She raised herself up on trembling haunches, claws dulled to stumpy ends from lashing at iron and steel, and prepared to face the next soldier who approached the cavern's entrance.

Chee-chee-ka.

The familiar sound of Peethral's rattle roused Sepia from her languid state. She exhaled, relieved to see her little pearl once again—to see the baby dragon who'd grown into a man.

"Peethral? My little pearl. You have come back to me!" cried Sepia, as she crawled forward to see the man outlined by moonlight splayed across his back.

"I have come for your head," he said.

Peethral did not have to explain the words he spoke. Sepia knew what she had done to the boy. She knew she would pay with her life the day he returned. It was as if she had battled the soldiers, kept them at bay and reserved her final ounce of strength, only to see her son one last time. She did not shed a tear as Peethral marched into the cavern and swung the axe back over his shoulder.

She hung her neck across the top of a large, flat stone Craven had used to skin the maids. She gazed into his eyes.

"You are beautiful, my little pearl," she said. "You have grown beyond anything I could have imagined. Do not forget the words of fire. Do not forget your mother."

Just before Peethral came down upon the Lady Dragon, she closed her eyes and said, "I am sorry."

~ * ~

Peethral dragged a large burlap sack across the ground as he passed by the tower of Tilladune on his way to King Randolph's throne-room. Craven did not speak as he looked down from the tower at the bloody sack. He had been a slave for the better part of his life, yet he loved Sepia and did not wish to take part in the celebration of her downfall.

Peethral slid the sack in front of King Randolph's court and bowed with a grin slashed across his face. King Randolph did not expect his decree to be fulfilled, and so he waved his soldiers to fetch the sack. The entire court stood in awe at the sight of a knotted, spiraling horn as the soldiers pulled it out and laid it down before the king.

"This is indeed the horn of the wicked dragon who lives on the mountaintop," said the king in disbelief. "The dragon is dead?" the king asked.

"It is," Peethral Latah said. "And now, you must keep your word. Before all of Tilladune, have I won your blessing?"

The king scoffed. "You have, my lad," he said. "You may marry the Lady Cymphonee. We are in your debt, Peethral Latah. You are free to live out the rest of your life as you see fit. Your wedding shall be a glorious day."

The people of Tilladune celebrated that night. Peethral Latah and Lady Cymphonee danced and laughed and embraced beneath the shelter of the pale moonlight. And whenever Peethral Latah caught the king glaring his way, he smiled a smile which was much more than a gesture of gratitude for the blessing to marry his one true love.

~ * ~

Many years passed and Peethral Latah and Lady Cymphonee were married. Cymphonee bore a child, a girl, which Peethral Latah named 'Sepia,' as a tribute to her ruddy cheeks and her short, curly, golden hair. But beyond the child's appearance, Peethral Latah named her Sepia because of the love he had for his mother, the dragon on the mountaintop.

He sang the songs of fire Sepia had taught him as a child. He shook the hawk-head rattle before the child's bassinet, under an open window, as Craven perched above his home, guarding her from evil spirits as she slept. And when he was sure that little Sepia would not awaken, Peethral crept out the window and climbed to the top of his thatched roof.

Craven sat with bear-skinned drums atop crossed legs and hummed when Peethral sat beside him. Peethral pulled out his mother's tambourine, and the two of them played. Beneath the moonlight they howled, and the wind whistled from the north, as if the spirit of something familiar sat with them to play.

"I am proud of you, my little pearl," Craven said.

"Blood is blood." Peethral placed the tambourine beside him and stared at the cloudy sky above. And there, in the center of the great white moon, was the silhouette of a one-horned dragon plunging into a sea of shimmering pearls.

~ * ~ * ~

S.H. Mansouri earned his BS in Biology and MFA in creative writing from the University of California, Riverside. He has published more than twenty-five short stories, one novelette, and optioned a television pilot. He lives in southern California with his wife and dog Atreyu.

Slay the Dragon: Ten Pence a Go

Samuel Poots

"So, this is the place, is it?" Sir Derek Peveley raised his helmet visor and cast a critical eye over the cave.

The mayor of the town, decked out in an ermine robe and gold chain, nodded. "Indeed, yes, oh noble sir. Here is the lair from which the dragon has terrorized my town for over fifty years."

Sir Derek looked back over his shoulder at the jostling crowd of people. "They don't look very terrorized. Is that man selling hot dogs?"

"Just eager for the tyranny to be lifted, Sir Peveley, sir," the mayor said, glaring at the enterprising sausage seller.

The cave certainly looked like the lair of a dragon. Acrid smoke drifted across the ground, parting to reveal the occasional glimpse of a skull. Scraps of molted dragon hide hung on the stones, flapping like pennants in the breeze. Low braziers cast the place in shades of hellish crimson. Inside, stalactites and stalagmites transformed the cave into the jaws of some hellish monster. It was definitely a dragon's lair. And yet...

Sir Derek regarded the crowd of expectant people. A number of them had gathered around his horse, admiring his armor and equipment. One gave his lance the critical look of a professional.

"Look at this," he said to a friend loud enough for his words to carry. "It's ancient! Probably won't last more than a few minutes against your average fire breather. If he liked, I could sort him out with some special dragon proof gear, no trouble."

Monster hunting was not exactly a booming business these days, Sir Derek knew well. His last job had been months ago, and that had turned out to just be rather large house cat. But even with monsters becoming so rare, surely people didn't queue up to see them? In his experience, they barricaded their doors and hid under the bed, which always made getting paid something of a chore.

He turned on his heel and strode over to his horse. The people gathered around the old nag melted away at his approach. He drew his sword out from its place behind the saddle's pommel, peeling away a colorful flyer for asbestos-lined shields lodged in the scabbard, and gave it a few experimental swings. Despite the specks of rust on the blade, it seemed to impress the people. There were even some smatterings of applause. He gave his horse a pat on the neck and then walked back towards the cave.

"You and your people should move back," Sir Derek said as he passed the mayor. "If the dragon feels threatened, it might run out into the open."

"Oh, yes indeed. I'll see to it right away." The mayor turned and began waving feebly at the people. "All right everyone, let's settle down. Move back please. Health and safety, you know."

Sir Derek clanked his way up to the entrance. He took a deep breath, trying to ignore the cold sweat prickling his skin, and took a step forward. A mighty roar echoed up from within. The noise silenced the chatter of the crowd which, far from cowering away, leaned forwards as one. One or two people began to chant his name. Sir Derek shook his head. The roar still echoed around his helmet. With a hand that managed to tremble only slightly, he raised his sword and stepped inside. The cave mouth swallowed him whole.

Smoke billowed about him, filling his nostrils with the smell of rotten eggs and scratching the back of his throat. He felt tears pricking the corners of his eyes and blinked to clear them. When he opened them again it was to find the world had vanished. Sir Derek looked back at the cave's mouth. The circle of light had simply gone. Before he could puzzle this out, another roar shook the stone walls. The dragon either had to be very close, or very large. Sir Derek wasn't sure which option was the least awful. His heart began to race, its rapid beat echoing in his armor to make a tinny music.

For a moment, he considered running, grabbing his horse and putting this town and its damned dragon far behind. No pay was worth getting cooked. Underground. Alone. He could just leave. They couldn't stop him. Except...except no pay was just what he currently had. The idea of another night eating stewed roots and scraps of leather...Sir Derek shivered. It didn't bear thinking about. He took a deep breath and headed off into the darkness.

Honor and duty are all very well, but the promise of a full stomach does wonders for a person's courage.

He held his sword to the side, dragging the tip along the wall in order to feel his way. A series of sharp tings marked where stalagmites clinked against his helmet. He ran a hand up, making sure the plume jutting from the top wasn't damaged. After a while, the sword slipped to the side, marking a point where the wall disappeared. Desperate for the comfort its presence had given him, he poked his sword around him in every direction. Nothing. He fumbled on the ground for a stone and threw it as hard as he could into the darkness. It was a long time before he heard the clatter.

Sir Derek jumped as a low grumble echoed around him. "Who dares disturbeth my slumber?"

The knight gulped. He could hear a strange rattling sound. It took him a moment to realize it was his knees.

"I…" He coughed and tried again. "I am Sir Derek Peveley." Warming to his subject, he put on his most heroic voice. "Proud knight of the Royal Order of the Gusset. And I am here to slay you, beast!"

A light burst into life. A fire burned dull and red between two sets of teeth. Two enormous eyes, glowing green from within. By the dual light of fire and eyes, Sir Derek saw the dragon.

"Oh my," he whispered. His sword fell limp in his hand.

The dragon chuckled around its mouthful of flames. "Thou art a tiny morsel. What is to stop me from cooking thou in that pathetic armor of thine?"

As though to illustrate the point, a jet of flame burst into life at the base of a stalactite. Sir Derek squealed. The thing's fiery breath had been so fast he had never even seen it leave its mouth.

"I'm—I'm willing to fight you," he said at last, raising his sword. "To the death, if necessary."

The dragon laughed. "Oh, it shalt not be my death, little knight."

Fire dripped from the corner of its mouth. Sir Derek watched, mesmerized, as the flames began to creep across the thing's scales.

"Many have tried before thee. Many with far better weapons and armor than those you are carrying now," it hissed. A huge claw came out of nowhere and pointed at the knight's chest. "Verily, thy might as well have wrapped thyself in tin foil."

Sir Derek bristled. "My father gave me this armor!"

The fire crawled down the dragon's neck, pooling at a wing joint.

"I can tell. It looks ancient. People always think old means better. What is wrong with modernity? Only a knight in the most modern of iron mongery could dare hope to stand against my flame—eth."

"Look, I didn't come here to get fashion advice from a bloody lizard," Sir Derek snapped.

Was it his imagination, or was the fire starting to grow bigger?

"Well I can tell thou needseth it, little knight. As it is, I'm going to—"

There came a pause, during which Sir Derek could have sworn he heard whispering. Then the dragon yelled, in an altogether different and less sinister voice, "Bloody hell, we're on fire!"

The dragon's ribcage swung upwards. A great cloud of smoke plumed out, from the midst of which stumbled three men. One of them turned around and gave the side of the dragon a kick. It made a metallic clang.

"Bloody thing," the man swore. He lifted his flat cap and regarded the dragon with a critical eye. "Ten year's guarantee that engineer gave us. All right, who was in charge of the fire?"

"That were young Eric," another man said, indicating a sheepish individual trying to hide behind a stalactite. "We figured we'd let him have a go, him being so keen and all."

"Damn it, Eric," the first man said. "What the hell were you playin' at, lettin' it get so much fuel?

"Ahem."

The three men turned to find the tip of Sir Derek's sword pointed at them.

"What the hell is all this?" Sir Derek asked, in tones as sharp and brittle as an icicle.

"Er, well, you see sir," the first man said to the sword, "it were by way of a—a fake dragon you see." He tapped the side of the dragon again. One wing fell off.

"I can see that," Sir Derek said. "What I want to know is, why?"

"Not really my place to say, sir," the man said. He placed a finger on the sword tip and tried to move it aside. It didn't budge.

"Well tough luck, because we're not moving until I get some answers."

The first man gulped and his eyes swiveled over to his

companions.

"We would, sir," said one, taking off his own cap. "Only the dragon's burnin', you see. And there's a lot of fuel still left in the reserves, you see. So, you see, getting out of here might be a good plan? If that's all right by you, your honor, see?"

The other two nodded. Sir Derek looked over their shoulders at the burning wreck of the dragon. The flames provided quite a good light, crackling merrily as they consumed what he saw now to be nothing more than a leather shell stretched over a metal frame. The sharp whiff of lamp oil filled the cavern.

"Fair point," he said, sheathing his sword. "I'll lead the way, shall I?"

He took off back down the cave tunnel, armor rattling. They ran pell-mell through the gloomy cavern. Sir Derek lowered his head, trusting in his helmet to protect him. From the collection of swears and shouts, he guessed the others were not as lucky.

He reached the end of the stone corridor, only to be brought up short. The entrance was still missing. All that he could see was grey stone.

"We're trapped!" he wailed.

Someone pushed past him. "Give it here, you tin plated idiot."

Sir Derek watched as the first flat cap clad dragon operative walked up to the stone wall ahead of them. He grasped the wall in both hands and pulled it aside. Sunlight flooded the cave, blinding in its brightness.

Sir Derek didn't wait for his vision to clear. He charged headlong through the opening. Someone shouted and then Sir Derek tripped. He landed on something soft, which went "Oomph!" Seconds later, an explosion shook the ground. The back of his armor became uncomfortably hot and the whole world turned into light and sound.

It took a few minutes for everything to stop shaking. Or at least, for Sir Derek's world to stop shaking. The inside of his helmet rang like a bell. When he tried to stand up, the world beneath his feet rolled and he fell again in a loud clatter.

"Oomph!"

Sir Derek looked down to find he had fallen on top of the mayor. He tried to apologize, but the words reaching his ears sounded muffled. The man, whose face had turned an alarming shade of crimson, nodded and mouthed something. Together, they picked one another up off the ground, an activity rather like pulling up a ladder you happen to be standing on. By the time they were both upright, noise had begun to leak back.

"What on earth happened there?" The mayor strode over to the cave opening, swaying only a little. A thick, grey curtain had been drawn across it, though now patches of it smoldered.

A young man, Sir Derek recognized him as Erik, stepped forward. "It were my fault, Mr. Mayor, sir. I got a bit overenthusiastic with yon bellows."

"This is ridiculous," the mayor said. He patted at his ermine robe, now a host to a dozen little patches of candle flame. "Do you know how much we paid for that damn dragon?"

Someone tapped him on the shoulder. The mayor whirled around, his face set like thunder. "Yes, what is it?"

The bad weather parted quickly as he found Sir Derek, standing so close the two were practically nose to nose. Sir Derek smiled. "A pretend dragon?"

"Er, yes," the mayor managed. "Did—did you like it? It took the lads ages to get the movements right."

"Why is there a pretend dragon in your dragon cave?"

"Well, you see," the mayor began, addressing the knight's right knee, "we really did have a dragon. Fearsome thing it was too." His eyes misted over in memory. "Knights and heroes would come from miles around just for the chance to look at it." He sighed. "Then it went and died. No dragon meant no heroes, and no heroes meant…well, not to put too fine a point on it…no money."

Sir Derek looked at the crowd, who backed away from his gaze. Some shoved items behind their back. One woman, he saw, was trying to hide a white breast plate on which the words "I Fought The Lothwick Dragon!" had been inexpertly painted. There was even a little dragon, although it might have been a red-winged goat.

"You're telling me," Sir Derek said, "you have been pretending to have a dragon, just to lure in heroes and sell them souvenirs?" A thought struck him. He bent down and picked up one of the skulls littering the cave entrance. He dropped it. It bounced.

"I can see you're upset, lad," the mayor said, taking him by the arm. "Why don't you and I take a quick walk back into town? The lads can clear up here, can't you lads?" He glared at the former dragon operators, who shuffled their feet and produced a chorus on the theme of "yeah."

The crowd parted for the two. People watched Sir Derek with the air of seismologists who have just noticed the ground is making odd noises. One kind man even took his horse by the reins, presumably leading it to a nearby stable where it could be cared for, brushed, fed, painted brown, and sold for ten shillings.

The mayor led Sir Derek down the town's main thoroughfare. Sir Derek saw many of the buildings featured rough carvings. Great wyrms stood guard over doorways. One or two sported brightly colored banners and flags, often bearing words like "Get Yer Dragon Fitein Stuff Ere!" and "Garunteed No Insinerashun!" Stalls lined the road, selling all manner of cuddly dragons or wooden hero figures. At the town's center stood a small chapel with a wooden statue outside. It showed a dragon swooping down on some hapless people, while a knight knelt in prayer. The knight had their money pouch offered up in the direction of the temple.

The mayor leaned back against the statue and, to Sir Derek's surprise, produced a pack of cigarettes. He lit one, striking the match on the carved dragon's rump. "Look, lad, I'm sorry about the false dragon. Really I am." One thumb rubbed at his chain of office. "But times are hard. We do what we have to."

"Resorting to falsehoods and mummery to get money out of heroes?" Sir Derek snapped. "What on earth would drive a person to such dishonesty?"

The mayor seemed to catch his thoughts. "Ha, chance would be a fine thing. Heroes aren't finding much work these days. When was the last time you got paid for a job, lad?"

Sir Derek didn't answer, but his stomach gave a treacherous gurgle.

The mayor went on. "Besides, it's not just heroes that come here you know. People come from all over just to see the famous home of the Lothwick Dragon." He spread out his arms. "We're famous, we are! Let's face it, with monsters getting so rare, this is the closest most are going to get to the old glory days. And, in the end, it results in far fewer dead adventurers. Most of them run away."

His grin slowly faded and he settled back against the fountain. "But I think it might have run its course. Heroes just don't have the money to buy from us anymore." He looked around at his town, its houses built from wood and wishful thinking, and Sir Derek was surprised to see a tear prick the corner of his eye. "We'll go back to just being another dot on the map, I suppose. Still, it was good while it lasted." He chuckled. "Far more fun than sheep, I can tell you."

Sir Derek followed the mayor's gaze around the square, at the array of brightly colored bunting. Nearby, a small stand sold misshapen toy knights. A few small strands of hair formed a rough plume on their painted helmets. He reached up to feel the remains of his own plume. Next to the knights sat a stock of cuddly dragons. A sign beside it declared, in foot high red paint, "Soovanears For Yor Kids!"

Something began to take shape within Sir Derek's mind.

"Mr. Mayor," he said, speaking slowly so as not to scare the idea away, "I think I might have an alternative."

~ * ~

A talon slashed down at Sir Derek. He parried it with practiced ease and rolled out from under the dragon's bulk. The creature reared, sending jets of fire up into the sky. From where they stood behind the dividing rope, the spectators gave a mighty cheer.

Sir Derek wiped the sweat from his forehead, before spinning around and bringing his sword into the dragon's flank. There came a loud clang as the dull blade made contact, followed by a round of sotto-voce swearing from inside.

"Sorry Mike," Sir Derek said.

"Watch it next time!"

The young knight hooked his shield into place on his back and jumped up to grab onto the dragon's rear leg. The machine bucked and writhed, shaking him like a rag doll, but he held on tight to the hidden hand holds. He allowed one hand to slip, smiling at the appreciative gasp this got from the audience.

"I'm going to go for the kill now, Mike. You and the lads ready?"

In answer, the dragon stopped bucking and unfurled its great leather wings. These began to beat, sending gusts of wind out among the watching crowd.

Sir Derek clambered his way up the thing's side until he stood on its back. The wide wings gave him more room to walk, while also hiding the special foot grooves from the audience. He walked steadily up towards the head and lifted his sword high, just as the dragon let out another burst of flame. The sword came down, sliding into the slot between the contraption's eyes. The fire cut off immediately. Grabbing the short length of rope that lay hidden behind the horns, Sir Derek swung himself down. Behind him, the dragon fell to the ground in stages, starting with the head, then the wings, before finally the body collapsed with a deafening crash.

The watching people exploded into applause. Sir Derek bowed and smiled. He waved at a group of kids, all holding up their Sir Peveley Action Figures™.

"Derek! Derek! Derek!"

He raised his hands and the crowd quietened down. "Thank you all ladies and gentlemen," he shouted, his voice carrying around the stands. "We hope you have all enjoyed your time here at the Dragon Land World of Adventure. Before you leave, we do have a special opportunity for all who want to be a hero like me." He gestured at the dragon, from which Mike and the other operators had emerged to take their bow. "Have your picture painted with our monster. Slay the dragon yourself, just ten pence a go!"

~ * ~ * ~

Samuel Poots is a writer from Northern Ireland who can usually be found clambering around the coast muttering about dragons. His work has been featured by Daily Science Fiction, Tales to Terrify, and Toasted Cake podcast and he is a recipient of the Arts Council of N. Ireland's Support for Individual Artists Award. If found, please give him a cup of tea and send him home via the nearest post office.

Memories of Dragons Slain

Ken Goldman

> *" "A man's real possession is his memory.*
> *In nothing else is he rich, in nothing else is he poor."*

Alexander Smith (1830-1867)
"Of Death and The Fear of Dying"

"Grandfather, will you tell me a story...?"

So it always began, this child's simple wish that brought the surge of memories. Like ocean waves they came crashing upon the shore of Sir Edmund's sleeping mind, so many he could scarce contain the swell.

He remembered alluring young damsels with skin of cream, golden haired princesses of noble birth no man could resist. Such maidens delighted in young Edmund's rescue of them from such terrible circumstances as would cause any man's flesh to crawl. And in the end, how the princesses loved him!

Remembered also were evil knights with whom the young warrior had crossed swords and who had fallen, blood spattered, at Prince Edmund's feet. In his hands he had held the black hearts of his adversaries, bleeding organs held high for all men to see, the dripping tokens of savage battles won and of detestable opponents bettered.

There had been plentiful ceremonies he recalled as well, sumptuous feasts spent seated at his Queen's side and in whose royal palace the heroic knight had been treated as a King himself. At times Her Highness' eyes caught his, lingering a moment longer than seemed appropriate for royalty. The recollection always made the elderly Edmund smile, but that memory he preferred keeping to himself.

Seemingly impossible quests that tested his mettle, bloody battles that confirmed his valor, and countless nights filled with passionate love making, Sir Edmund's memories came. He had lived several lifetimes' worth of adventures, enough to fill volumes.

But these recollections paled when compared to the dragons.

Yes, of course there had been dragons, fearful fire breathing beasts whose snapping leathery wings filled the skies with thunder as they terrorized the numerous kingdoms of the Southern provinces. Each among them spat hell fire through teeth like daggers as Edmund brandished his gleaming sword, having only that and his shield between himself and certain death. Yet he had succeeded in killing them all, every last hellish dragon among them.

The ancient knight tapped his temple. "So many stories, Grandson. A wealth of tales safeguarded for all time right here…." Time's winds could never carry off these memories. Clear as spring water they came, glorious each and all. His innumerable adventures remained fresh for the telling—and retelling—and that kept them alive and magical. Certainly the old man's chronicles enchanted young Philip, the child who now sat crab-like at his grandfather's knee in the respectful fashion that had become familiar to both.

"And what tale shall it be today, my grandson?" the silver haired knight spoke as if searching some extensive vault for just the right episode to share. The old warrior felt certain he already knew the young man's answer. Day for night it rarely wavered.

"The dragons!" the boy responded with no hesitation. "Tell me of all the bloodthirsty dragons, and how you killed each hideous monster in its own fashion!"

Edmund smiled. As always, the sharing of his adventures required some coaxing. This made his stories so much richer in the telling. "Each one of the dragons? Child, so numerous they were, too many flame breathing beasts to describe in one sitting. Perhaps the rescue of an imprisoned maiden from some inescapable tower would be more—"

Philip would not be put off. The boy seemed to enjoy the ritual of persuading the elderly knight. "…Then tell me of the most terrible dragon, Grandfather. Tell me of the most frightening dragon that ever was, and how you killed him with only your sword and shield!"

"…and my wits, Philip. For without a man's cunning his sword and shield mean nothing to even the bravest knight. Cunning does not mingle well with a softness of heart, and there come such times as only the most hardened of hearts will prevail. Why, once I killed a nest of young dragons while they slept, then poisoned their mother with her own venom. Concerning dragons, courage makes no room for sentiment."

The child drew closer as if to hear some magnificent secret, but such was the boy's manner whenever he took his place upon the old man's knee.

"Yes! Tell a story of a knight's cunning and bravery! Of a heart as hardened as steel!"

Edmund smiled, leaning forward and speaking low. "Each and all, they were terrible, the dragons, savoring the flesh of young maidens or the blood of aspiring knights, eternally as hungry as death itself. But if you ask about the most savage creature among them, the most blood thirsty, well, Philip, this tale of Needhogg will prove too challenging for the ears of a young man such as yourself."

"These ears belong to a one who is young only in years, Grandfather! Tell me!"

The aged knight knew he had the boy then. The spell now cast, all that remained was to relate his story…

~ * ~

…My tale of Needhogg begins with Princess Vivian of the kingdom of At-lan. Ah, child, her name alone inspired poetry! A fairer young woman never lived. But the lady's beauty was equaled by her utter lack of common sense, and too often she placed herself in danger's path. Why, once she allowed a young archer to shoot an apple from atop her head, then dared him to do the same with a grape! The Queen had often warned her impulsive daughter of the devil-like six horned black dragon whose breath alone could kill ten men where they stood and whom entire armies could not bring down. Even the most proficient of dragon slayers became the creature's playful sport, then his dinner. But secured within At-lan's gates, the Queen assured Vivian she need not fear, for Needhogg preferred to seek his victims as they traveled alone and therefore offered easy prey. Even the bravest knights feared this black dragon, and rightfully so, for Needhogg had eaten many of them.

But the Lady Vivian, well, Philip, she had no such acquaintance with common girlish apprehensions, having been sheltered from such emotions from the moment of her birth. And, in truth, the lady was more than a tad spoiled—indeed, I should say she was *insistent*—when it came to having her way. Despite her royalty, she threw tantrums whenever she saw fit. Although this indelicate trait had an odd charm, it might well have proved the maiden's undoing.

Vivian's most prized possession was a lovely golden steed, a gift from the Queen on her daughter's eighteenth birthday. The princess christened her animal Butler. You see, she considered the horse her servant much as she viewed everyone else. Nonetheless, the princess loved the steed and in no time, Butler became the envy of every person in the kingdom. The equine proved a most majestic animal, strutting each morning throughout the domain of At-lan while the princess sat proudly on his back for all to admire. How it amazed others to observe the animal's steadfast obedience whenever the Lady rode by! And yet…

Away from Lady Viv the horse possessed as wild a disposition as his mistress, an ungoverned spirit not easily restrained behind a kingdom's lofty walls. One spring morning before first light the young horse broke free of his stall, cleverly concealing himself among the horse soldiers for whom the gates opened during the darkest hours before the dawn. Butler quickly found his way along the paths leading far from the Queen's provinces.

When Vivian awakened and went to the stables to discover her Butler absent from his paddock…well, to say she was beside herself would seriously understate the young woman's misery. On foot she immediately set forth to search for her precious steed even as the sun climbed the dawning sky. In the morning's gray mist she scaled the castle wall as, to the great consternation of her mother, she had done so often as a precocious child. In no time Vivian ventured a good distance from the kingdom, and from the sanctuary of its shelter.

"Butler! Butler, where have you gone to…?" she cried into the forest.

Far off in his lair, Needhogg awakened to the sound of the lady's echoing shouts. He sniffed the wind, for a dragon's senses are extremely sharp. Yes! The morning breeze carried the scent of the blood of a young virgin. The creature took to the sky that very instant, headed for the green wood surrounding At-lan, hungry for the taste of maiden flesh.

~ * ~

"Did the dragon Needhogg eat the princess?" Philip asked.
"Grandson, who is telling this story?"
The child covered his mouth.
The old man smiled…

~ * ~

I was not there to witness, of course, but I can easily imagine the terrible spectacle that followed when Needhogg swooped upon the lady on her solitary journey. From what I have been told by those who looked to the skies that morning, the dragon held the steed, Butler, in his talons. So when Needhogg revealed himself in all his fiery ferocity to the princess, Vivian must have screamed mightily to see her cherished horse kicking and whinnying in such peril. But there was nothing the lady could do. Much worse, now her own escape seemed impossible.

I can only surmise how the dragon descended, flying in great circles so that the princess might clearly see her beloved Butler's nightmarish suffering, and one can visualize the lady's shrieks of terror as he swooped past again and again with the hapless equine imprisoned in its claws. Certainly, anguished tears filled Vivian's eyes. I would not be surprised had she thrown one of her infamous tantrums. I can almost see her ranting and shaking angry fists at the beast.

"Release my horse now, you accursed creature! Drop him, I say!"

In any case, an amazing thing, an inexplicable moment of reprieve followed. The dragon deposited the golden steed where the princess stood, as if to indicate 'Here, princess, is my gift of freedom to you, if only if you are bold enough to take it.' For one false moment of hope Vivian must have felt such commingling of relief and absolute terror as would be impossible to describe.

Unfortunately, the lady's relief could not have lasted long. You see, Philip, the dragon has not been born that can be trusted. The princess, completely ignorant of this fact, mounted Butler saddle-free, clinging to his neck with every hope of returning to her palace safe and untouched. But Needhogg was not terrible simply owing to his unearthly powers. No, Grandson, 'twas the dragon's awful cruelty that made him the true monster he was. To such a creature, death deprived of pain proves no sport. I picture the dragon allowing the princess time for her escape with Butler in full gallop, and from high above Needhogg observing the amusing scene even while crackling fire flared within his nostrils. Doubtless, the beast shot a great plume of flame from his opened jaws, a powerful conflagration targeted directly at Butler and his lovely rider. Right from under the princess as she rode, the accursed monster roasted the poor horse to a blackened crisp! And within that same moment Needhogg held the princess captive in his talons before she ever touched the ground!

Can you see the absolute horror in the captured princess' eyes as she struggled, pummeling Needhogg's claws desperately with her fists while shrieking her throat raw? Can you, Grandson?

Soaring high above the trees the dragon carried off the damsel to his lair, no doubt to kill her in the most appalling manner imaginable. Would he pick apart her bones piece by piece to savor the woman's pain and misery as he chewed off first arms, then legs? Possibly he might torture the woman with gusts of fire to scorch every inch of her young flesh slowly, so agonizingly slowly, until she was shriveled like burnt paper? Or might he allow her to live for a day or two, only to observe him dining upon the flesh of the failed saviors come to her rescue? Needhogg's evil ways seemed incalculable to those poor souls who had the unenviable fortune of crossing his path.

~ * ~

Philip clung to the elder knight.

"But you did cross his path, didn't you, Grandfather? You did find Needhogg and slaughtered him. How? How did you kill him?"

The old man whispered into the boy's ear.

"Oh, yes, I found him. And I have spent the better part of my life wishing I had not..."

~ * ~

Upon discovering her daughter and her steed absent from the kingdom all day, the Queen, fearing the worst, summoned me to her throne. She seemed agitated beyond terror, for a royal daughter is prone to more dangers than anyone, and the Queen feared kidnappers and murderers along the bridle paths leading from At-lan. Her Highness refused to entertain the thought that Princess Viv had been taken captive by the dreaded dragon Needhogg, although I knew that terrible consideration had certainly entered her mind.

"My Vivian's horse is absent yet his saddle remains on its nail, Edmund. Vivian is nowhere to be found. Perhaps her Butler had escaped and my daughter has gone in search of him. Find her for me before any danger befalls her. Please! I promise you will receive riches beyond your imaginings when my daughter returns to me."

A woman's tears are awful enough to behold, Philip. But a Queen's tears are unbearable. I made my vow to her that moment.

"I desire no riches, your Highness. By my own blood, I do promise I shall find your princess daughter!" Clothed in armor and emboldened by my heavy sword, I mounted my horse and was gone from the kingdom within the half hour.

Some daylight remained, and it proved a simple task to follow Vivian's path. The steed Butler had his own particular hoof markings, and fresh tracks of his hooves proved simple enough to pursue. Whether the Lady had mounted her horse or not, I had no doubt that where these tracks led, so had gone the princess. Lady Viv's shoes imprinted the trail further along proving me correct. But where these prints terminated confirmed my Queen's worst fears. The great patch of scorched earth could mean but one thing, yet I dreaded to speak the name aloud.

"Needhogg…"

I did not know whether the princess remained living, but I resolved to travel to the dragon's lair to discover the answer for myself. The journey would be treacherous and I had to leave my horse behind, for Needhogg lived in a cave upon the highest mountaintop in all the kingdom. The watchful climb to his lair took days and proved an adventure in itself, but that narration will keep for some other time, for my grandson is impatient for his dragon tale, eh?

The creature's den appeared huge and as intimidating as Needhogg himself, a home fit for such a monster as he. Littered with the bones of his many victims, saturated with the fetid stench of rotted flesh, the lair seemed an alcove of Hell itself. As I entered the cave's recess, some foul slime dripped upon me, doubtless the innards of the most recent among Needhogg's kills. For one terrible moment I feared this to be the remains of the princess, but from deep within the bowels of the cave I heard the screams of the terrified woman. Reverberating tenfold against the walls Lady Vivian's shrieks produced an incessant wail.

"EEEEEEEEEeeeeeeeeeeeeeeeeeeeeeeeeeeeeeeeee!!!!!"

Nearby lay Needhogg dozing. The woman stood caged within his clenched talons, the claws creating a prison as inescapable as any made of steel bars. To free the damsel would be impossible without awakening the creature. How strange Needhogg had no difficulty napping through the lady's wails. I suppose a woman's shrieks serve as sweet music to a beast so abhorrent, for Needhogg slept soundly.

Princess Vivian detected me. Her shrieking stopped and for one terrible moment the woman called out *"Prince Edmund! My rescuer! God be praised!"* I raised a finger to my lips, attempting to silence her before she spoke more, for words articulated seemed far more perilous than those screamed.

"Shhhhh, princess..." I whispered, then quickly silenced myself for my own foolishness. Fortunately, Needhogg did not stir, and the Lady suppressed herself. But how to kill the dragon without placing Lady Viv in peril, I had not a clue. To drive my sword into his throat would awaken him, assuring no human would leave his lair alive this day. He would tear the doomed woman to shreds before any rescue could begin, and his fiery breath would then finish me off as well.

I looked about me for an idea and, *God be praised!* —I discovered one!

The cave's great ceiling loomed high where Needhogg slept, and along its walls jutted overhanging shelves of flat slate that I might, with persistence, scale. Located on each shelf I saw huge boulders, and on one ledge high overhead a massive rock capable of crushing the skull of the creature. If I could climb to it and then...

If only I could manage to dislodge it...

But climbing to such height would be impossible encased in thick armor, and the metal would certainly be heard clanging against the rock. Of course, lacking armor I stood completely defenseless, but this chance I decided I must take. Removing my breast plate carefully so as not to make a sound, I stripped to my bare chest.

Lady Vivian's eyes widened. She looked at me as if staring at a man gone mad.

"What are you do—?" she began.

"—Shhhh! Lady, please...*Shhhhh!!!"* I whispered.

The woman bit her knuckles to keep herself silent, but she could not restrain a squeal of consternation as I scaled the cavern's wall. A few pebbles were kicked free as I climbed, falling close to the sleeping dragon. But luck remained with me, and, excepting a succession of snorts, Needhogg remained motionless in his slumber. My climb—punctuated by the lady's gasps—proved less than an hour's work. Reaching the apex, like a spider I crawled upon the highest shelf to carry out my plan.

The dragon stirred.

"Hurry! Hurry!" the princess pleaded, again endangering her own rescue.

And again my fingers went to my lips to squelch her words. I set about to propel the boulder that would destroy Needhogg, threw every ounce of my weight against it, but the accursed thing would not budge. Groaning with the effort, I wedged my sword beneath the stone, utilizing every muscle in my body.

"Unngbhh!"

Not one inch did the boulder shift!

Needhogg snorted. His eyes flickered. The princess stared at him aghast.

"The dragon…*See! He awakens!"*

I hissed my words at her. "My Lady…*please!!!"*

But already Princess Viv had roused Needhogg from his slumber, and perhaps a minute's time remained before the monster fully awakened. I had to act instantaneously if we were to live. But the Lady would not keep her silence.

"You fool! Move that rock now! Rescue me, damn you!"

Needhogg awakened! His attention traveled first to the woman still imprisoned within his talons. She screeched like a startled mouse, but only for a moment. The dragon hoisted the princess close to his great eye, examining the squirming damsel as he opened wide his jaws to take her like a delicate morsel into his cavernous mouth. It would not be unlike Needhogg to toy with a victim he had no intention of eating at that moment. Suspended between the dragon's teeth Vivian found the strength to point in my direction.

"Fool! Fool! Fool!!!"

Needhogg's head turned upward toward where I stood exposed on the shelf.

He saw me! I had to act, I had to act now!

The boulder slipped, toppling from the ledge. It smashed directly into the dragon's head, crushing his skull with the princess still inside his mouth. The force of the plunging rock slammed the dragon's mouth shut, and those dagger-like teeth severed the woman in two! Lady Vivian's legs first dangled, then fell sloppily from his jaw, while the rest of her disappeared down the dragon's gullet. Needhogg gulped, then collapsed on the spot. The princess served as the last meal the dragon ever would eat! And he enjoyed only half of her! *Only half of her!!!*

~ * ~

Philip stared at the old warrior, completely bewildered. The ancient knight now laughed hysterically.

"Grandfather…You…You did not rescue the princess? Lady Vivian —she was eaten?"

Edmund's laughter softened to crazed cackling.

"Rescue her? Philip, the Lady would have killed us both! She deserved no rescuing from me!"

The dragon slayer did not seem convinced of his own words. How was it possible, a brave knight failing to rescue the imperiled fair princess? The child's mouth hung open.

"But the princess—You failed to save her?"

"All right, then! I admit I was unable to rescue her! I could not! That damned dragon was death itself!"

"But you—you did kill Needhogg, didn't you?"

"Kill him? Well, you see…"

"You slaughtered so many dragons, Grandfather. Every dragon you ever met. You told me how you killed them all…all of them! You told me!"

The old man's eyes seemed to go dull as if a candle within had been snuffed out.

"Not all of them, Philip. Needhogg, after I escaped—he awakened! I had only stunned the creature. He would kill again…and again. A dragon is insatiable!"

The boy's lips quivered.

"Needhogg—He lived???"

Edmund could not look at the young man.

"Did I not tell you this tale was never intended for a child's ears? He lived. Yes."

"But—But the Queen—You promised her!'

"Promises made by mortal men are themselves only flesh and blood, Philip. Promises die, Grandson. But dragons…Dragons can so easily kill promises!"

Philip's eyes grew moist with disappointment. And suddenly the old warrior was shrieking the name he so hated to utter.

"Needhogg!!! Needhogg!!!!"

The grizzled knight's agitation frightened the boy. Philip tried to shake him.

"Grandfather! Are you all right? Grandfath—!!"

Sir Edmund seemed to have fallen into some kind of frenzy. He would not stop screaming.

"Neeeeeed—hogggg!! Needeeeeeeeed—hogggggggggggg!!!!"

~ * ~

"…Nurse! Nurse Campbell!" Philip DePrinze called from his Grandfather's bedside. A stout black woman came charging into the room. "Mrs. Campbell, I think he's hallucinating again. He was resting quietly for an hour and then suddenly—"

"Old age will do that. Some memory just kicks into the brain and sets 'em off like that." She managed to get a pill into the man's mouth, got him to drink some water. The medication calmed her patient a little. "He'll sleep in just a while. But are *you* all right, Mr. DePrinze?"

"Just a little shaken. I hate to see the old guy get like this."

The nurse placed a hand on Philip's shoulder. This bedside scene was nothing new, and conversation usually helped.

"I'm told back in Atlanta your grandfather used to be a policeman?"

"A damned good cop. Officer Eddie they called him, Sir Eddie for short. Decorated for bravery, the whole nine yards. He always had this thing about going after the bad guys, at least until a bullet took out a chunk of his hip. It's been over thirty years now."

"Guess he couldn't catch *all* them bad guys, eh?"

"Not like in the movies. He used to love taking me to the matinees when I was a kid. Then we'd come home and he'd tell me his stories. Cops and robbers, and the cops always won. But real life isn't like that, is it?"

They looked at the old man still muttering in his bed.

"Needhogg…Needhogg!!!"

Mrs. Campbell shook her head.

"Such a shame what time does to a man reduced to this assisted living where he can't even wipe his own nose. Most folks in the home got no one what gives a sweet damn about them. I seen this sort of thing every day here when the surviving spouse is left all alone. It's nice when family like you comes to call, Mr. DePrinze."

Philip tried for a smile but didn't quite get there.

"Since my mother passed away I'm all the family my grandfather has. He used to joke about how he enjoyed spoiling his wife. She was feisty to the end, but he loved that woman more than anything in this world. Diabetes took my grandmother years ago. They had to amputate both her legs, and it just killed him to watch his Vivian die like that, as if there was anything he could do about it. The old guy never got over it. He lived alone in their old house on Dragons Lane until we had to bring him here last year. I pray those memories of Dragons Lane with his Vivian are still somewhere inside him."

Mrs. Campbell nodded. "Memory is all he's got, I guess. And there ain't a whole lot the Alzheimer's ain't took."

"Neeeed-Hoggggg! Neeeeeed-Haaaaaaaaaaaaaaaggggggg!"

Philip scratched his head.

"He keeps yelling that. What's he saying?"

The nurse took the old man into her arms, rocking him like a child and holding him tightly.

"You know, Mr. DePrinze, workin' here 'long as I have, you learn that sometimes a little affection is all an elderly person really needs. Ain't that right, Mister Sir Eddie? You just need a hug, ain't that right, sugar?"

~ * ~ * ~

Ken Goldman, former Philadelphia teacher of English and Film Studies, is an Active member of the Horror Writers Association. He has homes on the Main Line in Pennsylvania and at the Jersey shore. His stories have appeared in over 925 independent press publications in the U.S., Canada, the UK, and Australia with over twenty due for publication in 2021. Since 1993 Ken's tales have received seven honorable mentions in The Year's Best Fantasy & Horror. He has written six books: three anthologies of short stories, YOU HAD ME AT ARRGH!! (Sam's Dot Publishers), DONNY DOESN'T LIVE HERE ANYMORE (A/A Productions) and STAR-CROSSED (Vampires 2); and a novella, DESIREE, (Damnation Books). His first novel OF A FEATHER (Horrific Tales Publishing) was released in January 2014. SINKHOLE, his second novel, was published by Bloodshot Books August 2017.

Many of Ken's stories appear in various online anthologies, and many on Kindle and/or in print can be purchased at Amazon.com Stop by and scream hello!

Dragons are Forever

Jean Martin

John was alone.

When he thought about it, he understood he had been alone for years. He just hadn't noticed before the shutdown.

His two boys were grown. JJ moved to Seattle after he graduated. Kevin and his wife had built a McMansion out in the suburbs, which John was, sometimes permitted to visit.

His wife, Alice, who had always been devoted to JJ, was living in Seattle now too. She liked it out there. She had her own place, close to where JJ and Wendy lived. She belonged to a bunch of book clubs and a fitness group and took gourmet cooking classes, when she wasn't babysitting her grandkids.

His parents were gone. His oldest brother, Gregg, had been dead for ten years. Larry, the middle brother had died two years ago.

John still lived in the house he'd inherited from his parents. He liked it there. He liked the big cherry wood mantelpiece in the living room and the carved molding in the dining room.

He liked the big old kitchen where his mom had baked her molasses cookies and where he and Alice had made Thanksgiving dinners for the family every year.

The house really was too large for him now. But he didn't want to sell it, and spend his days squabbling with his neighbors in some condo.

That was before the shutdown.

In that time before everyone was wearing masks, he had had a group of friends he ate lunch with twice a week. He went to the library every Friday to pick up some new books, and talk to his friends there. He went to the gym three times a week. He saw people there.

That was the thing. He saw people. He had no close friends. He hadn't had any, really, since college.

He'd married Alice three months after they graduated. After that, they had dinner with other couples once in a while. Now and then they got together with other families.

He had friends at work, people he talked to there, anyway,

until he retired.

Since then, he'd been filling up his days and staying occupied.

He had his social media accounts, where he traded jokes, cartoons and sometimes videos with people he didn't see.

Kevin called every Sunday, to see that he was all right.

Alice sent him emails, now and again, with pictures of JJ's kids.

Once a week, he went to the supermarket and said hello to the clerk who rang him up, the guy who bagged his purchases, and the security guard at the door.

Otherwise, he was alone. It was just him, the TV, the radio and the computer.

Until that night, he heard a voice out on the porch calling "Jackie".

No one had called him Jackie since his mother died.

"I'm out here Jackie." The voice sounded familiar. He remembered it from his childhood.

"Jackie," it was deep and soft and comforting, somehow.

There were big French doors leading out to the porch. When he looked out, he could see the tail, curled on the flagstones, and a tip of wing by the porch glider.

He stepped outside, into the warm starry night, and stood and stared for a few minutes.

"You aren't real," he said.

"Who told you that?" The dragon demanded.

"Everyone." John said, suddenly. "They all said you were pretend. They said I was too big for make believe and..."

"I see," the dragon said solemnly.

He flapped his wings, and the porch glider swung, in the breeze they created.

"They were wrong," John said.

"They were indeed," the dragon said.

"I missed you," John said.

"I missed you as well. Now, we have things to do. Captain Creeg has kidnapped the Lord Mayor of London Town, and we must fly to his rescue."

"Yes! Right away!"

John clambered up a lowered wing, and onto the green, scaly back. He clung to the dragon's neck, as he galloped across the back yard and launched himself into the starry sky.

They flew over housetops, and treetops, to the seaside, and then over the white capped waves. The dragon glided through the air above the ocean.

There it was, with the Jolly Roger flapping in the wind on the topmast. The Sea Witch, Captain Creeg's ship, with Captain Creeg himself, in his black coat and his feathered tricorn hat, up on the quarterdeck watching them through his spyglass.

"Avast!" he shouted. "Keep yon scurvy dragon from my ship ye lily livered landlubber!"

"Surrender!" John shouted. He felt a little foolish, really.

"Never!" the pirate roared. "Gunner! Prepare to fire a broadside!"

The pirate gunners were loading their cannon, preparing to fire, as John and the dragon landed on the deck. The dragon let out a powerful roar, and swept the guns overboard with his tail.

Pirates scattered everywhere, while Captain Creeg cursed them as cowards and scurvy swabs.

John didn't think. He grabbed a cutlass, a fleeing pirate had dropped, and leaped onto the quarterdeck.

Did he really duel with Captain Creeg?

Did he actually disarm him?

Did he truly run down into the ship's hold, and free the Lord Mayor of London Town in his gold laced coat?

It seemed very real, as he and the Lord Mayor climbed up onto the dragon's back.

He felt the powerful muscles rippling as the dragon flapped his wings and flew them all the way to London Town. Not the city he had visited with Alice, with the aluminum and glass high rises, and the giant ferris wheel. This was a storybook city full of half-timbered houses, with a castle at the center where a king and queen in jeweled crowns, and a princess with long, golden hair welcomed the heroes and the rescued mayor.

There were fanfares and salutes, and a banquet with roast beef, and candied carrots, and a whole roast pig for the dragon.

John tasted all the food, and the fruity red wine he drank from a jeweled goblet.

He felt the castle's stone floors under his feet. He smelled the onions on the Lord Mayor's breath.

His knees hurt a little as he knelt in the throne room and was made a knight of the realm.

The dragon was rewarded with a chest full of gold, one more to add to the store in his cave, John remembered.

Then they flew off, over the sea, over the mountains, back to his street and his house, and the porch, where the dragon landed, gently, and John climbed down.

"I'd almost forgotten you," he said.

"But not entirely," the dragon told him.

"Will you be back?" John asked hopefully.

"Of course."

John rubbed the dragon's long, scaly neck. The dragon made a soft sound a little like a cat purring.

"Good." John felt strange. It took him a few minutes to understand he was happy. It had been a long time since he had genuinely enjoyed anything.

He stood on the porch, waving, as the dragon flew off into the night sky.

He presumed it was a dream, but it was a lovely dream. So much better than the dreams he'd had about filling out endless forms or looking for things he could never find.

He slept soundly for the rest of the night, and in the morning, he did two loads of laundry, and finally thawed out that pot roast he'd bought two months ago and hadn't felt like cooking.

While he was in the kitchen, he found a length of bright blue string he had saved because it was bright blue and he couldn't bring himself to throw it out. He slipped it into his pocket, understanding what he was doing was foolish.

But the dragon was back on his porch that night.

This time, John ran out and wrapped his arms around the dragon's long, scaly neck.

"Look what I've got for you!" He pulled the blue string out of his pocket.

"String!" the dragon smiled, large and long toothed. "You remembered!" He held it up by one of his long claws and admired it in the moonlight. "It's beautiful! Let's go to the giant's castle and see if his wife still makes cherry pie."

Once again, John climbed onto the dragon's back, and they flew off across the starry sky.

The giant's wife did, indeed, still make cherry pie. She and the giant were pleased to see John and his dragon friend again.

The slice of pie John ate was huge, sweet and sour at the same time. Strange, he never tasted anything he ate in dreams.

They flew home over villages with thatched cottages, where red cheeked men and women waved and smiled.

They flew over storybook castles with pennants flying from the turrets and knights and fair maidens cheered them from the battlements.

Then they were back again on the porch. Again, John wrapped his arms around the dragon's neck.

"Thank you for the string, Jackie." He flapped his wings and smiled again. His teeth were long and sharp, but not threatening.

"Glad you liked it," John said.

Then the dragon flew off again, across the starry sky.

In the morning, John found a red cherry pie stain on the front of his shirt.

The blue string was no longer in his pants pocket.

But it couldn't be real, could it?

He'd been a lonely kid. His two brothers were so much older than he was. Both of them natural athletes, sports stars with letters on their jackets. They had a lot of friends, and not much time for their baby brother.

All the other children on the street were either years older, than John, or years younger.

He'd had friends in school, but it was like now, when he saw them during the day, and was alone when he came home.

Except for the dragon.

One night he'd seen him, out in the back yard. He'd slipped past his parents, glued to the TV watching Tic Tac Dough, out the back door and onto the porch, to see a real live dragon, and meet his first real friend.

They'd flown away on their first adventure, to rescue a blonde-haired damsel held in a tower by a sinister knight, with a pointed black beard and a black doublet.

After that, they were inseparable. Flying off to fight pirates, hunt for treasure, visit giants, princes, dwarfs and mermaids.

Until his parents decided he was spending too much time playing by himself.

They signed him up for Little League and Pop Warner Football.

A new family moved onto their street with a son his age named Robert. Robert didn't care for dwarfs or pirates. But he loved sports. They would spend hours pretending to be sports stars in their back yards.

John forgot about his friend the dragon. He settled into an ordinary life, focusing on all the ordinary things, school, sports, clothes, pop songs that were played five times an hour for two weeks and then forgotten.

He watched the games on TV.

When he was older, he went out drinking with his friends, and thought the guys who read Tolkien and played Dungeons and Dragons were strange.

That next night, John cooked the pot roast and split it with the dragon, who ate his half in one happy gulp.

"What did you do, when you stopped spending time with me?" he asked.

"I played with kids my own age," John said.

"Was that fun?"

"Sometimes," John said thoughtfully. "Mostly I was worried somebody would laugh at me."

"Why would anyone laugh at you, John?"

"Lots of reasons. Mostly to keep other people from laughing at them."

"I don't think I will ever fully understand people." the dragon mused.

"I'm not sure I understand them either," John said.

They both laughed.

There would be more adventures, in their fairy tale world, with the wizards, dwarfs, giants and pirates.

He spent less time on his social media sites, sharing cartoons and videos.

One day his phone rang, and he was surprised to see his son was calling.

"Hi Kevin," John said.

"Hi dad." Kevin sounded relieved. "You, okay?"

"Yeah," John said. "I'm fine. I've just been busy. Were you worried?"

"A little," Kevin admitted. "I hadn't heard from you. I was scared you might have covid."

"No, I'm pretty careful," John told him. "Never out without my mask." *Almost never*, he thought. But he didn't say it. "I ran into an old friend, and we've been spending a lot of time together."

"A friend from college?" Kevin wondered.

"Before that," John said.

"Sounds good. I was worried about you. Glad to hear you're okay. I'll tell JJ."

"You do that," John said.

"I'm kind of busy right now," Kevin said. "I'll get back to you later, okay."

"Okay," John said. "I know how it is. Say hi to Nicole and the kids for me."

"Yeah,"

The call was over.

John laughed.

His boys' lives had been carefully organized, for fear they might grow up to be drug addicts if they didn't spend their days playing sports and taking classes. They weren't interested in dragons, or pirates or kings.

His grandsons all played soccer and Little League, in between coding classes and organized playdates.

Until the shutdown, of course, when they were stuck at home living on their computers.

That night he got an email from Alice, who was also concerned, because she hadn't heard from him.

When he emailed back to say he was fine, and he'd met an old friend, she sent him a long account of her concerns for Reston, JJ's youngest boy, who was happy going to school online and didn't miss soccer at all.

"He's going to be a loner if this keeps up," she worried.

In Alice's universe, loners were people who murdered their parents, and kept severed heads in their freezers.

"Maybe not," John answered. "He seemed like a good kid, the last time I saw him. He sounded like he had his head on straight."

The last time he'd seen Reston, the kid was five. He liked "Sesame Street" and his older brother called him a baby.

Reston needed a friend, John thought.

John and the dragon flew off that night, because Captain Creeg was sailing for their fairy tale London, to raid the city and loot the king's treasure.

The dragon flapped his powerful wings and blew the pirate ship out to sea, and the whole town cheered as they flew off.

"How would you like to go to Seattle?" John asked as they flew over the mountains.

"Where's that?" the dragon wondered.

"It's near the sea, I think you'd like it. "

"Near the sea," He glided down into the yard, and climbed carefully up on the porch. "Yes, I think I would like that."

"There's somebody there you should meet." John climbed down from the dragon's scaly back.

"It would be good to have another friend," the dragon agreed. "Let's go there sometime."

John smiled as his old friend flew off into the night sky.

$\sim * \sim * \sim$

Jean Martin has a BS degree in Journalism from Ohio University, and has been laughing about it for longer than she cares to admit. She lives, at present, in McKeesport, Pennsylvania, with an orange tabby cat named Samwise, who likes bagpipe music.

If you, for some strange reason, like this story. You can find her story "The Sun Makes the Wheels Go" in this year's PARSEC Triangulations. Ms. Martin is a shameless self-promoter.

More Great Anthologies from WolfSinger Publications

Crunchy with Ketchup – edited by Carol Hightshoe

It has been said that one should never meddle in the affairs of dragons—for you are crunchy and taste good with ketchup.

Come enter the dragon's lair.

Take your chances with other would-be heroes and heroines who decide to face off against one of the biggest, baddest predators ever.

Witness a dragon civil war.
Hear the true story of the Battle of New Orleans.
Find out what it's like in the belly of a dragon.
Discover why cats can spell disaster when stealing a dragon's egg.
Meet a group of dragon riders who protect us from nuclear devastation.
Follow legends of modern dragons, only to find something very unexpected.

And more…

Cat Tails: War Zone – edited by Rebecca McFarland Kyle and Dana Bell

Cats have been our companions since long before they graced the temples of Ancient Egypt. In addition to being members of our families, they have also stood with us through difficult times. From keeping pests and vermin away from our food stores to providing a comforting paw when we have been wounded; cats have been our sidekicks and friends in many different battles.

Cat Tails—War Zone contains twenty-five stories from Ancient Egypt to the far-flung future, about some amazing cats who have served as compatriots during war times. But beware, for they can also be tricksters sent to teach lessons.

The real heroes are the volunteers of SHADOW CATS, an

Austin, Texas-based rescue that has saved the lives of 9,000-plus cats since 1997. Trappers, veterinarians, nurses, and adoption social workers volunteer to trap, neuter and return ferals, provide care for ill, injured and behaviorally-challenged cats, find perfect adoptive parents, educate on proper feline care, and advocate for real change in communities.

Proceeds from this book will continue their efforts.

Unintended Consequences – edited by Carol Hightshoe

For every action there is an equal and opposite reaction –
Newton's Third Law of Motion.

While Newton was talking about motion when he developed the above law, it can also be said that for every action or decision there is a consequence: sometimes good, sometimes bad.

Many times consequences can be foreseen and planned for. But there are times they are never seen. It is these unforeseen or Unintended Consequences that can have the biggest impact on individual lives.

An android working to pass as human.

A woman who loses her pre-destined 'soul mate' on world where they were marked at birth.

A Queen who uses magic to make her subjects more cooperative and helpful to each other.

A wife who authorizes a radical treatment for dementia to be performed on her husband.

And 16 more who will learn about the unintended consequences that will affect their lives.

Just Desserts – edited by Rebecca McFarland Kyle and J.A. Campbell

Whether you like your revenge with the molten fire of a fine old Scotch or the cool sweetness of a tasty meringue, the nineteen tales within these covers should offer something to assuage you.

Narcissistic co-workers, thieves of affection, and bad neighbors are given their due in ways imaginative and sublime.

Love 'em, Shoot 'em – edited by Dana Bell

One should never be afraid to love or shoot the one they care about. A famed markswoman once said that. Or so it's claimed.

Imagine a town with a dog sheriff from another planet.
A zombie attack clean-up woman.
An attractive alien who likes to play love goddess.
A magical concert with dead musicians that gets out of hand.
Or those of the old west who meet aliens.
Those from the far future hunted for not volunteering to die.
A woman who learns a lesson with a twist during war time.
And more…

Come along with our writers and travel the diverse trails of their tales, of loving and sometimes shooting, in these pages of Love 'em, Shoot 'em.

Extinct – edited by Dana Bell

What if those ancient creatures so beloved in fiction, myth, and science had not disappeared? What if they were real? What might have been developed to handle them, and how might man have felt about the thundering giants in yesterday's, today's, or tomorrow's worlds.

Imagine a sanctuary established for dinosaurs that displaces humans.

What if Raptors were used on a distance planet as scouts for the new colony?

Could Dodo birds have left a record about what happened to them? Dragons helping settlers? Inconceivable!

A conqueror learns a hard lesson from a goddess and two children create their own 'monster'.

Lovely, unique, tales of lumbering giants of old, ancient rulers of the skies, and many others once thought to be myth or legend appear here in Extinct?

Tales From the Fluffy Bunny – edited by Carol Hightshoe

Welcome to the Fluffy Bunny

We welcome everyone—especially those with a story to tell. Adventurers, mercenaries, guardsmen, merchants, noble and peasant. Whoever. If you have a tale to share, then come in and have a seat. First drink and a hot meal are on the house.

What's a tale without an audience to appreciate it? So, even if you don't have a tale to share, come in, pull up a seat and enjoy these 17 tales of how a warrior or their weapon earned their name.

Visit us at www.wolfsingerpubs.com for more information

www.ingramcontent.com/pod-product-compliance
Lightning Source LLC
Chambersburg PA
CBHW061515020726
47502CB00006B/2085